P9-BYW-261

STATE OF EMERGENCY

Steve Pieczenik

JOVE BOOKS, NEW YORK

If you purchased this book without a cover, you should be aware that this book is stolen property. It was reported as "unsold and destroyed" to the publisher, and neither the author nor the publisher has received any payment for this "stripped book."

STATE OF EMERGENCY

A Jove Book / published by arrangement with
S & R Literary, Inc.

PRINTING HISTORY
G. P. Putnam's Sons edition / October 1997
Published simultaneously in Canada
Jove edition / February 1999

All rights reserved.
Copyright © 1997 by Steve Pieczenik.
This book may not be reproduced in whole or in part,
by mimeograph or any other means, without permission.
For information address: The Berkley Publishing Group,
a member of Penguin Putnam Inc.,
375 Hudson Street, New York, New York 10014.

The Penguin Putnam Inc. World Wide Web site address is
http://www.penguinputnam.com

ISBN: 0-515-12525-3

A JOVE BOOK®
Jove Books are published by The Berkley Publishing Group,
a member of Penguin Putnam Inc.,
375 Hudson Street, New York, New York 10014.
JOVE and the "J" design
are trademarks belonging to Jove Publications, Inc.

PRINTED IN THE UNITED STATES OF AMERICA

10 9 8 7 6 5 4 3 2 1

To Birdie, my love, my soul, my lodestar.

And to Sharon and Stephanie, my intrepid voyagers.
Each generation must redefine and reconstruct
its own form of democracy.

ACKNOWLEDGMENTS

Although the actual act of writing is very much a solo act (at times even painfully so), it still requires at its very core a multitude of information, assistance, and reality testing to make the novel both interesting and enlightening. In particular, I want to thank a group of people and institutions without whom the completion of this novel would not have been possible. First and foremost, I want to thank my wife, Birdie, whose endless revisions, dedication, and insights make this book as much hers as it is mine.

I want to thank the wonderful people at the Putnam Berkley Group, including Phyllis Grann, and all those other dedicated professionals who supported the book in terms of marketing and distribution, and helped to make this book the best it could be. In particular, I want to thank my editor, Senior Editor David Highfill, for his gracious professionalism and his tireless dedication to sculpting the book into a reading experience that would hopefully elicit both enjoyment and wonderment.

I want to acknowledge the invaluable assistance of Professor Martin H. Greenberg, Ph.D., and Larry Segriff for their meticulous fact-finding expeditions in the areas of military warfare, Native American Indians, the Colorado River, and the working of hydroelectric plants. John Helfers served as doctor-in-residence for my congenital inadequacies to operate my computer (to which I had at best an ambivalent relationship) properly. Tami Wood deserves my gratitude for the endless revisions that she had to input into the computer.

Special thanks to University of Wisconsin Professor of American History Jerry Rodesch on his clear and scholarly dissertation on the topic of states' rights, secession, and the Constitution. To my friends in the foreign and domestic National Security Areas, who shall remain at their request unidentified, I want to thank them for their invaluable assistance on militia groups, "False Patriots," the Posse Comitatus, citizens' courts, and the overseas national neofascist movements. The Mormon Church and their representatives deserve special mention for their invaluable assistance and graciousness in allowing me to access those parts of the church that were relevant to my book, in particular the Family History Library. Thanks to the Department of the Interior, the professionals at Glen Canyon Dam, and the citizens of Page, Arizona.

All inaccuracies, distortions, misrepresentations, and mistakes are solely mine, for which I ask your indulgence and understanding while reading the book.

INTRODUCTION

On July 4, 1995—Independence Day—Dick Carver, a pleasant rancher and county commissioner in a western state, took the law into his own hands. His weapon: a rusting, yellow D-7 Caterpillar bulldozer. His target: the federal government. His goal: to stop the intrusion of the federal government into his daily life.

Carver's parents had settled in the Big Smoke Valley in 1938. Over time, the family homestead had turned into the small town of Carver Station. Carver and his family raised cattle on approximately 860 acres of their own—an atypical feat for a rancher in any county in which the federal government owns 93 percent of the land.

Until the 1970s, relations between the ranchers and the federal agencies in Carver's state had been cordial. Grazing permits on federal land, for example, were approved automatically. Since then, however, Carver found that decisions that affected the daily life of his county's citizens were increasingly made by federal agents, environmental activists, and urbanites who resided several thousand miles away.

On July Fourth, Carver climbed aboard his Caterpillar to clear a weather-damaged road across a national forest. He wanted to do it, however, without the permission of the federal government. While ranchers frequently use federal lands without permission, Carver's actions were different on this day because he purposefully committed what he knew to be an illegal act as a manifestation of civil disobedience. He was arrested and then released after paying a fine.

Carver, a model citizen without any major political ambitions, soon became one of the principal leaders of the self-described "county supremacy movement," which spread like wildfire throughout the far West. The Justice Department currently estimates that at least thirty-five counties, primarily in Arizona, New Mexico, Nevada, and California, have declared their authority over federal lands. Other federal agencies push this number to three hundred counties.

Not all acts of defiance against federal authority are as peaceful as the one committed by Carver. Pipe bombs were found in the federal Gilda Wilderness of New Mexico. An unknown assailant fired shots at a Forest Service biologist in California. Federal agents arrested a man after he tried to buy explosives that he allegedly planned to use in blowing up an IRS office in Austin, Texas. In Carson City, Nevada, a bomb destroyed the family van of a forest ranger while it was parked in his driveway. This was the second explosion in which the same forest ranger was the apparent target. What each of these acts had in common was an underlying complaint against the actions of individuals who represented the federal government. Even the temperate Chairman of the Western Governors' Association stated publicly, "When you're a governor and you see what the federal government does to your communities, you want to strike back and say, 'No more!' "

Unfortunately, these acts of rebellion mirror the rise of another new phenomenon spreading throughout the Farm Belt and the West called the "citizens' court." These makeshift courts are composed of ordinary citizens without the presence of an elected or appointed judge, defense attorney, or prosecutor. Instead, ordinary citizens take those roles. When a decision is reached, the sentence is executed by unofficial "agents" of the court. These courts declare thousands of people to be state, not federal, citizens. They retry cases which they find have been unfavorably handled in the regular courts. On the basis of the decisions emanating from the citizens' court, they attach liens to the property of their enemies, mainly public officials who oppose them. They attempt to publicly sever their ties to the established judicial system, which they no longer trust. Ultimately, they take pride in putting public officials on notice.

In Jordan, Montana, thirty-six men formed a citizens' court and briefly occupied a courthouse, offering a $1 million bounty for the arrest of local officials. In retaliation, the Montana State Legislature recently made it a felony to impersonate or intimidate local officials. In Colorado, close to a dozen people have been charged with threatening and harassing public officials. In Wisconsin, where the official court system plans to aggressively pursue four hundred cases involving parental custody, the attorney general has warned that any organizers of citizens' courts run the risk of incurring severe criminal charges.

Supporters of the citizens' court range from hard-core white supremacists to struggling wheat farmers who claim that their raison d'être is solidly grounded in the Constitution. In language reminiscent of the radical Posse Comitatus tax protest group of the early 1970s, they insist that the federal government is illegitimate and that the citizens' court may be the only way to preserve their individual freedoms, guaranteed by the Constitution.

In *State of Emergency*, I have attempted to take these real-life stories of individual defiance against the federal government and weave them into a novel. I try to show that, in our own lifetime, there may be a real possibility that this once benign, now increasingly violent, trend toward anti-federalism can lead to civil war. As far-fetched as this may seem, one only has to look at the growing trend of secessionist movements arising within the United States and around the world. Staten Island considered seceding from New York City because its citizens wanted autonomy. So did sections within Los Angeles and Miami. There are continuous political pressures to divide California into two separate states. Native American tribes are demanding land entitlements all over the United States. Quebec's recently failed attempt to secede from Canada was defeated by a narrow margin in a widely publicized referendum. The Basques continue their acts of terrorism in order to force

Spain to grant them independence. The Corsican Nationalist Movement demands independence from France. Recently, political parties in Italy have called for a division of that country into two separate entities along the lines of the wealthy industrial north and the impoverished agricultural south.

In my first published novel, *The Mind Palace*, an account of the abuse of psychiatric hospitals for political incarcerations from a Soviet psychiatrist's point of view, I predicted the downfall of the Soviet Union ten years before it occurred. In *Blood Heat*, a story of biological warfare, I predicted the use of biological weapons as a major concern in international security. In *Maximum Vigilance*, I showed, in part, that aberrant personality traits in the President of the United States can place the country in danger as they play themselves out in international crises. In *Pax Pacifica*, I illustrated the possibility that mainland China could become a major superpower and attempt to intimidate Taiwan and try to draw the United States into a military confrontation.

My point is not to demonstrate how smart I may or may not be, but to demonstrate to you that I am willing to spend two to three years of my life writing about something that initially might appear trivial at worst, interesting at best, but that, in time, turns out to be quite significant.

In the case of *State of Emergency*, I hope to entertain you and perhaps enlighten you as well. More than anything else, I hope that my prediction of an imminent civil war within the United States is strictly a function of my imagination. I hope the novelist in me presides over the realist, lest I be identified as a cynic or, worse, a modern-day Cassandra.

STATE OF EMERGENCY

PROLOGUE

ESCALANTE CANYON, UTAH

Thursday, July 3rd, 9:00 A.M.

"On behalf of the President of the United States and the Secretary of the Interior, both of whom were sorry that they could not be here on this momentous occasion, I have been authorized to transform 1.7 million acres in nearby southern Utah into the Grand Staircase–Escalante National Monument." Secretary of State Barbara Reynolds spoke into the microphone on the makeshift wooden platform framed by the overwhelming beauty of the canyon behind her. She paused and waited for the applause from the environmentalists in the audience to subside. As she suspected, only the four governors seated in the front row looked uncomfortable with what she was announcing to the country over national television. They had been told only two days before that this event was to happen. To say that they were not happy would be an understatement. Their collective feelings could probably be summarized by the remark made by the governor of Utah to his executive assistant months before, when he had first been informed that this federal landgrab was being orchestrated, "This is the most arrogant, illegal presidential act I have ever witnessed in my lifetime."

"The President has asked me to tell all of you assembled here today that he has always been an environmentalist," the attractive African-American woman in her mid-forties continued, "growing up in a town nestled in the national parks of North Carolina—even if he didn't always know it.'' She smiled when she heard the intended chuckles and snickers and decided to thank her speechwriter when she got back to Washington with a big box of chocolates.

She looked down into the audience at the frozen faces of the governors. She knew they were furious, but she also knew there was nothing they could do to stop the President's action. The three male governors had their heads together, as if they were in a football huddle. The governor of Colorado, an attractive, middle-aged, blond-haired woman, nodded as she clapped perfunctorily. To Barbara, it signaled that the governors had heard the message and understood the marked political consequences this action would have on all future relationships between the federal government and its states.

''We, in the administration, feel that this is a visionary act which will preserve for our children and our children's children the natural beauty of the southlands of Utah.'' She paused again, wondering how many mining executives were watching the broadcast in their plush offices, gnashing their teeth, mentally tallying their lost future revenues.

''With Presidential elections only five months away, couldn't one construe this as a preelection gambit by the President,'' a CNN investigative reporter yelled out from the crowd, ''to curry favor with the environmentalist groups which he neglected for the past four years of his administration?''

Barbara hesitated to reply, having been assured by her staffers that there was to be no Q&A. But she decided that there was more to be gained by responding. ''I think that would be a little too cynical,'' she replied. ''Let us just say that the President has worked on many issues over the last four years and now feels that the time is right for him to focus on an issue in which his heart is truly invested.''

''By what authority has he committed such a precipitous action?'' an anonymous voice called out, encouraged by Barbara's response to the first questioner.

''As you may know,'' Barbara responded, certain that the irate young man was a disgruntled lobbyist or state official, "there has been a long-standing bipartisan tradition over environmental protection. The President employed the same rules that President Theodore Roosevelt used to save the Grand Canyon over ninety years ago—the Antiques Act of 1960—which allows the President, without any consultation with Congress, to designate any properties as 'antiques' and therefore a 'natural treasure' which must be preserved."

Barbara knew, of course, that what she hadn't said was a lot more significant than what she had just told the audience. The governor of Utah seated before her understood perfectly well that the President, by using the Antiques Act, was, in fact, robbing him of legislative powers, as well as revenue-producing land. Each of the other governors was already fearful that his or her state could be next and was counting potential lost monies from mining, shipping, water, or grazing fees. From the expression on their collective faces, there was no doubt that they each understood that the President had just thrown Utah out of his political calculus. With only five electoral votes, Utah was solidly behind the President's opponent, anyway. So it was a no-brainer. By making the Escalante Canyon and the Grand Staircase Cliffs and the Kaparawits Plateau a national monument, to be owned and administered by the federal government, the President would retrieve the millions of environmental votes that he was in the process of losing. It was nothing more than good politics.

"If you look at the rugged, majestic beauty of the Grand Canyon formed by nature's own evolutionary magic," Barbara continued, "then you can well understand what motivated the President to do what he just did today. Let me quote to you from his own words why he made the Utah lands a national monument. 'When I was a teenager in the early 1970s, on a trip with my family, I found myself all alone in the Grand Canyon. Even today, some three decades later, in hectic and in lonely, painful times, my mind drifts back to those hours alone in the canyon.' "

As the ceremonies ended, and the reception line scripted by her advance team began to form, three governors walked up to Barbara to shake her hand. Only the governor of Utah did not join the line. Instead, he turned his back and walked away. Little did the country know, he thought, that this day was much more than the day Utah was robbed of its rightful lands. This day was the beginning of the second civil war in America.

1

NYE COUNTY, NEVADA

Thursday, July 3rd, 10:10 A.M.

The bulldozer ripped through the forest like an army of rapacious termites. Shifting the handles of the crawler tractor back and forth, middle-aged, beefy-faced County Commissioner Larry Teague felt ambivalent. How could he destroy the very trees his grandparents had helped to plant when they first came here from the east coast almost a hundred years ago? Yet how could he continue to live with the imperialism of the federal government, which was turning his county and state into nothing more than a colony? All he knew was that his county needed the road he intended to plow, and he was tired of the runaround he was getting from the bureaucrats in Washington.

The trees in front of his CAT had belonged to his family until they bequeathed them to the state of Nevada some forty years before, in order to maintain the wild-game preserve on which he, his family, and his buddies went deer hunting every November. But at some point in time, for reasons which had become increasingly unclear, these valuable acres of timberland were expropriated by the Federal Bureau of Land Management.

So here he sat, comfortably ensconced within the steel-framed cab of the tractor, making certain that the behemoth beneath him created a large swath of destruction. A handful of heavily armed Nevada State Police stood guard around him, unwitting accomplices in a far more dangerous and uncertain political game than they realized. They were about to defend the state of Nevada's claims to these federal lands.

By temperament and profession, this portly married man with four grown children was described by all who knew him as "an accountant's accountant." He was exceedingly comfortable with debits and credits, profit and loss statements, and balance sheets. Far from being either a social creature or a political animal, he was called (by his wife and close friends) "extremely awkward" in new social situations and "extremely stubborn" when it came to making political compromises. A solid family man and churchgoer, as a county commissioner he had earned the respect of Nye County for extricating the county from imminent bankruptcy by refusing to implement federal legislative mandates which most of his neighbors considered inane. In short, he was by most local standards an exemplary, law-abiding citizen whose only act of defiance since childhood was to "lose" an overdue library book so that he could keep it.

How could it be possible, he wondered, as he rammed the ripper into the rocky red soil, that he was now in a confrontation with the United States of America? He had been honorably discharged from the U.S. Army as a second lieutenant just after the Vietnam War. He was also one of the elders of the local chapter of the Veterans of Foreign Wars. He was a loyal Republican who voted in every election, including primaries party loyalists dismissed as perfunctory. He was born in the United States of America, and for all practical purposes he expected to die in his country as a true patriot.

Watching the state police surround his crawler tractor with their shotguns raised, Teague was suddenly concerned that he had ignited a far more dangerous incident than he had intended. A handful of Nye County citizens stood side-by-side with the Nevada State Police cheering him on. Most were armed.

All Teague had ever wanted to do as county commissioner was to reinstate the right of a legitimate tax-paying entity, in this case Nye County, to exploit its own resources for what was deemed essential for the well-being of its citizens. This was not intended to test state power or federal jurisdiction over these lands. His start of a new road through the forest was simply his action as a county commissioner who would tolerate no unwanted costly delays from whatever source they might arise. As far as he was concerned, the federal government was simply an impediment to achieving one of his campaign promises—that Nye County would finally open an existing weather-damaged road that went through the forest. For the last two years, commuting from one end of the county to the other had been unnecessarily difficult. At the time, he had considered it a pretty reasonable promise to make and a highly feasible goal to attain. Now he was no longer so sure.

In the distance he saw three forest rangers, with their distinctive brown round-rimmed hats and Smokey the Bear uniforms, waving their arms frantically, telling him to stop. He looked away and focused on the hydraulic cylinder lifting the tractor's steel blade as it ripped through the roots of century-old trees and heaved them into the air. They landed a few feet in front of the rangers.

The Nevada State Police focused their attention on the forest rangers, their shotguns pumped. The captain, a wiry, intense man, had lectured his men in the principles of caution and restraint. But he was still concerned that one of his men would accidentally precipitate a conflagration that could end up in one of those Waco-type incidents.

The forest rangers approached the tractor, screaming at the top of their lungs to stop. But their words were lost in the metallic cacophony of the shank protector rising about the ripper cylinder while the push arm of the crawler tractor pulled the bulldozer's track shoes forward.

Behind the forest rangers were a handful of U.S. Alcohol, Tobacco, and Firearms agents, semiautomatics drawn. Teague recognized from TV their distinctive blue windbreakers with the large yellow ATF letters emblazoned both on the front and back of their jackets. Images of the failed assault on the Davidian cult in Waco, Texas, permeated the ATF's collective consciousness as if they were borne of the same professional nightmare that they could never escape. "Err on the side of caution" was the current ATF policy that prevailed over both the six months' basic training exercises of new officers and their subsequent field experiences. Although the men standing in this field had role-played a scenario in which federal agents confronted local officials, this was the first time any of them had been involved in this kind of situation in the field.

The explosion in Oklahoma City, in which 163 people died, had been included in each officer's briefing before coming to this site. Its implications for anti-federal government sentiment had been spelled out very clearly.

Teague turned off the bulldozer's engine. Who knew what these Washington, D.C., hotshots would do next? Maybe they would invoke eminent domain and expropriate the whole fucking forest.

With the bulldozer quiet, the silence was deafening. The Nevada State Police, forest rangers, and ATF officials stood in their places as if frozen, their guns ready. Only the small uncomfortable movements of the civilians created a rustling sound—until a shot rang through the air like a clarion call announcing Armageddon.

2

SALT LAKE CITY, UTAH

Thursday, July 3rd, noon

Governor Josiah Brigham IV felt proud of his thriving city nestled within the snowcapped, craggy peaks of the Wasatch Range of the Rocky Mountains. Sitting in the backseat of his Cadillac limousine with its Choose The Right license plate, driving down Main Street toward Temple Square, the trim, well-coiffed, former high school running back recalled with nostalgia the stories his parents and grandparents would tell him about the hardships the Mormons endured during the Depression. But with the grace of God, hard work, and most important, shrewd, farsighted planning, his ancestors were able to become one of the most important economic forces in the entire country. He was proud that the endless history of Mormon successes was due, in large part, to people like him, men who did not believe in limits when one combined an individual's aspirations with a collective purpose. And like his Mormon ancestors, he was willing to defy all laws of convention in order to achieve his goals.

Did not the founder of the Mormon Church, Joseph Smith, start his career with a water divining rod and eventually land in jail? Despite what looked like an aberrant, if not erratic background, Smith had succeeded in accomplishing what no other man had done in the nineteenth century—he created a new religion. And most cleverly, a religion which incorporated the beliefs of the Old and New Testament, but went on to state that the Book of Mormon was a later, more complete, revelation from God.

My God, thought Brigham, what would it be like to control the minds and hearts of eight million people? Perhaps he could never achieve that type of glory, but as sure as the Wasatch Mountain Range would have snow this coming winter, he, too, would achieve greatness.

It was hard to believe that only a few hours earlier, in front of national television, a different episode in history had repeated itself. And with no adverse repercussions. The federal government had committed another of its many arbitrary acts of authoritarianism by expropriating 1.7 million acres of land in his state. As a result of that action, Brigham knew his political and economic powers were diminished. He could no longer fund state projects to maintain the public schools. Or the highways. And what about the needs of the poor and the elderly? The state was almost as bankrupt as they were. Instead of receiving billions of dollars in royalties from the coal mines on the Kaparowits Plateau, and the tourist revenues from the state parks, he would now have to beg the federal government for money to keep the state afloat. He would have to raise taxes, an act that he swore throughout his gubernatorial campaign he would never do. As an extreme fiscal conservative, he would lose his political cachet. Next election, for sure, some dog catcher without any previous political experience and no fiscal smarts or expertise would defeat him with the promise to lower Brigham's tax increases.

The taking of his state's land by the feds was the last straw. In the long run, states' rights would have to prevail over federalism run amok. From a political point of view, as far as the President was concerned, Utah might as well not exist. Thank goodness, Brigham thought, that he wasn't the only governor who felt that way.

Some of his critics would certainly portray him as the equivalent of the ambitious corporate entrepreneur, using the church as the vehicle for his own advancement. But he couldn't help the fact that he had a hard time coming to terms with the true faith of his religion. At least he had all the accoutrements of being a good Mormon—a relatively successful marriage of twenty-five years, four college-bound children, and strict public adherence to religious practices. As a former mayor of Salt Lake City, he was "a fast-comer" in the religious, financial, economic, and political center of Mormonism. And as one of the senior elders of the church, and as governor of Utah, he bridged a religious and secular gap which most governors in the other states envied. In his heart of hearts, he was probably a "Jack Mormon," the name for someone who left the church because he no longer believed in the religion. But for him, the Mormon Church was a political convenience which he deftly manipulated to suit his purposes.

Brigham's limo slowed to a stop at the first traffic light at the edge of the city. The last thing he remembered for the five seconds he blacked out was the flashing red and white lights of an oncoming ambulance. Only the honking of the car behind him made him realize that he had had another episode of petit mal seizure, a neurological condition during which he would lose consciousness for a few seconds.

He reached into his pocket and took out a bottle of Dilantin and swallowed a pill. He'd better take his medicines regularly, he thought, if he wanted to be able to handle his epilepsy during the stress of the next few days.

The skyscraper of the Church Office Building of the Latter-Day Saints, more commonly known as the Mormons, loomed outside his car window. It was from that building that the extensive wealth of the Mormons was being managed, enhanced, and distributed. The six-spired Mormon Temple now came into view, the elegant embodiment of a church which dominated the state.

From victim to victor, he thought. In 1847, Brigham Young created this city on the arid land known as Salt Lake Valley over the protests of three Indian tribes, the Ute, the Shoshone, and the Cosiute. The Indians were eventually converted to Mormonism or exterminated. But that was the way of the world. Only the fittest survived. Had not President James Buchanan sent federal troops to destroy the Mormons because of their practice of polygamy? Of course, it was really a way to distract the nation's attention away from the bloody wars occurring between Kansas and Missouri over the issue of the abolition of slavery. But thanks to Brigham Young, the Mormons were able to outwit the feds and slaughter them at the battle of Meadow Lands. And didn't the Republican Party under President Abraham Lincoln try to divert the nation's attention away from the ongoing civil war by continuing to attack the religious practices of the Mormons as "unChristian-like"?

Yes, the Mormons had spent a century being victims of the federal government. Yet they never complained. Instead, they focused on those areas of self-growth and development that they could personally affect.

And so it was with some sense of pride that Brigham stared at the landmarks of the city through which he was riding. Salt Lake City had grown quickly from a brilliant Mormon plan that laid out the city in twenty ecclesiastical wards, each of ten acres. The business district developed southward from the Temple on Main Street. By 1870, the population of farmers in the state had decreased as significantly as the city of Salt Lake had grown. The Utah Central Railroad created a boom in mining, milling, and smelting. During World War II, Salt Lake City was a strategic military center, serving as the focus for several installations including Fort Douglas, Kearns Army Air Base, Hill Air Force Base, and Tooele Ordinance Depot. Each contributed to the eventual wealth of the Zion National Bank, which now owned much of the real estate that Josiah was passing—the Salt Palace Convention Center, Beneficial Towers, the ZCMI Mall, and the Crossroads Mall.

It was not until 1983, during his first tenure as mayor, that the residents of Salt Lake City became nationally known for their volunteer efforts in flood control. And it was his first cousin, Joseph Smith III, who, according to Brigham's plans, would soon be headed toward Page, Arizona, was the genius who had figured out the flood-control systems for the Glen Canyon Dam. During Josiah's second mayoral term, he had helped to renew the city's economy so that it could be a viable contender for the Winter Olympic Games of 1989. In his third term, he basically prepared himself to run for governor. The rest was history. He won by a landslide which buried his opponent in anonymity. That was the way Brigham liked to play—tough and hard. Winner takes all.

At Temple Square, the ten-acre parcel at the heart of Salt Lake City, Josiah stepped out of the limousine. He walked past the Salt Lake Temple, its six major towers and ornamental spires signifying the restoration of priesthood authority, and continued past the dome-shaped Tabernacle, renowned for its huge metal elliptical arches that were an incredible innovation in its time.

Cutting across Temple Square, past the Seagull Monument which commemorated the miraculous work of the gulls that saved the crops of the early pioneers, he crossed West Temple Street and entered a nondescript five-story gray granite building. The Family History Library contained all the necessary research tools required to do genealogical research.

On the ground floor, visitors were being taken on a guided tour past the computers, card catalogues, and microfiche systems which were designed to "access" the ancestors of anyone in the United States or, for that matter, around the world. But this was not a benign effort to establish family ties. The church's interest in family history was based on the fundamental doctrines of Salvation, Agency, and Exaltation. The purpose of tracing a family's history was to obtain names so that Temple Ordinances could be performed on behalf of deceased ancestors who did not have the opportunity to hear the restored gospel during their mortal life. The basic religious principle behind the Family History was to allow a living believer to convert thirty-five generations of his or her ancestors. The Mormon Church could do no less than redeem the dead.

Herbert Oaks, seated behind a huge wooden desk with a placard reading "Chief Librarian," was a heavyset man with a full beard and twinkling hazel eyes. He exuded an air of insouciance and comfort that belied an underlying thirst for power. For him, information was power. And the more information one had, the more power was accrued. Oaks was the governor's intellectual and spiritual soul mate.

"How is everything?" Josiah asked in a whisper.

"We've transferred most of the information from here to

the Vault," Oaks responded, "and we're now in the process of cross-indexing."

"Are we on schedule?"

"Follow me and judge for yourself," Oaks replied, knowing that the governor had no choice but to be impressed. This was no small achievement Oaks had accomplished. Using high-tech electronics, he had gathered information on living Americans and their ancestors from over six million records and books. Religion. Date of birth. Ethnic/racial identity. Political affiliation. Arrest record. Bankruptcy and foreclosure data. Television-show preferences. Movies rented. Credit cards used. Insurance claims made. Death certificates. Probate data. And countless other documents. If the information was publicly available, or could be privately purchased, it was in Oaks's files. And now he had transported the 500,000 microfiches, and 4.5 million rolls of microfilm to the Vault. He took pride in the fact that no one but a tireless, ruthless, and ambitious Mormon could have accomplished this task.

The two men walked out of the building together, stepped into the governor's limousine, and rode in silence twenty miles southeast of downtown Salt Lake City, stopping one mile from the mouth of Little Cottonwood Canyon. They walked toward the Vault, a mountain excavation reaching six hundred feet into the north side of the canyon. Constructed between 1958 and 1963, at an outrageous cost at that time of $2 million, it contained two main areas. The office and laboratory section lay beneath an overhang of about three hundred feet of houses, shipping and receiving docks, document-evaluation stations, and administrative offices. The Vault proper was situated farther back in the mountain behind the laboratory. It consisted of six chambers, known as vaults, each 190 feet long, 25 feet wide, and 25 feet high, which were accessed by one main entrance and two smaller passageways. Two of the vaults contained banks of steel cabinets filled with microfilm. Optical discs, computer scanners, fax machines, and endless rows of computers filled the four remaining chambers. The information contained in the Vault had been collected from churches, libraries, government agencies, private organizations, and countless other business and nonprofit organizations.

''Speed up the project,'' Josiah said, nodding his head with unspoken satisfaction. ''I'll be meeting with the other governors very soon, and I want to make certain that we can go on-line as planned.''

''We'll try,'' Oaks replied.

Josiah looked at Oaks sternly. His silence spoke for itself. There was no such thing as ''trying.'' There was no margin for error.

3

LINCOLN, MONTANA

Thursday, July 3rd, 1:15 P.M.

"The Anaconda Copper Company, often referred to as 'the company,' once owned this entire state," Montana Governor Tom Snoddy said to a select group of Wyoming state legislators led by Governor James McMinn. They were all standing on a rubble of exposed ore, surrounded by the beautiful vista of undulating tree-covered mountains covered by a clear blue sky. "At the turn of the century, the company employed three-quarters of the wage earners in the entire state. In addition, the company owned huge copper mines, millions of acres of timber land, railroads, hotels, municipal utilities, and five daily newspapers."

"But that all disappeared once the federal government moved in," James interjected, directing his comment to his own state legislators. "What just happened in Utah—the expropriation of 1.7 million acres of land—already happened here in Montana. And it is about to happen to Wyoming in a very short period of time, if we don't act quickly to pass our State Resolution for Secession."

"We understand, James," Wyoming State Senator Don Tallent offered. "We have, for quite a long time. The necessary papers of secession have been drawn up for months by the Special Committee of the Wyoming State legislature. The men with me today are the five key members of our state legislature who will represent the will of the legislators . . . and public. . . . God only knows that we are a small enough state. With only 500,000 citizens, it's not very hard to take the pulse of its people. All that remains is for all of us to sign it."

"Thank you, Senator," James responded, hopeful that all of the time he had spent over the last few years convincing the powerbrokers in his state that secession was their only fiscally responsible route was now going to pay off.

James McMinn was a tall, unassuming, gangly man dressed in faded blue jeans and cowboy boots, carrying a manila folder filled with the all-but-signed secessionist papers. With very little time left, he had brought the five key legislators in his state to see what had happened since the federal government had preemptorily taken over millions of acres of a state like Montana and made them into a "national monument," just as it had done in Utah. He believed in the adage that a picture was worth a thousand words. More important, he wanted his good friend Governor Snoddy to underline the catastrophic consequences of federal intervention into his state. The Wyoming legislators understood the issues intellectually. But they had to see it.

Four of the five state senators didn't have to be convinced. One was a Libertarian, who believed that there should be no government, whatsoever, at any level. Another senator was an Independent, who had been instrumental in starting the grass-roots campaign in Wyoming for the 1996 Perot presidential campaign. The third was a former 1960s hippie, who was still wedded to the notion that the federal government was dangerous to the well-being of the individual, especially one with a "free spirit." This senator, from the Liberal wing of the Democratic Party, was still fixated on a century of atrocities committed by the federal government. If asked, he had a litany of abuses at the tip of his garrulous tongue, including the FBI's files on prominent individuals like Dr. Martin Luther King; the CIA's conspiracy to transport heroin into the black ghettos of Los Angeles in order to make money to fund other covert operations; the Department of Defense's use of Americans as guinea pigs in nuclear testing; and the CIA/DOD cover-up of the American soldiers' exposure to nerve gas during the Gulf

War. Ironically, the fourth senator was an archconservative Republican, who just didn't trust the bloated government bureaucracy, especially ATF, Department of Interior, and the Bureau of Land Management. He believed, like all true Conservatives, that a government is best which governs least. A minimalist government should stay out of the citizens' bedrooms, pocketbooks, and schools.

The fifth senator was the crucial person to convince. He had been an apolitical physician who had become increasingly interested in politics as he watched his specialty of psychiatry vanish during the first Clinton administration. According to him, the President's wife, Hillary Rodham Clinton, as "tzarina" of health, had singlehandedly destroyed the entire medical profession within a two-year period. Yet as much as he personally despised the former President and his wife for their arrogance, ignorance, and duplicitous betrayal of the American people, he was not yet ready to commit himself to an act of secession—which was equivalent in his mind to an act of treason.

James knew it would not take too much to push the fifth senator over the point of no return. James had already made his case to these and other "friendly" legislators. He was now employing his good friend Governor Snoddy to make that same case in another setting. The irony of it all, thought James, was that although Snoddy might be able to convince Wyoming's senators to have their state secede from the United States, he himself didn't have a snowball's chance in hell of persuading Montana's state legislators to do the same. They were so individualistic and so anti-government that they didn't even trust Snoddy to serve as a replacement for the feds. They were anti-county, anti-state, and anti-federal government. Snoddy had a better chance of convincing his own constituency by first helping Wyoming secede, and then showing how effective the state had become as a self-sufficient entity. Hopefully, at a later time, his state could effect the same course of action.

"The hottest political issue we have going for us right now, gentlemen," Snoddy continued, pointing to the clear stream of water flowing in front of them, "is known as I-122. Simply stated it goes as follows: the tree-huggers, environmentalists, and the federal government are trying to push Proposition I-122 through our legislature in order to weaken and, if possible to eliminate, the 1995 state laws that the feds feel weakened Montana's water-quality standards for dozens of carcinogens. If I-122 is passed, which I am afraid to say looks quite possible, it would be the final death knell for the mining industry, which today still employs over ten thousand Montanans at excellent wages and, by the way, pays five hundred million dollars in state taxes and royalties. I think you gentlemen would all agree that is no small change."

"What would be the effect on the state if I-122 passes?" James asked, lobbing in the softball question so that his companions could hear the numerical consequences of federal intervention.

"That's a good question, James," Snoddy responded, pretending to imagine the calculation that he had already rehearsed in his mind. "First, we would lose five hundred million dollars as a yearly revenue base. That, in turn, would force me to shut down half of my public schools as well as one branch of the state university system, several community colleges, numerous nursing homes and halfway houses, major general hospitals, and a maximum security prison. So now you got all the nuts, sluts, and muscle boys roaming throughout Montana without anything to do or anyplace to go. My welfare costs increase three to four hundred percent, my police force is cut in half. Crime rises, and the citizens correctly scream out that they are not safe. So what do I have left?"

"To increase taxes at a time when your state is bleeding," Tallent responded.

"Worse than that," Snoddy responded. "Stagnation and then chaos. At the same time, exorbitantly high taxes would be levied but never collected. And flight into a nearby citizen-friendly state occurs. I'd probably have to call in the National Guard and declare Montana bankrupt, if the bankers from Wall Street would not allow us to renegotiate our lower credit rating."

"If you—Wyoming—secede from the Union," Snoddy continued, "many of our citizens would go to Wyoming."

''How could we prevent the sluts and nuts from entering Wyoming?'' the Libertarian senator asked.

''Well, Cato,'' Snoddy responded sarcastically, referring to the pseudonym of one of the founding fathers of the Libertarian Party, ''you've got your own National Guard, which will patrol your own borders and allow only those people you deem appropriate to enter. You'll be constructing what any other independent sovereign state would—a security system, self-taxation, and the building of an infrastructure for an autonomous state. I'd sure like to be in that enviable position.''

''But in all fairness, Governor Snoddy,'' the former psychiatrist asked deferentially, ''if you look around you, there are certainly a lot of eyesores here—open ore pits, contaminated waterways, defoliated forests, and strip-mining areas—that the federal government had nothing to do with, except to try to prevent the mining companies from creating even further environmental disaster.''

''You're right, Doctor,'' Snoddy responded, sorry that the issue came up, but having rehearsed his and James's response if it did. ''In Butte, Montana, we had what was called 'the richest hill on Earth' when it was producing $25 billion worth of copper. It is now a monstrous, festering eyesore on the landscape. Butte's Berkeley Pit, closed as an open pit copper mine in 1982, is presently filling up like a toxic cauldron of heavy metal–laced water—28 billion gallons and still rising. Clark Fork River is contaminated for nearly a hundred miles from Silver Bow Creek to the city of Missoula, one of the largest Superfund sites in the nation.''

''But in all fairness to you, Governor,'' James interrupted, fearful that Snoddy hadn't overplayed his part, ''I understand that the Pegasus Gold Corp. and its Zortman Mining Inc. subsidiary has agreed to a nearly unprecedented $100 million settlement with the state to clean up a lot of the pollution.''

''That's correct, James,'' Snoddy responded, ''but that's without any federal intervention. As a matter of fact, had the feds gotten their ugly noses into this mess, they would have made it more costly and almost impossible to conclude a mutually satisfactory deal.''

"So what you're saying, Governor," Tallent concluded, "is that 'you takes your chance and you pays your price.' "

"That's about it, Senator," Snoddy agreed. "It's not a simple choice to make for you guys. I myself have been a decorated war veteran and an extremely loyal citizen of this country. But I'm afraid that I came to the same conclusion as my good friend Governor McMinn, that the federal government has become a major force of terror. It perpetuates incompetence, corruption, demoralization, and fiscal irresponsibility. I can no longer feel part of this great country of ours. I wish I could. I wish I could do something about it. But no matter which way I turn as both a responsible citizen and a state official, I'm frustrated and alienated by a federal bureaucracy that no longer serves the people. It only serves itself by increasing our taxes and playing social worker to the world. For less than that we Americans started a revolution in 1776. Fortunately, gentlemen, you have the ability at this point in history to choose your destiny. I don't—yet. But whichever way you go, we in Montana will be as good neighbors as we can."

"Thank you, Governor," James said, thinking that Snoddy's last speech would have even convinced his dead grandmother to vote his way.

From his manila folder, Governor James McMinn pulled out a packet of secessionist documents, which had been prepared by the Special Committee of the Wyoming legislature. Each state legislator walked up to him and signed his name. When it was his turn, the psychiatrist looked around at his colleagues and then stared into James's hazel eyes. He took the ballpoint pen offered him and signed his name. *"In hoc signo vinces,"* he muttered.

"In this sign, you shall conquer." James translated the Latin proverb for the group, adding "Amen" as he signed his own name as governor of Wyoming.

4

PAGE, ARIZONA

Thursday, July 3rd, 1:30 P.M.

''What's going on here?'' Governor Andrew Paul asked the man wearing the blue windblazer with the Federal Emergency Management Agency initials on the back. Andrew, a short, spunky man with a chiseled physique befitting the Marine he once was, watched as thousands of Page citizens streamed out of the city in cars, trucks, and vans in an orderly fashion. The people who recognized Andrew waved to him. Some of them even came up to thank him personally for having organized such an orderly exodus out of the town. What they didn't know was that he had no idea what they were talking about.

''FEMA has ordered that we evacuate this town within the next eight hours,'' Robert Gottlieb, the fit, commanding director of the regional FEMA office, responded. Robert recognized the governor from local newspaper articles.

''How come I wasn't informed about this evacuation?'' Andrew asked indignantly.

''Sir, I believe your office was notified several weeks ago,'' Robert responded with a tone of indifference combined with a hint of politeness. ''Your subordinates must have probably forgotten to inform you.''

''What do you mean that my subordinates forgot to inform me?'' Andrew asked.

''Sir,'' Robert replied officiously, ''I'm certain that if you go back to your office you will see the written orders that we submitted to your office several weeks ago."

"I see every piece of paper that comes into my office," Paul replied, becoming increasingly more angry.

"I'm sure that you do," Robert responded nonchalantly.

"Who is your superior?" Andrew asked. "I insist on talking to him. Right now."

"I'm sorry, sir," Robert responded calmly, "but he has taken off this long weekend and left me in charge of this evacuation. So you can say, Governor, that you are, in fact, talking to my boss." He smiled as he talked, and Robert could see that his insouciant attitude was driving the governor crazy. Just as he expected.

"This whole evacuation is totally unacceptable," Paul began to shout. "I order you to stop it immediately!" What angered Paul the most was the attitude conveyed by Robert—that FEMA really could care less what he, Governor Andrew Paul, had to say about a major evacuation within his own state. Where were the local Arizona newspapers when he needed them? Paul wondered. He didn't see any journalists. In fact, the entire evacuation route was cordoned off with yellow tape and FEMA agents. There were no Arizona State Troopers, Arizona National Guardsmen, or local police. From everything Andrew could see, this was strictly a federal operation. Something was wrong. Very wrong. But before he did something rash, or said something he would later regret, he had to find out more. The last thing he could afford to do was to undermine the plans that he and his three gubernatorial colleagues were about to implement.

"Sorry, sir," Robert responded firmly. "We are under federal orders to evacuate this town as quickly as possible. In the opinion of FEMA, Page is in serious danger of being destroyed by the floodwaters from a faulty dam."

"What flood?" Andrew asked incredulously. "What faulty dam? What are you talking about?" Suddenly Andrew began to sweat. There was more going on here than met the eye. Could the feds be setting him up? he wondered. Was he going to have to take the fall for his colleagues?

Robert responded as if he had rehearsed the answer many times. "Engineering inspectors from the U.S. Department of the Interior, specifically the Bureau of Reclamation, which is normally responsible for the maintenance of Glen Canyon Dam and power plant, informed FEMA that there were some serious structural problems in the dam and that we had precisely eight hours to evacuate the citizens of the town if we wanted to avoid a major catastrophe. From there, an Executive Order was cut from the White House to activate the FEMA team. So here we are, Governor.''

''What structural problems?'' Paul asked. ''None of my state engineers who monitor the power plant mentioned anything to me about this.''

''Again, sir,'' Robert said politely, ''I can only repeat what was told to me. I'm sorry, but I'm not an engineer.'' Robert saw that Andrew was becoming more irritable, just as it had been anticipated. The plan was working. Now, if he would only tip his hand about what he and his fellow governors intended to do with the Glen Canyon Dam.

''When is this flood supposed to take place?'' Andrew asked.

''Within the next twenty-four hours,'' Robert replied, challenging Andrew to respond.

Andrew now knew that he was being tracked by the feds. Not just by FEMA, the Department of Interior, or the Bureau of Land Management. But by someone more senior in government. Someone who suspected that Andrew was involved in something they didn't like, and they were taking action to prevent it. What else did the feds know, Andrew wondered, and what more would they do? He would have to talk to the other governors and see whether this called for a change in plans. No, on second thought, that might not be smart. Not until he knew how the feds found out. Was there an informer in his ranks? He decided that he wasn't going to say a word to anyone. He would just play along, both with the feds and the governors. He could envision the newspaper articles already: ''Arizona Governor helps the federal government to save the citizens of Page. The Governor worked in secret so that he would not create a panic.'' On the other hand, if the plans to secede succeeded, he had saved his state from both a human and environmental disaster. Either way, it could turn out to be a win-win situation for him. And for a governor with greater aspirations, what could be more appealing than to play both sides against the middle without being accountable for the outcome? It was a politician's wet dream.

5

DEPARTMENT OF STATE, WASHINGTON, D.C.

Thursday, July 3rd, 3:50 P.M.

The State Department Medical Department, known affectionately as "Med," was located in the bowels of the nine-story building. Despite the fact that it was considered one of the essential support units of the diplomatic corps, it had never acquired the appropriate recognition that its twenty Board-Certified physicians, twelve nurses, and twenty-odd paratechs, secretaries, and orderlies felt it deserved. The Director of the Medical Department held the equivalent rank of Deputy Assistant Secretary of State, when it should have been Assistant Secretary of State, and reported directly to the Undersecretary for Management, instead of the more appropriate level—the Secretary of State. In the context of Washington's power structure, Med was the State Department's "stepchild."

Med was responsible for the physical and mental well-being of over nine thousand Foreign Service employees, both stateside and overseas. It was structured like any medical department at any mid-size hospital. There was the Director of Medicine, usually given to some physician who was both an outstanding medical practitioner and who had served at least three tours of duty overseas. Beneath the Director of Medicine were two Deputy Directors, who were also physicians, one for domestic concerns, one for overseas problems. The Deputy Director responsible for overseas problems had a staff of fifteen Regional Medical Officers, general practitioners who were stationed strategically all over the world so that they could handle any medical emergency. RMOs were usually based in the principal capital of a geographical region but spent seventy percent of their time on an airplane, visiting embassies throughout their region. Once they were in a particular location, the RMO would assist the full-time nurse who was stationed at that embassy in evaluating the more difficult medical cases. If a case required more or better medical intervention than could be provided by the host government, the RMO was authorized to evacuate the patient to the nearest hospital, where he or she could receive the necessary treatment. The "medivac" could cost anywhere from a thousand dollars to almost fifty thousand dollars, depending on the severity of the case and the distance that the patient had to be transported.

Like most local stateside hospitals, the Medical Department was an unending drain on the overall budget of the State Department. The cost of the medical services was hard to contain, and the number of unforeseen variables could only be guessed at in the yearly budget. In addition to taking care of Foreign Service officers, Med was responsible for the welfare of all the personnel located in thirty-three different agencies, which were housed in any overseas embassy—the FBI, Commerce, the United States Information Agency, the Drug Enforcement Agency, Agriculture, etc. Only one government agency provided its own medical services to its own personnel—the CIA. Consistent with their paranoid character, the CIA trusted neither State nor any other institution to take care of CIA personnel.

Alison Carter, M.D., was one of those twenty-year career "meds" who would come in to see his patients or finish his paperwork even on a national holiday like July Fourth. By all accounts, he was considered a doctor's doctor by colleagues and patients alike. He was there for anyone, anywhere, the last of a breed of General Medical Officers whose life was dedicated to medicine and patient care. He exuded warmth and concern. It was hard not to think that he cared about whomever he dealt with. Six feet in height, meticulously dressed in a tweedy sports jacket and khaki pants (contrary to the standard dress code of the FSO—striped gray suit), he always wore either a bow tie or regular tie that made you want to laugh. Or made you feel that this physician was, above all else, a caring human being. He had a twinkle in his hazy blue "bedroom eyes" that made him extremely attractive to women. But beneath the sharp features of his Swedish-stock face, he had a certain coolness and reserve that on occasion could transform into a stern and authoritarian forcefulness. In his college days at Columbia University, he was captain of all three major varsity teams—football, baseball, and rugby. But it was rugby that he enjoyed playing most of all. It required all the agility and body contact of football but without the advantage of helmet and padding. His tolerance for physical pain was legendary. He once walked around one week after a rugby game with a two-inch gash in his thigh without having said a word about it until it was discovered by his girlfriend, a frail, hysterical Barnard literature graduate who insisted that he have his wound attended to immediately. Depending on whom you talked to, many described him in both manners and appearance as a cross between Robert Redford, Marcus Welby, M.D., and James Stewart. He could care less, however, about those sorts of ersatz Hollywood descriptions and simply attended to his two passions—medicine and rock 'n roll.

On this day, Alison Carter, M.D., decided that he would go into work wearing a silk Batman and Robin tie that he had found at a Big Entertainment kiosk in the Georgetown Park mall while looking for rock 'n roll memorabilia. He had heard that a poster of Buddy Holly and the Crickets was selling for seven hundred dollars, a considerable bargain. It was one of the last posters distributed before the fateful tour in which Buddy Holly, along with the "Big Bopper" ("Hellooo Baby!") and Richie Valens ("La Bamba"), died in an airplane accident on February 3, 1959. There was no reason for wearing this particular tie, other than the fact that it seemed timely. And he doubted that he would encounter anyone in the office at this time to question his sartorial decision. The staff had taken off early for the holiday weekend.

Alison preferred being called Al, tired of being defensive that a vengeful, alcoholic, high school principal of a father from upstate New York had bestowed upon him a woman's name. But like Johnny Cash's "Boy Named Sue" hit record, defending the name Alison had produced within him a strong sense of self, an iron will mixed with mischief and playful self-deprecation. He outgrew his father's act of vengeance and used the name to become the very opposite of what his father had intended him to become—angry, bitter, vengeful—just like himself.

Instead, Al was entering middle-age with his boyish good looks, thinning red hair, and one failed childless marriage. He enjoyed his life immensely. Besides his great love for medicine, patient care, the Foreign Service, and rock 'n roll, he had an "addiction" to chewing gum. Irrespective of kind, taste, age, or quality.

On any given day, Al usually carried two to three packs of sugarless bubble gum in the inside pocket of his jacket, which he would chew at the rate of one piece every hour. All day long. His most embarrassing moments came when he felt compelled to blow bubbles and then finish the feat by cracking the gum. By this time in his life it was not something he thought about consciously but was a compulsive behavior to which he considered himself a slave. The minute he began to chew a new piece of bubble gum, he invariably had to test out its elasticity by blowing a bubble. If the bubble he blew expanded beyond a two-inch diameter, he was ecstatic for the rest of the day.

Chewing his favorite strawberry bubble gum, Al walked down the empty dark lower level corridor to his ten-by-six office, a tiny hole in the wall that was considered prestigious only because it had a below-ground window guarded by a window well that faced State's C Street diplomatic entrance. Because of the holiday, he didn't expect many patients in the medical clinic, which really served as a regular doctor's office. But he had received a message from the seventh floor to stand by. And when someone from the seventh floor wanted you, it was the equivalent of the chief of a hospital asking to see an attendant. He scanned an office crammed full with stacked medical files, computer printouts, and all kinds of rock 'n roll memorabilia and relaxed into an oversized leather chair that had seen better days, his foot on his desk, arms folded behind his head, and blew a large bubble.

"Sam the Sham and the Pharaohs," a voice said as the door of his office opened slowly.

" 'Wooly Bully!' " he responded, waiting for the next volley in an ongoing battle of rock 'n roll trivia.

" 'I've got a gal named Daisy/She almost drives me crazy/Whooooo. . . .' "

" 'Tutti Frutti,' by Little Richard," Al responded nonchalantly, "recorded on Specialty Records."

"And the writer?"

"Richard Penniman," Al replied, "the real name for Little Richard."

"And . . . ?"

"He recorded a score of rock 'n roll classics for Specialty," Al answered, popping the bubble. " 'Long Tall Sally,' 'Slippin' and Slidin',' 'Ready Teddy'. . . ."

"Okay," the voice interrupted, "a dinner if you can name his backup band."

"Forget the dinner, Madame Secretary," Al said, taking his feet off the desk and moving her toward a chair opposite him. "It's a slam dunk."

"Then let's see you slam it in," Barbara dared, taking a piece of bubble gum from his pack.

"He had the finest New Orleans rhythm 'n blues band—Earl Palmer on drums, Lee Allen, tenor sax, Alvin 'Red' Tyler, his baritone sax, Frank Fields on bass, and guitarists Edgar Blanchard, Justin Adams, and Ernest McLean."

Barbara slowly blew a bubble that was large enough to be a winner and burst it. "I want you to do me a favor."

"I'm all yours," Al responded. "Let's rock 'n roll."

6

DEPARTMENT OF STATE, WASHINGTON, D.C.

Thursday, July 3rd, 4:05 P.M.

"What's up, Barbara?" Al asked, sensing that the Sec State's appearance in his basement office on a holiday weekend was not going to be a routine request for personnel information. He walked over to a drawer with medical equipment, withdrew a sphygmomanometer, and placed the blood pressure cuff on her left arm. With his stethoscope in his ears, and the black rubber bulb in his right hand, he blew the cuff up beyond the numbers her hypertension might indicate.

"How in God's name can we talk?" she demanded, "if you're wearing that damn stethoscope in your ear?"

"That damn stethoscope is singing some tunes that don't sound like 'ram-a-lam-a ding-dong.' " Al ignored her righteous indignation. "As a matter of fact, it's telling me that you are under a lot of stress and we're going to have to up your anti-hypertensive dose of meds."

"Oh no, you're not!" she said emphatically.

"Down here in the boiler room," he said, deflating the blood pressure cuff, "I'm in charge. Upstairs on the seventh floor, the captain's deck, you're in charge."

"Are you getting uppity with me, Dr. Carter?" Barbara asked.

"I'm not one of your pin-striped bag carriers." Al continued to ignore her comments. "I'm just a simple doctor, relegated to the bowels of this stately ship, so that I can have the privilege of treating some of your 'best and brightest' people steering foreign policy.''

Al had been Barbara Reynolds's doctor for ten years, starting when she first came into the Foreign Service and served as Assistant Secretary of Security and Consular Affairs. He had traveled all over the world with her from Harare, Zimbabwe, where she caught malaria (despite his insistence that she take Lariam weeks before and after the trip), to St. Petersburg, Russia, where she caught giardiasis, a water parasite, after he had warned her not to drink anything that wasn't boiled or 12 percent proof alcohol. Only when she became ill would she follow his directions. By that time, of course, it was too late. Sometimes he wondered if she didn't do it out of spite, just to prove him medically fallible.

Like most understanding, compassionate doctors, he understood her initial reluctance to listen to him because it was an organic part of the unique physician-patient relationship. On the one hand, the patient wanted the physician to be omniscient and all-powerful in order to be helpful. On the other hand, the patient also wanted the doctor to be wrong, or not as powerful as the patient would like him to be, so that the patient could have some control over his or her own life. It was a push-me, pull-me type of relationship, which Al understood all too well. So he proceeded with whatever procedures he thought appropriate despite Barbara's protests. But beneath the verbiage of a tough, independent woman, he knew that she felt comfortable letting down her facade in front of him. Of course, only in the guise of a patient.

''I want you to help me manage a major crisis.''

''Your hypertension is getting worse,'' Al said. ''Your blood pressure is up to 170 over 120, and that's with antihypertensive medications. That's the crisis.'' Al stood up and examined her right eye and then her left eye with his ophthalmoscope. He was looking for the light reflections off the arterioles exiting the optic nerve of the retina, and he didn't like what he saw. The area around the optic nerve was enlarged and red. This meant that Barbara's brain was beginning to swell and put pressure on the nerves servicing her eyes. The shininess and narrowness of the arterioles servicing the optic nerves looked constricted and tortuous. This meant that a great amount of blood pressure was required to make the blood flow through these narrow passages.

"Dr. Carter," Barbara pronounced emphatically, "you didn't hear me. I need your help and it's not about blood flow. Then again, maybe it is."

"If you don't take a vacation and get that pressure way down, you are going to have a major vascular crisis. It will be called a stroke." He wrote out a prescription for a stronger than normal anti-hypertensive drug. "And you will wind up in the hospital for a long time. It's no joking. . . ."

"Al," she interrupted, "listen to me. This is important. I want you to act as my personal emissary for a very unusual assignment. You're one of the few people I can trust who doesn't have some kind of political, bureaucratic, or personal agenda to get in the way. Politically, you don't belong to anyone and you can't be compromised—to my regret, sometimes. Bureaucratically, you're inept, anyway. How long do you think you would have survived in this tight-assed environment chewing bubble gum and singing rock 'n roll? If I weren't sitting upstairs, my dear doctor, you wouldn't be hidden away down here."

"A little threat goes a long way with me." Al laughed, popping a bubble. As both knew, implied threat or guilt had very little effect on him. In general, he was immune to the Machiavellian machinations of a normally functioning bureaucracy.

"Moreover, I can invoke that wonderful doctor-patient relationship of confidentiality which, as you and I know, is sacrosanct," Barbara added. "So I can tell you all kinds of things and you can't tell anyone else what I just said. Isn't that true?"

"What's true is that you have malignant hypertension," Al responded, ignoring her serious tone, "and it's out of control. I don't have to explain to you that blood pressure like that in African-American males or females can be lethal."

"You don't have to scare me," Barbara replied calmly. "I know quite well what I have. I've been taking pills long enough to know what it means."

"Do you still get intense headaches?" he asked. "How about a numbing sensation in either hand?" He wondered whether he should hospitalize her as the only way to be certain that she would get the proper medication and rest.

"You didn't answer my question," Barbara repeated. "Will you act as my personal emissary? Just say yes. I have a lot to tell you."

"Barbara, listen to me," Al said, taking her hands into his. "We've known each other too long to kid each other. . . ."

"The country is coming apart at the seams," Barbara interrupted again, knowing he was right but not wanting to hear the actual words. "Malignant hypertension." It scared her. The term sounded as if she had a terminal illness. Incurable. Metastatic. Her kidneys, heart, eyes, and brain would all be affected. Her father had died of malignant hypertension at the sprightly age of fifty-two. Her paternal grandfather had died at age sixty from what had been diagnosed then as "a heart condition." She had been treated for hypertension for at least twenty-five years. It was the only reason that she resented being an African-American. Being black and having high blood pressure was a deadly combination. And no one knew why. Maybe that's why she liked to be around her rock 'n roll doctor. Al cared. He cared enough about her as a person that he could periodically force her to do something that she was not capable of doing for herself. Taking proper care. But she was the Secretary of State. And medical problems, no matter how serious, were incidentals that weren't relevant to job performance. No one cared that during the battle of Waterloo, Napoleon Bonaparte suffered from excruciating kidney stones. All that history recorded was that Napoleon met his major military defeat there. His kidney stones were at best a footnote to history. And so it would be with her malignant hypertension, if the United States would begin to fragment during her watch.

"The country is always coming apart at the seams," Al

replied. "Don't change the conversation. The country really can run without you or me. Believe it or not. We are not indispensable."

"Listen to me, Alison Carter . . ." Barbara said, invoking his full name because she knew it would annoy him.

"So we're getting down and dirty," he responded. "Now I know you're trying to avoid taking my advice."

"I've got only a few days to prevent this country from falling apart," Barbara continued. "Do you think that high blood pressure is going to stop me from doing that?"

He stood up, shaking his head. "The headaches are getting worse, aren't they? What am I going to do with you? When I held your hands in mine, you didn't even feel the pinpricks I was applying to them."

"Of course I did," she responded defensively. "I just thought you were cozying up to me and squeezing my hands."

"Barbara," he bent over and whispered in her ear, "you can try to fool me, and you can certainly try to convince yourself that everything is all right. But your body doesn't lie."

"What do you want me to do?" She stood up, face-to-face with him. "Resign my office and check myself into a hospital?"

"The simple answer is yes."

"And the simple response is no way, Jose."

"So as usual we are at a stalemate," he responded. He had played this charade of who's-in-charge so many times before that he knew it was useless to prolong it any further.

"You still haven't answered my question," she persisted.

"What was that?"

"Will you help me out?"

"Of course I will," he replied reflexively. "What other disease do you not want me to help you treat?"

"Can I invoke doctor-patient confidentiality?"

"Wait," he replied facetiously. "I have to shut off the tape recorder."

"No, Al!" she blurted. "I mean it!"

"What in God's name do you think happens when we talk?" he asked in a hurt tone of voice. "It's always confidential. That's how I've been trained as a physician, and that's a value I've carried over into my personal life. So, continue.''

''I need you as a personal emissary, friend, and confidante,'' she continued.

''You got it, lady. But I hope it's for an important mission, like an Elvis sighting. . . .''

''No such luck,'' Barbara interrupted. ''I need you to help me prevent a war.''

7

DEPARTMENT OF STATE, WASHINGTON, D.C.

Thursday, July 3rd, 4:30 P.M.

''We have no choice but to respond,'' Barbara continued, pouring a glass of her favorite Jack Daniel's. ''Josiah Brigham, the governor of Utah, and three yahoo governors from Colorado, Wyoming, and Arizona have presented the White House with an ultimatum—allow our states to secede from the Union peacefully or we'll create such continuous havoc for the federal government that Washington will wind up begging to accept our demands.''

Al said nothing for several minutes, unsure whether Barbara was playing one of her frequent practical jokes. A glance at her strained facial expression, however, assured him of the seriousness of the situation. And he was stunned.

''Good. I see that you do believe me,'' she continued. ''So let me add that, as we speak, our good friends are taking over Glen Canyon Dam in Arizona in an attempt to hold our country hostage to flooding the entire area. And have hinted at bigger catastrophes to follow, unless we give them the response they want.''

''And what is that?'' Al asked, almost dreading to hear Barbara's answer.

''They want the President to sign an Executive Order immediately—already drawn up for him, you understand—that grants the states their demand for secession. It was delivered to the White House earlier today and gives him three days to respond. Luckily, the President and the Vice President were already out of the country. But he was informed of the demand and stated that he is counting on me to diffuse this explosive situation. So, I'm in charge for the next three days. Until he returns. And I need your help.''

''I'm still having a hard time comprehending the magnitude of the governors' request and threats,'' Al responded, grabbing the glass away from Barbara and spilling it out into a nearby plant. He knew that she needed something to anesthetize the sickening feeling that was taking over her gut—and now his—but pills and booze didn't mix. She should know better.

''Can you back off from the details for a moment and put the problem in context?'' he continued. ''You can imagine the questions that are racing through my head. The first problem,'' Al began, ''mind you, no small problem, is of states' rights as the basis for secession. I just find it unbelievable. If my entire life experience has taught me anything, it is that constituents resent state authority as much as they resent the feds. Quite frankly, folks these days are as much anti-state as they are anti-federal government.''

''So far no argument from me,'' Barbara responded.

''That's easy for you to say,'' Al said, ''but do you really understand how much negative feelings most citizens have against state government? In the western states, the most resented government unit is the State Department of Natural Resources, which regulates hunting and fishing. Throughout the country there is the resentment over state taxing authority, and transportation policy, and . . . I could go on and on. The fact that after a secession a state might have even more power over every citizen's life would send shudders through people's alienated bodies.''

''So far,'' Barbara interjected, ''you've said nothing that surprises me. But you didn't see the governors' reactions when we took away 1.7 million acres from one state's power base. We're still talking about different levels of power and different functions. At this point in time, I can only worry about the federal level.''

''Barbara,'' Al implored, ''it's not that simple. Even state legislators with secessionist sentiments have to be convinced that there is more to gain than some financial benefits for the state and the absence of federal intrusion into their operations. Water, electric power, and land rights just don't seem reasons enough to precipitate a possible war among the states."

"Excuse me, my dear friend," Barbara said, "but do you recall what the original civil war was fought over?"

"Slavery."

"Right," Barbara said facetiously, "and if you believe that then I'll send you a box of your favorite chocolates every week for the rest of your natural born life. Doc, that war was fought over two simple things: money and power. The Southern states wanted to exercise their constitutional rights to secede from a union that they didn't feel allowed them to live the kind of life that they were used to. There was as much slavery and racism in the textile factories of Massachusetts but they called it 'inexpensive labor.' The Northerners were just a little more clever than the Southerners. They had the wife of a preacher write a propaganda treatise called *Uncle Tom's Cabin.* Because it was so well written, probably for the first time it allowed the reader to empathize with a black man. And it allowed President Lincoln to use more lofty 'Christian concepts' like man's inequity to man as the basis for going to war against the South when he damn well knew that it had nothing to do with slavery."

"Isn't that being a little bit too cynical?" Al asked.

"No!" Barbara reaffirmed. "It's called reality. You see, the issue of states' rights has never really been settled, regardless of the war we fought between 1861 and 1865. Just look at secessionist movements all over the world right now. Quebec wants to secede from Canada. The north of Italy wants to secede from the rest of the country. Catalonia and the Basque provinces want to dissociate themselves from Spain. Czechoslovakia became two countries. Yugoslavia has become three. And here in the States, the northern part of California wants to have nothing to do with the southern part of the state. I've even seen proposals for California to be divided into three states. Sure, states splitting off into smaller entities is different from states becoming independent countries. But look at NAFTA. We no longer have state interests that correspond to artificially imposed political units. Now it's economic, geographic, and cultural factors that tie different regions of the country together. Or with Canada. Or Mexico. For regionalism to exist and flourish, a great many state legislators and citizens want Washington, D.C., to disappear. Our federal government has become a hindrance and not an asset in this new 'state of affairs,' so to speak.''

''And you think I can . . . infiltrate . . . the secessionist movement and flush out the treasonous elements who are consolidating power in the four states?'' Al asked, not sure whether Barbara's expectations were based in too much reality or too many drugs.

''Yes,'' Barbara replied. ''If anyone can, I have confidence that you can. Listen, we've crisscrossed the globe together for years. And don't give me that 'I'm just a humble doctor' routine. You've always given me invaluable assistance in critical situations, and I don't mean just medical. Sometimes I think that it's you who should be Sec State. You've dealt with international crises. You have a better understanding of human nature than my ten best Foreign Service officers put together. You have no political axe to grind. I trust you implicitly. Shall I go on? You know more about my body . . .''

''Enough,'' Al interrupted, slightly embarrassed by the passion behind her words. ''Flattery will get you everywhere. But is what you are asking do-able?''

''To put it bluntly, it's now or never,'' she responded.

''What do you mean?''

''The secessionist movement is spreading, unnoticed, and uncoordinated, throughout this country,'' Barbara replied. ''But wherever it is, it's based on one basic doctrine—the sovereignty of the state.''

''I certainly remember some of it from American History One-oh-One. Let me guess the arguments,'' Al said. ''Our early theoreticians layed the intellectual foundation for secession. Thomas Jefferson wrote about the nullification by the states of unconstitutional federal laws. James Madison, to counter, declared that such acts, unless 'arrested on the threshold, may tend to drive these states into revolution and blood.' "

"Now I know why you were magna cum laude," Barbara added.

"You flatter me," Al interjected. "Believe me, I was never that good a student. But keep laying on the flattery, I love it." He smiled, pleased with himself and ready to continue testing his memory. "Now John C. Calhoun's ideas were much more carefully developed into a specific system. Again, basing his argument on the theory of the Constitution as a compact among sovereign states, he said that when a state believed the federal government had overstepped the boundaries of its constitutional authority, the state could call a special convention which could nullify federal law . . ."

"But the Fourteenth Amendment to the Constitution asserted the doctrine of national sovereignty," Barbara continued, "by defining citizenship and making the national government the guarantor of individual rights. So the national government—that is, the federal government in Washington, D.C.—was given a direct constitutional relationship with individuals and could no longer be construed only as a compact among states."

"Put those original doctrines all together, which some modern-day scholars interpret as the real issue behind the Civil War," Al concluded, "and the constitutional right of states to secede can be quite appealing. It was espoused by some of our most respected founding fathers."

"You got it! Place these theoretical justifications for states' rights," Barbara continued, "in the hands of ambitious governors and paranoid citizens and we ease our way not only into secessionist movements but militia groups and Posse Comitatus, the refusal to pay taxes of any form. Combine them with normal alienated citizens and what do we have? The new 'patriot'—the False Patriot—who can justify all of his or her actions according to the original precepts of the Declaration of Independence, which spells out exactly what should be done if the contract between a citizen and a sovereign state is violated. . . . Nothing less than revolution."

"Aren't you becoming a bit paranoid yourself?" Al

asked, concerned that the stress of Barbara's position and physical condition might be leading her to overreact to some disgruntled politicians. "I know that disaffection with the feds . . ."

"It's considerably more than disaffection," Barbara stated emphatically. "Will you believe me when I tell you that over the past months, small but powerful groups of malcontents, manipulated or being manipulated by powerful legislators, have put together legal documents of secession? In four states that I know of?"

"How do you know that?" Al asked, his face flushed red.

"Come on, Al," Barbara responded. "It's my job to know. That's why I've asked you to help me. The President and the Vice President left it up to me. Their overseas trips allow them 'plausible deniability' if anything goes wrong."

"You realize I need some time to think about this, don't you?" Al asked. "I also need as many briefings and background documents as you can give me to read."

"Time is of the essence, as the lawyers say," Barbara responded. "You'll have what you need in a few hours. And then I need you on a plane."

8

LAKE POWELL, ARIZONA

Thursday, July 3rd, 1:45 P.M.

Richard Solomon, a handsome, self-effacing spokesperson for the BLM was not enjoying his day on the water. For one thing, he became slightly seasick whenever the boat rocked back and forth at slow speeds. For another, he wasn't sure that he could pull off the next two hours without the media catching on.

For the first twenty minutes on board, everyone had reviewed a highly polished version of the facts about the Colorado River and the Glen Canyon Dam project which the BLM felt it necessary to publish. It mentioned that the dam, built in March 1963, contained the Colorado River at its most northern part and provided over 1,320,000 kilowatts of electricity to Arizona, Colorado, Utah, Wyoming, New Mexico, California, and Nevada. It held an impressive volume of 26,214,861 acre feet of water, second in size only to the Hoover Dam, constructed in September 1935. As in most projects of such massive proportions, the basic reason for its very existence was political, part of an unrelenting congressional pork barrel. The proud sponsor was the distinguished senator from Arizona, Carl Hayden.

The briefing document continued with the history of water use in the area, originally based on the concept of ''first in time, first in use.'' But by the early 1920s, water in the developing Southwest had become too precious a commodity to leave to an unregulated stampede of states. The seven states through which the Colorado River flowed wanted assurances that each would have access to its share of the river's water. The Colorado River Compact of 1922 divided rights among those states. As a condition of the compact, the upper basin states were required to allow a 75-million acre flow to pass to the lower basin states every ten years. Years after, to further enforce the correct distribution of water, the Colorado River Storage Act of 1956 required the building of a large dam and reservoir very near the dividing line between the upper and lower basins. The Glen Canyon Dam was intended to store water for the upper basin and to guarantee the accurate delivery of the mandated amount of water, on schedule, to the lower basin.

During the late 1960s, the growing community of environmental activists began to protest the impact that the dam was having on the areas around the river. The environmentalists were the first to notice that the color of the water entering the canyon no longer ran the muddy red of the ancient Colorado but had become a clear green, completely free of sediments. This simple change in river color signaled a fundamental change in the very nature of the riverine ecosystem. Through experimentation, it was found that the clear river meant that the energy available from the sun would no longer reflect off the surface of the water; it would penetrate the water deeply. The effect of this new phenomenon was that old species of fish were being replaced by new ones, like the highly prized rainbow trout, carp, and catfish. Unlike the fish that had been there previously, the new ones were able to adapt to perpetually cold water.

It was the environmentalists, however, whom Richard knew he had to appeal to, so the remainder of the information focused on how the streamside habitat of the river corridor changed more slowly but no less drastically. As the dam stabilized the river's peak flows, annual floods that previously had damaged the riverbanks were eliminated, allowing for a vigorous growth of new vegetation to develop. As a result of this newly added vegetation, populations of lizards, toads, small mammals, and birds flourished. Paradoxically, even as the dam made this new streamside abundance of vegetation possible, its long-term existence was threatened by the new river. The vegetation was rooted in and dependent upon pre-dam sediments deposited by the river. Now that its load of silt was trapped in Lake Powell, the river had become a corrosive force, with little suspended sediment to replace the vast amount it carried away. One of the most deleterious, far-reaching effects of the dam, contended the environmentalists, was their observation that there had been a gradual decline and in many cases a gradual disappearance of sandbars, or beaches, available to support wildlife producing riverside vegetation. The possibility that the dam-controlled river could scour itself to bedrock, removing the newly gained wildlife habitat in the process, was now becoming evident.

"The increased recreational use of the river corridor," Richard announced to the group of selected journalists, local TV news anchormen, and most important, CNN correspondents, "has compelled us to create the Colorado River Research Program. The BLM is currently undertaking twenty-nine separate scientific studies which focus on human use of the river and its natural resources."

The group approached the dam aboard the 120-foot cabin cruiser confiscated by the FBI from a drug smuggler and loaned to the BLM. Richard had to marvel at the clear blue waters of the 186-mile-long Lake Powell and Wahweap Bay. At some turns in the lake, his eyes played tricks on him, and he could swear that the steel-arch bridge that spanned the two sides of the Glen Canyon was merely painted on an expansive concrete surface. He knew, of course, that the bridge was separated from the dam by 865 feet. This pristine image of lake and sky was enveloped within a rust-colored sandstone frame which constituted the Glen Canyon, itself forged several millennia ago from the Colorado River gorging the earth's craggy bedrock.

"Mr. Solomon," an attractive CNN reporter said diplomatically, "you've made a very convincing presentation that the Glen Canyon Dam has been the largest single influence over the Colorado River and that the dam has dramatically altered the natural cycles of flooding in the river through the Grand Canyon . . ."

"What are you getting at?" Richard asked, atypically impatient. He was a tall, middle-aged man with a physique befitting a man who played tennis five times a week. Calm down, he said to himself, everything is going well. He had to remind himself again what the purpose of this mission was, and it was certainly not to antagonize his important media guests, which numbered around fifty. Most of these hotshots were with him because it was a wonderful junket in the Southwest which they could charge to their employers as a business expense. From Richard's point of view, it was a win-win situation. He got them to listen to and report a non-story.

"Well, Mr. Solomon, to put it bluntly," the CNN correspondent contended with a respectful yet forceful tone of voice, "the person who invited each of us on this trip informed us that we would be privy to something important today."

"That's true," Richard replied, looking at the CNN correspondent, an attractive, short brunette. "Starting tomorrow, on July Fourth, the BLM is going to flood the area downstream of Lake Powell."

"Why are you going to do that?" the CNN correspondent asked, slightly alarmed at the prospect.

"We are going to re-create, under controlled conditions, the flood of 1983," Richard responded, looking at the inquisitive and confused faces around him. "From 1963 to 1983, little, if any, attention was given to the potential for downstream floods once Lake Powell was full. Unlike the managers of the Hoover Dam, who were required by law to prevent downstream flooding and degradation of resources and property, Glen Canyon Dam managers had no such mandate."

"So?" the CNN correspondent asked, annoyed that the "important" promised event was no more than history re-created, and was suddenly sorry that she would be spending part of her July Fourth weekend on the plane, traveling home, when it should have been spent with her family.

"A higher-than-average snowpack in the Rocky Mountains in the spring of 1983, an unusually rapid snowmelt, and unseasonal rainfalls in May and June of that year, combined with full reservoirs throughout the upper basins, were to have profound consequences for the Colorado River in the Grand Canyon,'' Richard continued, as if he believed that his audience was truly interested in the information.

''And?'' she persisted.

''The resulting flood of June 1983 was unprecedented for the river corridor environment that had developed under controlled, stable conditions since 1963.'' Richard spoke slowly, pleased that the media was getting restless. ''What we discovered was that the river's ecosystem was changed in one month of uncontrolled flooding more than it had been by all the recreational activities of the previous twenty years combined.''

''So what you're trying to say''—the CNN correspondent emphasized the words ''trying to say,'' making certain that Richard understood that without her help he was not getting his message across—''is that the hand of man, and not nature, now controls the operations of the Glen Canyon Dam.''

''That's precisely correct,'' Richard said, enchanted that the most cynical correspondent was biting the bait hook, line, and sinker. Within a few minutes he would convince the group that the flooding of the downstream area was environmentally necessary. A ''non-event'' in the course of political history. Just another prosaic federal government experiment. Only he knew that nothing could be further from the truth.

''By tomorrow, as each of you very patient people are celebrating Independence Day, we will begin to implement the Glen Canyon Environmental Studies authorized by the Bureau of Reclamation, the Secretary of Interior, in cooperation with the National Park Service, U.S. Fish and Wildlife Service, U.S. Geological Survey, and the Arizona Game and Fish Department. The goal is to analyze the effects of the dam on downstream resources. By flooding the downstream areas we are going to study the best ways to manage the dam for the benefit of plants, animals, and human beings. We will be temporarily evacuating anyone whose property might be in the path of the waters and undertaking some deferred maintenance on the dam itself while we have the chance. In short, we're covering several bases at once.

"Look at it this way. The Colorado River has become a single, complex plumbing system, with Glen Canyon and Hoover dams the controlling faucets. In the arid Southwest, the Colorado River is life for millions of people, and empires of agriculture, manufacturing, mining, development, and recreation. The Colorado River is the most used, the most dramatic, and the most highly litigated and politicized river in this country, if not the world."

When he finished speaking, Richard could see that he had lost the interest of most of his audience. So far, so good, he thought.

9

NYE COUNTY, NEVADA

Thursday, July 3rd, 11:05 A.M.

''Who fired that shot?'' Larry Teague asked as he scanned the nervous faces of the forest rangers and ATF agents. He doubted the shot had come from his own Nevada State Police, who were greatly outnumbered by their federal adversaries. Climbing down from the tractor, he walked slowly toward the federal agents. Everyone standing in the forest at that moment knew that one wrong word or impulsive act could spark an incident which would have less chance of being contained than did the county's disastrous forest fire of 1972.

''None of us did,'' Nevada State Police Captain Robert McElroy yelled to Teague. A former Marine major, whose nickname was the ''sphincter commander,'' he was a perfectionist when it came to training, command, and execution. ''I would venture to say that it was probably one of those feds.''

''Bullshit!'' ATF Agent Sandy Evers shouted back. He was a ruddy-faced, flaxen-haired, former New York City policeman, who was now a ''double dipper,'' drawing his pension from the city while he drew a paycheck from the federal government. Because he knew how to extract the maximum advantage from both systems, he certainly had no interest in seeing either one destroyed. He was one of those atypical law enforcement agents who had always believed that civilian concerns should dominate any system in which force or the restriction of civil liberties was involved.

"Then what the hell was that sound?" McElroy asked. "A nine-millimeter Beretta or an elephant fart?"

"Sounded more to me like an elk eructating," Evers replied.

Everyone broke into laughter.

"I bet most of you guys don't even know what that means."

"Hey, boss," McElroy asked, looking at Teague. "Do you know what that means?"

"Captain," Teague replied, "I think we should really concentrate on the matter at hand." He added matter-of-factly, "Belch." Again everyone started to laugh. A smile crept across Teague's face. "Now, can I talk to someone who is in charge of this matter? Are you in charge of all these federal agents?" Teague asked, pointing to Evers.

"Yes, I am." Evers motioned to his agents to lower their guns and walked toward Teague, cradling his shotgun with both arms.

"My name is Larry Teague," he said, extending his hand to Evers. "Pleased to meet you. I'm Nye County Commissioner. I have been duly authorized by the county to clear this land so that we can restore a much-needed road through these woods."

"I know who you are," Evers said, shaking Teague's hand. "But I think we have a real problem here. I have been authorized by the Department of Justice, the Department of Interior, and the BLM to make certain that Federal Law 232 is not violated, which prohibits any person or persons from tampering, damaging, or destroying federal lands. The fine is $10,000 and five years in prison for damaging federal property and another $50,000 and ten years in prison for obstructing the law. Which is what you are presently doing."

"So you want us to stop," Teague said soberly.

"That's pretty much the idea," Evers said. "It's not much more complicated than that." He added, "Leave, and take your state troopers with you, and we will forget this ever happened. Chalk it up to some kind of misunderstanding."

"And if I continue? . . ." Teague said.

"Please," Evers interrupted, "don't even think it. I'm trying to defuse a situation that I know neither of us wants to occur."

"I see," Teague responded. "Do you think we can explore what the options are?"

"The options are quite simple, Mr. Teague," Evers said with some exasperation. "You either vacate these premises within the next few minutes or we have no choice but to arrest you."

"It's that cut and dried, huh?" Teague asked.

"I'm afraid that's pretty much the case," he responded. "My orders are to stop you from whatever you're doing," Evers responded, trying to moderate his officious tone, "and make certain that neither you nor anyone else destroys the natural beauty of this area." He looked at his five ATF agents with their guns pointed in the direction of Teague and his police. Evers couldn't help thinking how beautiful and peaceful it was in this part of the woods. There was a crispness and freshness in the air that he had forgotten could exist at all. Having worked in the Los Angeles regional office for the past two years, he was starting to get used to city smog and pollution. What a pity, he thought, that this halcyon setting could become the scene of a major bloodbath. He turned toward the five Nevada State Police officers, focusing his attention on McElroy. He saw beads of sweat forming around the rim of his gray broad-rimmed hat. How could he not feel scared? he wondered. He could feel his own sweat spread over his back against his ATF jacket. Was there really any difference between him and McElroy? Both were working-class boys who had become professional law-enforcement officers. McElroy had probably served in 'Nam, as he had. McElroy probably had a wife and kids, as he had; maybe even a second wife with a new set of kids because he was too young when he first married early in his law-enforcement career. If he were any good at his job, Evers thought, McElroy had probably received a meritorious award for service beyond the call of duty, as he had. This was crazy, he thought. Why should he subject himself and his officers to a potential gunfight against well-intentioned police officers who were sworn to uphold the law? But which law? The law of the land? Was it federal law or state law? Perhaps neither one was worth dying for.

"I think it's quite clear, Mr. Teague," McElroy said, impatiently shifting his weight. "These feds are intent on shooting it out." Once said, McElroy's men started repositioning themselves.

The ATF agents responded as if they were playing a silent chess game by repositioning themselves so that they would be able to take advantage of their numerical superiority.

God forbid, but if there were a gun battle, thought McElroy, he and his men would be outmanned and outgunned. It would be a duck shoot, which left him with only one reasonable alternative—retreat.

"Mr. Teague," McElroy called out, "we have to talk." He walked over to where Teague stood in front of the bulldozer.

"Larry," McElroy lowered his voice, "there's no point in wasting lives."

"What are you telling me?" Teague asked.

"This is a no-win situation," McElroy replied. "A lot of good men could get hurt, maybe even die. There must be something you can do to prevent this."

"Are you suggesting that I back down?" Teague asked.

"That's what I'm recommending," McElroy responded. "I thought they would back off the minute they saw state troopers assisting you. But these feds are gung-ho. Remember what they did in Waco and Ruby Ridge with that white supremacist. They'll throw in everything they've got until the very last one of us is dead."

"But you knew this beforehand," Teague said, somewhat irritated. "What's different now?"

"Looking down the barrel of a fellow law-enforcement agent's gun," McElroy replied, "makes you think twice about what you really want to do, and whether it's worth killing a fellow American over some small piece of forest."

"Sometimes you have to just stand and fight for what you believe in," Teague answered.

''This is not one of those times, Larry,'' McElroy responded.

''Gentlemen,'' Evers screamed out. Sensing the difference of opinion between Teague and McElroy, he was determined to take advantage of it. He motioned to his men to continue outflanking the state police. ''I'll give you ten seconds to put down your weapons.''

10

GLEN CANYON DAM, LAKE POWELL, ARIZONA

Thursday, July 3rd, 3:35 P.M.

''Daddy, what time is it?'' ten-year-old Samantha ''Sammy'' Smith asked as she watched the lunarlike landscape whizz past her. She peered through the back window of the hot Chevrolet with both incredulity and fear. How insignificant she felt as she stared at the red barren rocks jutting into the overwhelmingly blue sky. For Sammy, this entire moonlike landscape held a frightening fascination. While it reminded her of the three-dimensional holograms she loved at Disneyland, these strange forms left her with an overwhelming sensation that she could not survive the experience of being part of it.

''Sweetheart, don't bother your father,'' her heavy-set thirty-eight-year-old mother, Rachel Smith, née Jenifer Olditz, replied. ''He's trying to concentrate on his driving.'' She flashed a quick glance at her husband, a balding, intense, yet kind man who never raised his voice above a whisper.

''That's all right, Sammy,'' Joseph Smith V replied. ''It's almost four o'clock. We're only a few minutes away from the dam.''

''Daddy?'' Sammy asked.

''Yes, darling,'' Joseph responded, detecting a sense of both confusion and urgency in her voice. ''What is it?''

''I don't understand it, Daddy,'' Sammy said, anxiously

twisting the ring that her father had given her on her tenth birthday.

"Sammy," Rachel reiterated, "don't bother your father. If he gets too distracted you may cause him to have an accident. Now you wouldn't want to do that, would you?"

"Mommy," Sammy responded plaintively, "how do you expect me to learn anything if I don't ask any questions?"

"She's right," Joseph responded in his clearly restrained, mellifluous voice. He was disturbed by his wife's overprotective attitude toward him, hovering about like a mother hen, guarding him from any type of intrusion.

"I don't get it, Daddy." Sammy completed her thought before her mother could interrupt her. "How could it be almost four o'clock now, if it was almost four o'clock one hour ago?"

"That's very clever, Sammy," Joseph responded. "Do you remember where you were when you asked me that same question one hour ago?"

"You're being silly, Daddy," Samantha responded coyly. "I was sitting here in the backseat of the car just like I am right now."

Rachel turned around and tapped her disobedient daughter on the knee. "Show a little more respect for your father. He isn't one of your friends. Next to Jesus, he is probably the most important man in your life right now."

"I know that, Mother," she replied. "But I want to know how we lost one hour by traveling one hour more."

"The answer is really quite simple," Joseph replied. "One hour ago we were in the state of Utah, where we live. The minute we crossed the Arizona state line we had to turn our watch back one hour later. Like daylight saving time, we lose one hour."

"Where did the one hour go to?" Sammy persisted, pulling on and off the CTR ring which marked her membership in the Mormon Church.

"We're here," Rachel happily interrupted, aware that even her husband would be unable to keep responding to the torrent of questions that always came from Sammy. Joseph pulled into a space in the visitors parking lot in front of the Glen Canyon Dam. "Isn't it beautiful?" Rachel asked. "Let's hope that we can still make the last guided tour of the day. It's a special Independence Day tour."

They rushed through the parking lot toward a single-story sandstone building marked by two signs at its entrance.

"What do these signs mean?" Sammy asked, reining in both her parents as they tried to pull her forward.

"We'll find out on the tour," Rachel responded with annoyance. She hated to think that they might miss it, after having driven so far.

"What it says here," Joseph answered, stopping in front of the glass doors to the building, "is that the United States Bureau of Reclamation is responsible for the maintenance of Glen Canyon Dam and power plant, the regulation of Lake Powell's water, and the production of hydroelectric power."

"What does that mean?" Sammy asked.

"This dam," he replied with a bemused expression on his face, "supplies a lot of electricity for many, many people in several different states."

"How many people?" she asked. "Where we live, too?"

"I don't know how many, darling," he responded, caressing the blonde flaxen hair that draped her cherubic face. "A lot of people receive electricity from this dam. I think this dam supplies electricity for most of our state, and maybe Wyoming, Arizona, Colorado, and New Mexico."

"Can't we talk about this later? We're going to be late for the tour." Rachel spoke with some annoyance in her voice.

"What does the other sign say, Daddy?" Sammy said, ignoring her mother's admonition.

"This arrow-shaped sign," Joseph answered, avoiding his wife's glare, "says that the National Park Service acts as host to visitors who enter the dam through the Carl Hayden Visitor Center."

"Does that mean we'll have a guide?" Sammy asked disingenuously, knowing that the real excitement of the trip was going to be the forest rangers who appeared with Smokey the Bear on television.

"Yes, it does," Rachel responded, reasserting her control

by yanking Sammy's arm forward, an act which met with Joseph's immediate disapproval.

They ran quickly into the Visitor Center Receiving Room, a circular lobby washed in crimson light that shone through thick glass windows facing the setting sun. In the middle of a lobby dominated by photographs of the history of the construction of the dam was a topographic model of the area adjacent to the dam. The area was described as "Lake Powell Country." Smaller displays revealed different facets of the dam's construction and operation. A Norman Rockwell painting hung on one wall, depicting the awe of a Navajo family at their first view of the dam and the bridge.

Joseph Smith quickly purchased three tour tickets and guided his family to the hallway elevator where a perky, red-headed tour guide dressed in her Smokey the Bear costume had just started the tour. Rachel Smith took a deep breath and felt she could finally relax. They had made it.

"Please move in a little closer," the guide asked, beckoning the Smiths forward to join her small group of tourists. "Where are you folks from?"

"Salt Lake City, Utah," Sammy announced loudly, raising her CTR ring, "and we're Mormons."

Several nondescript people smiled.

"Hush, Sammy," Rachel admonished her, embarrassed by her daughter's outburst.

"But it's true. We are Mormons," she responded defiantly as the elevator descended 110 feet to a hallway leading to the crest of Glen Canyon Dam.

"We are now in a one hundred and eighty-foot tunnel," the tour guide announced in a high-pitched reverberating voice, "that was blasted out of the sandstone cliffs of Glen Canyon. If you look up around the doorway," the guide said as they exited from the tunnel, "you'll see rock-bolts or 'fasteners' that keep the sandstone in place."

"What would happen if you loosened those bolts?" Sammy asked, fascinated by the notion that the dam had to be held together by fasteners.

"It would be quite serious," the guide responded. "The dam could burst." Nervous laughter spread through the group of visitors. Only a child could articulate the adults' primordial fears, no matter how improbable the situation. The guide added, somewhat defensively, ''Thousands of these two-inch-diameter rock-bolts were installed by daring 'high-scaler' men suspended from long cables attached to windlasses on canyon rims. They drilled holes from fifty to eighty feet into the Navajo sandstone, inserted the bolts, then forced concrete grout around the bolts to secure them within the walls. When we go back to the lobby at the end of the tour, be sure to look at the photographs of the dam under construction.''

''But isn't the dam bursting now?'' Sammy asked, looking outside at water which was seeping from some of the rocks at the side of the dam.

The group's attention turned to the seepage that horrified Sammy.

''The porous sandstone walls of Glen Canyon Dam contain natural fractures,'' the guide replied, trying to control her own mounting anger, ''that allow groundwater, or what looks like 'leaks' from Lake Powell, to seep from them. While such moisture can weaken the rock and cause exterior rocks to come loose, the long rock-bolts inserted into the walls near the dam prevent any major problems.'' She looked at the group, ignoring Sammy and hoping that her explanation might shut her up. ''All the water that finds its way to the face of cliffs adjacent to the dam is caught in troughs at the base of the wall and is routed directly to the river below.''

''But it's still leaking,'' Sammy added, not quite understanding what the guide had just said.

''That's enough,'' Rachel reprimanded Sammy. ''Can you keep quiet for five minutes?''

''But it's leaking, Mom,'' Sammy replied.

''Enough, Sammy,'' her father added.

The tour guide nodded her head in appreciation and proceeded along a narrow bridge toward the dam's power plant, a huge concrete building that contained the hydroelectric generators.

The Power Generator Room, with its eight huge generators, was physically impressive to the entire group. It was in all respects a testimony to man's determination to harness the forces of nature. At the same time, this room was a clear statement of man's presumption that he could defy the natural order of the world in order to fashion it according to some imaginary, grandiose design. This was a temple of spiritual blasphemy, concluded Joseph Smith V, the great-great-great grandson of Joseph Smith, the founder of Mormonism.

"The eight generators in this room," the guide said in a voice of regained confidence, "produce 1,320,000 kilowatts of hydroelectric power for several million people in seven different states."

"How do these machines produce electricity?" asked a scrawny, elderly woman who clearly wanted to co-opt the pesky Mormon girl.

"Thank you for asking that question," the guide responded. "It's the one I always like to answer because it's at the very heart of the entire dam."

"Why is she so happy to answer that old lady's question," Sammy asked her father, "and not mine?"

"Shh . . . hhh . . . hhh . . ." he whispered, firmly placing his hands on her shoulders.

"The huge rotors within the generators," the guide continued, "spin quietly at one hundred and fifty revolutions per minute. These rotors are turned by steel driveshafts connected to Francis-type reaction turbines located thirty feet below in the power plant's foundation. There, torrents of Lake Powell water gush from enormous penstocks to strike turbine blades that rotate the shaft."

Sammy broke away from her father's hold and walked over to a nearby area where she could see a group of men wearing yellow and white helmets directing the lifting of a huge rotor by two enormous three-hundred-ton overhead electric cranes suspended from the ceiling.

As Sammy bent backward to look up at the cranes, a thundering noise from outside shook the very walls of the Visitor Center. The cable holding the rotor snapped and the rotor dropped from the overhead cranes, crushing several men. The building shook. Screams filled the cavernous space.

11

PAGE, ARIZONA

Thursday, July 3rd, 3:40 P.M.

The eight thousand citizens of Page, Arizona, located on the southern end of Lake Powell, dutifully worshipped in fifteen different houses of worship to a God whose sacrosanct silence reassured them that they would enjoy continued prosperity, peace, and general well-being. Along with their belief that their newly constructed McDonald's was the finest hamburger joint in the world, there was not an iota of a doubt that the Glen Canyon Dam, holding a volume of 26,214,861 acre feet of water, could ever disappoint in its primary functions of containing the Colorado River and providing electricity to several states.

Even the local pastor of the First Congregational Church of the Lost Parishioners had to admit to one of his admiring worshippers that he sometimes fantasized about relocating his sparse altar to the top of the 710-foot dam as a way of thanking those twenty-odd thousand people who had built it back in the early sixties, some forty years ago. The pastor was even more blunt in his affirmation of the Glen Canyon Dam as one of "God's miraculous creations." As far as everyone in Page was concerned, the dam had become a shibboleth of faith. It had attained ecclesiastical powers of conferring sanctity and damnation. Swearing on one's mother's grave as evidence of virtue and truth had been effortlessly substituted by swearing to the dam's fortitude and longevity. If a transgression had been committed, often the words, "May you drown in the dam," were used instead of the more conventional threats of bodily harm or blasphemy.

Only Robert Benson, the seventy-year-old town eccentric who used a red toothbrush on odd days and a blue toothbrush on even days, proclaimed occasionally, "Damn the dam." Heresy to the citizens of Page. But what could one expect from a person who was rumored to have sustained cerebral contusions either at the age of fifty-five when he started to skydive, at the age of sixty-three when he discovered bungee jumping, or at the age of sixty-eight when he began to parasail in Mexico. But "Robby," as he was affectionately known about town, was both tolerated and adulated because he was one of the original engineers who had designed the dam. No one seriously believed Robby's assertion that there was something "structurally wrong with the damned dam." Hadn't the dam been performing perfectly for the last thirty years? Everyone knew that if anything were wrong with "the damned dam," the feds would take care of it. Wasn't that the job of the Bureau of Reclamation and the U.S. Department of the Interior?

Pagenites, as the citizens of Page were known to the people of Flagstaff, Scottsdale, and Tucson, would often take out a quarter and hold it up in front of Robby's face and invoke the well-known incantation "In God We Trust." Robby, in turn, would grab the quarter and throw it in the direction of the Glen Canyon Dam, proclaiming in the loudest voice possible, "Damn the dam! Damn the feds! And damn God!"

It was in that particular order that he repeated his blasphemy. First against the dam. Then against the government. And finally against God Himself. The ultimate blasphemy, of course, was the fact that Robby gave the dam greater importance than he gave God. But perhaps that was his salvation as well, since every Pagenite could personally testify to the dam's existence. It was there. It was visible. It dominated each Pagenite's landscape, life, and livelihood. Everyone in town had seen the feds inspecting the dam. And, of course, every April 15th, every responsible citizen of Page knew that the federal government which received their money was putting some of it back into the town's coffers by taking care of the dam. In short, proving the existence of the dam was an easy act of faith. And Robby's damning it made no sense to anyone—except to Robby himself.

But something had been bothering Robby over the last few weeks. He had noticed an inordinate number of visitors to the dam. Normally, he would go down to the Visitor Center once a week to watch strangers at the dam, his "magnificent obsession." Then he would take one of the guided tours which left every hour on the half hour. By this time he was on a first-name basis with every National Park Service guide.

Robby calculated that he had been on 2,355 tours to date. Frequently finding fault with what guides said, he corrected factual errors, criticized a guide's presentation, or added some tidbit of information that he determined might increase the educational experience of visitors. Of course, he invariably found himself in a struggle with his guide to demonstrate who knew more about the dam. On 1,497 occasions he had been asked by the guide to either "restrain himself" or "leave the tour." Of course, the latter was the far more palatable alternative. Therefore, it would be more precise to state that he had completed, in full, only 858 tours.

What was evident to everyone who knew him, however, or saw him on the tour, was the fact that he was obsessed with the dam. It was as if he were part of the very structure of the dam itself. Neither entity was complete without the presence of the other. Although he was an avowed agnostic, he nevertheless believed that there was a spiritual bond between him and the dam. If that was considered crazy by his fellow Pagenites, then so be it.

To Robby, the dam was both a life force and a death machine. It provided clean water and electricity to those who believed in it and had learned how to harness its power in a disciplined way. If the dam was shut down, for whatever reason, approximately fifteen million people in seven states would lose their electricity. On the other hand, if the water held by the dam was released, over eight thousand Pagenites, to say nothing of another one hundred thousand people in the villages downriver, would most certainly drown.

On July 3rd, Robby, a medium-sized man with a shock of gray wavy hair, entered his dented Jeep Cherokee, placed a wine cork on the dashboard, and drove down to the dam. The cork was a reminder to go on one more guided tour of the dam, as meticulous and methodical a reminder as one might expect from an eccentric former structural engineer. This wine cork, probably from some Napa Valley chablis, was as much of a memory jogger to Robby as string tied around a finger to someone else.

As he approached the dam, he still marveled at the clear blue waters of 186-mile-long Lake Powell and Wahweap Bay gently nestled at one end of the lake. From Robby's point of view, this was as close as one got to godliness. No amount of human engineering could have created such a formidable vista.

Despite the twinge of guilt he felt for having been part of the team that had had the audacity to think that it could manipulate mother nature to some politician's grand design, Robby still maintained a certain reverence for the memory of Senator Carl Hayden, the leading advocate of water reclamation and storage in the west.

He parked his car in the visitors' parking lot and walked over to the four signs of commemoration near the Visitor Center. He stood in front of them and read aloud the words on the two faded brass plaques as he did on every trip to the center. In a voice that was reverent and subdued, he said, "For Outstanding Civil Engineering Achievement, Awarded in a National Competition, Glen Canyon Dam, by the American Society of Civil Engineering." Then he moved over and read the next plaque aloud: "American Institute of Steel Construction Annual Award of Merit, Most Beautiful Steel Bridge, Class I, 1959."

Without warning, the sound of thunder reverberated through the clear skies, and the cement beneath his feet began to shake wildly. He clutched the handrail for support. If this were an earthquake, he thought, it would surely register 6.4 on the Richter scale.

12

GLEN CANYON DAM, LAKE POWELL, ARIZONA

Thursday, July 3rd, 4:20 P.M.

Had Armageddon arrived? The Day of Judgment: Revelation 16:16. Robby had felt as if he was on the plains of Megiddo, the scene of the decisive battle between the forces of good and evil.

He surveyed the area and was surprised to discover that there seemed to be very little overall damage. As might be expected, people were running around, confused and screaming for help, but no one had been hurt.

Where in God's name did the shaking sensation come from? he wondered. Before he could think of possibilities, an unusual sound he now heard began to bother him. It sounded like a swarm of killer bees hovering overhead. Turning his eyes toward the direction of the sun, he saw the outline of a group of helicopters approaching. He shaded his eyes with his hand and counted what looked to him like four Blackhawk attack helicopters carrying a broadside of 2.75-inch rockets. He immediately recognized this constellation of forces as part of the Utah Air National Guard. What in God's name were they doing here? he wondered. Another military simulation? Could they have caused the dam's tremor? Within minutes the helicopters were directly over the dam's parking lot. Robby watched in amazement as a group of fully outfitted soldiers dressed in brown-camouflage uniforms rappelled down ropes hanging from the helicopters, like grapple hooks mysteriously suspended from heaven.

"Hey, what's going on here?" he asked as three soldiers surrounded him, their M-16s at the ready.

"Please come with us," a young, cherubic-faced second lieutenant with a high-pitched voice said, motioning him to proceed toward the Visitor Center. "I'll need some identification."

"What is this all about?" Robby asked again, angrily handing over his wallet. One of the soldiers rifled through it and handed it back to him.

"Sir," the second lieutenant reiterated, "would you be so kind as to proceed toward the Visitor Center with a minimum of discussion and obstruction."

"No, I won't," he responded, looking at the group. Each man was fully armed as if ready to enter battle. "What do you want from me? I built this goddamn dam!" He raised his voice. "Because of me you're able to land on this concrete. Otherwise, you'd be landing on those ragged rocks."

"We understand," the second lieutenant said calmly, refusing to be baited into argument. Rounding up the visitors was supposed to take precisely five minutes. There was to be no unnecessary dialogue with civilians, according to briefing instructions. The lieutenant noticed a group of adults standing near the Visitor Center who were giving the soldiers a difficult time being interrogated. As controlled an operation as was planned, there was more pandemonium than expected.

"Please. . . ." The word was pronounced with such forcefulness that Robby could not misunderstand the second lieutenant's meaning. Go along with the command or take the consequences. Ironically, he concluded, he was the one in control of this situation. He could make it either easy or hard for them, depending on the price he was willing to pay.

He allowed himself to be prodded forward toward the Visitor Center where an extensive deployment of soldiers was guarding a confused group of tourists and park service employees alike. He made a quick estimate of about two to three hundred soldiers, and raised his hands above his head.

"There is no need to keep your arms up above your

head,'' the second lieutenant said. ''You are not a prisoner of war. Please relax and just do as we ask.'' The two soldiers accompanying them remained silent, scanning the pathway for any potential surprises.

''Listen, if this is about the time I placed a call to the National Guard Command Post in Utah,'' Robby said nervously, ''claiming that I was a descendant of one of the Navajo Indian chiefs, I really wasn't going to blow up your base if you didn't return the land to me and my Indian cousins.''

''Thank you for the confession,'' the second lieutenant replied, ''but it isn't necessary.''

''Is this about the time,'' he continued, trying to make some sense out of this ridiculous scene of American soldiers holding Americans at gunpoint, ''I called up the sheriff's office and informed him that I was Sergeant Bob Laws from the Royal Air Force and told him that I had met his father in a bar in Reykjavik, Iceland? It was a prank phone call. No harm was intended.''

''Is there any possibility, sir, that you might shut up any time soon?'' the second lieutenant asked. ''It would certainly be very much appreciated by me and my colleagues.''

''Does this have to do with my not paying the part of my taxes which goes to entitlement programs, like Social Security or Medicaid?'' Robby refused to relinquish his questioning. Without waiting for any answer, he proceeded, certain that he had now found the reason for what appeared to be a massive roundup of ordinary American citizens. They were in one or another form tax dodgers who had refused to pay part or all of their federal income taxes. He recalled that Al Capone, the notorious Chicago gangster of the 1920s, was put in prison for tax evasion and not for the numerous crimes he had committed. That was it—failure to pay federal income taxes. He and his fellow ''hostages'' were being held for civil disobedience.

As they walked to the Visitor Center, Robby became frightened by what he saw. Hundreds of soldiers dressed in camouflage battle uniforms were herding civilians into the circular lobby. Surprisingly, there wasn't as much of a commotion as there was at the dam itself. Only the occasional infant's cry or cavorting behavior of the few toddlers broke the monotony of this very orderly, polite, almost apologetic human roundup. The scene reminded him of all the World War II movies he had seen depicting the roundup of Jews by the Nazis during the Holocaust. The Nazis had appeared very much in control, like sheepherders quietly herding their flock along the preordained road of genocide. But for what purpose was this happening today? Who was at war . . . and with whom?

Robby watched three AH-64A Apache attack helicopters slowly approach the broad, arching, twenty-five-foot-wide crest of the dam. They were majestic, he thought, descending like behemoth black whales suspended by whirling currents of air created by the syncopated rhythms of rotary blades.

"It's almost like ballet," Robby said to no one in particular, "the way those Apaches seem to come down ever so gently on top of the dam. I bet they wouldn't crack an egg."

"That's a nice way to put it, sir," the second lieutenant responded sarcastically. "I'll make certain it gets into our recruiting pamphlet."

"There's no need to get snotty with me, young man," Robby responded. "I meant it."

"I'm sure you did, sir," the second lieutenant said, taking off her combat helmet and unleashing a flow of luxurious auburn hair.

"Christ, you're a woman," Robby said, startled.

"Yes, sir," she replied. "Very much a woman." The two soldiers accompanying the lieutenant laughed.

"Well, I knew women were in the . . ." he sputtered.

"That's all right," she replied. "I'm used to this type of reaction."

"Come on, Lieutenant," Master Sergeant Archie Davis said. "We've secured the Visitor Center, the crest of the dam, and the Ganry Crane. We've only got a few minutes left to neutralize the civvies in the power plant."

"What's going on here?" Robby asked, bewildered. "Why are you guys . . ." He paused to correct his faux pas. "Excuse me. Is this some kind of military exercise? Like one of those hostage sieges where the police and military practice how to take back the dam once the people inside have been taken hostage?"

"Mr. . . ." She hesitated. "I'm Second Lieutenant Ellen Brown . . ."

"Mr. Robert Benson," he interrupted. "Robby, for short."

"Mr. Benson," Ellen said.

"Call me Robby," he responded. "I like that better." He paused to extend his hand in a gesture of friendship but realized that she wasn't interested in reciprocating.

"Mr. Benson," Ellen said forcefully, "please allow us to do our jobs with a minimum of interference. It will guarantee your safety and the increased likelihood of our success." Her wholesome, button-nosed, pink-cheeked facial features belied a steely determination. Ellen checked her watch. She was, as Archie had correctly informed her, behind schedule. She would have to make up two minutes and forty-seven seconds; otherwise, she stood a serious chance of jeopardizing the mission.

Suddenly the sky cracked with a loud sonic boom. Robby fell down and covered his head with both hands as if it were some type of air raid exercise. "We're under attack!"

"No, Mr. Benson," Ellen barked. "Get up! It's only one of our F-16s showing off. They fly as low as possible to make certain they've scared anyone away who doesn't know what it is."

"Planes, helicopters, soldiers," Robby said, standing up. "What in God's name is this all about? The 'evil Soviet empire' has completely dissolved and the Chinese have retrenched from their decade of expansionism. So whom are we fighting?"

Ellen squirmed uncomfortably but did not respond.

"If we're not fighting anyone," Robby continued, "then what is going on?"

Ellen ignored the question. As she helped Robby get to his feet, the Apache attack helicopters took off from the crest of the dam and released their broadside of 2.75-inch rockets. Both sides of the canyon shook.

13

DUPONT CIRCLE, WASHINGTON, D.C.

Thursday, July 3rd, 5:00 P.M.

The surf sounds of the Beach Boys filled the small storefront clinic on P Street across from the Dupont Circle Metro stop. Al continued examining the two-inch laceration over Jaime Rodriguez's right eye, a sixteen-year-old Hispanic teenager who was a frequent visitor to the Free Clinic. Before Al left his office at State, only thirty minutes earlier, he had promised Barbara that taking his shift at the clinic was the only thing he would do before leaving for New York. It would also give her time to get together information for him to read on the plane.

Working at the Free Clinic for a few hours a week, being a general practitioner, treating a spectrum of ordinary diseases in an extremely varied and needy population was very important to Al. And a replacement for these two hours, at the last minute, on the eve of July Fourth, would be very difficult to find. The Foreign Service officers were extremely privileged to receive the benefits they did. They earned them, and it was part of their employment package. But he was at the clinic for more selfish reasons. When he worked here, he felt grounded, both physically and psychologically. While he enjoyed being a medical doctor to the Foreign Service world, he also felt the need to belong to an urban community, where people knew him and recognized him by sight. He liked being a member of a neighborhood where he could shop at his local grocery store and the owner would ask him jokingly, "Which part of the globe did you go to this time? Or is that classified?" And he loved treating his community for free.

When Al returned from overseas trips he always looked forward to entering his one-bedroom bachelor apartment on New Hampshire Avenue, decorated in unkempt eclecticism with artifacts from around the world. He lived in the Greenwich Village of Washington, D.C. And on any warm evening, he could walk around his neighborhood and listen to bongo players beating out the Latin rhythms, watch the men of different colors and ages playing chess on the park tables while the homeless slept undisturbed on nearby park benches. If the city fathers felt flush, the huge fountain in the middle of the Circle might be shooting water into the pool surrounding it.

Wanting to feel an even stronger part of the neighborhood, Al provided his medical services to his neighbors. This way he could convey to them a sense that he wasn't simply a transient visitor or a voyeur, but a true, permanent member of the community. With a couple of physicians who lived in the vicinity, Al had started the Free Clinic years before. From the start, they were flooded with patients. Many were illegal immigrants who would not go to a normal E.R. for fear of being asked for legal documents.

Al liked Jaime and treated him with respect. He knew everything and everyone in the neighborhood. He was the "eyes and ears of the street."

"Doc," Jaime said, "my eyes are killing me. No offense, but that music you're playing is murdering my eardrums even more. If you're not careful, I'm goin' to need a pair of hearing aids."

"Help me, Rhonda, help, help me, Rhonda," Al sang along with the lyrics from one of the Beach Boys' golden oldies. "That's the price you have to pay for free medical care these days."

"Is this some dream you've always had?" Jaime asked, watching carefully as Al prepared the sterilized instruments and placed them on the suture tray. "Becomin' a surf deadhead?"

"That's my next career," Al replied as he put on his rubber gloves. "I'm going to be a big rock star someday."

"Sure, sure, whatever you say, man," Jaime responded, watching the doc stretch on his powdered white plastic gloves.

"Jaime," Al asked, "what makes you think you're such an expert in music?" He jabbed a needle of 10cc novocaine into the tissues surrounding Jaime's wound.

"Oow!" Jaime shouted out to the empty clinic. "You got a heavy hand, doc. I didn't mean to sound you down, man. I was just tryin' to tell you that you are a great doc, but a little bit short on the vocal range. You don't have to butcher me for that."

"Didn't you ever hear the expression," Al asked, pushing down the syringe plunger, "that music soothes the savage beast?" Tonight was a slow night, Al thought. Usually, when he worked this shift, he would have a waiting room filled with over thirty patients. And he would see everything, from TB in illegal Chinese immigrants, to gunshot wounds in African-American teenagers, to malnourishment in the elderly.

"So, Jaime, what are some of your favorite songs?" Al asked as he slowly passed the curve-shaped needle and thread through one fold of skin and then another.

"Bem, Bem, Mari . . ."

"The Gipsy Kings," Al interrupted. "Vamos a Bailar."

"Man," Jaime exclaimed, "for a gringo doctor, you sure know your *canciones.* I also got to say, and please take no offense at this, but you sew like a woman. Real nice and pretty-like."

"No offense taken." Al laughed. "And what's wrong if I sew like a woman?"

"Well," Jaime answered as the last stitch was pulled through his wound, "everyone knows that men don't sew . . . especially not the way you do."

"Would you like me to sew like a man?" Al laughed again, covering the wound with a gauze pad.

"What do you mean, doc?" Jaime asked in a high-pitched voice.

"I can make that scar look very masculine," Al replied.

"All I have to do is to rip out these sutures and hold the two flaps unevenly together with a butterfly Band-Aid. That could give you what I call the 'boxer's look'—jagged edges with blood oozing from the wound from time to time. The *mujeres* would *mucho* love you. Or I can give you one of those 'mean dude' looks. You know the one I mean. The *bandejo* look. Always looks like you finished last in a fight."

"Hey doc," Jaime said, reaching into his pocket, "what do I owe you?"

"Three Chuck Berry albums, one Frank Valli, and the Four Seasons," Al continued, "and . . ."

Jaime shook Al's hand as if he were a fellow gang member. "I've got to rob too much shit to get those records."

"So I see that you still take an active part in the acquisitions division of the Jaime Rodriguez Investment Banking Firm."

"Are you making fun of me, doc?"

"No, Jaime," Al replied. "I'm just wondering how long you can continue this life of hit-and-run?"

"As long as I have to scratch some bread for me and my family," Jaime responded.

Al smiled at the response. He knew from previous experience that Jaime was lying. But it was not his role to call Jaime on the carpet.

"Jaime," Al asked, "how did you get that scar?"

"Doc," Jaime responded, looking around, "we still got this patient-doctor confidentiality?"

"That's correct," Al replied.

"Anything I say to you," Jaime continued, "can't be repeated to nobody else, right?"

"That's right, Jaime," Al reaffirmed. "It's just like confessing to a priest."

"Okay, Holy Father." Jaime laughed. "I got this cut in a fight with a bunch of 'spear-chuckers' . . ."

"You mean African-Americans," Al interrupted.

"Yeah," Jaime continued. "Afro spear-chuckers. They started to sound me out. You know the routine. 'Hey spick, your mother does this, your mother does that.' "

"So you fought?"

"No, man," Jaime responded indignantly. "I'm used to that. We sound each other out all the time. Nothin's different with that . . ."

"So what made you get into a fight?" Al was perplexed. The rituals of territorial imperative required a certain amount of aggressive posturing. But it rarely led to an outright fight. Otherwise, there would be constant bloodbaths all over the neighborhood. Something unusual had to have provoked Jaime into a fistfight which he knew he would lose.

"Here, take a look at this!" Jaime handed Al a crumpled piece of paper. "Don't bother to read it, doc. I can tell you what it says."

Al scanned what looked like a propaganda leaflet. The bold headlines read "Illegal Hispanics Kill African-Americans. Brothers Unite Before It's Too Late. Kill the Wetbacks Before They Kill You."

"We spicks and the blacks have always had our differences," Jaime said, "but we could always figure out a way to split the difference between us. Or fist it out. And that's true. Until the next incidence. But it ain't never been like this before on the streets. Not like this. Man, that piece of shit you're holding in your hand lists out a bunch of black names and addresses that my Hispanic brothers were supposed to have killed. Man, no way possible."

"What do you mean?" Al asked, noticing that on the bottom of the piece of hate mail was a telephone number the reader could call for further information. He didn't recognize the area code: 801.

"You think we Chicanos are crazy?" Jaime asked rhetorically. "The last thing we want to do is to go around and kill anyone. This mass killing stuff, that's crazy, man! We don't want to bother no one, and we don't want no one to bother us. If we had some big list of blacks to kill, you know better than I do, doc, every immigration officer in the country would be out to deport us faster than you can say Taco Bell."

"Jaime, are you telling me that somebody is trying to start something between the Hispanics and the blacks in Washington?" Al asked.

"I don't know, doc." Jaime pulled another crumpled paper out of the same pocket. "I got one of these in my house. My cousins have got a couple like these. Man, the cops can barely find me to give me a warrant. But I get this piece of crap right to my front door. Sent to me personally. That's one hell of a delivery service."

"You got this personally?" Al asked skeptically. "How did they know your address or your name?"

"Beats the shit out of me, doc!" Jaime handed another crumpled paper over to Al to read. It contained largely the same wording as the other hate letter, except this one warned the Hispanics of the United States "to kill the blacks before they kill you."

"The blacks of this country are afraid that the wonderful, hardworking people of Spanish heritage will take away their jobs because you work more efficiently and cheaper than they do," Al read out loud. "Don't let the lazy black welfare parasites take away your jobs just because you are of a noble Spanish heritage."

"Hey, doc," Jaime said. "I got to get goin'. You keep the mail. Thanks for everythin'." He had just heard the distant sound of police sirens somewhere near the Circle and didn't want to take any unnecessary chances. "I've got a lot of power dinners to attend and important people to meet. You know what I mean?"

"*Hasta luego,* Jaime," Al said, wishing that he would look out for himself better than he did.

After Jaime left, Al reread the flyers. The area code on both were the same, only the telephone number was slightly different. Al dialed one of the numbers and listened to a recording spewing forth the same hate message that was on the flyer. He then dialed the telephone operator. "Could you tell me where the area code 801 is located?"

"Yes, sir. That's Salt Lake City, Utah."

14

BRECKENRIDGE, COLORADO
WESTERN GOVERNORS' COUNCIL MEETING

Thursday, July 3rd, 5:25 P.M.

Nestled within one of the glistening Rocky Mountain snow-peaked crests, Breckenridge was one of those gentrified year-round resort towns, which had a history as a former mining town. Only one hundred years before, a dirt road had run through the center of town, lined on both sides by houses of ill-repute. Now the street had been transformed into an upscale mix of mock cowboy saloon-restaurants and stain-glassed A-frame stores stuffed with either the latest skiing apparel during the winter season or outdoor backpacking equipment during summer. Less glitzy than either Vail or Aspen, Breckenridge had become the mecca for middle-class families, who had enough disposable income to bring their children to learn the basics of skiing without having to worry about either their safety or a jet-set social scene.

Tomorrow, Independence Day, a traditional display of patriotism was planned. About fifty people, firefighters from two local fire departments, state troopers on horseback, members of the VFW, and a local Boy Scout troop, would parade down Main Street. But today, four state governors rode on horseback, across the pine tree–covered mountain ridges, outside of town. This accounted for the well-hidden black limousines and the dozens of vigilant Colorado State

Troopers who scanned the crowds for potential troublemakers.

The four unescorted governors rode far up into the mountains, where the horse trails twisted around trees at unusually steep angles. They climbed along narrow, rocky paths which paralleled the black diamond ski trails of the resort. It would have been obvious to an onlooker that each of the riders had had extensive experience on a horse. The skill of one rider, however, stood out among all the others. To those who knew Colorado Governor Cheri Black, it was no surprise that she looked and rode better, and was a hell of a lot smarter than her counterparts, the governors of Utah, Wyoming, and Arizona.

''Bullshit,'' she responded on her portable cellular phone that she held in her left hand while holding the horse's reins in the other. ''Let me tell you, Mr. Secretary of Transportation, I don't give a rat's ass what the feds think about what West Virginia, Connecticut, and New York want. There is $150 billion in the highway trust fund created by the 1991 Intermodal Surface Transportation Efficiency Act. West Virginia got $1.35 last year for every dollar paid into the gas tax while Colorado got ninety cents back for every dollar we put in.'' She had tracked down the Secretary of Transportation before he left for the weekend in order to see what happened to her $20 billion request for highway funds that she had submitted six months ago and to which she had received no reply.

''Tell those bureaucrats of yours,'' she continued, ''that the goddamn highways and bridges in the Northeast are no more important than ours.'' She paused to listen to the response which she had heard over a thousand times.

''No,'' she answered, ''it's not true what your regional offices in the Northeast say.'' She mimicked the whining voices of the federal bureaucrats. ''We here in the North need a proportionately greater share of the federal highway funds because our highways tend to be older and are used by a larger share of out-of-state motorists.''

The governors riding alongside Cheri laughed quietly and goaded her on. She was well aware of the fact that she was entertaining them. But the more important point was that she was impressing upon them how tough she could be with the people back in Washington, D.C. That's why she had made this call today.

"I know this is a national holiday, Mr. Secretary," she continued, "but I'm here in Colorado, at the tail end of the annual Western Governors' Council Meeting, and speaking for the governors of several western states, we are sick and tired of the way you and your people in Washington have been treating us. It's rude, high-handed, and arbitrary. When we give you a dollar for the highway trust, we expect a dollar back. We have no intention of subsidizing that already-bloated bureaucracy of yours. Furthermore, Colorado and the other western states are expanding in population at a much faster rate than the northeastern states and the amount of money we receive from you is completely inadequate to meet the needs of creating new roads, bridges, and highways."

The governors silently applauded her.

"Let me just end our discussion by telling you that if we don't get our appropriate allocation of the highway funds, the state of Colorado isn't making any more contributions. We'll just use our own money to build our own roads and charge you all to travel on them."

She paused to hear the Secretary's final argument. "Yes, sir, it may well be unconstitutional for us to refuse your mandates, but we will just have to see what the consequences are. Won't we? Have a good July Fourth weekend, Mr. Secretary." Cheri snapped her cellular phone shut and placed it in the pocket of her black leather jacket. Then she kicked her horse's flanks and spurred him forward. The Secretary of Transportation didn't have to tell her what was or was not constitutional. She knew it a lot better than he did. She had written her doctoral dissertation on "States' Rights: The Constitution Revisited" in the Department of Political Philosophy at Rice University. But that was a long time ago.

After a failed marriage, she decided to dedicate her life to politics, challenging herself to implement those beliefs she had acquired in school. She was as much challenged by the intellectual concerns of a political reality as she was by the everyday, nitty-gritty applications. As an action junky, she was always willing to take a risk in order to achieve the result she wanted. Her personal philosophy revolved around the concept of character, and all her graduate education could be reduced to the proposition that you either ''had it'' or ''didn't have it.'' Without the proverbial ''it,'' you were bereft of courage, creativity, and integrity and therefore easily swayed by the opinions of others. Those with ''it,'' according to Black, stood alone and determined. With courage you could literally move mountains—or at least ride them defiantly. And it was in the world of politics that she felt you could measure a person's mettle.

Governor Cheri Black was an unusual combination of masculine toughness and feminine intuition woven in a filigree of Southern coquetry. Single at the age of forty-five, she lived with her own code of morality, a combination of Catholic rigor and Baptist mischief with all its inherent contradictions. She believed no man was fair game if he was married, engaged, or in love. She lived by the illusion that she was completely independent and had bought into the stereotype of the woman of the nineties—act like the man you would like to marry. Throughout her rise to power, her ambitions were scarcely hidden. She went from the local school board, to the first female elected county sheriff, to the politically appointed position of Chief of the Colorado State Highway Police. In that position, she became highly visible throughout the state by cracking down on drivers with out-of-state license plates who, it turned out, were transporting drugs throughout the region. The informal instructions to her officers were simple: come up with a reason to stop anyone who drove a suspicious-looking car. The police translated that quiet edict into a practice of stopping anyone who looked or acted like a ski bum, hippie, or illegal immigrant. The previous governor of Colorado, part Indian, Irish, Polish, and self-invented bravado, continuously reprimanded her in the press. Cheri simply smiled and proceeded as before.

At the proper political moment she decided to run for the governorship against her mentor of fifteen years. Throughout the campaign she harped on the issues she knew well:

the state's rights to police its own borders and restrict illegal immigration. One factor that contributed to her overwhelming success in the polls was her stand against encroaching federalism and her infectious motto "Colorado for Coloradans." What helped elect her were the TV spots portraying her riding a white stallion while dressed in black leather boots, hat, and whip. They conveyed the message that she meant business.

Cheri, like most of the citizens of Colorado, felt that the quality of life in the state would increase only if the state went its own way. It could collect its own taxes, run its own social services as it liked and, if need be, maintain its own Secretary of State for foreign affairs. The state was already becoming a major trading partner with Mexico, Canada, Western Europe, the Far East, and Latin America. If necessary, it could stand alone. Or Colorado could join in an alliance with those neighboring states with which it had a common interest. Every time a Colorado for Coloradans ad appeared on television, it could be counted on to fill the coffers of her party—with much of the money coming from out of state. A public referendum requested by a militant group in the state that demanded secession from the Union had been shot down in the last election, but the number of citizens endorsing the position had become significant.

Seated comfortably on her saddle, twelve thousand feet above sea level, Cheri knew that this was her time. The governors from Utah, Arizona, and Wyoming had been meeting with her for almost a year. This little outing, coming at the end of the annual governors' meeting, would seem innocuous enough to the other governors. It would be interpreted merely as four gubernatorial colleagues with similar interests wanting to spend some additional time together. Cheri, alone, realized this was her moment to make history. She was playing a dangerous political game, and the consequences would be dire for both her and the country if she failed.

"Whoa!" Cheri shouted as she pulled on the bit of the Arizona governor's horse. Two seconds more and both horse and rider would have slid off the trail onto tree stumps and large jagged boulders. "How can you run your state if you can barely control your horse?'' she asked.

''Damn it, Cheri,'' Andrew shouted back as he reined in his horse, ''don't start moralizing as I'm about to meet my Maker.'' His negligence masked his level of anxiety about today's meeting and the possibility of a traitor among them who was reporting directly to the feds. He decided to wait and see what transpired. In the meantime, he would try to minimize the damage to his state, its citizens, and his political future.

''Hang onto those reins, Andy,'' Cheri responded, slapping the rear of Andrew's horse and forcing it back to the middle of the trail. ''Don't start getting skittish on me now.'' She maneuvered her horse behind Andrew's to prevent his horse from sliding downhill. One wrong move and they would all find themselves on the bottom of a ravine.

''Maybe you should let Andy fall,'' joked Wyoming Governor James McMinn, positioning his horse so that he was completely out of harm's way.

''Not very Christian of you, James,'' Utah Governor Josiah Brigham IV interjected. His horse caught up to Cheri's and bumped hers, making it look like an accident.

''Hey,'' Cheri replied, ''don't tell me that you can't control your horse, either.''

''Sorry about that,'' Josiah responded, reaching over to pat her shoulders and back in contrition but really attempting to feel whether she was carrying any weapons or wearing an electronic bug. He didn't trust anyone, but he was suspicious of Cheri in particular. Why would the governor of a state which had two symbols of the federal government in which the Coloradans had great pride—the U.S. Mint in Denver and the U.S. Air Force Academy in Colorado Springs—be the rallying point for this act of secession? Unlike Utah, which had a landslide win on the secession issue, Coloradans had given their referendum less than thirty percent of the popular vote. Yet Cheri was the de facto leader of their movement. If she were a Mormon, he thought, pulling his horse away from hers, he would have made certain that she remained in her proper place—at home, raising lots of Mormon kids. But for the moment, all he could do was watch and wait as their plans took shape.

"Josiah," James replied, "did I ever tell you that I was the anti-Christ? My pleasure in life is to make life miserable for others," he added. "Especially you."

"Cut that crap out, Jimmy," Cheri shouted. "We have too much ahead of us without you cowboys scrappin' it out in the dung heap." She looked around with a certain amount of disgust at the men whom she considered to be her charges on this trip. "Am I going to have to tame the bunch of you guys?"

"What are you going to do?" Josiah asked. "Give us hell and brimstone?"

"Or are you going to spank us?" Andrew asked as he loosened the reins and jumped off his horse.

"Hey, guys," Cheri responded, dismounting, "if you need breastfeeding, you're about twenty years too late. I gave up the idea of nurturing babies a long time ago when my husband decided to leave the house and get a pack of cigarettes and forgot to return." She loved to use that imagery. It was one of her favorites. She considered hyperbole to be one of her verbal fortes.

"That's too bad," Josiah said. "I could use a little TLC." Following the lead of the others, he dismounted.

"Josiah," Cheri replied with a biting sarcasm, "the last thing you need is TLC. What you need is for someone to pull you off that mighty self-created throne and convince you that your shit doesn't smell any different from ours." Before she finished her statement, she realized that she was sounding unnecessarily provocative.

"I figured with all your wives, Josiah," Andrew said, holding the reins of his horse, "you would be loved up the ying-yang." Like most conversations, he was always one or two beats behind.

"Andy," Josiah replied, "I'm not certain which one is dumber—the horse next to you or . . ."

"Now, now, boys," James interjected.

"I just wanted to set the record straight for my good friend from Arizona," Josiah said, walking toward Cheri to help her remove the paper cups, a bottle of lukewarm Dom Perignon, and some mixed nuts from her saddlebag. "There is no such thing anymore as polygamy. We don't practice it or preach it."

"You sound a bit touchy," James said. "I'd be extremely proud of that particular part of my heritage if I were a Mormon." He joined Cheri, Josiah, and Andrew as they prepared their celebration on the edge of the trail.

"James," Josiah responded laughingly, "don't worry. We would never even consider the idea of your becoming a Mormon."

"Is that a fancy way of saying," James asked, "that I'm not an automaton wandering about the world proselytizing others by relating fanciful stories from a newly found Testament?" His retort was delivered with more than a bit of sarcasm.

"James," Cheri ordered, "apologize to Josiah right now! What we don't need is divisiveness within the ranks. From this moment onward we must work and play together as if our lives depended on each other. And believe me, they do."

They sat in a semicircle, cups of champagne in hand. Each knew that what would transpire among the four of them today would determine whether there could be an effective secessionist movement. And whether it would lead to civil war.

"So where do we begin, chief?" Josiah asked Cheri, hardly disguising his jealousy. When he was not being vindictive, he knew that she was the best choice to be the leader of this group. She had the trust of the group that he lacked. Within the highly structured setting of the Mormon Church, Brigham had no equal when it came to bureaucratic manipulation and leadership. But it had never carried over in his dealings with other governors.

"At 1630 hours," Cheri said, checking her watch, "National Guard troops from our respective states descended upon the Glen Canyon Dam in Page, Arizona, and secured the dam as well as Lake Powell."

"I think you might be fifteen minutes too late," Andrew said. "My staff reached me by cellular just a while back and informed me that certain units from the Utah National Guards literally jumped the gun by fifteen minutes."

"Is that so, Josiah?" Cheri asked sternly.

"I can't corroborate that until I get back to the limo," Josiah replied defensively, "but I would never be presumptuous enough to even entertain the idea of contradicting my esteemed colleague from Arizona."

"Cut the horseshit, Josiah," Cheri interjected. "I don't care whether it did happen or why it happened, but I do care to make certain that this kind of screwup won't happen again. Is that understood?" She wondered whether he was trying to ruin the mission just so that he could discredit her leadership.

"Sorry," Josiah responded. He didn't want to argue with her. He had his reasons. In time they would become apparent.

"Does that mean you are in agreement with Cheri?" James asked, mistrustful of Josiah's response.

"What's your problem, James?" Josiah asked angrily, "spending too much time in the Grand Tetons?"

"Very funny," James responded, appreciating the double entendre nature of his comment. The Grand Tetons, the major mountain ranges in Wyoming, had looked like women's breasts to the original explorers of the mountains.

"Before we regress into mistrust, deceit, and betrayal," James said, "can we review the basic strategy of our impending action? At least we'll be reading from the same script."

"You're right, James," Cheri responded. "The basic strategy is quite simple. First, we declare that all the waters leading into Lake Powell and the Glen Canyon Dam are the property of our respective states. Then we demand that the federal government withdraw all federal personnel from the dam and reassign all federal water and land rights to the respective states."

"They, of course, will refuse," James interjected.

"That's right," Andrew said. "That would make the states more powerful than the federal government, which the green shades in Washington would never allow to happen."

"That also means a military confrontation," James elaborated, "between the National Guard under the command of the governors of Arizona, Utah, Colorado, and Wyoming against the Commander-in-Chief of the United States and his federal troops.''

''What happens if the government federalizes the National Guards by Executive Order?'' Josiah asked. ''The soldiers would then face immediate court-martial and serious prison time if they obeyed any orders given to them by us.''

''You forget that the National Guard are citizens, too,'' Cheri replied. ''Citizens who have voted to secede.''

''But, even at our best,'' Josiah continued, ''our National Guard soldiers are no match against federal troops. All the government has to do is deploy the First Marine Division at Camp Pendleton to deal with any of the military threats. The Marines are only four hundred and fifty miles away from Lake Powell. As an ex-Marine, I can assure you that one brigade of Marines would be more than enough to deal with 25,000 guardsmen. The Marines would simply set up ambushes along the routes of approach to the dam in order to neutralize the National Guard.''

''And what about the fighting abilities of the National Guard?'' Andrew asked, more nervous now than he had been over the last six months. ''Most members of the National Guard are poorly prepared to fight and are in possession of only light infantry weapons. Over these past few years the Guard had done little more than maintain domestic order and help out in case of natural disasters and emergencies.''

''You both worry too much,'' James responded, annoyed. ''We all know that the highly trained citizens' militia forces in each of our states will be fighting, if necessary, with our National Guard units. With these groups we've got ourselves an extremely credible fighting force with a very impressive arsenal of heavy, sophisticated weapons.''

''Now you're getting into the spirit,'' Cheri added. ''Once we have achieved a military standoff, which is the most desirable outcome of Phase One, we implement the second part of our strategy, the controlled flooding of Glen Canyon Dam. That will certainly ratchet up our credibility with Washington. And it will show our willingness to use our power.

‘‘Our declaration of secession from the United States of America—state by state—will follow . . .’’

‘‘And if there is a problem,’’ Josiah interrupted, ‘‘we move to Phase Two, which I will share with you at the Lodge.’’

‘‘Let’s hope,’’ Cheri continued, ‘‘that we won’t have to precipitate a constitutional crisis in Congress. Otherwise, we will all be preparing for a second civil war. That’s all there is, folks,’’ Cheri concluded. ‘‘Happy July Fourth.’’

15

GLEN CANYON DAM, LAKE POWELL, ARIZONA

Thursday, July 3rd, 4:30 P.M.

''For the third time, what's going on here?'' Robby asked.

''For the fourth time, stop asking questions,'' Second Lieutenant Ellen Brown responded.

''Should I consider myself a hostage?'' As far as Robby knew, hostages were innocent civilians who were taken against their will, and then bound, gagged, and tortured. While thankful that nothing of the sort was happening, it was also a little disappointing that he was being treated very undramatically—no handcuffs, no blindfolds, no beatings—nothing he could ever relate to friends and family with a sense of importance. They entered the Visitor Center, as Robby had anticipated, but instead of being herded together with the other tourists they walked briskly to the Power Generator Room.

The damage that had occurred from the falling rotor was unnerving. A young girl was being extricated from the debris, having remarkably avoided anything but superficial cuts and bruises.

''Those yellow giants used to be some real beauties,'' he said, suddenly nostalgic. ''Those generators in their time were state-of-the-art. The rotors spin at 150 revolutions per minute and are turned by steel driveshafts connected to Francis-type reaction turbines located thirty feet below the power plant's foundation.''

"Mr. Benson," Ellen interrupted. "We've done a standard computer search on every one of the civilians here, and I'm well aware of your expertise."

"You know what made this dam really unusual?" Robby continued, trying to match her pace.

"What was that?" she asked, realizing that it was futile to try to silence him just now. After using the Social Security number in his wallet to check his federal records, it had been decided by her commanders that she work closely with him. Whatever else he might be—eccentric or not—he really was one of the original engineers who had designed the dam. Probably no one knew the dam better. So it was decided to use him rather than let him stir up trouble with the rest of the civilians. Until the Corps of Army Engineers arrived, Ellen had been placed in charge of the power room because she had taken a few courses in mechanical engineering during her sophomore and junior years at Stanford University.

"This was the first time," Robby responded eagerly, "that powerful generators like these . . ." He paused, trying to collect the thoughts flooding his mind. If he could only tell the pretty young woman how grateful he felt for her attention, even if she was his captor. ". . . were trucked in parts into this room on specially built low-bed trailers that descended, reptilianlike, through two miles of tunnel connecting the power room with Glen Canyon's rim."

"Very interesting, Mr. Benson," Ellen replied, distracted as they approached a chicken-wire cross-hatched grille. In the room behind that grille, she thought, was the equipment that ran the power and water-generating facility for the dam.

"If you really think about it," Robby continued, oblivious to her indifference, "it was really ingenious the way we thought to put the generators here."

"I'm sure it was, Mr. Benson."

"The standard way of moving this type of generator," he continued, "was to lower it from above into a roofless powerhouse. We simply reversed the process."

"Fascinating," she responded reflexively. "Absolutely riveting."

"I know you don't think this very interesting, but I can't

tell you how grateful I am that you are willing to listen to me. Not to kill me."

"Don't worry," she said, aiming her gun at the lock, "I have better things to shoot at."

"You know," he said, gently lowering her raised gun, "I have this feeling, maybe it's just an old man's foolish hope, that down beneath your hard exterior there's a part of you that likes me." This said, he put his ear to the lock, spun it a few times, and it opened.

"How the hell did you do that?" she asked.

"By being gentle," he responded, breaking into a Cheshire smile.

"You certainly have a way about you, Mr. Benson," she said, reholstering her gun. "Let's hope we don't have any more problems."

"You shouldn't," he said, "if you let me handle them. Unless you insist upon waving your gun around. Remember, most of the people in this part of the dam are operators who are basically mechanical engineers. The only guns they play with are rifles during hunting season."

Robby saw an unfamiliar face in the room that opened up before them. He wore a white helmet and was reading meters which indicated the performance levels of the turbine generators behind the panel.

"Hey, what's going on here?" the helmeted engineer asked, surprised by the presence of a military officer and a civilian in a restricted area.

"Mr. Benson," she said, patting her gun, "please handle this matter according to your own principles of conflict resolution."

"You two don't belong here," the engineer shouted. "Get out, otherwise I'll have to call the guards. Anyway, what the hell is the U.S. Army doing here?"

"Everything is okay," Robby said calmly, offering his hand in friendship. "I'm Robert Benson, one of the original engineers who designed this dam."

"I don't care if you're the President of the United States, mister," the engineer interrupted. "You and that officer don't belong here. So I'm going to ask you, politely, to get off these premises. ASAP. Otherwise . . ."

"Otherwise," Ellen responded defiantly, determined to resolve this impasse quickly, "what?"

"Please, Lieutenant," Robby intervened, placing himself physically between Ellen and the engineer. "You're not making this situation any easier."

"Didn't you hear me?" the engineer shouted. "Vamoose! This area is forbidden to unauthorized personnel. And you aren't authorized."

"What's your name?" Robby asked in a soothing voice, trying to calm down the engineer.

"What the hell is the difference," he replied, "if my name is Tom, Dick, or Harry?"

"Well," Ellen responded, "pick one goddamn name so that we can proceed." She checked her chronometer. "As it is, I'm already three minutes behind schedule."

"I don't care if you're a lifetime behind schedule," the engineer said. "I want you both out of here." He picked up the red phone hanging on the wall. "I think our security guards can handle this matter."

"It won't help you to call anyone," Ellen said, yanking the telephone out of his hand. "We've taken over the entire dam. So would you please move aside so that I can complete my assignment with the least amount of collateral damage."

"What the hell are you talking about?" the engineer asked.

"Robby," Ellen said, clearly annoyed, "your techniques of conflict resolution aren't working."

"Please don't give us any trouble," Robby reaffirmed, "otherwise this sweet, delicate-looking Army lieutenant will have to use force. And I've assured her that it wouldn't be necessary. If you don't listen, you won't make me look good. She'll be forced to hurt you, and you may end up dead. So please do as she says. Otherwise we'll have a lot more problems than we ever bargained for."

"What is this," the engineer persisted, dumbfounded, "some Army emergency planning exercise?"

"Yes," she responded with alacrity. "That's it. We are practicing a special Army maneuver in case the dam and power plant are taken over by enemies."

"What enemies?" he asked stubbornly. "The Russians?

They're too poor. The Chinese? They could care less about this dam. Are you some kind of environmental nut who wants to shut us down because we killed some algae?''

''You lose, Mr. Mister,'' Ellen responded impatiently. She pulled a Beretta from her holster. ''Unfortunately, this is not twenty questions. So please step aside.''

''The hell I will,'' he responded, crossing his arms in a defiant stance.

''Please listen to her,'' Robby implored. ''Despite her angelic looks, she's quite determined.''

The mechanical engineer turned around and started to run down the long green hallway. Ellen chased him through heavy metal doors marked ''Danger. High Voltage.'' As she pursued him, he hid behind one of the eight austere-looking generators that regulated the speed of the dam's eight turbines. Ellen had been briefed weeks earlier that the generators were sensitive. These were oil-pressure cabinet-actuators. She also knew that one misplaced bullet could accidentally destroy any one of the generators. And then she would have destroyed her own mission. On the other hand, if she let the engineer escape, he might compromise the entire mission by blocking her access to the Main Control Room.

''Shoot me!'' he shouted. ''And this dam shuts down!'' He darted out from behind the generator and started to turn a valve that controlled the amount of lake water that entered the turbine's spiral cases.

Ellen realized that if she didn't stop him he would shut off the electrical power produced by the dam. The seven states that received electricity from the dam would be in complete darkness.

16

WATERGATE COMPLEX, WASHINGTON, D.C.

Thursday, July 3rd, 6:15 P.M.

It was rare to see a Secretary of State, followed by DSAs, walking leisurely on the bike path in front of the infamous Watergate Complex, a series of semicircular buildings along the Potomac River. Barbara Reynolds was accompanied by her distinguished-looking Secretary of Defense Phil Grahn. But not even one motorist driving by had slowed down to crane his neck. So much, Barbara thought, for being a Washington celebrity.

"I'm glad you were able to see me," Phil said hesitantly, "admittedly in somewhat of a strange setting, but I wanted to make certain that no one could overhear our conversation. And what could be better than a little open-air tête-à-tête?"

"What did you find out?" she asked.

"Just as you suspected," he responded. "There are major National Guard troop movements in a series of states. We're talking about a combined total of about 25,000 men, all heading toward what seems to be Lake Powell, Arizona."

"The Glen Canyon Dam," she responded without hesitation.

"Yes," he said in a surprised tone. "How did you know?"

"I checked with my Bureau for Intelligence and Research," she replied, hesitant to tell him the entire story just yet.

"So you picked up an inordinate amount of military traffic," Phil said, "and wondered whether I had authorized it. Am I right?"

"That's pretty much the idea," she responded. "Just checking that the intel was correct. I figured that you could tell me who authorized the troop movements and why."

"Well," Phil continued, "the intel is correct. And the answer to your second question is that the governor of each of those states called in their respective National Guards. The reason for that is still unclear to me, but two hypotheses quickly come to mind."

"Let's hear them," she urged.

"The first hypothesis"—Phil stopped walking so that he could face her—"is that the troops are involved in some regional exercise."

"How likely is that?" she asked.

"It would be highly probable only if the governors held their National Guard maneuvers with the Pentagon's knowledge," he responded.

"So that didn't happen," she said.

"No," he responded. "Not only did they not clear anything with the Pentagon, but when each of the National Guard commanders were queried about what was happening, they responded that their governors had ordered them to remain on maximum alert and be prepared to move out without an exact destination."

"How unusual is that?" she asked.

"Very unusual," he replied. "More often than not, a mission statement accompanies that type of readiness."

"So, Phil," she said, staring straight into serious eyes, "would it be fair to say that the governors are working together to attain a mutually beneficial goal?"

"Roger on that one," he answered.

"And what could that goal be, Phil?" she asked, certain of the answer but waiting for Phil to discover it for himself.

"It would have to do with the Glen Canyon Dam," he replied.

Barbara thought for a moment. "You mean to secure it?" she asked.

"That's right," he responded.

"Against what?" she asked.

"That's a good question," he replied, unwilling to utter the words that were on his mind.

"There are no foreign enemies in Arizona that we know of," she said facetiously. "Or are there?"

"No," he said, reiterating. "None that I know of."

"Therefore," she added, "we would have to assume that it's some type of domestic enemy—either real or imaginary—like the . . ."

"Federal government," he concluded.

"Precisely," she added. "But it sounds ludicrous. Governors seizing a dam. The only thing they can realize by their action would be to confront the federal government with the threat of shutting off water and power to millions of people . . ."

"All in the name of . . ." he said.

"States' rights." She finished the sentence.

"What we have then," he said deliberately, "is hypothesis two. The potential of a civil disturbance . . . for lack of a better term."

The silence between them for the next minute was deafening.

"I guess this confirms the message I received earlier today from the governor of Utah, on behalf of the governors of Colorado, Wyoming, and Arizona. They really are going to push the envelope and try hard to hold Washington hostage to a secessionist movement."

"The whole thing is ridiculous," Phil responded.

"I guess it's not an accident that the foreign minister of France is in Wyoming," she said. "Yvette is always looking to stir up trouble around the world, ostensibly in the name of France."

"I think we should notify the President," he said.

"In principle," she responded, "the answer is, of course."

"But . . ."

"But as you know, both the President and the Vice President are out of the country," Barbara affirmed. "The President is in Asia to cement our relations with the ASEAN countries."

"And the V.P.?" he asked.

"He's in Europe," she responded, trying not to laugh, "cementing relations with Germany, France, and Italy. I doubt that most of Congress is even in town. You can probably find most of them on a recess junket."

"So, it's you and me, kid," he retorted, trying to conceal his cynicism. Something was wrong. The whole situation just didn't smell right. The President and the Vice President were conveniently out of town, and at that very same time, on the most important holiday weekend of the year, major military maneuvers were being exercised without his sanction. Barbara knew more than she was letting on to him.

"Actually, it's just me," she responded. "Danforth asked me to keep an eye on things while he and the V.P. were away." Barbara and President Danforth had had a twenty-year relationship that went all the way back to Stanford law school.

"Well then, Madame President, what do you want to do?" he asked.

"As little as possible, for now," Barbara responded. "Certainly nothing that would attract any attention from the media. If any questions arise about National Guard troop movements, respond by explaining that these are normal military exercises to test our National Guard Reserves in those particular states."

"What if the governors," he asked, "go public with a different story?"

"That's one of the things we will have to deal with if and when it comes up. I'm sending Al Carter up to New York to see if Yvette can shed any light on this, before we confront the governors with force." It was a gamble, she thought, but one that was worth taking. "How many days would you need to mobilize federal troops?"

"Days?" he asked. "I could deploy in a matter of hours. The Ready Brigade of the First Marine Division at Camp Pendleton is only 450 miles away from Lake Powell. Trust me, one brigade of Marines, setting up ambushes along the routes of approach to the dam, would be more than enough to deal with 25,000 exposed Guardsmen without air cover."

"Phil," she said, "I'm going to ask you to trust me."

"You know I do, Barbara," he responded.

"I don't want you to deploy the Marines. Just be ready to deploy whatever Army units are around the dam and in Arizona. But most important, I do not want you to do anything at this time. Is that understood?"

"You want me to hold back my most effective units to prevent a civil disaster," he reiterated, "and at the same time, make it appear as if the U.S. Government is responding reasonably?"

"You've got the idea," she replied.

"May I ask why?"

"You may."

"But I have a feeling that you won't tell me," he said.

"Trust your feelings, they're right on the mark," she said. "That's why I prefaced my comments to you with the question, 'Do you trust me?' "

"You're asking for a hell of a lot more than trust," he said, sounding exasperated. "I presume that you also do not want to federalize the National Guard troops by Executive Order?"

"That's right. But again, please don't ask me why."

"Barbara," he said uncomfortably, "you and I have worked with several administrations in different capacities. We've had our differences. But I never questioned your integrity."

"Thank you."

"But do you mind if I tell you exactly what's on my mind?" he added.

"Not at all."

"I think you're crazy," he said. "I don't know what's going on. But I hope to God this isn't something that you and I will ever regret having been part of."

"Phil," she said, taking his arm and proceeding with their stroll, "you may well be right. I am crazy. Others have accused me of insanity."

"Then that makes me crazy, too, for going along with you," he added. "A real *folie à deux.*"

"If necessary, I only want a show of force," she emphasized. "I'll know more after Al returns. Based on what he finds out we may be able to negotiate a happy ending to this madness.''

''And what if he fails, we fail, and there are no deals?'' Phil asked.

Before she responded, Barbara Reynolds sighed. ''Civil war,'' she whispered. ''And this time it won't be fought to free the slaves. This time it will be fought to preserve the United States of America.''

17

GLEN CANYON DAM, LAKE POWELL, ARIZONA

Thursday, July 3rd, 4:45 P.M.

Her options were limited, Ellen decided. Too much collateral damage would result if she shot the engineer. On the other hand, if she didn't stop him, he could shut off all of the electrical power produced by the dam.

Robby shifted from side to side like an autistic child ready to receive his medication. He shook his head violently, warning Ellen not to shoot. Glancing at her watch, she was disturbed that so much time had passed.

If she did nothing, the entire dam would shut down in just a few minutes. Ellen aimed her gun at the point at which the brachial artery traversed the engineer's right shoulder cuff . . . and fired. The engineer screamed. He clutched his shoulder and released the valve handle. Ellen rushed over and threw him against the wall, shoving the Beretta beneath his lower jaw.

"Please," he pleaded, "I'm not a violent man."

"I really don't want to hurt you," she said. "Just turn the valve back where it was and let us into the Main Control Room."

The engineer responded by adjusting the valve.

"Here, take this," she said, handing him a gauze pad from a pouch fastened on her belt, "and press it tightly against your wound. It will stop the bleeding." She examined the wound. "It's a clean shot. No major arteries or nerves have been damaged."

"I can't get into the Main Control Room," he protested. "I don't have the proper identification with me."

"Well, you better figure out how else to get us in," she said. "You've got exactly thirty seconds to do it before your other shoulder is out of commission." She looked at her watch. "Twenty-nine . . . twenty-eight . . . twenty-seven . . ." She pressed her gun hard against his left shoulder. "The Main Control Room."

"All right," the engineer said, envisioning his body with all of its limbs useless. He took a key from his pants pocket and opened the grilled gate.

Two men sat at consoles in the MCR. Max and Sam, the Laurel & Hardy of the MCR, had been monitoring the brightly lit panel board of flashing colored lights that controlled the entire electronic network of the dam.

"What the hell is going on here?" Max, the white-helmeted, stocky supervisor asked when he saw the intruders. A former Marine sergeant, he was sorry not to have his old M-15 at his side.

"Watch where you're going!" Sam, the asthenic deputy, shouted, jumping up from his swivel seat.

"Take it easy, gentlemen," Ellen said, trying to assure them as she pointed her Beretta at one and then the other. "All I need is a modicum of cooperation, not two bodies filled with nine-millimeter lead. You can ask Robby whether or not I can be reasonable. Or ask your pal here, whose shoulder is filled with metal debris, what happens when you don't cooperate."

"Max," the engineer said, tightly pressing his right shoulder, "don't try anything foolish. She'll use that gun if she needs to."

"Oh, come on," Sam interrupted. "What are we supposed to do? Turn over the entire dam to this gun-happy female?"

"Gentlemen," she responded, "the quicker you follow my instructions, the faster I can complete my mission, and the happier we will all be."

"Please, listen to her," Robby reaffirmed. "There's a battalion of soldiers . . . maybe three battalions . . . maybe fifty battalions . . . crawling all over this dam. We are completely outnumbered. If you don't listen to her . . ."

"What do you want?" Max asked, examining her face.

"I want you to open the dam and flood the river," she replied calmly.

Confusion marked the faces of all the men in the room. If they followed Ellen's orders, entire towns would be washed away. Lives and property would be lost. Images of cascading, unchecked waters flooding everything in its path were horrifying.

"Do you know what you're asking me to do?" Sam asked, wondering whether she would shoot him if he tried to stall.

"I think you heard me," Ellen repeated. "Flood the river."

"It's just not mechanically possible from these controls!" Max stated, hoping he could pull off a bluff.

"If I'm not mistaken," she responded impatiently, "you have a combined series of Francis turbines, Kaplan turbines, and Pelton turbines working in seriatim. Those panels just in front of me should be controlling the drunner, the bottom ring, the runner blades, the wicket gate, spiral case, the stay case, and the stay cane. If you shut down those panels on the top right side, facing us, you will find that you may indeed accomplish the very task I just requested."

Max remained mute, impressed by her knowledge of his hydroelectric system.

"Female second lieutenants," Ellen bluffed, "can also be summa cum laude engineers from Stanford University."

"Sam," Max shouted, "she's bluffing. Any soldier can spout out a few terms here and there. That's part of their training. It doesn't mean jack shit. Just part of their psychological operations plans to intimidate us."

"Max," Sam replied soberly, "I think . . ."

"Gentlemen," Ellen interrupted, walking over to the console. "I'm bending over backwards to act reasonably. But if you insist . . ." She punched a few buttons on the panel and they all heard a loud grinding noise. "I've just shut down your Pelton turbine. But it sounds like your bucket ring needs adjusting.''

''Gentlemen,'' Robby implored, holding up the half-fainting engineer. ''I beg you. Help out the lieutenant.''

''He's right,'' the engineer reiterated feebly. ''It's time to stop playing games.''

''Damnit!'' Max shouted. ''Since when does a snot-nosed female second lieutenant tell me what I should or should not do?'' He walked toward the console and pushed a few buttons. The control panel stopped humming. Lights stopped flashing.

''Thank you, gentlemen,'' Ellen said. She looked down at her watch, smiled, and looked up at the map. ''Which part of me is it that you resent the most? The fact that I'm a female Army officer or that I'm a Stanford engineering graduate?''

''It's none of those things,'' Max responded, continuing to push buttons.

''So what is it that seems to bother you about me?''

''The fact,'' he responded somberly, ''that you seem to be having so much fun.''

''I'll remember that the next time,'' Ellen said. She spoke into her portable telephone. ''The Main Control Room is completely secured.''

18

ABOVE THE ATLANTIC OCEAN

Thursday, July 3rd, 9:15 P.M.

''What would you like to drink?'' the pleasant middle-aged stewardess asked.

''Nothing,'' Alison Carter responded, gathering together the documents he was reading and clutching them tightly against his chest. ''On second thought, you could give me a glass of water.''

Like most government officials, Al was flying in the highly uncomfortable economy class of United Airlines, squeezed next to a relatively large passenger, who had never taken his eyes from his laptop computer. Al had recently started hating to fly, suspecting that the newer aircraft were designed for anorectic waifs who had little need for fresh air. But government regulations mandated that a federal employee must take economy class on an American carrier for trips of less than fourteen hours in duration. And to make matters even worse, whatever bonus miles were accrued were automatically transferred back to the State Department's account. Perhaps he should feel privileged to have received a bag of peanuts on this nonstop flight from Washington National Airport to LaGuardia Airport, which was to arrive shortly in New York City.

He removed his headset and clicked off his Walkman. Thank goodness for rock 'n roll, he thought. He listened to it continuously while he worked. The louder and more intense, the better he could concentrate. In order to stay awake and work on this flight he was listening to a tape of Mitch Ryder and the Detroit Wheels. Their hit "Devil With a Blue Dress On" was just the kind of song that incorporated the basic words and raw emotion of a Little Richard with the whirling persistence of a Jerry Lee Lewis. He chuckled to himself, wondering what Barbara Reynolds would say if she knew that he had just finished reading the classified files she had given him to the best background drumming of the 1960s.

On the surface, his mission appeared quite simple. He was to meet informally with French Prime Minister Yvette de Perignod, as the personal representative of the Secretary of State. He was to inform Yvette, whom he had known for many years, that Barbara was concerned that France was meddling in the internal affairs of the United States. Off the record, of course. According to the documents Al had just finished reading, the French seemed to be targeting, with an impressive amount of financial investment, those states which were considering secession from the United States. Barbara had asked him to try to find out whether the meddling was due to an official government policy or to a personal agenda fabricated completely by Yvette, who was well known for her anti-American, ambitious stance as well as a potential contender for chief of the forthcoming Europe Union. Nothing would serve her own interests better than a divided, fractious America. It wouldn't take all that much for the EU to surpass the States in gross national product and become the major economic and political force in the Western hemisphere.

The stakes were so high, Barbara had repeated to him when she handed him the documents, that there was no one else she would trust with the assignment. Al was a personal friend who was completely loyal to her, a doctor whose professional medical ethics stressed integrity and confidentiality, and a career professional who was skilled in crisis management. And Al's psychiatric training would be helpful in exploring Yvette's mental stability. As Barbara explained, later corroborated by a CIA psychological profile, Yvette had a history of being an *agent provocateur.*

Al remembered Yvette vividly from his early days in the Foreign Service as a young RMO in Africa. Fifteen years before, Yvette was merely a political consul at a French embassy located in the capital of a former French-speaking African colony. He recalled how, over the years, Yvette always embroiled herself in turmoil wherever she could find it. She had been thrown out of at least one country for fomenting political, economic, and social unrest against the authorities. Of course, as expected, the French government denied any complicity; they would always let it be known through informal channels that she was acting on her own behalf, without official orders, a renegade diplomat over whom they had no control because of her strong personal ties to the nobility of the *ancien régime.*

According to the French Foreign Ministry, they had tried on several occasions to remove her from the service, but without any success. The reason was her strong ties to the right wing nationalist party in France, founded by Le Pen. By firing her, the President of France knew he ran the risk of destabilizing his own fragile coalition government consisting of both Socialists and the Right Wing. It had been intimated, but it was never proven, that Yvette was supporting a separatist movement within France, encouraging the southwest region of the country, which included the cities of Marseille and Toulouse, and which contained over two million North African immigrants, to split off from the central government.

In her cover memo to Al, Barbara suggested that Yvette might be meddling in the affairs of America because of her frustration with the lack of progress toward ethnic purity in her own country. An agent provocateur who knew no political boundaries. And like most Frenchmen, Yvette maintained ambivalent feelings about the United States.

Barbara's classified files revealed that Yvette's own economic and political ties to the power brokers in the States trying to secede from the United States federal government were strong. If these states were successful, Yvette's business friends would benefit through tax exemptions, economic preferential treatment, and minimal regulation. In effect, by becoming personally involved in the dissolution of the United States of America, Yvette would become a major international economic and political player. A significant percentage of her personal fortune was invested in French multi-conglomerates that were located just in these states.

The more he read, the more it became apparent to Al that Yvette was not above abusing her position as Foreign Minister if it meant protecting and leveraging her personal fortune in America. Under cover of an official policy, she could make an already strained relationship between France and the United States extremely volatile.

Al learned from her dossier that Yvette's attitude toward the United States was one of noblesse oblige. It was clear that she felt that only because of France's intervention in the American Revolutionary War were the British defeated. General Lafayette and his soldiers, as well as the French Navy, had propped up General George Washington, universally considered a less-than-mediocre military commander of a pathetic rag-tag Revolutionary army.

Much of the ten-year separatist activity in Quebec, Canada, had been officially supported by Yvette's Nationalist Political Party and unofficially funded by Yvette through an organization she had personally established in order to propagate "true French culture" throughout the world. Since her work with the Ministry, she had been effective in insinuating her organization into former French colonies in Africa, North America, and Southeast Asia, particularly Cambodia, Vietnam, and Laos.

As he adjusted his headset, Al realized that Barbara's second agenda for sending him to see Yvette in New York City while she was visiting the United Nations was going to be even more problematic than his unofficial assessment of France's official policy. Barbara wanted an evaluation of Yvette's mental state. Although his residency had been in internal medicine, his undergraduate degree had been a double major in psychology and history. A psychiatric rotation during internship and years of handling the personal problems of American families abroad qualified him to assess "mental health," whatever that meant. According to CIA reports, Yvette had a history of cyclical mood swings. They called them "mercurial." Al interpreted it to mean a manic-depressive disorder in which she could be euphoric and grandiose one moment and then depressed and de-energized the next. She could be erratic, decide at one moment to do one thing and then the next moment change her mind completely. In short, this was not a lady with whom to tangle. Her behavior could be both destructive and dangerous.

His clinical sense, however, told him that something was missing in the diagnosis of Yvette he was handed. And his New York City street smarts told him that something was missing in Barbara's explanation of what was going on. Alison hoped the next day's meeting with Yvette might give him the answers he needed.

19

DEPARTMENT OF STATE, WASHINGTON, D.C.

Friday, July 4th, 12:05 A.M.

"United by hate against the federal government and everything it stands for," Secretary of State Barbara Reynolds explained, "these secessionists are, as far as I am concerned, 'False Patriots.' And that's how I will refer to them for the remainder of this discussion." She spoke judiciously, making certain to choose her words carefully. This was not a time for histrionics or grandiloquence. She was addressing a handpicked group of senior government officials, all of whom had worked intimately with her at one time or another. She had bypassed the chain of command in order to cull those individuals whom she knew would be effective. They would minimize bureaucratic turf battles and comprehend precisely what they were about to be asked to do. She only hoped that, physically, she could make it through the meeting. Her head was pounding as if it were being hammered on an anvil. She had taken her anti-hypertensive pills right before the meeting but knew that their effects would be limited.

The group of twelve seated around the table was composed of military officials, Foreign Service officers, domestic law enforcement agents, and an assortment of other facilitators, like Al, who made things happen. Perhaps it was this latter fact that distinguished these dozen men and women from the rest of their peers. They were willing to bend the rules to the degree necessary to accomplish the task at hand. Officially, they were banned from committing an illegal act. Informally, they were allowed to go as far as needed as long as there was no paper trail or compromising action that could be traced back to the source. They all operated with the same credo: "Get it done!" The unspoken corollary was no leaks and no excuses. And they trusted one another implicitly.

"The situation is dire," Barbara said in a controlled voice, pacing up and down the oval briefing room. "We have exactly seventy-two hours to meet the demands of the secessionists and avert another tragedy. In short, by midnight Sunday." She swallowed two more Fiornals to try to alleviate her pounding headache.

"Can you tell us a little bit more about the governors, what they want, and how they intend to get it?" asked Brigadier General Jason Montague, a middle-aged Special Forces Army commander. Jason was a self-made street kid who had worked his way up from the slums of Chicago through high school, wrestling and boxing while holding down a perfect 4.0 grade average and working part-time at the slaughter houses. After entering West Point on a full scholarship, and repeating his sterling academic and athletic performance there, he went on to serve in Vietnam and the Gulf War. Eventually he headed up the combined operational forces in Somalia and Bosnia. He gained his reputation as both a thinker and a fighter when he was asked by the President to write a white paper, reconfiguring the Army for the twenty-first century.

Jason, like most of the officials in the room, addressed his colleagues by their first names. In this room they were a body of equals. However, as in all egalitarian systems, there was one person who was, in fact, more equal than the others.

"Unfortunately, Jason," Barbara responded, "we have very little time and I am by necessity going to have to give you only thumbnail sketches. More information will follow throughout the day."

"At least someone has some thumbnails," Secretary of Defense Phil Grahn laughed, seated next to Barbara, ready to assist her on strategic issues related to military operations. When it came to tactical issues, he knew she preferred the scholar-soldier, Jason Montague.

"The secessionist movement seems to have two distinct components," she continued, "which conveniently join together both ideologically and geographically in the states of Utah, Wyoming, Colorado, and Arizona." She walked back and forth across the newly remodeled briefing room, taking mental note of how many minority men, women, gays, and lesbians were in the group. Close to forty percent, she calculated. No affirmative action. No preferential treatment. No excuses. No rationalizations. They were all here because of one simple fact. They were the best. And that was the way it should be.

"From what we can gather from our intelligence sources," she continued, "there is a domestic component and a foreign component. The domestic component, possibly headed by Colorado Governor Cheri Black, includes three other governors. Utah Governor Josiah Brigham IV, a deacon in the Mormon Church, may be second-in-command. But we do not know whether any differences of opinion or tensions exist within the group. Certainly something to watch out for and exploit. Those two governors are the major players on the domestic side. Arizona Governor Andrew Paul is perhaps the weakest and most compliant of the group. Wyoming Governor James McMinn is irreverent, shrewd, and may be playing off both sides to see which side will eventually win. He's the one who is providing the actual location for the governors' meeting and most of the security."

"If Governor Paul appears to be the weakest," Jason interrupted, "maybe that's the reason these governors chose to destroy Page, Arizona."

"That certainly is one possibility, Jason," Barbara retorted. "Remember, the Glen Canyon Dam controls the water and electrical power for those states. I'm beginning to think that the next 'incident' will be of significantly greater proportions, but it will also occur in one of those four states again. This way the governors can both precipitate and manage the crisis better than if they created it in a state where they don't control the National Guard, grass-roots politics, or the physical terrain.'' She paused for emphasis. ''They will not avoid a military confrontation. They believe that they have the resources, manpower capability, and political support within their own states to carry out a secessionist movement.''

''You said there was a second component to this madness,'' Angela Rodriguez, FBI Special Agent, said. ''I was wondering what that is.'' Angela, one of the first Hispanic women to enter the senior ranks of the FBI, was a specialist in criminal behavior, mass psychology, and hostage negotiation. She had distinguished herself in her handling of several cases, one in which a high-risk strategy had successfully secured the release of several American hostages taken captive in Lebanon by the Hezbollah. She had worked with Alison Carter in several operations, and they both shared a similar philosophy. While she was highly respectful of Barbara, something was bothering her. If this was such a dire situation, then where was Al?

''The second and equally significant component,'' Barbara continued, ''is the fact that the governors are supported by at least one foreign government we know of, France, in the person of Prime Minister Yvette de Perignod. There is some classified evidence to suggest that Yvette has met with several officials in England and Germany to discuss political problems in the U.S. In my way of thinking, that makes her a renegade diplomat. In my personal opinion, I think Yvette is representing both her own and her government's overseas interests.''

''Why England and Germany?'' someone asked from the audience.

''Because these three countries are major investors in the United States. Contrary to common opinion, the Japanese aren't the primary investors in our economy. It's the British, followed by the Dutch, the Germans, the Japanese, and then the French. I gather that these countries feel that these states are America's future, that they will be the most productive and successful ones in the twenty-first century. By backing the secessionist movement, these countries are hoping to gain immense economic and political benefit. Collectively, these five countries already control trillions of dollars' worth of investments in the four states. With NAFTA, they can cross the border between Mexico and the U.S. and Canada and the U.S. They can go all the way from the very north of Canada, where they can mine uranium, and pass it through the U.S. into Baja Mexico with no tariffs, no surcharges, no customs, and no trade impediments whatsoever. In short, they've created a new country. Not one based in history, political allegiance, ethnicity, or custom, but one based on physical contiguity and economic enhancement."

"What you are describing, Barbara," Jason said, "is the new colonial empire of the twenty-first century."

"That's correct, Jason," Barbara responded. "And our mission is to prevent that from happening."

The room was completely silent. Everyone shared the same thought. They would do whatever was necessary to prevent a civil war and, in the worst case, an international incident. The only problem was that no one believed in miracles and that's what they would need to accomplish everything Barbara had said, and they needed to do it within the next three days.

20

DEPARTMENT OF STATE, WASHINGTON, D.C.

Friday, July 4th, 12:20 A.M.

''The grass-roots movement for the False Patriots,'' Special Agent Angela Rodriguez said as she pointed to an illuminated screen hanging in the front of the room, ''consists of dozens of right wing fanatical groups, ranging from the Christian Coalition to the Aryan Supremacy Group. They are united today by one common ideology, a complete hatred of the federal government.''

''Angela, how extensive is the membership?'' Brigadier General Jason Montague asked. ''And what's its profile?''

''Membership is broadbased,'' she responded. ''Members are found in all regions of the country and in all walks of life.''

''Can you flesh that out?'' Sec Def Phil Grahn asked.

''Yes, sir,'' Angela replied, pointing to a list of job affiliations which were flashed onto the screen. ''Let's begin with the more innocuous ones. As you can see, we have real estate agents, preachers, commodities traders, elk ranchers, electricians, retired military personnel, and health professionals.''

''Is there any profession,'' Barbara asked, ''which is not represented?''

''For all practical purposes''—Angela answered as carefully as possible—''we've pretty much identified the aforementioned professions as the primary feeders. Paradoxically, there seems to be a disproportionate number of former military personnel and civil servants. Over the last six months the FBI has had success in infiltrating a score of hate groups that call themselves tax protesters, millennialists, survivalists, populists, freemen, constitutionalists, neo-Nazis, skinheads, Klansmen, Identity believers, Christian Reconstructionists, secessionists, abortion foes, and anti-environmentalists. Many have paramilitary components to their group. A group that seems to come out of Salt Lake City, Utah, called A.P.R.L., the Association for the Privilege of Religious Liberties, has been disseminating hate posters, flyers, and simulation games on the Net which teach you why you should hate Jews, Blacks, Hispanics, and Catholics. Of all the groups, this one is the most ingenious. They use the latest technologies. Faxes, online Websites, interactive software that teaches you how to interrogate, imprison, and torture. The goal is definitely how to pit one group against another to create conflict."

"A modern-day Goebbels," Jason interjected.

"In terms of the dynamics of these people," Angela continued, flashing to another slide with the names of specific organizations, "the secessionist movement makes everyone feel welcome. It appeals to people who feel isolated, aimless. The movement provides them with a sense of mission and a comradery that they cannot find anywhere else. It has great appeal to people who view themselves as victims. It offers them an expansive, faceless enemy—the federal bureaucracy—as a scapegoat. Who among us hasn't fantasized the destruction of the IRS after having just paid taxes?"

Everyone in the room started to laugh. It was a scary notion to see how easily everyone could empathize.

"Many who join the False Patriots," Angela continued, "are religious fanatics whose faith is focused on the time when Christ will supposedly return to collect his followers as the world is destroyed. A.P.R.L. places a particularly heavy emphasis on the Christian way of doing things."

"So," Barbara interrupted, "they are the type of believer who will join the organization in order to witness the inevitable battle between good and evil."

"That's correct," Angela responded. "However, there

have been many joiners who have rationalized their affiliation as a protest against the rise of blacks into prominent positions in the U.S. government. Now we may be witnessing a shift, as they express their hostility toward both the federal government and the Jews, whom many of them believe control it.''

''Angela,'' Phil interrupted, ''don't we have an incident occurring right now in Nye County, Nevada?''

''Earlier today,'' Angela responded with alacrity, ''we had a standoff involving normally law-abiding citizens, including Larry Teague, the Commissioner of Nye County, Nevada, and several ATF agents, forest rangers, and FBI officials. The dispute is over who owns a particular parcel of land: the federal government or the county.''

''What's the latest info on that situation?'' Barbara asked, concerned that no single incident sidetrack their mission.

''The latest Sit Rep indicates that no one has been hurt,'' Angela responded, consulting her notes, ''but that a citizens' court is going to be held on the matter.''

''Please make sure that there are no precipitous actions taken on our part, but continue to monitor the situation,'' Barbara ordered. ''We don't want to trigger a second Ruby Ridge.''

''It's under control, I can assure you,'' Angela responded rapidly, as if she had been rehearsing the answer.

''What do you mean?'' Barbara asked, her adrenaline pumping. She stood up and paced the front of the room. The entire situation was beginning to get out of control, she thought. It was always the insignificant incidents which precipitated the major problems. A standoff in the woods of Nevada could get as much press coverage as— If one smart-ass reporter tied seemingly unrelated incidences together, the rest of the connections would be easy to make. And the country would panic. Then she would have a real disaster on her hands. From the beginning, her trump card was the fact that she was in control of the situation. But now she was beginning to feel on edge.

''As far as we know,'' Angela continued, ''our undercover agents are on top of everything that is happening. We've gotten word that the Nye County Common Law

Court is going to be convened by a farmer named Darrell Hayeck, along with the support of County Commissioner Lawrence Teague and Nevada State Police Captain Robert McElroy. We'll monitor it closely."

"So this is one of the matches," Barbara said in a loud but clearly ominous voice, "that can light gunpowder."

"We have evidence to suggest that . . ." Jason interjected, collating a group of papers on the table in front of him.

"We also have evidence . . ." Angela continued, not wanting Jason to give the Sec State the impression that only the military had intel on the situation. It would not look good for the FBI. In the bureaucracy, one man's victory was another man's defeat. And she wanted to make certain that Barbara knew that the FBI was totally in charge of the crisis. Collegiality was extended first to your own agency and then to your next bureaucratic kin. Angela didn't want to appear too eager or too anxious, yet she had to make it clear that the Bureau received its proper share of credit.

"Please allow me a few minutes," Jason interrupted, walking to the front of the room and displacing Angela as the focus of attention. "Military intelligence informs us that militia groups and organizations are prepared to attack federal installations around the country. They're just waiting for right cause." He proceeded to read from a list in his hand. "The groups include: the Police Against the New World Order, from Phoenix, Arizona; the militia from the New Covenant Bible Church and Ministries, Birch Tree, Missouri; the American Renaissance Militia, from Louisville, Kentucky; the Christian Patriot Crusaders for Stone Kingdom Ministries, Asheville, North Carolina; E Pluribus Unum Patriot Group, Columbus, Ohio; Flying Colors, Northpoint Teams, Topton, North Carolina; Necessary Force, the Missouri's Fifty-first Militia, Kansas City, Missouri; Militia of Montana, Noxton, Montana; the National Vanguard, Hillsboro, West Virginia; the New American, John Birch Society, Appleton, Wisconsin; the Private Intelligence Network, Easley, South Carolina; The Special Forces Underground, Kansas City, Missouri; Aryan Nations, Hayden Lake, Idaho; a still unidentified group working out of Salt Lake City, in conjunction with A.P.R.L. and possibly the Mormon Church. The Mormon Church has publicly denounced any groups preaching sedition, secession, or violence. So I'm pretty certain it's not coming from the church proper. But there can always be a renegade Mormon group somewhere. . . . There are about one hundred and twenty more groups. I think you get the idea. We have quite a comprehensive list.'' That last sentence was intended to garner credit for his agency.

''We've also been compiling a list of radio stations which will act as a 'call to arms' for these militia groups,'' Carl Williams, a tall, lanky, bespectacled National Security Agency analyst, shouted out, reinforcing Jason's thesis that militia all over the country could mobilize with short notice. ''Personally, I am extremely disappointed to announce that the stations include some of your favorite oldies but goodies, Barbara,'' he said with his typically wry sense of humor. ''KCCA, 107 FM, Arizona; KCVL, 1240 AM, Colville, Washington; KDNO, 98.5 FM, Delano, California; KFYI, 910 AM, Phoenix, Arizona; KHNC, 1360 AM, Johnstown, Colorado; KVOR, 1300 AM, Colorado Springs, Colorado; WBTJ, Pensacola, Florida; WHRI, Noblesville, Indiana; WINB, Philadelphia, Pennsylvania; WJCR, 90.1 FM, Upton, Kentucky; WJYM, 730 AM, Bowling Green, Ohio; WMKT, FM, Charlevoix, Michigan; WRNO, New Orleans, Louisiana; and WWCR, Nashville, Tennessee. Following up on what Angela and Jason said before about the militia group out of Utah, there seems to be a disproportionate amount of hate radio transmissions coming from Salt Lake City. The Mormon Church has certainly denounced them in several of its Sunday broadcasts from the Tabernacle. But the odd thing is that the actual transmission signals seem to be coming out of the very same complex of buildings in which the Tabernacle is located. Figure that one out,'' he added rhetorically.

''Anyone you leave out?'' Barbara asked, trying to lessen the tension in the room.

''As far as we can tell, we've heard nothing from MTV, ESPN, CNN, The Disney Channel, or the 700 Club,'' Williams continued, getting the laugh he had hoped for.

''I think it's time,'' Barbara responded calmly, ''that we

take to the airwaves. Michael, the first thing I want you and your crew at the NSA to do is to jam the radio transmissions coming out of the stations Carl listed. Make it look as if there was electrostatic interference from heaven. We can't take a chance that the current incident, which seems to be limited to four states, will gain a wider audience."

"But, Barbara," Michael interjected, his face turning red, "that's completely illegal."

"So is NSA monitoring American citizens around the world," she responded, a Cheshire smile on her face. "And we do it every day."

Michael's face turned bright red.

"He's right," Phil confirmed. "We're in complete violation of the law."

"Blame heaven for electrical interference," she repeated. "It's not the first time God will have worked miracles. These False Patriots always seem to use the Holy Book against us. Now, it's our turn at the pulpit." She felt good and righteous saying that. She always knew that God would be a formidable ally. Now, she would demonstrate just how formidable.

A firm knock at the door of the briefing room startled the group. Could an incident already have occurred as they sat there planning how to avoid one? Fortunately, it was only Barbara's secretary announcing that the Chinese food had arrived.

21

DEPARTMENT OF STATE, WASHINGTON, D.C.

Friday, July 4th, 1:25 A.M.

One of the unspoken enticements of Barbara's midnight meetings was the Chinese food brought in from Bethesda from her favorite North China Restaurant. The inside joke among the group was that if anyone wanted to know whether a crisis was imminent, they only had to stake out the C Street entrance of the State Department to see how many delivery vans arrived throughout the night. What foods were delivered, and how frequently, was the key to unlocking the secrets of U.S. national security.

"The first phase of our counteroffensive," Barbara announced, while trying to gracefully eat a pancake overstuffed with moo shu chicken, "is to neutralize the False Patriot groups in Utah, Colorado, Arizona, and Wyoming as quickly as possible. To that end I am assigning Special Agent Angela Rodriguez to coordinate what I will call 'Operation Grass Roots.' The basic strategy of our offensive is to cut off the groups' financial resources and personnel, thereby limiting the political support they can give to the governors. And do it in less than forty-eight hours. Angela, use as many federal agents as you need. Deputize, if you need to."

"I'll do my best," Angela responded. The assignment seemed overwhelming, but that was the beauty of working with a group of people you trust to pull 150 percent for you and a no-nonsense leader like Barbara who was willing to cut all the necessary corners to achieve her goal.

"Barbara." Allan Youdelman, a well-dressed man in his late fifties, stood up to address her. "There is an extremely swift, effective way to cut off the financial underbelly of the False Patriots and their governors." Allan was a meticulous senior bureaucrat in the Treasury Department who had a thorough understanding of federal subsidies and payments.

"Let's hear it. But make it simple," Barbara replied, reaching for a carton of crispy beef.

"It couldn't be more simple," Allan said, walking to the flipchart standing near the wall. He listed the names Teague, Hayeck, McElroy, and the words "other False Patriots." In a pedantic voice reminiscent of his days as a college professor, he addressed his audience. "What do these people and about sixty percent of all these secessionists who are anti-federal government have in common?"

"They're assholes," someone muttered.

The room broke up in laughter.

"That, of course, may be one point in common," he replied, "but there is a similarity of far greater strategic value."

"None of them paid their taxes?" Phil guessed, knowing from prior meetings that when Youdelman presented a solution to a serious problem it would be well researched.

"Good guess," Allan responded, enjoying the fact that he had piqued the interest of the Sec Def. "That may well be the case. What they usually do is file their income tax form and then not pay any taxes due. And no one is any the wiser unless they are audited by the IRS. But then it's too late to collect. By that time they have spent all of their money. And they get charged by the government for a civil crime as opposed to a criminal one."

"Allan," Barbara said with a hint of impatience, "remember the caveat: make it simple. Please, let's get to the point."

"One of the great paradoxes of all these False Patriots," Allan continued, ignoring Barbara's criticism, "is that despite the vehemence of their anti-federalist rhetoric, many have been recipients of federal subsidies. We know that some are federal government workers who have received a federal paycheck or secured a retirement annuity. But the names I've written on the blackboard go one step further. They continue to receive substantial farm subsidies from our favorite Uncle Sam."

"Flesh the point out, Allan," Barbara instructed him. "What are you getting at?"

"I did research on farm subsidies in Nye County," he responded, "and found that all the principals involved in this anti-federalist movement, at one or another time, received substantial subsidies from the federal government not to grow anything on their land. I have no doubt that they have been using this money to finance their political and paramilitary activities against the feds." Pausing, he scanned the room to reassure himself that he still had their attention. "Teague and Hayeck together account for about $750,000 in direct subsidies. Since 1985, Teague, Hayeck, and McElroy have received $4.5 million from the Department of Agriculture to hedge their bets against droughts, hailstorms, and low market prices for their wheat, barley, and wool. It was only when they had to pay back taxes or face foreclosure by the local bank did they start to form this anti-federalist campaign."

"Are you suggesting," Barbara interrupted, "that we cut off subsidies to any persons with known or suspected connections with the secessionist movement?"

"The sooner it's done," Allan replied without hesitation, "the quicker we will be able to blunt the movement. Citizens of Nye County alone received more than $50 million in subsidies over the last fifteen years."

"Aren't these the same people who went on television a few years ago and pleaded poverty because of bank foreclosures? And in some cases received court stays of judgment?" Jason asked, disgusted by the double standard that seemed to be operating among the False Patriots: take what you can from the feds but piss on them when asked to be held accountable for your actions. So this was the end product of the dependency that Washington had fostered, he thought to himself.

"Jason is precisely right," Allan replied. "These three

individuals took the subsidies and spent it on two Lincoln Continentals, one helicopter, two motor homes, and gambling trips to Las Vegas and Aruba. Two other Nye County farmers bought up about seven thousand acres of land which were completely overleveraged. No one paid taxes for years. And when the IRS demanded to be paid, there was nothing left to pay with. Some of the land was ultimately foreclosed on by the local bank.''

''I know it may not do the trick in the short run, but I want you to identify each one of these groups and their members,'' Barbara ordered Youdelman. ''I want the IRS to go over their tax forms with a fine-tooth comb and put them away if they don't come up with what is owed to the federal government. Cut off their farm subsidies, Social Security payments, pension fund payouts, and any other item that smacks of federal handout. Call it whatever you want to. Get whatever court orders you need. Just stop the flow of federal funds to them.'' Turning toward a lawyer from the Treasury Department, seated next to Allan, she said, ''I want every one of these so-called patriotic organizations to lose their nonprofit status if they have it. Pay strict attention to the heavy interest owed on their back taxes. I also want them tied up with an immense amount of paperwork.''

''Don't you think,'' Phil asked, ''that we're going a little too far? We really may be doing what they've been accusing us of doing—stretching the federal government's authority and power.''

''Phil,'' Barbara responded, with a clear tone of hostility, ''we are—or soon may be—at war. As the acting senior official of the government for the next three days I will suspend any due process venues to the degree that I am able to.'' She added, ''I will assume full and personal responsibility for any . . . extraordinary measures we may have to undertake.'' She recalled an ancient adage of crisis management: Choose your enemy well; for in the process of combating him, you may well become like him.

22

DEPARTMENT OF STATE, WASHINGTON, D.C.

Friday, July 4th, 2:15 A.M.

''Unfortunately, eliminating the financial basis of the False Patriots will take awhile to execute and be felt by them,'' Barbara continued. ''We have to implement the short-range part of the strategy, our military options, now. Jason, please share some of your thoughts with us.''

''Over the past several hours,'' Jason said, clicking on the slide projector, ''my staff and I have been preparing a military options plan requested by Barbara. I must apologize for the fact that we've tried to do in two hours what we usually spend two months planning. However, thanks to the unusual interagency cooperation, we have acquired extremely good intelligence about the secessionists and their cohorts. As most of you know there is a federal law that prohibits the CIA, the Defense Intelligence Agency, the National Reconnaissance Agency, and the NSA from tracking or electronically 'sweeping' American citizens. Thanks to Secretary of State Barbara Reynolds and the senior representatives from the Justice Department and the National Security Council at the White House, we have received an exemption from that law.

''At present, we are collecting the different types of intelligence that allow us to monitor both the civilian and military movements of the governors who are staying at the Rockefeller Lodge. Our collective intelligence indicates that the Lodge is the command and control center for the entire secessionist movement. At the same time, we have a pretty good idea of the military, paramilitary, and militia group deployments in the four states. Thanks to the efforts of the FBI, DIA, ATF, various local law enforcement agencies, and the CIA, we have both overt and covert Human Intelligence. The NRO have provided us with satellite images of the various National Guard troop dispositions in the different states as well as the location of the governors. All this intelligence has been enhanced by signal and electronic intercepts by the NSA which allow us to monitor the governors' conversations among themselves and with their respective field commanders.

"As a result, we've been able to develop an outline of a three-pronged military strategy which we call 'Operation Trident.' " He looked around the room at his own people, hoping that they felt that his presentation reflected the result of a major team effort. "Our basic strategy is to disarm the soldiers who, earlier today, took over the Glen Canyon Dam. For that purpose, we will deploy the Ready Brigade of the First Marine Division at Camp Pendleton. They are only four hundred and fifty miles away from Lake Powell. One brigade of Marines would be more than enough to deal with the 25,000 National Guardsmen defending the dam, assuming they are unprotected from air attack. At the same time, we will mount the second phase of the operation, which will be to parachute the Eighty-second Airborne Division from Fort Bragg, North Carolina, into the Grand Tetons region to secure the Rockefeller Lodge. They are on standby alert and should be there in a few hours. We will hold everyone there incommunicado long enough to try to find out where the next major catastrophe is going to happen and when."

"Do you feel comfortable," Phil asked, "that you can realistically accomplish these goals?"

"Yes, sir," Jason replied with self-confidence. "I'm employing the campaign principles we picked up in the Gulf War, particularly that of 'parallel warfare'—striking all the relevant targets at the same time. Our intention is to surgically strike and extract the cancer while containing its spread. We will deprive our adversary of his eyes and ears, leaving him senseless in a swift retaliatory counterattack. Without belaboring the point Angela made, the next phase of our strategy will be to assist her FBI agents and Federal Marshals in a preemptive strike on the False Patriots' paramilitary training sites. Please correct me, Angela, if I've missed anything.''

''Don't worry, Jason,'' she replied, ''you're doing just fine.'' He was the type of team player who, while supportive of his team members, made certain that in the long run he would be first among equals. Not that he didn't deserve that position, she thought. But he always appeared so ''military,'' so serious. She couldn't help but believe that underneath his ribbons and medals he was basically quite mischievous.

''As of now,'' Jason proceeded, ''our primary targets are the Kingman Group in Arizona; the Colorado State Militia in Colorado; the Army of Israel in Utah; and the Aryan American Citizens in Wyoming. Once we have this crisis under control, we have plans to go nationwide. In Idaho, the contiguous state to Wyoming, which supplies the greatest number of militia, we'll hit the Idaho Patriots with a combination of FBI, Federal Marshals, and First Armored Cavalry Division from Fort Sam Houston. Secondary targets will include two groups in Alabama, the Gadsden Minutemen and the Central Alabama Militia. In California, one of the largest sources of paramilitary soldiers, we will be neutralizing the Placer Company Militia, the Militia of California in San Diego, and the National Alliance of Christian Militias. And in Texas, Washington State, and Wisconsin, we'll try to shut down the North Texas Constitutional Militia, the Washington State Militia, and the Waupaca and Vernon County militias. And the list goes on . . .'' Jason paused for a moment, looking at the shocked faces in the room. As expected, few people at the meeting had realized how broadbased and far-reaching was the dissatisfaction of their fellow Americans. And all these groups needed, Jason thought, was a charismatic leader who could mobilize them into an effective political/military force. Through the use of modern technology these groups could really become a formidable fighting machine. Right now the individual militias could be picked off one group at a time. But his past counter-insurgency combat experience had taught him that the absence of a single militia leader was only a short-term problem waiting to explode into a larger one.

"What type of resistance do you expect from these militia groups?" Barbara asked, looking at both Angela and Jason.

"In terms of weapons," Jason replied, "we can expect a wide variety, including Stinger missiles, LAW rockets, plastic explosives, automatic rifles and pistols, hand grenades, blasting caps, and military grade ammunition." Pausing, he added the caveat, "Remember, every person in this country has available to him a wide assortment of military information, war manuals, and blueprints, including the formula for ANFO, the ammonium nitrate and fuel oil bomb that tore apart the federal building in Oklahoma City. Although I'm not trying to frighten you all, or create a doomsday scenario, we know that these groups also have access to biological weapons, including bubonic plague, anthrax, and a variety of other bacterias."

"We expect to encounter a leaderless resistance," Angela continued. She didn't mention her shared concern with Jason about the imminent emergence of a single leader, because there was already enough on the table to deal with without worrying about the future. "The underground strategy used by these False Patriots was described by the revolutionary white supremacist Louis Beam in the 1992 edition of his newsletter *The Seditionist.* Beam proposed that those patriots who were 'serious about their opposition to federal despotism' should stop holding public meetings and start organizing underground 'phantom cells,' small independent units that could instigate actions against the government without having to coordinate plans with a central leadership. The intention was to cull out the 'hangers-on' who were not willing to take action. But more important, they wanted to create an 'intelligence nightmare' for law enforcement authorities, especially the FBI, where we would be stymied by the lack of a unified network and a clear hierarchy of leadership. The leaderless resistance is organized with four layers of activists. First are full-time 'citizen soldiers' who come out only to strike against the occupying power and disappear. Then there are the auxiliary groups, which organize civilian support through recruiting, propaganda, counterintelligence, and providing safe houses. Third is the auxiliary's 'home guard,' small armed units who guard weapons caches and train recruits. Fourth are the 'underground' secret auxiliary units."

"It seems as if you are telling us that on the domestic scene," Barbara offered her conclusions, "we are organized to neutralize both the actual secessionist movement and the leaderless resistance cells of the False Patriots." She glanced around the room, lingering on the faces of the career Foreign Service officers. For the most part, they were hardworking, selfless, and loyal. The biggest mistake every previous Sec State had made was to fire or reassign those Foreign Service officers who technically did not perform up to standards. She knew all too well that more often than not the standards were arbitrary, vague, and unjust. So she had changed as much of them as she could with some help from Al. They had adopted a paradigm based on the medical model that Al had learned during medical school. See one; do one; teach one. Everyone in a decision-making capacity who worked with Barbara had been involved in a crisis before, had been part of managing one, and was prepared for the tough job ahead. She just hoped that they would be able to calibrate their own energy and fatigue levels so that they didn't burn out before the crisis had been resolved.

"There are several points that we have not covered yet," Barbara continued. "Thanks in large part to the brilliant cooptation of the media at Lake Powell by our BLM spokesperson, Richard Solomon, as well as the inherent laziness of reporters, we are keeping journalists and cameramen completely away from this crisis. Dick devised a double-pronged smoke screen that deals with both environmental concerns and structural problems at Glen Canyon Dam. The reporters and the citizens of Page, Arizona, will be able to pick whatever excuse for the flooding—when it comes—that appeals to them. We've had only a few inquiries from Congressional staffers, but they seemed satisfied with our answers. Thanks for doing a great job, Dick."

Everyone applauded as the shy, lanky, silver-haired man

reluctantly stood up to receive the well-deserved accolades from his peers.

"But this may not work for long," Barbara added. "Dick is still in the final stages of developing yet another one of his unique strategies for redirecting the media's attention away from the crisis. I understand that this gambit will entail some interesting type of diversion. Clearly, it is too premature to reveal anything more." She recalled an incident that occurred about fifteen years before, involving Marine guards who had fallen asleep on duty at the U.S. Embassy in Moscow. It had been alleged in the American press that Top Secret information had been stolen from the embassy during the "nap." In reality, the entire incident had been directed by the U.S. government in an attempt to divert attention away from the principal activity of the U.S. government at that time, which was to uncover a mole within the CIA. It had taken fifteen years, but the FBI had finally uncovered a Russian mole within the CIA—Richard Ames.

"Let's also thank Robert Gottlieb, who with his FEMA agents evacuated the entire town of Page, Arizona, and dozens of smaller ones, in record time and without incident. No small feat. Thanks, Robert."

The group applauded, once again impressed by the capabilities of their peers.

"And I know you are all wondering why Al Carter isn't sitting here with us tonight. Well, he's on a fact-finding mission in New York City, where he will be speaking later today with Yvette de Perignod, who is heavily involved with our renegade governors. I'll keep each of you posted on his communications with me.

"Next, ladies and gentlemen," she continued, "there is the matter of what I call 'international pressure.' " She nodded her head as if she already knew what their response would be. "You don't think for one damn second that this Secretary of State"—she pointed to herself in an exaggerated manner—"is going to tolerate French interference in the internal affairs of this great country in the guise of its 'unauthorized' emissary, Prime Minister Yvette de Perignod? Or the quiet, unofficial complicity of England and Germany? I think it's time for tit for tat. Any suggestions?"

''How about if we tried to create some domestic turmoil in those countries?'' Gary Messing asked somberly. ''It seems appropriate enough. A little wake-up call from our covert operational units might strike just the right tone in Europe. We don't have to precipitate a major war. Just a subtle retaliation and warning.''

''Spoken like a true Vice Chairman of the National Intelligence Committee,'' Barbara responded with a broad smile on her face. ''Would you like to elaborate on some of the wake-up calls you might have up your sleeve?''

''I think we can make it sufficiently unpleasant,'' Messing responded with a sadistic smile, ''so that our 'good allies' will think twice before they ever attempt to destabilize the U.S.A.''

''Just remember, I don't want anything involving loss of life,'' Barbara admonished Messing. ''That I will not tolerate. Also, I don't want anything that will require a Congressional 'finding.' We just don't have the time, nor would I trust anyone in Congress to keep his mouth shut on such a sensitive issue. And for God's sake, nothing that will create anything more serious that a diplomatic demarche against us.''

''I can assure you,'' Messing said, ''that we will create enough discreet back-pressure so that these three countries will think twice before they embark on another destructive adventure like this one.''

''Then I think that that's it for now,'' Barbara concluded. ''We don't have any time for mistakes. From now on, it's the real thing. And remember, according to yesterday's telephone call from Brigham, we have less than three days left to deal with the governors' demands before we're hit with another disaster.''

23

UNITED NATIONS PLAZA, NEW YORK CITY

Friday, July 4th, 7:45 A.M.

From time immemorial, the French have always elicited an unusual ambivalence from both pundits and diplomats alike. No less a satirist than Mark Twain once proclaimed in a moment of New England despondency that "God made man a little lower than the angels and a little above the French." Even the famous French sociologist Crozier stated: "French society throughout its history has shown a tendency to resist change until the last possible moment, to allow an intolerable situation to build up and then, when the strain and inconvenience are too great, to change together in a vast reshuffle, under the impulse of a few pioneering individuals." But perhaps it was the great French statesman, General Charles de Gaulle himself, who provided the final coup de grâce when he was rumored to have said, "It's a pity that the grandeur of France belongs to the Frenchman."

Fortunately for the French, most of the world visualized France through the commercial prisms of gastronomic delights, haute couture, and idealized romantic settings which inflamed passions and promises of *liasons dangereuses.*

Dr. Alison Carter, however, had no such illusions about France, or its Foreign Minister, Madame Yvette de Perignod, the grande dame of international diplomacy.

"The world is in a state of chaos," proclaimed the stately

Yvette to Al as they left the United Nations Plaza and strolled leisurely down the street.

"*Je suis d'accord.* I agree," Al replied in the excellent French he had acquired during his overseas RMO assignments. As he looked at his companion he was surprisingly impressed by her quiet self-assurance and aristocratic demeanor. Things had obviously changed over time. His memories were of a more frenetic, histrionic woman with grand gestures and languid insights.

"*Tu me comprends?* You understand me?" she asked, turning around to make certain that they were still being trailed by the protective detail of six fully armed security guards.

"*Je te comprends.* I understand you," he replied, comfortable using the informal *tu* form of "you" as opposed to the *vous* form, which normally would have been the more appropriate form used by two senior diplomats. He needed to awaken the bond of trust that had existed between them years before. Sooner or later, he would have to deliver his "unofficial" message from Barbara and assess Yvette's response. In official diplomatic parlance, he would be presenting a demarche, an official protest by his government. Whichever way he said it—officially or unofficially—he knew it would certainly strain his already inchoate relationship with Yvette and possibly affect French-American relations.

For this meeting to be successful, Al was relying on the goodwill which had accrued during the years when Yvette and he had worked together to prevent a second "killing field" in Cambodia. Working in an informal capacity for a former U.S. Secretary of State, he had been sent to Cambodia to help develop strategy. Together with Yvette's French minions, Al had devised a risky diplomatic formula that used the United Nations Perm Five Security Council, composed of England, France, China, Russia, and the United States, to create a twenty-thousand-man United Nations Peace Keeping Force, called UNTAC, to neutralize the infamous Khmer Rouge. And it had worked. Of course, he had sidestepped the entire East Asian and Pacific Bureau at the State Department. But the successful outcome of the

First Paris Peace Conference on Cambodia resulted in the newly created democratic regime of Cambodia. The country, unfortunately, was still being ruled by a manic-depressive constitutional monarch.

Al wondered if anyone had ever told Yvette about the wonders of lithium. So far, she certainly hadn't evidenced any bipolar illness that he could see. But it wouldn't be the first time that CIA assessment of a world leader would be wrong. It never hurt to have a medical license readily available when dealing with international leaders, he concluded. Al smiled, recalling how he had broken a major impasse at a Middle East peace negotiation by giving an Israeli leader a medication which cured his back pain, and prescribing a beta blocker for a heart arrhythmia that one of the Arab leaders developed during the talks.

Given her current status, Al was impressed that Yvette allowed him to address her in the *tu* form. As long as that continued, and she addressed him informally, he was still in her good graces. It would never do to become one of the legions of foreign diplomats and special envoys who over the years were relegated to the status of persona non grata by the "last courtesan," as Yvette was sarcastically identified in the dark corridors of power. He certainly didn't care that prodigious sexual appetites had served her well in her ascendancy to power. He just knew there was a fine line to walk.

"*Et maintenant on va parler.* And now we are going to talk," she continued, "*mais tu es trop maigre, tu sais.* But you are too thin, you know." She really was concerned about him. While he was still tall and thin, the years had taken a toll on the good doctor. He walked with stooped shoulders. He looked too haggard. Perhaps he was having romantic problems, which she knew could be debilitating. True to her Gaelic heritage, she would never inquire about his financial status or marital infidelities. These matters were best left to the confessional booth.

On a personal level, Al thought, they could not be more different. Yvette was in her mid-sixties. He was in his late forties. She was still strikingly beautiful, with a Modigliani-like face that was no stranger to the wonders of plastic surgery. But like all women who are extremely comfortable with themselves and appreciate whom they have become, she allowed her *nez de Bourbon*, with its characteristic bump, to remain a prominent feature of her otherwise faultless face. Her hazel eyes shimmered in the bright New York light with green fluorescence. Her hair, still jet black, was pulled back into a chignon. Her svelte body had been pampered, massaged, exercised, and, possibly, liposuctioned so that it could conform to a petite dress size.

For Al, Yvette embodied all the wonderful contradictions inherent in the French and their sacrosanct culture. Although he had grown up in the unfashionable area of Manhattan called lower Harlem, on 108th and Amsterdam Avenue, he always had the drive to learn about the finer aspects of life. He taught himself French, Spanish, and the black ghetto patois. He understood, perhaps as no other American envoy had, that too many Frenchmen had taken too seriously the political rallying cry "France not being France without greatness." As far as Al was concerned, France tried too hard to forget that she was the primary beneficiary of American generosity during and after both great wars. Unfortunately, the political and economic asymmetry had resulted in a marked ambivalence between the French and the Americans which was manifested by a constant, stormy relationship. As France prospered, the French had needed to reassert their independence from the Americans. This had shown itself by their proclaiming an independent *force de frappe*, a nuclear power independent of U.S. or NATO control, and by developing an autonomous economic entity that would compete against the U.S.

"Madame Prime Minister," Al began, assuming the more formal role of the official diplomat, "as you know, I am here because my country and yours seem to be having very serious political and economic problems. Despite our long-standing agreements to lower our trade barriers," Al continued, preventing her from interrupting him, "your country insists on violating the General Agreements for Trade and Tariff agreements. Your country just dumped government-subsidized French products on our soil. Automobiles. Heavy manufacturing equipment. At the same time, you won't allow us to penetrate your consumer markets with our products.'' Al looked at her face closely, wondering whether she knew that he was not really there to represent his country's economic financial interests.

''*Mais qu'est-ce que tu dis? Tu te rencontes ce que tu dis?* But what are you saying? Do you realize what you've just said?'' she asked, stopping their walk to stare into his bedroom eyes. If she were only a few years younger, she thought, she would not have hesitated to proposition him. Despite the fact that he appeared tired, he had an internal vibrancy that never ceased to entrap her within its force. He was compelling without being obtrusive or even threatening. And he had a professionalism that never confused his personal affections for her with the interests he represented. Perhaps that was his medical training shining through. His overwhelming sense of responsibility to the patient—or diplomat—at hand. Whichever it was, his word was his bond.

''*Je vais t'expliquer l'essence de ce sujet.* I'm going to explain to you the essential element of this subject,'' Al replied, trying to decide how to frame his argument.

''*Alors, dépêche-toi! Explique-le-moi!* All right then, hurry up! Explain it to me!'' she said, annoyed by the change in the nature of the conversation.

''This year,'' Al responded calmly in a rehearsed tone of voice, ''the U.S. exported to France a total of $12.5 billion of goods including machinery, electric equipment, soybeans, chemicals, and aircraft and aerospace equipment. In contrast, the U.S. imported from France an estimated $26 billion of products including iron, steel, chemicals, aerospace and telecommunications equipments, beverages, wines, liquors, textiles, cosmetics, and gourmet foods.''

''Oh, come, come,'' Yvette said, shaking her head. ''Some years we export more and some years we import less. That's part of doing business. As you Americans say, 'That's part of the give and take of everyday life.' ''

''Unfortunately,'' Al responded, ''this imbalance has been going on for a few years. Pechiney Ugine Kuhlman, a massive conglomerate, bought companies in Utah, Arizona, Colorado, and Wyoming,'' Al continued. ''Rhone Poulenc, a large chemical company, bought major holdings in Ogden,

Utah. Saint-Gobain and Thomson, part of France's Fortune 500 companies, are relocating in Salt Lake City as well as importing billions of dollars of consumer groups at preferential prices, while our companies must overcome a much higher tariff, making their products prohibitively expensive and noncompetitive.''

''I'm not clear what you are objecting to.'' Yvette spoke with more than a hint of exasperation. ''Is it the fact that we are buying companies in America? Or is it that we don't think your products are as good as ours? Or is it the fact that the American consumer has a certain fondness for French products?

''Listen, my dear Dr. Carter,'' she continued, jabbing her thin spindly fingers into his chest. ''You didn't fly over here to inform me about our country's surplus trade balance. As you Americans like to say, 'Get to the point.' ''

''What do you mean?'' Al asked disingenuously, realizing that his brief performance as a diplomat had been a complete bust.

''You know exactly what I mean,'' she responded, annoyed that he was trying to be coy with her. ''Barbara Reynolds sent you over here to see whether I was intact, so to speak. Both body and mind. And she wanted you to find out whether I had any intentions of supporting a group of states which, not by mere coincidence, match the places you just singled out for inordinate French investments—Wyoming, Utah, Colorado, Arizona.''

''Really?'' Al asked, totally taken aback by her biting bluntness.

''Doctor,'' she continued, ''neither coyness nor innocence becomes you. So please, at least treat me with some modicum of respect, by granting me the fact that I have been, as you Americans are so fond of saying, 'several times around the block.' ''

''And the answer?'' Al asked.

''You shall soon know. Remember, I—or should I hide like you did behind the diplomatic 'we'?—am a creature of opportunity. Monetary. Political. Social. Whatever advances my many interests. But unlike your boss, Ms. Barbara Reynolds, whom, for your edification, I happen to know extremely well, I do not have any hidden agendas. I will support those states because it is a unique opportunity for me personally, and possibly for France. It will afford me, if we are successful, of course, personal, financial, political, and social advantages far beyond anything you could imagine. If I know Barbara, she sent you to evaluate whether I was doing anything against my government's wishes. And the answer is again quite simple. Yes, I am involving myself as a private citizen in the domestic affairs of another country. That's, as you Americans like to say, a 'no-no.' Well, my whole life has been one big no-no. If for some reason I lose my gambit and your federal government wins, then I have still lost nothing and France will have lost nothing. Because as weak as our president may be, yours is weaker, and he will, I assure you, pardon a seventy-year-old spinster who has in the past served American national interests quite valiantly. So on those grounds alone, it is a win-win situation for me."

"I appreciate your candor," Al said, checking his watch. He didn't want to miss the flight that was leaving in an hour back to Washington.

"The last question for you to answer," Yvette interrupted, "is whether I am crazy or not. Is that not so?"

Al smiled.

"You don't have to answer the question because I would not want you to break your patient-client confidentiality," Yvette continued. "Am I not right, Dr. Carter? Isn't that why Barbara sent a physician and not a diplomat to see me? She wants to know whether you think that I am crazy. And if so, how best to handle me."

"You certainly are . . . perspicacious," Al said, completely lost for words. He had a knot in the pit of his stomach that told him he had just been set up.

"That's a very fancy word, Dr. Carter," Yvette responded. "Despite what you may think of the French, we are not all snobs, or pretentious, or fools blinded by our own past. Let me give you a word of advice before we end our little walk. Be careful, Dr. Alison Carter. It is Secretary of State Barbara Reynolds whom you have to worry about. Not me. I've just told you what my agenda is and will be. Opportunism and more opportunism. But what is Barbara's agenda? I'm not sure that this meeting was entirely necessary. Have you ever been to the Rockefeller Lodge in the Grand Tetons? I will be there tomorrow as the personal guest of Governor James McMinn. Where will you be?"

Al's face blanched. He was taken completely by surprise.

"Didn't your precious Madame Secretary tell you anything about that? And why is she suddenly in charge of running your country over the next few days? You are a good, competent physician. Your profession is to heal the body and the mind. Please take care of yourself. You are, again as you Americans like to say, 'way out of your league.' "

24

NYE COUNTY, NEVADA

Friday, July 4th, 10:05 A.M.

''The Nye County Common Law Court is in session,'' declared Darrell Hayek, a beefy red-haired farmer dressed in a starched white shortsleeve shirt, freshly ironed blue jeans, and red bow tie. He sat behind a folding rectangular table in front of four dozen of his neighbors, each dressed in standard Nye County attire—plaid shirts, dungarees, and cowboy boots. They were all seated on metal chairs set up in rows in the gymnasium of the county's high school, which this year had half of its graduates going on to five different junior colleges, four agricultural schools, and a handful of trade schools. The sense of pride each attendee had about his community was evident in the conversations about their children, the bountiful harvest, and the decreasing cost of fertilizer.

As Darrell banged his wooden gavel on the fake wood veneer, he hoped he could maintain both his composure and authority throughout the proceedings. County Commissioner Larry Teague and Nevada State Police Captain Robert McElroy were seated in front of him along with four state troopers. Darrell was both impressed and somewhat intimidated by their willingness to attend this mock trial.

''We are convened here today,'' Darrell said in a moderate tone of voice, ''to determine what exactly happened between Larry Teague, our county commissioner, and the feds in yesterday's confrontation.''

''Darrell, stop blowing all that hot air,'' Brian Sullivan shouted out from his seat. ''We all know what we are here to do. Let's get on to the adjudicating.''

''Cool your heels, Brian,'' Darrell said, banging his gavel to demonstrate his self-anointed authority to preside over the hearing. ''Well get to the judging. And the sentencing, if need be. But first we have to hear the case. Then we can deliberate on the options available to us.''

''You sound like one of those federal judges now,'' Brian added. ''This is the people's court, and we can decide on whatever rules should or should not prevail.'' A murmur in the audience indicated that several people supported Brian's statement. As a middle-aged bank executive, he was known and respected by most of the community.

Listening to Brian's complaint, Darrell knew that to anyone outside of the community this unassuming group of mostly men looked as if they were attending just another uneventful Rotary Club meeting. But nothing could have been further from the truth. In countless towns, hamlets, and villages scattered throughout this state, similar groups of citizens were meeting at this very moment over some issue involving unjust federal laws or infractions committed by overzealous federal agents. These mock trials were the outgrowth of the self-proclaimed citizens' courts, and most of them looked just like this one. No lawyers. No real judges. No properly constituted jury. These citizens' courts, as Darrell knew all too well, had grown out of the individual and collective grievances of citizens all over the country, like him, who had a personal grudge against the federal government for one or another reason. These were grievances that were never properly addressed or rectified by the feds. They just continued to grow in number and build up in hostility until there was no outlet other than the impromptu courts.

In Darrell's case, his four-hundred-acre farm had been foreclosed on by the federal government. All he knew was that when the Nye County Bank closed and was taken over by the Federal Deposit Insurance Corporation, he was unable to come up with the necessary money to pay off the entire $300,000 note he owed to the bank. It never seemed right. He had always paid his mortgage. Yet despite his on-time payment for the past ten years, his fifteen-year note was still "called." The FDIC had said he should try to get another bank to remortgage his farm. But times had gotten tough for everyone—especially small banks throughout the county—and Darrell couldn't come up with the money. He was now making a living, if he could call it that, working for minimum wage at a fast-food restaurant.

This citizens' court was Darrell's way of venting his frustration and anger toward the federal government. He knew that everyone seated in front of him and in other mock trial rooms around the country had a similar story and shared a similar hatred and distrust of the feds. The citizens' court was a by-product of what was fast becoming a national states'-rights movement. He knew of fourteen other states in which ordinary, once law-abiding citizens had set up courts which were now intent on directly challenging the federal government. Darrell was enough of both a realist and a patriot to realize that this new political theater was directed at dramatizing their collective grievances.

Typically, the organizers of these courts would deny that they were conducting trials of public officials in absentia. In reality these courts had declared thousands of people to be "state, rather than federal citizens." They had retried cases that had already been tried in regular courts, and attached liens to the property of public officials who opposed them. In one case, a murder contract had been issued against a federal judge.

Darrell had witnessed this phenomenon of civil disobedience and citizens' courts increase markedly since the April 19, 1995, bombing in Oklahoma City. Although he found that act personally repugnant, he understood the anger toward the federal government that lay behind it and the pent-up hostility over the role that federal agents played in the debacle at Waco, Texas, and Ruby Ridge, Idaho. Since that time, citizens' courts had really come into their own. About three dozen men had formed a common-law court in Jordan, Montana, and offered a million-dollar bounty for the arrest of federal and local officials. The Montana State Legislature retaliated, Darrell recalled, by making it a felony to impersonate or intimidate local officials. But the law was proving very hard to enforce.

It all boiled down to the same thing, thought Darrell. The backers of these new courts, ranging from white supremacists to struggling farmers like himself, all believed in the Constitution. Accordingly, like the radical Posse Comitatus tax-protest group of the 1970s, he believed that when the federal government partakes in illegitimate activities, the citizens' court may be the only way to rectify a bad situation. And that led Darrell to support the right to trial by popular jury that is preserved in the Constitution. Like many others, he argued that lawyers should be forbidden in the courts. While he was aware that his adversaries accused him of practicing vigilante law, which in time would inevitably lead to vigilante action, he explained his actions as implementing the true intention of the founding fathers.

"Brian, I can appreciate your impatience," Darrell responded, not wanting to provoke an argument with someone who stood for the same things he did. "But as responsible citizens of this honorable state of Nevada . . ."

The audience broke out into applause and cheers on being called "citizens of Nevada." Darrell nodded his head as if he were accepting an award. At least he felt comfortable that he was back on track. For a moment there he was worried that his neighbors had become frustrated and, God forbid, anarchic. He didn't want them to act before they heard all the evidence. Recently, he had begun to appreciate how professional politicians must feel like a cross between an entertainer and a teacher in order to keep the attention of their constituents focused on the issue at hand.

"Hell," Brian shouted back, "it's not my impatience you have to appreciate. It's this little baby that you have to thank." He raised a .38 Smith & Wesson.

Once again the crowd broke out into catcalls and applause.

"Brian," Darrell said sternly, "you are going to give our distinguished guests the wrong idea." He continued, aware that the audience was getting restless. "Let me reintroduce all of you to our County Commissioner, Larry Teague. Sitting next to him is State Police Captain Robert McElroy. Both men distinguished themselves in a major confrontation with the feds yesterday. After taking their testimony, we will decide what we, as citizens, should do next.''

''Why should we wait?'' a middle-aged housewife called out. ''We know what happened. Let's just pass sentence.''

''Mary,'' Brian responded, ''Darrell is right. We can't afford to look or act like a kangaroo court. We need some due process.'' He added with a chuckle, ''Or at least the semblance of it. So let's hear what the commissioner and the captain have to say.''

The audience mumbled its approval. Darrell stood up and motioned for Teague and McElroy to proceed to the desk.

''Ladies and gentlemen,'' Teague addressed the crowd in a trembling voice. ''What Bob and I have to report to you today is not very good news. Yesterday, the state of Nevada and, in particular, Nye County, suffered a major defeat.''

The audience sighed in unison. This was not the type of news they were expecting to hear. They all had assumed that if the county commissioner came to give testimony, it would be good news.

''What happened yesterday,'' Teague said in a disconsolate voice, ''was a major standoff where Robert and I decided that it would be futile to engage the feds in a firefight.''

''What's the matter?'' someone from the audience shouted, disgusted. ''Were you afraid of getting killed?''

''As a matter of fact,'' Robert responded, ''I made a tactical decision, in consultation with Larry, to withdraw in light of the superior firepower.'' He added sternly, ''Sir, if you had ever been in combat, you would know not to ask that kind of question in that stupid tone of voice.''

The audience applauded.

''As Robert told you,'' Darrell added, ''we didn't want to shed blood needlessly and, quite frankly, the head of that ATF unit was quite sympathetic. He traded our capitulation in return for dropping major federal felony charges against all of us.''

"What charges would have been brought against you both had you not given up?" Brian asked.

"There would have been quite a few," Larry answered, "all centering around obstruction of justice, destroying federal property, and attempting to subvert the federal government. In short, we were talking about eighty or ninety years in prison for me and Robert."

"I don't understand," Brian said agitatedly. "You went out there with a bulldozer in order to confront the feds who you knew were going to be waiting for you. So why did you bulldoze those trees if you knew this is what was going to happen?"

"That's a good question, Brian," Larry replied. "Because Robert and I asked each other that same question. We came to the conclusion that it was important to test the limits of federal tolerance for states' rights. And we concluded that the feds had none."

"So what should we do now?" Darrell asked.

"I think the answer is quite obvious," Brian said, standing up again, and feeling good about being able to influence his neighbors—who were also mortgagees. "As the presiding judge of this citizens' court, Darrell, you have no other choice than to pass sentence on the federal agents involved in yesterday's episode. I assume you got all of their names, Larry?"

"Yes," Larry responded. "We made certain that we knew who was there." He handed a piece of paper to Darrell. "That's a list of all of them, with their work addresses and telephones. We've begun to do this as standard operating procedure."

"Does anyone have anything else to say," Darrell asked the audience, "before we pass sentence?"

"All I've got to say"—Mary, the housewife who spoke earlier, stood up to speak—"is that we shouldn't waste any time retaliating against these messengers of Satan."

"Thank you, Mary," Darrell said, trying to cut her off.

"Washington, D.C., is Satan's own land," Mary added, determined to be given time to talk to her neighbors. "The interstate highway that surrounds Washington, D.C., is built in the shape of a human skull, the eye of which is CIA headquarters, and the length of that road, which I believe is called Route 495, is 66.6 miles long which is exactly the mark of the anti-Christ.''

''I think that's a bit far-fetched, Mary,'' Larry said, fearful that the court would deteriorate completely into a farce.

''As the appointed judge of Nye County's Citizens' Court,'' Darrell said, ''I am asking for a show of hands if you believe the federal agents named on this sheet of paper are guilty of having violated the rights of our honorable citizens of this great state of Nevada.''

Everyone in the gymnasium held up his or her right hand.

Darrell slammed the gavel on the table, but it was barely audible with the loud applause coming from the audience. ''The court will consider the appropriate sentence and each of you will be informed.''

25

DEPARTMENT OF STATE, WASHINGTON, D.C.

Friday, July 4th, 10:30 A.M.

Barbara Reynolds was a whirling dervish spinning around the seventh floor of the State Department with the religious fervor of a zealot, preordained to represent the magnificent potential of all African-American womanhood. Born in the late forties during the tail end of Harlem's Renaissance, she was part of what was then called ''the black aristocracy,'' a distinguished class of doctors, lawyers, other professionals and performers who had been completely ignored by the broad sweep of white American history.

Above all else, she was imposing—six feet tall in medium-sized heels, brown hair cropped in a medium Afro, always dressed in the latest fashion from Avenue Montaigne in Paris, and a summa cum laude graduate from Radcliffe College. If she liked you, she didn't simply grab your hand and shake it. Instead, she would envelop you in an embrace of genuine caring. And she was no less than passionate about everything she cared about. In both spirit and character, she was the opposite of the character the brilliant playwright Molière had described in his farce *The Misanthrope:* someone who loved the whole world but loved no one man. Barbara was someone who cared for individuals. Unlike the liberal label she carried along with her skin color, she refused to be stereotyped as someone who should espouse human rights, women's rights, African nationalism, affirmative action, and sundry other subjects that could easily fit into a category of issues that African-Americans "should be concerned about." She was a fiscal conservative as well as a socially conscious humanitarian. What that translated into in terms of political affiliation was that she was no one's fool or anyone's ideological chattel. Her beliefs were those her physician father and Latin-teacher mother had given her throughout her education in both public and private schools. She was an independent who owed nothing to anyone. In fact, she resented being labeled by liberals as the first African-American female Secretary of State. Even with her liberal leanings she had been selected by a Republican President precisely because he had said that he wanted someone who was an individualist. And Barbara had always been strictly accountable only to her own version of Jeffersonian democracy, which held that government is most effective which governs least.

Republican President Sean Danforth intended to be fully preoccupied by domestic concerns and needed Barbara to be the czarina of foreign policy. They had agreed on their first meeting that the National Security Council, the State Department, the Central Intelligence Agency, and the Department of Defense would continue to be downsized and reconfigured so that they worked harmoniously and still met the national security needs of the United States.

Barbara shared the view that the past several Secretaries of State were bereft of any strategic capabilities or tactical sense. Worse yet, these were the very same men who then picked as their advisors men who were clones of themselves and placed them into crucial foreign policy–making positions. By doing so, they had unfortunately amplified the Secretary's very own deficiencies. What any Secretary needed were people who could contradict him, if need be, or reality test his assumptions.

Barbara understood the basic tenet of leadership: you always surround yourself with people who are brighter or more capable than you are and then leave them alone. But she was all too aware, having to help clean up foreign policy and bureaucratic messes of past Sec States, that most of her white, Protestant predecessors, with their self-assurance and ignorance of basic human dynamics, were in truth complete disasters, irrespective of what they wrote in their biographies.

She sat behind her cluttered mahogany desk bracketed by all the accoutrements of seventh-floor power: a black STU-3 secured telephone; an intercom box that allowed her to reach anyone around the world in seconds through the Op-Center; an encoded computer terminal; an overhead projection machine; and many more electronic gadgets that she knew would be of little use to her in the immediate future. If she wanted to know how to use one of her machines, she had only to call in the Diplomatic Security agents standing outside her door. Of course, if it were totally up to her, she would get rid of all the DSA agents. The administrative costs of running the State Department had gotten completely out of control, and one of the reasons was the cost of maintaining a protection detail for the Secretary of State. Since no Sec State was indispensable, what was the point of treating them as if they were? It would be a lot safer if she just traveled in random taxis with, at most, one agent to maintain a comfort level. Being driven around in a bullet-proof limousine, with a backup detail of one to two dozen agents, was both a futile and ludicrous exercise in protective indulgence. The truth was that if anyone wanted to kill the Sec State it was relatively easy to do so and no amount of protection could prevent it.

Her moment of quiet and relaxation was interrupted by the ringing of her STU-3 telephone.

"Yes?" she asked, somewhat annoyed.

"Dr. Alison Carter is waiting to see you," the secretary replied.

"Show him in, please," she said, eager to hear what *bons mots* he was bringing back from New York.

" 'To Know Him Is to Love Him,' " Al announced as he walked across the room and sat down in one of those elegant, leather-bound chairs that were never intended for comfort. Barbara's big smile told him that she was happy to see him.

"If it isn't my own Little Richard," Barbara responded. "And just for the record, the Teddy Bears sang it. They recorded it, as best as I can remember, in the late 1950s." She paused and looked closely at his tired face. "Was the meeting with Yvette that bad?" she asked. "Do you need some TLC after that strenuous trip back from New York?"

"Who wrote it?" Al asked, wanting to play a little before they got down to serious matters. For him, the language of rock 'n roll was the equivalent of the language used in diplomacy, filled with ambiguities, double entendres, oblique references, historical imperatives, and subtleties of unspoken emotions and attitudes. And for the most part, Barbara and he were as good as they got in this game of titles, songs, recording artists, trivia, and nostalgia.

"Now you're pushing pretty hard on the memory cells," Barbara replied. But she knew that once he told her the answer, she would berate herself for being so stupid. He was pitching her a softball, but she still wasn't yet able to hit it.

"Come on, Barbara." Al started to sing the opening verse, "To know, know, know him, is to love, love, love him . . ."

"And I do . . ." she interrupted.

"I'll give you a hint." He took out his sunglasses and put them on. Then he patted down his hair over his forehead. "Who am I now?"

"A bleached Stevie Wonder?" she laughed.

"Good try," he responded. "Close, but not quite."

"Phil Spector," she shot back. "You don't think that you could fool an oldies but goodies devotee *comme moi*?"

"Remember the 'Spector sound'?" he asked. He was referring to a special type of multitracking recording where the rhythm sections sounded like invading armies of percussion instruments. The sound was loud, fierce and, up until that moment in time, the most magnificent explosion of mayhem set to a rock 'n roll beat.

"You know I do," Barbara responded. "Are you trying to tell me that Yvette was that difficult?" Phil Spector, the famous rock 'n roll impresario, was known to be difficult, controlling, demanding, and completely elusive. He skyrocketed to success after having produced such famous records as "He's a Rebel" with the Crystals, followed by twenty hit records within the next three years: "Then He Kissed Me," "Be My Baby," "Today I Met the Boy I'm Gonna Marry," "Walking in the Rain," "You've Lost That Lovin' Feeling," "Uptown," "Baby I Love You," and many more, impressive combustions of rhythm and blues. Records produced by a one-man conglomerate who disappeared into reclusiveness and anonymity soon after his successes. The mention of Phil Spector could only mean one thing to Barbara—elusive problems. To be fair, she wouldn't be surprised to hear that Al had found Yvette elliptical at best, paranoid at worst. The name Phil Spector was synonymous in the record business with the word "paranoid." He was a small, fragile man who hid behind very dark sunglasses.

"She claims that you are the one who is mentally sick and ambitious," Al replied, "and implied that you were creating this whole situation so that you could fulfill your own political agenda." As he talked, he assessed her nonverbal responses—breathing rate, face coloring, eye movement, and body movements. As he expected, Barbara was completely nonplussed by Yvette's accusations.

"Maybe this will satisfy any doubts that she may have instilled in you about me," Barbara persisted. She handed Al a dossier marked "Top Secret/No Dissemination."

The folder consisted of bank drafts from financial institutions all over the world, including the Cayman Islands, the Isle of Man, the Bahamas, Switzerland, and several other well-known offshore money centers. There were no names listed on any of the papers, only account numbers.

"By using a special warrant issued by the Secret National Security Court called the National Security Letter," Barbara continued, watching Al's quizzical expression. "I had the authority to enter each of the governors' bank accounts overseas. It's potential evidence if the time comes for prosecution. The drafts show that the four governors involved in the secessionist movement are each receiving significant amounts of money from French companies on whose boards Yvette de Perignod serves. So what do you think of my mental status now, Dr. Carter?"

"If you don't mind my asking, how do you know that

those bank account numbers match with the governors' names?''

''I see,'' she responded coolly. ''Perhaps you spent one hour too long with Yvette.''

''Now, now, Barbara,'' he said, surprised at her tone of voice. ''Don't become defensive. I think that's a reasonable question to ask.''

''You don't trust me?''

''Of course I trust you,'' he replied. ''But trust is not the issue here.''

''What is the issue?'' she asked stridently.

''The issue, as I see it,'' Al responded nonchalantly, refusing to be baited into some sort of power contest with her, ''is one of cold, asceptic evidence versus feelings, egos, and unstable temperaments.''

''I hope by that last comment,'' Barbara interjected, ''the one about 'unstable temperaments,' you don't mean me.''

''You accused Yvette of being unstable,'' Al continued, watching Barbara's face flush red, her eyelids blink rapidly, and her fingers tap the mahogany table. ''And she, in turn, without ever hearing your accusation directly, deduced correctly from my presence as your personal emissary that you presumed her to be equally unstable.''

''What are you saying, Al?''

''I'm saying that I found no evidence of any mental illness in Yvette,'' Al responded, ''yet you have a CIA psychological profile that clearly diagnoses her as 'mercurial' and 'bipolar manic-depressive.' And she accuses you, without any reason or provocation on my part, of being 'ambitious' and 'mad.' ''

''So?''

''So,'' he continued coolly, ''you asked me to act as an emissary on your behalf, which I did. Given both your reaction to my comments and her reaction to my comments, I have only one thing to conclude.''

''And what is that?''

''That one, I am not a diplomat,'' Al answered, ''and two, I clearly have failed at whatever it was that I was sent to do.''

"Failed?" Barbara repeated the word. "How did you fail?"

"Clearly, you're not happy with my response to your question," he replied, "and Yvette is angry with me for simply being there and inferring, quite correctly, that you sent me there to evaluate her." He corrected himself. "No, it wasn't just an evaluation that I was sent to do. I was sent to warn her that you and she had a personal vendetta that was being played out in an upcoming civil war."

"What do you mean by personal vendetta?" Barbara asked, pushing back her chair and standing up, agitated. "This isn't a personal vendetta I'm engaged in. You don't get it! This was a mission to ward her off from helping a group of seditious governors . . ."

"Then why send a simple, ordinary RMO," he asked, "and not your Ambassador to France? Or the Assistant Secretary for Western Europe?"

"Because I could not trust the bureaucracy," Barbara replied, becoming upset. "You know that. I told you that before you went over there. I don't trust the goddamn system. It has more leaks, duplicity, and inertia . . ."

"As your personal physician," Al interrupted, walking over to her, "I must warn you to calm down. Getting angry increases your blood pressure."

"Damn my blood pressure," she stated. "The destiny of my country is more important than my lousy blood pressure."

"Can we discuss this matter tomorrow?" Al asked, holding her arm and walking her over to the couch so that she could relax.

"I don't have tomorrow," she responded nervously. "I barely have today."

"Just sit down," he said. According to his watch, her pulse was racing at 128 beats a minute. He walked over to the mahogany cabinet where he kept a spare sphygmomanometer and wrapped it around her left arm. He pumped the black bulb quickly and watched the numbers on the dial jump upward like a slot machine. The steady rhythm of her blood pressure started to settle comfortably around two numbers—210/140. A few points higher on either number and she would be having a stroke, if she was lucky. And dead, if she wasn't.

26

DEPARTMENT OF STATE, WASHINGTON, D.C.

Friday, July 4th, 10:45 A.M.

"I've got to take you to the hospital," Al said.

"Just give me my bottle of anti-hypertension medication," Barbara responded, trying to catch her breath. "It's in the left top drawer of the desk."

Al walked over to the desk and took three blue pills out of the bottle, which would have the immediate effect of lowering her blood pressure. He also poured a glass of water from the wet bar and handed it to her.

"What would I do without my good doctor?" she said, swallowing the pills.

"The same thing you do with him when he's here," Al responded. "You ignore him."

"I've got a terrible headache," she added, her face ashen.

"Just lie down quietly on the sofa and let the pills take effect while I'm examining you," he said. He did a cursory neurological examination, to discover whether she was in the process of having either a Transient Ischemic Attack, a condition where the blood vessels servicing the brain close down or constrict, depriving the brain of badly needed oxygen, or worse, whether she was having a stroke.

"So what's the prognosis, doc?"

"Not good," he replied calmly, as he took her blood pressure again. It was starting to come down slowly. Just by her relaxing, it was down to 190/130. When the pills kicked in, he calculated, it would go lower. Paradoxically, he was also concerned that her pressure might fall too far down and precipitate a stroke by creating a sudden shock to the nervous system. Either way, he had to hospitalize her. He had no other choice.

"Where's the rock 'n roll spirit?" she asked, starting to regain her energy. "A few numbers here and there can't make the difference on how I'm going to live my life."

"You're not going to have much of a life," he asserted, "if you keep playing with those numbers."

"So I'm a walking Las Vegas," she added. "What's new with that? We're all playing against the odds. Al, you and I know damn well that if I walked across the street a truck could hit me, and I could die with the cleanest arteries and the most perfect blood pressure."

"You know what the odds are when you walk into any casino around the world?" he asked rhetorically. They had had this conversation numerous times before.

"A sucker's bet," she reasserted. "That's what you're telling me? I'm playing against the odds that I'll make it through this crisis? Right?"

"You got it," he responded. "I can't make it any simpler than that." He took her blood pressure again. This time, as he expected, it was 150/100, approaching the normal range. "It's coming down."

"That's because you're such a good doctor," she said, stroking his arm as he deflated the blood pressure cuff. "If it makes things easier for you to understand, I admit that Yvette is right. I'm crazy. I'm ambitious. I'm also mad and irrational about those things I care about, especially my country. But, believe me, she is no less committed to the positioning of France as a major superpower, even if it means the destruction of the United States of America. I have no doubt that she will align with anyone or any cause that will accomplish that goal. Call it a personal vendetta. Call her General Charles de Gaulle in drag. But whichever way you want to explain it, the outcome will be the same. Civil war."

"Isn't that a slight exaggeration?" he asked.

"If I'm wrong, then I have erred on the side of being

overprepared and overanxious," she replied. "But if I'm right, then at least I can say that I tried to prevent it. This will be a civil war ostensibly based on states' rights and economic and political sovereignty. But what it will really be about is hatred. Ethnic, religious, gender, color, sexual preference. All of our differences will feed the hate machine. People may be using the name of the Constitution, but for many it's a code word for Aryan supremacy, militia terrorism, rabid anti-Semitism, anti-Catholicism, anti-Muslim, anti-anything these hatemongers will define as 'appropriate' and 'Christian.' Even Christians won't be safe because they're going to have to believe in the type of distorted religiosity that the hatemongers want everyone to believe in. And God only knows what that is. Because sure as I'm destined to have another pressure attack, the only thing that these hatemongers believe in is their own venom, and their right to express it against any group, if they are in any way different. Do you read me, Dr. Carter?"

"I read you loud and clear," he responded, once again taking her blood pressure. Just as he suspected, it had climbed back up again. This time it was 170/120.

"Ain't that peculiar?" she asked laughingly. "The greater you believe in a cause, the more you are likely to die for it?"

" 'Ain't That Peculiar?' " Al repeated, taking the stethoscope out of his ears. "Recorded by Marvin Gaye on the Motown label, written by the infamous Smokey Robinson and his Detroit associates."

"In one hour," she smiled, "you'll fly out from Andrews Air Force Base to the Rockefeller Lodge beneath the Grand Tetons, near Jackson Hole, Wyoming. Our renegade governors have just finished attending the annual Western Governors' Council meeting, and are going to have a private tête-à-tête at the Lodge. I want you to join them, find out what they are up to, and see what you can do to avert a constitutional crisis. I need to resolve this by Sunday, before the President returns. You can reach me twenty-four hours a day. The Sec Def is on alert, as well as my usual group. Just knowing you're still with me in this will keep my pressure down."

" 'Three Times a Lady,' " he sang, gently kissing her on the forehead. He quickly disposed of the thought that this would be the last time he would ever see her.

"Stop that, you flirt," she said, restraining herself from crying. "I'll give you all the necessary instructions . . ."

"Lionel Ritchie wrote that song," he interrupted, averting her tearful gaze. He was trying to maintain a professional composure. "Ritchie was then still part of the Commodores."

" 'Our love is made for love,' " she muttered to herself as Al walked out the door, " 'when we're cruisin' together.' "

"Smokey Robinson sang and wrote that," Al shouted back defiantly, making certain that she knew that he was still the rock 'n roll trivia champion. He leaned his head against the doorway as he closed the door and wiped the tears away from his eyes.

27

GLEN CANYON DAM, LAKE POWELL, ARIZONA

Friday, July 4th, 2:25 P.M.

Robby and Ellen stood side by side on the catwalk overlooking the swelling Colorado River. He shook his head in total disgust as torrents of water rushed from the hollow jet valves and spillways with a force that he had never seen before.

"The gods are angry," he said. "First we harnessed the forces of nature and now we are unleashing them. Man is getting too big for his britches."

Ellen said nothing. Only two days ago, everything seemed so simple and sensible. Now she was uncertain about what she had really done and what the consequences would be of her actions. All she knew was that she was following orders. And they were explicit orders—to flood the canyon. And she had no choice in the matter. That was the trade-off she made when she joined the military reserves—personal freedom for security. At the time of her voluntary induction, she had been more than eager to make that exchange. Now she had some serious reservations.

"I'm going to lose a lot of good friends," Robby said, tears welling in his eyes. "They won't even know what hit them. By the time the water reaches Page, it will be too late for anyone to do anything. Everyone will drown."

All Ellen could think about was that this wasn't what she had joined up for. Americans killing Americans.

"We have no one to blame except ourselves," Robby continued. "We did this. I was as much a culprit as you."

"How could you have stopped me?" she asked.

"I should have refused to help you out," he responded.

"There is nothing you could have done to stop me," she added. "Believe me."

"You're probably right," he said, saddened to his core. The innocent would be dying because of man's arrogance and self-destructive nature. Construction of this multi-billion-dollar dam was merely a testimony to the venality and hypocrisy of the American political system. It was, as far as he knew, pure and simple pork barrel. Senator Hayden, who had been known for his interest in the reclamation and storage of water, was the primary catalyst behind the creation of both Glen Canyon Dam and Lake Powell. Others had argued that the dam was nothing but a payoff for his support for other senators' pork barrel projects. Which, of course, was standard operating procedure for Congress. Robby recalled the outcries when the Glen Canyon Dam was built in the wrong place. If anything, it should have been built farther up river, closer to the state of Colorado. This way there would be more power generated with less environmental damage. But that may have all been simply a lot of Monday-morning quarterbacking, Robby thought. How cruel the gods were. First, they played on man's hubris, on his willingness to build a dam that would stop the flow of water that nature had intended. Then when civilization was flourishing because of the electricity generated by the dam, the gods played on man's basic evil nature. The same water that had provided the sustenance for new life had become a weapon of death.

Ellen saw the pain in his eyes but preferred not to address it. It would only heighten the sadness and confusion that she was feeling. They stared in the silence of their own private thoughts.

Robby couldn't stop the waves of guilt which overtook him. He didn't want to play the role of the old Hebraic prophet who might have cast a curse upon the Pagenites, warning them of God's retribution for ungodly behavior. He was neither Hebraic nor a prophet. He was only a mortal man knowing hours ahead of time that his friends and neighbors would die. His city would be awash with water. The street lined with churches—Catholic, Methodist, Baptist, Episcopalian, Lutheran—that at one time distinguished Page from its neighboring towns, would be submerged. Whatever faith the Pagenites may have had in their 5,370,000 cubic yards of concrete poured for the dam would completely disappear in a torrent of man-made mayhem. Perhaps God, as Robby had worshipped Him, would also disappear in this whirlpool of unrelenting destruction. He thought of the six million Jews who had died in the Holocaust. The two million Armenians slaughtered in the early part of the twentieth century. The two million Cambodians killed by Pol Pot, one of their own leaders. The hundreds of thousands of Hutus and Tutsis who had slaughtered each other for reasons long forgotten. Or the atrocities committed by the Serbians, Croats, and Bosnians in the name of religion. For the agnostics, this incident was one more proof that there was no God. Or if there were a God, then that God had forsaken His children.

How many more towns downstream would be flooded? he wondered. He made a quick calculation and came up with a number—about two hundred small-sized towns with populations of less than two thousand and another three hundred towns with populations of five hundred people or less. It would be a massacre of immense proportions. But worst of all, he had made it possible. Without saying a word to Ellen, he tried to boost himself up over the railing. She pulled him back and warned him that she would shoot him if he tried to commit suicide.

28

ROCKEFELLER LODGE, GRAND TETONS, WYOMING

Friday, July 4th, 3:30 P.M.

The Rockefeller Lodge, one of those few examples of unostentatious wealth and environmental sensitivity which so often characterized its namesake, was an expansive, rugged, stone-hewn hunting lodge. It nestled elegantly beneath the foothills of the imposing Teton Mountains. After a period of time in private hands, the main Lodge and its surrounding smaller cabins, stables, and acres of forest were donated to the people of the United States for their enjoyment. To admit that the Lodge and its surrounding scenery were breathtaking was to do this corner of the world injustice. It was as if the Italian, French, and Swiss Alps had conspired to create an even more majestic setting, resettling at the site of a pristine lake, populated with elk, moose, and deer. The Rockefeller Lodge in Wyoming was truly one of the last repositories for both the contemplative and the action-oriented naturalist.

Dr. Alison Carter, of course, was neither. The heart of Manhattan was where he had spent his childhood. His father was a dedicated general medical practitioner who believed in primary care long before it became a federally mandated fashion in medicine fifty years later. A soft-spoken, intense, dedicated physician, his father had helped to create one of the first HMOs in America, the Health Insurance Plan. Originally, it was designed to help provide inexpensive medical care to teachers, blue-collar union members, and city employees. Long after his father's untimely death at the age of fifty-three, HIP had become a financial behemoth with its original charter of caring for blue-collar workers lost somewhere in the ledger of necessary profits.

As might be expected from a firm, frugal, disciplinarian father, Al attended all of the run-down public schools that the neighborhood could provide. He started grade school at P.S. 165, where he was engaged in more fistfights than classes. After a while, he learned to survive by befriending his opponent. Al's boyish face, replete with freckles and red hair, seemed to attract bullies. Although far from being physically imposing as a child, he never shied away from a fight that someone else provoked, or allowed a bully to take advantage of one of his friends. Al was known as a fair player who lived life according to the old principle of live and let live. What really saved him at Booker T. Washington High School, which presented ceaseless taunts of "doughboy" or "white bread," was the fact that he knew more about black rhythm and blues and rock 'n roll than most of his African-American classmates, kids in the school who prided themselves on being hip.

For Al, jogging was an essential survival mechanism. Fast in mind and body, he learned to jog away from potential problems, like when he was alone on the basketball court and outnumbered. One time, he tried to co-opt a gang leader who would not leave him alone by tutoring him in a subject in which he was failing. The co-optation ended when the class ended.

After high school, Al went to Cornell University on a New York Regents Scholarship. Four years later he was admitted to Cornell University Medical College, located in the fashionable East Side of New York City, where he attained the distinction of receiving the second lowest grade average in the history of the medical school. A maverick even then, he felt that the first two years of medical school were pretty much a waste of time. So he didn't attend the classes he considered a waste of his time and bought "dummied-down" nurses' handbooks on those courses. To the surprise of everyone involved, including the Dean of the medical college, Al managed to pass biochemistry, anatomy, histology, physiology, pathology, virology, parasitology, pharmacology, and neurology without having seen a test tube or touched a cadaver. He proved the point, at least to himself, that the essential prerequisites for the clinical years could have been just as easily learned from a computer program or simplified handbook. However, it was in the last two years of medical school that Al excelled, especially when it came to clinical diagnostics and patient care. Despite Al's initial defiance of the school curriculum, the Dean admitted to him that Al would become "quite an impressive clinician."

As he walked up the wide stone steps of the Lodge, Al wondered whether it was really essential to always see the dark side of human nature when he was acting on behalf of the Sec State. Yet it had always been hard for Al to accept the concept that man was basically good. Although now a non-practicing Catholic, he still retained remnants of belief in Original Sin. But unlike the Church, he felt no obligation to exonerate, forgive, or grant mercy. He had turned into a theological cynic who believed that man's basic need to mess up his own and other people's lives was rooted in his compulsion to avoid dealing with life's miseries, sorrows, and desperations. Scenes of remarkable natural beauty, like the Tetons in the distance, always reminded him of his own mistrust of man's intentions and capacities.

Al walked through the intricately carved wooden door and over to the registration desk to discover that no room had been reserved under his name. A typical State Department foul-up. As he leaned against the counter, taking stock of his lodging options—there was a small motel fifteen miles away—he noticed several men dressed in dark suits, standing next to uniformed Wyoming State Police Officers. He also recognized the uniforms of state police from Colorado, Utah, and Arizona on men lounging in sofas scattered around the lobby. This was one of the largest security contingents he had seen in a long time. Since cutbacks in the federal budget, he had become used to a paucity of security around the agencies he visited. The few DSAs in the lobby were probably there to protect Yvette. Just another waste of taxpayers' money, he thought, because she was here on a private visit. For Al, the DSAs were unnecessary because no Secretary of State or, for that matter, no other senior foreign policy official, was indispensable. The DSAs always attracted more attention than they were worth.

"Zut alors!" Yvette greeted Al with her usual double-cheek kiss. "*Qu'est-ce que tu fais ici?* My God, what are you doing here?" she asked disingenuously. Her face showed only a trace of confusion over his presence at the Lodge.

"I thought it was time for me to see one of our most famous landmarks before it was too late," he responded sarcastically. She knew perfectly well what he was doing here. As she took his hand into hers, he noticed a group of officials enter the hotel, some of whom he recognized from photographs in newspapers.

"My, my," Yvette said, "that sounds so ominous. This is not the place to be morbid. Of course, you're staying here at the hotel."

"I'm afraid there is no room," he responded, nodding his head in the direction of the large group now assembled in the lobby.

"What nonsense," she responded, waving her arm dismissively. "How could the Secretary of State's personal emissary not have a room? Preposterous!" She ordered the hotel manager to assign him a room next to hers by reassigning one of her deputies to a motel in the outskirts of Jackson Hole.

"I certainly appreciate your hospitality," Al responded, wondering whether she had been responsible for removing his name from the registration book in the first place.

"Nonsense," she added, "that's the least that good friends and allies can do for one another."

"Yvette," an attractive woman in cowboy boots said as she approached the desk, "I think it's time for us to start the meeting."

"You're absolutely right," Yvette replied. "But before we do, let me introduce you to Dr. Alison Carter, who is with your Department of State."

"How do you do," the woman said, stretching her hand

out to him. "I'm Cheri Black, governor of Colorado." In the grasp of his handshake, she decided that she liked what she saw. But in all truth, there were very few attractive men whom she did not find appealing.

"Pleased to meet you," Al said, mutually attracted by the dramatic sense of self that went with her strong handshake.

Cheri, in turn, introduced him one by one to the states' governors as they filed by. Governor Josiah Brigham of Utah. Governor Andrew Paul from Arizona. Governor James McMinn from Wyoming.

"How's the camping in Breckenridge this time of year?" Al asked sarcastically, having been informed by Barbara of the official governors' meeting that had ended prior to this unofficial meeting at the Lodge. What a great cover, he thought, for these governors to get together. Just their own little regional planning meeting.

"Great!" Cheri replied, dismissing his tone as unnecessarily provocative. "Even though the weather is a bit chillier than I like, tourism is up throughout the state. Thank you for asking, Doctor."

"Now we must adjourn to our conference room to begin our discussions," Yvette interjected, "concerning the dismemberment of the United States of America. Won't you join us, Al?"

29

ROCKEFELLER LODGE, GRAND TETONS, WYOMING

Friday, July 4th, 3:45 P.M.

Al looked closely at the two Utah State Patrol officers who patted him down before he was allowed to enter the conference room. Both were memorable. The taller of the two had a Class-3 prognathous jaw which jutted out like a pelican's beak. The shorter man was only about thirty years old, but totally bald. Probably genetic.

The conference room was sparsely decorated. Yvette and the governors took their seats around a rectangular, cloth-covered table. In the center of the table sat an assortment of bottled mineral waters and glasses. One brand of mineral water represented each of the four states. Equality of thirst, Al thought.

He decided not to waste any time. Following his introduction to the group by Cheri he decided to address Yvette's inflammatory statement and put to rest the suspicious looks he was getting from the governors.

''Dismemberment of the United States?'' Al asked, looking, in turn, at each governor and Yvette. ''Is this some kind of joke?''

''Unfortunately this is not a joke,'' Josiah responded from his seat opposite Al. ''We, in this room, have come to a collective decision that the United States of America can no longer exist as it is presently constituted.'' His deliberate diction betrayed all of the arrogance of an ambitious politician.

"What do you mean?" Al asked, certain that this must be some variant of the Mad Hatter's Tea Party. Yvette averted his gaze.

"Dr. Carter," Cheri said, "I understand that by training and profession you are a crisis manager."

"No, I would not say that was entirely correct," he responded, trying in vain to pick up some nonverbal clues from Yvette's facial expression about where the discussion was headed.

"Maybe we were misinformed," Josiah interjected, "but we were told by the Secretary of State's office that you were a crisis manager and an expert in resolving, or should I say preventing, potential domestic and international problems."

"You were misinformed, Governor Brigham," Al responded, trying to avert the problem of compounding misperceptions and misunderstandings. His gut told him that the title of crisis manager itself would create unrealistic expectations which would allow the governors to make completely unreasonable demands upon him. To him, the title was little more than a narcissistic trap for those who needed some self-identity. "I am a simple, vanilla-flavored medical doctor," Al added, "with some experience in national or international crises."

"He's far too modest," Yvette interjected.

"Then why are you here?" Andrew asked.

"As a crisis manager, of course," James answered for Al. He glanced at Al's innocent, Corn Flakes box-cover face. Either this was a shrewd man playing dumb and self-effacing to throw us off balance, he thought, or he was one of the dumbest State Department officials around.

"May I be presumptuous enough to ask," James added, "what instructions you were given by the Secretary of State? Other than, I presume, to enjoy yourself in the Grand Tetons."

"I would be happy to share my instructions with you," Al responded. "But I'm afraid you will be quite disappointed with their brevity."

"And why is that?" Josiah asked impatiently.

"Because my only instructions were to help the Secretary of State resolve this crisis," Al responded, "to the best of my ability."

"That's it?" James asked skeptically.

"That's it," Al replied. "My basic professional concern these days is to take care of the health of the Secretary of State and Foreign Service officers around the world. Nothing more. Nothing less. If you need an official title, I am a Regional Medical Officer, in governmentese called an RMO."

"So you are here as a fancy messenger boy," Brigham added provocatively.

"Right on the mark, Governor, but the word 'fancy,' " Al responded with forced goodwill, "is a bit too extravagant."

"Oh come on." Josiah stood up, frustrated by this entire discussion. "This is not possible. We are in the process of committing an act of sedition and treason against the federal government, and we are being led to believe that the best response the government has to offer is to send us Dr. Marcus Welby?" He paced back and forth on his side of the table. "Something is wrong here. It doesn't make sense. With no offense intended, Dr. Carter, I'm certain that you are an excellent medical clinician, but this is crazy."

"I wouldn't make the assumption that I'm an excellent clinician, Governor," Al responded calmly. "Since your collective grievances against the federal government, as I understand it, is one of incompetence, I could well be part of that very problem."

"Very clever, Dr. Carter." James was impressed how Al was able to take a hostile comment directed at him, turn it around, and convey the image that he was in full compliance with everything that the governors had to say.

"Well, what we have here, in these United States of America, is a major crisis in which confidence in the federal government is, to put it politely, nonexistent," Cheri interjected forcefully, fearful that the conversation would bog down very quickly into a discussion of Al's identity and role.

The governors each nodded his head in approval. Yvette

sat stone-faced, betraying nothing of her own interests or concerns. Al wondered why she was even there in the room when she could have just as easily played her master puppeteer role without being present. Something didn't smell right, he thought.

"And . . ." Al asked, anticipating her response.

"And," Cheri responded empathically, "that means that what we have is a non-legitimate federal government. We no longer have a government as originally conceived by our founding fathers, but a series of regions with their own identities, etched out by invisible forces of global markets for goods and services."

"These regions represent natural economic zones which have been created by countless individual financial decisions," Josiah added, interrupting Cheri, "rather than some arbitrarily drawn political borders which were defined hundreds of years ago as states."

"Sometimes those economic units are formed by parts of states," Cheri continued, "such as those in the area of the four corners—Arizona, Utah, Colorado, and New Mexico. At other times those economic units are formed by economic patterns that overlap existing national boundaries such as the area between San Diego, California, and Tijuana, Mexico. Maybe it's easier to see it on the international level. We might consider the strong economic relationships among Hong Kong, southern China, and Taiwan as one viable economic unit that supersedes their national boundaries. Or the ASEAN nations—Singapore, Thailand, Malaysia, and Indonesia as another formidable economic entity. The same kind of economic region," Cheri continued, "that was created by the North American Free Trade Agreement connecting the United States, Canada, and Mexico into one single market."

"So," Al concluded, "now I understand why the governors of Utah, Colorado, and Arizona are here. But what happened to the governor of New Mexico? And why is Wyoming Governor James McMinn here at all?" He nodded to each governor as he mentioned his respective state. "And what type of economic region," Al continued, "is created by the presence of the Honorable Prime Minister of France?''

"The New Mexico governor could not attend this meeting,'' Cheri lied. "He was stricken ill.''

"Then why didn't he send a representative?'' Al asked, completely unconvinced that the economic regional argument was entirely valid.

"Remember the conversation you and I had in New York yesterday, when you complained about France's extensive investments in America without significant reciprocity?'' Yvette reminded him.

"Yes, I do,'' Al replied. "But I also remember that you minimized those concerns.''

"That's true,'' Yvette said, "but that was all part of the kabuki of international diplomacy. As I told you, I am at this meeting in an unofficial capacity without any knowledge of my government.''

"What do you call this meeting?'' Al asked, looking around the table. "A conspiracy of allies?''

"Don't you think that's a bit strong?'' Josiah asked, carefully sipping his glass of water.

"You are the one who is talking about dismemberment,'' Al responded angrily, "with three other prominent governors. Now if this meeting doesn't constitute treason, sedition, and a declaration of war against the federal government of the United States, then please tell me, Governor Josiah Brigham, what would?''

"I think it is fair to say that a group of interested parties are engaged in a series of discussions exploring the different alternatives available to deal with the new political and economic realities and opportunities extant in the United States.'' Josiah responded as if he had memorized the lines.

"I think we should stop beating around the bush,'' Andrew said.

"Andy,'' James said, "I think that you're being too hasty. Dr. Carter is a man of intellect and logic. It's important that he understand the full implication of what we are doing so that he can transmit our position accurately to the Secretary of State. I would prefer that we spend whatever time is necessary to ensure that Dr. Carter understands all of the nuances and subtleties of what we are about to do and that our decisions were made after months of struggling with the problem.''

''Well stated,'' Josiah added. ''I agree with Governor McMinn. In most instances less is more, but I'm afraid that this is not the case in our present situation.''

''Clearly,'' Al said impatiently, ''there are a few missing pieces here. Would somebody mind filling them in so that you can get down to the business of the day, which I am beginning to think will entail some form of extortion.''

''My, my,'' Cheri said. ''Let us not get so touchy—so early in the day. Contrary to what you might think, we are not a group of hoodlums aiming a gun at you, demanding your wallet or your life.''

''No,'' Al responded angrily, finding it increasingly difficult to control his temper. Somehow the role of special emissary was dissolving and he was beginning to personalize the entire situation. ''You don't have to stick a gun into my ribs, because it's clear that you've already taken what you want or are about to, without having to resort to weapons.''

''That's really quite flattering of you,'' Cheri said, ''but the point of fact is that we will be using force, or I might say a variation of that, in order to accomplish what we want.''

''So, Governor Black,'' Al said, staring into her determinedly beautiful face, ''is it fair to say that we are about to enter into a state of civil war?''

Several of the governors around the table coughed or cleared their throats. Clearly, Al thought, whatever else they might be doing, some of the governors were still uncomfortable with it.

''I think, Dr. Carter,'' Cheri replied, searching the faces in the room to see whether anyone was going to dissent, ''that your conclusion is correct.''

''Which part?'' Al asked provocatively. ''The one where we are about to enter or the one where we are already in a state of civil war?''

''Technically,'' Cheri responded, feeling the rush of adrenaline course through her veins, ''both statements are correct, depending, of course, on your response. Or more precisely, the response of your government."

"I see," Al said sarcastically. "Now it's become 'your' government. That's already quite a self-indictment."

"I think we should stop this Mickey Mouse approach," James interjected forcefully, "and tell Dr. Carter exactly what we are up to so that there will be no misunderstandings."

Everyone at the table looked to Josiah and Cheri for a response.

"Approximately twenty-four hours ago," Josiah said, "several hundred National Guard troops from our respective states were deployed to Page, Arizona, in order to secure the Glen Canyon Dam."

"That's the one that dams up the Colorado River and Lake Powell, isn't it?" Al asked, beginning to realize the full scope of what Governor Brigham was telling him. And that Barbara Reynolds had not deserved the hard time Al had given her.

"That dam," Cheri added, "supplies close to 1.5 million kilowatts of power to . . ."

"To," Al interrupted, addressing each governor as he talked, "Utah, Colorado, Arizona, and Wyoming via the Green River tributary coming off the Colorado River, as well as power to New Mexico, parts of California, and Montana."

"Bravo! I told you, ladies and gentlemen," James said, clapping his hands ever so lightly, "that Dr. Carter was a highly intelligent individual who simply had to be supplied with the proper facts for him to fill in the rest of the picture."

"If I understand this correctly," Al said, impressed by the sheer audacity, if not stupidity, of this enterprise, "you are basically holding the dam and its water and power allocation hostage to the federal government? And somehow you think the government will allow your states to secede peacefully from the United States of America and create a new region of sorts? How am I doing?"

"So far so good," Cheri replied.

"Only we've added something to the scenario to demonstrate our commitment to our cause, to add credibility to our capabilities,'' Josiah added, not to be outdone by Cheri.

''I can't wait to hear about it,'' Al responded, with a distaste he could no longer hide.

''We are currently in control of the Glen Canyon Dam—its electricity and its water,'' Josiah continued. ''And the federal government will soon become very much aware that we are not playing games.''

''Dr. Carter, we don't want to give you the impression that four crazed governors have cooked up an unrealistic scenario that wouldn't even play well on late-night television,'' Andrew added, trying to sound like the most contemplative of the group. ''Our state legislators are behind us. Our states' voters are behind us. If we don't act now, our citizens groups and militia will do it for us—but believe me, it will be bloody.''

''Therefore,'' Al continued, trying not to show his surprise and anger, ''the first demand would be the right of each of your respective states to secede from the Union.''

''That's the first and most important demand,'' James added.

''This is the most preposterous idea I've heard since some writer declared that the breakup of communism in Russia signaled the end of history. Why don't you just go through the legal system?'' Al asked.

''You may not know this, but for the past ten years,'' Josiah responded, ''we have been in a continuous state of political, economic, and legal battles with Washington, D.C. We can no longer afford it. We've exhausted all of our legal means. Each one of our respective states had reached the Supreme Court on one or another states' rights issues, whether it's cattle grazing or water rights or enforcement of federal laws. . . . And we've lost every one of those cases. Confrontation is our last recourse.''

''And the alternative?'' Al asked, looking for any grain of hope.

''That's why you are here,'' Josiah responded. ''Civil war or peace. It all depends on you.''

30

NYE COUNTY, NEVADA

Friday, July 4th, 3:50 P.M.

''ATF Agent Sandy Evers,'' shouted Darrell Hayeck through a hand-held megaphone, ''please step outside with your hands held up high.'' Darrell and a disciplined corps of fifty ''citizen soldiers'' dressed in camouflaged uniforms stood ready to enforce the verdict of the citizens' court. They crouched three hundred feet from a log cabin, its front yard cluttered with children's toys. Darrell's mind quickly flashed to the CNN replays of the Ruby Ridge fiasco when FBI agents had surrounded Randy Weaver and his family in 1992, the day after Weaver's son, Samuel, and a deputy U.S. marshal were killed in a shoot-out. Ironic, he thought, that the reverse was now occurring. He would try to avoid the mistakes the FBI had made.

''I think the suspect is moving toward the door,'' Police Captain Robert McElroy said, looking through his Zeitz binoculars. ''Hold your fire.''

''Yes, sir,'' the sniper replied, peering through the crosshairs of his rifle's scope. He wore the standard SWAT uniform—flak jacket, high-powered rifle with scope, and obligatory blue baseball cap with the SWAT insignia, worn backward.

''Do you really think that this is necessary?'' County Commissioner Larry Teague asked nervously.

''We tried it your way,'' Darrell responded, clearly annoyed by Larry's peevish attitude, "and that didn't work out all that well. Do you have any other ideas?"

"I want it made very clear to your men," Larry said, mistrusting Darrell's intentions, "that we are simply here to arrest Sandy Evers. Is that right? Remember he has a wife and several children."

"Don't be such a worrywart," Robert responded. "This isn't Ruby Ridge." He lay stretched out as flat on the rocky ground as he could.

"Why don't we just go down there," Larry asked, "and knock on Evers's door?"

"Because we can control the situation a lot better from the heights of this ridge," Robert answered.

"Wait a minute," Darrell said. "It looks as if Evers is opening the door." Raising his megaphone, Darrell shouted, "Evers, come out slowly, throw out your weapons on the ground, and then lie down and suck some ground."

Larry looked around at his neighbors playing soldier and shuddered. He saw fifty citizens eager to flex their muscles. Someone was bound to precipitate a firefight and there would go their entire cause. Citizens' rights over the feds would be completely discredited, just like the FBI's reputation for handling hostage situations. But there was nothing he could do. Darrell was out of control.

Like most of his neighbors, Larry was a cautious man, who had a deep respect for the Constitution and the integrity of the government of the United States of America. He was no revolutionary. Certainly no rabble-rouser or anarchist. Darrell, on the other hand, was by nature a cynic, who said that he was, by nature, a libertarian. But Larry sensed that beneath all of his fancy philosophy and pious posturing, Darrell was only concerned about Darrell. In short, he was basically a politician, concerned primarily with his own welfare, speaking in words that rationalized all his self-serving behavior in terms of the community's interests. All Larry had wanted from the group was a clear statement of protest against encroaching federalism and national paternalism. An article in the newspaper would have been a good start. He and others like him—ordinary American citizens—just wanted to control their own destiny. He was by nature a temperate man. But he was afraid that he was now engaged in a nontemperate act.

"Hold your fire," Robert yelled to the men, as Sandy opened the door to his cabin, walked out, his hands raised above his head.

"I'm unarmed," Sandy screamed out, stepping outside. "There is no one inside. No firearms. No ATF agents. So take it easy."

"Strip down to your shorts," Darrell yelled, descending from the ridge with the other soldiers, his gun drawn. "Take your belt, pants, and shirt off—slowly."

"I'm not a goddamn criminal," Sandy responded angrily. "I'm an ATF official. My word is my bond. If I tell you that I don't have any weapons, then that's the case."

"Right now," Darrell said, looking Evers straight in his eyes, "you are a convicted felon who must serve out his sentence as proclaimed by the Nye County Citizens' Court.

"Mr. Evers," Darrell continued, "you have been found guilty of violating the rights of the citizens of Nye County, Nevada, as well as usurping state lands in the name of the federal government."

"Is this some kind of joke?" Sandy asked, standing in his boxer shorts, his arms above his head. He looked around, incredulous, at the number of men who surrounded him. "I hope all you gentlemen are aware of the consequences of your actions. Trying to impede a federal official in the course of his official duties constitutes a major federal offense punishable by $50,000 and four years in prison."

"Darrell," Larry interjected, "Evers has a point. I think we are going a bit too far. It's one thing to hold court and publish our findings, but it's completely another matter to punish a federal official for executing his duties."

"Larry," Darrell responded, motioning to several of the men to tie up Evers, "may I remind you that it was you who started this when you confronted the feds. So stop complaining."

"I think Larry is right," Robert said, worried that he had taken part in a seditious act, which may have gone too far. "Let's not be hasty. I think we've made our point. We don't accept the outcome of our confrontation. So now that we've put the fear of God into Evers, I think it's time for us to go home."

"I don't know what you guys think you are doing," Sandy said forcefully, "but you are coming very close to obstruction of justice and harassment of a federal official. Federal prosecutors and judges are not very partial to that."

"Mr. Evers," Darrell said, "you're not by any chance trying to frighten us into compliance, are you?" He motioned to his men to lead Evers to a large tree in front of the house.

"Come on, guys," Sandy said nervously as they stood under the tree that had dominated his property for over one hundred years. "This isn't some Hollywood cowboy film. Can we be real for a moment?"

"What exactly would you like us to get 'real' about?" Darrell asked, taking a pair of handcuffs from his back pocket and handcuffing Evers's hands together.

"Get real about this stupid handcuff," Evers shouted, losing his composure for the first time. "What the hell do you think that all this is going to do?"

"I find your arrogance completely intolerable," Darrell said, throwing the handbound Evers down on the ground. "Are you sure there is no one else in the cabin?"

"You can look if you want to," he responded, surprised by the anger in Hayeck's voice. "My wife and two kids are in town."

"I bet you never imagined," Darrell continued, "how disturbing you and your colleagues' actions were the other day."

"Come on," Sandy replied, looking at Larry and Robert with pleading eyes. "We had a standoff, that's all. No one lost face. No one got hurt. No one was imprisoned. I beg you to stop all this nonsense."

"He has a point," Robert said, looking at Larry for backup. What they were doing was against all the principles of right and wrong that he and his sister were taught in parochial school. "I think we've made our point. Let him go and let's take this matter up to the state courts."

"I agree with Robert," Larry said. "Let him go!" He

placed his hand on the handle of the Beretta he wore on his hip. There was no doubting his resolve.

"So now," Darrell responded, "you're creating a division within my group."

"Hayeck," Sandy said, trying to stand up, "whatever differences you or your neighbors might have with the federal government can be addressed in a better way. This kind of childishness is not going to get you anywhere."

"You're right," Darrell said, pulling the trigger on his gun.

Evers fell straight down to the ground, blood cascading down his face.

31

GRAND TETONS, WYOMING

Friday, July 4th, 5:30 P.M.

"United we fall . . ." Cheri said as she and Al descended the steps of the Rockefeller Lodge toward the stables. "In 1787, many of the drafters of the Constitution argued that America was better off remaining a loose confederation of states, and that a strong national government was not desirable."

"But that was an agrarian society," Al responded, having become better versed in American history as a result of this assignment. "The Constitution, as you know, was written primarily by farmers, for farmers," he offered coyly. Al had concluded early in the meeting that if he were able to convince Cheri, he would be able to influence the other governors. Both Cheri and Josiah were obviously vying for leadership of the group. He needed to capitalize on their rivalry. Yvette, however, had been surprisingly passive at the meeting. Only during discussions about the termination of America as a superpower did she seem engaged. Intense side conversations between Yvette and Josiah had taken place during recesses, leaving Al no time to bring up to Josiah the issue of the Salt Lake City–based flyers.

Al had suggested the current break in the meetings after having listened to impassioned speeches from each of the governors for the last two hours. Now he wanted to digest the information, collect his thoughts, and formulate a strategy that would allow him to defuse the crisis. The Lodge was obviously meant to serve as both a planning and operation center for the governors. So far, the discussion had not revealed any of the governors' plans. Al and Barbara had discussed a last-ditch scenario if the governors remained unreasonable, and forming a bond with Cheri was to be considered an effective start. If he were to break her away from the other governors . . . A short horseback ride with her during the break in the meeting would be a good way to begin forging that special relationship.

"Dr. Carter," Cheri continued, "despite your humility, your background is impressive. Physician. Crisis manager."

"I do what I can," Al responded.

"I assume as a physician," she inquired, "you have done some form of family counseling. Or marital reconciliation."

"On occasion," he said, "I've had to do it. It's all become part of medicine now."

"Then," she responded with a broad smile, "think of our problem as an extended family crisis in which you, as the physician, are trying to focus on what are the real issues, who are the real culprits, and who are simply the unwitting accomplices."

Al sensed that she was trying to tell him something that she couldn't say outright. Out of character, he thought, for her usual direct, assertive manner. She was attractive to him in a variety of ways, but it was at a very basic sensual level that she was particularly appealing. He was the kind of man who could appreciate the difference between a woman who was sensual and one who was merely sexy. The former had what the people in his neighborhood would call that intangible "something" which made her stand out in a crowd, despite the fact that she was not necessarily beautiful. "Sexy" was a term that Al applied to those women who were self-consciously feminine. A sensual woman, by Al's definition, was rarely self-conscious. What came to mind, of course, was the famous rock 'n roll lyrics: "You don't look like a movie star, and on your money we won't get far, but baby, you got what it takes . . ."

"Then, Dr. Carter," she continued, sensing that he was

looking at her as a woman, rather than as a governor, "would you . . ."

"It's Al," he reminded her, realizing that she was aware of the effect she was having upon him.

"Al, then. Would you say that after our meeting you now have a major crisis on your hands?" she asked, looking at the way he moved his body as they walked. She definitely found his insouciant manner attractive. And the lines of fatigue etched beneath his eyes gave him a wonderful vulnerable look. His soft-spoken manner was appealing despite a certain cockiness.

"Cheri, I think it's fair to say that I have a major crisis on my hands."

"Then," she asked, "why are we standing here acting as if nothing had just happened? I would imagine that time has now become an indispensable commodity for you."

"It has," he replied. "But I'll deal with it . . . in my own time." The truth was that he had no other choice. He believed the solution to the crisis resided somewhere in the inchoate relationship between the two of them. He was trusting his "clinical sense," that fifth dimension of medicine that good doctors acquired after years of practice.

His mind drifted to a famous Roman senator's words as they passed by the horses running freely in the corral: if sensuality were happiness, beasts were happier than men; but human felicity is lodged in the soul and not the flesh. Even Cheri's question about what he should be doing right now, rather than wasting his time with her, was an incredible turn-on. Proving his competence to her was going to be a welcome challenge.

"You're the professional," she responded. "I'm simply part of the problem."

"I see," he said, looking intensely into her hazel eyes. "Maybe you're also part of the solution."

"Oh, oh," she laughed. "I smell a honey trap."

"What do you mean?" he asked disingenuously.

"I think," she replied, "you know exactly what I mean. You're trying to work some of that diplomatic charm on me. If your first rule of crisis management is to try to seduce your adversary, then we are going to have quite an interesting next few days. You certainly have to be commended for effort but seriously questioned as to professional judgment."

"Doesn't impress you, huh?" Al asked as they approached the stables.

"What do you think?" she asked, running her hands through her hair. "You're supposed to be the professional. You tell me."

"I would say 'supposed to be . . .' " He began trying to figure out how not to sound too glib.

"Now, now, Dr. Carter. Al"—she reprimanded him with her index finger—"are you going to try to play with my mind? You may find that quite interesting but extremely time-consuming."

"So what would you recommend, Dr. Black?" he asked, stroking the diamond-shaped forehead of a mangy brown horse. "Should I immediately fly back to Washington and meet with the Secretary of State and explain how dire the situation is?"

"That sounds to me exceedingly reasonable," she responded, stroking the same horse's mane.

"Why?" he asked, gripping her hand.

"What do you mean, 'why'?" she asked. He was clearly starting to make her feel uncomfortable.

"Why?" he reiterated. He let go of her hand and continued to stroke the horse more rapidly.

"Oh, come on," she said, stepping back and looking at him as if she had never seen him before. "I don't believe this. You've just been informed that your country is on the verge of a civil war. And you're telling me that there is no reason for you to inform the Secretary of State. I don't get it."

"You seem to be more excited by this whole matter than I am," Al said nonchalantly. "You're the one who's threatening us. We're not threatening you or your colleagues."

"Oh, now I get it!" she said, as if she had just witnessed an epiphany. "This is some kind of clever psychological manipulation. One of your famous PSYOPS, is it?"

"I think that's a fascinating thesis," Al said, laughing, "but isn't that a little bit grandiose? Aren't you implying that you are the critical element in all of this? And if somehow I bring you over then I've resolved the entire crisis.''

''Jesus Christ,'' she responded, shaking her head. ''I don't know what the hell you think you're trying to do. But whatever you call it, it's not going to work.''

''Cheri,'' Al said, grabbing her shoulders and holding her firmly at arm's length, ''I'm not denying that we have a major problem on our hands. But at this very moment there is really very little that I can do about it. You guys have this all thought out.'' He watched her reaction, hoping to see some compliance or acquiescence but only saw increasing mistrust in her eyes.

''Is this the point at which you smoothly slip in all that State Department charm?'' she asked, enjoying the feel of his firm fingers digging into her shoulders.

''I can't make you do anything that you don't want to do,'' Al reaffirmed, relaxing his grip.

''There is one thing,'' she said sweetly, ''I would like you to do.''

''What is that?'' he asked, hopeful that his strategy was working.

''Would you mind letting go of me?'' she asked.

''Touché,'' he laughed. ''You see, there is nothing subtle about who I am and what I do.''

''I think you are what we call one 'dangerous steer' who might end up goring himself,'' she added. ''If you know what I mean.''

''You might be right,'' he responded. ''But what's the fun of having someone else gore you if you can do it to yourself?''

''What does that mean?'' she asked.

''Ask not how someone can screw you over,'' he said somberly, ''without finding out first how you can screw yourself.''

''To thine own self be true, huh?'' she asked, playing along.

''Something like that. Shakespeare,'' he responded. ''But with one minor addition.''

''What's that?'' she asked.

"Be certain that your opponent knows as much about you as you do about yourself," he said.

"Why?" she asked, incredulous. "That's totally counter-intuitive."

"That's right," he responded. "But at least this way you know exactly what your opponent knows about you."

"Or what you want him to know about you," she said, impressed by his mind.

"Information control," he said with a broad smile, "is the first premise of crisis management." He made that one up on the spur of the moment. It certainly sounded credible and authoritative. A simple extrapolation of the intuitive premise that "knowledge is power."

"Very clever, Dr. Carter." She smiled, wondering if this was going to be a winning or losing boxing match. And for whom.

"Now that you see how I work," he added matter-of-factly, "there is just one little issue left between you and me."

"I'm afraid to ask," she said, impressed by the self-confidence of someone who professed inexperience. "What is that?"

"How can you and I together," he whispered in her ear, "prevent this civil war?"

32

GRAND TETONS, WYOMING

Friday, July 4th, 6:00 P.M.

''What's your definition of treason?'' Al asked as he mounted the brown-as-mud horse.

Cheri ignored the question and swung herself effortlessly over her specially crafted saddle. ''Let's kick up some dust.''

They trotted through the open corral, heading westward into the blood-orange sun. At this time of the year, the Grand Tetons stood as a magnificent testimony to the natural beauty of the country. Its outline mirrored the finest of America's character. Independent. Proud. Tough. The mountain range was chiseled into ragged sparkling granite spirals covered with parchments of snow. Dense rows of trees covered the side of the mountain, providing an impressive shelter for an array of moose, deer, wolves, and snakes, all of which lived in a wonderful predatory ecology, where the simple dictate of Darwinian survival, eat or be eaten, permeated the cool, brisk air.

''What would you call a group of co-conspirators,'' Al asked, breathing heavily as they slowed the horses to a walk, ''who try to overthrow their government through extortion and threat?''

''There's a certain connotation to the word treason that I resent,'' she answered. ''I don't see myself as treasonous. No, as a matter of fact,'' she added, ''I see the federal government as having violated its constitutional trust with the American people. The government is there to serve us, not the other way around. And it has become an intellectual, ideological, and financial oppressor. All that I and my compatriots, or 'co-conspirators' as you insist on calling them, have done is to defy that oppressor. That, to us, is an act of patriotism, not treason."

Their horses jumped over the small logs in the forest, while they ducked, bobbed, and weaved to avoid the intrusive branches jutting from the trees. Al clearly was not as good a horseman as Cheri. He admired the spirited way she rode, indifferent to the obstacles in front of her. Her riding, thought Al, reflected her style. For him, it was a clear indication of how she handled all of life—she was a highly calculated, disciplined risk-taker.

"I'm sure that your views are shared by many people in this country," Al shouted, trying to be heard above the heavy breathing of his horse, "but I still can't accept your method of getting change made."

"That's not for you to judge," she responded, spurring her horse forward.

"And how would you have me judge you and your fellow governors?" Al asked, catching up to her as her horse slowed down.

Without answering, she patted her horse's mane and brought him to a halt.

Al followed, thankful for the respite. "Not to put too fine a point on the matter," he continued, "but it seems to me that you and your colleagues have sold this country out for no other reason than money—or as the economic analysts might say, 'a brighter economic future.' "

"If that be treason," Cheri said unabashedly, "then we are as much traitors as George Washington, Patrick Henry, John Adams, and Thomas Jefferson. I might remind you, they all supported the American Revolution because they didn't want to pay the prohibitive taxes that the British government had levied on the colonies. All we have done is exactly what the original founding fathers of our country did—declare our inherent right to be financially, politically, and ideologically separate from an oppressive mother country. But in our case the oppression comes from within—Washington, D.C.''

''So this whole secessionist movement is driven by the desire for economic and political autonomy?'' he asked.

She stopped her horse so that the importance of her words could not be mistaken. ''You seem to think that this 'whole secessionist movement,' as you call it, just sprang up out of nowhere as a result of a few malcontent governors.''

''I don't think you're far off,'' he noted.

''What you see in that Lodge was a long time in coming. As a matter of fact, it's been percolating for about two hundred years. Let's start first with the famous theorists. This secessionist movement was the result of unresolved constitutional issues, leading to famous patriots like Thomas Jefferson who advocated the abrogation of 'unconstitutional federal laws,' going all the way back to the 1790s.'' She stopped, and was impressed by his attentiveness. ''Do you want to hear the rest of the history of what you call treason?''

''I'm all eyes and ears,'' he responded, walking his horse alongside hers.

''Theories justifying secession under the U.S. Constitution are based on doctrines of state sovereignty: that the Constitution is a compact among sovereign states for a limited set of purposes and that sovereignty—which is indivisible—continues to reside in the states, not in the national government. Had enough yet?'' she asked.

''Keep going,'' he replied. He wanted to understand the mindset that could rationalize sedition and treason. In so doing, he might uncover the wrinkle in their logic which he could then exploit.

''The classic arguments for this position are in the resolutions passed by the legislatures of Virginia,'' Cheri continued, trying not to sound pedantic, ''drafted by none other than former U.S. President James Madison, and in Virginia, written by another former U.S. President, Thomas Jefferson. In effect they said, and I quote, 'The rights grants by the people may be resumed by the people at their pleasure.' Madison argued that the state was entitled to 'interpose' itself between the federal government and its inhabitants of unconstitutional federal laws. Jefferson proposed that the states 'nullify' unconstitutional federal laws. Both gentlemen, as you can plainly hear, advocated the use of force where necessary. Madison went so far as to declare that 'These and successive acts of the same character, unless arrested on the threshold, may tend to drive these states into revolution and blood.' And most Americans, at that time, accepted a right of revolution and appealed to force as a matter of principle much more easily than we do now.

"Advocacy of secession was brought up at the Hartford Convention of 1814 to 1815 and in the War of 1812. Others, like John C. Calhoun, a respected Vice President of the United States, argued that when a state believed the federal government had overstepped the boundaries of its constitutional authority, the state should call a special convention which could nullify federal law."

"You certainly know your history," Al said, still listening attentively.

"I would hope so," she responded. "I received a Ph.D. in political philosophy and, of course, as a governor, I had to research this issue very carefully before I joined the movement."

"Please continue," he encouraged, admiring her obvious passion for history, one which he shared.

"Since the Civil War, these issues have remained unresolved and continue to pop up their ugly heads whenever you have alienated American citizens or separatist movements." The more she talked, the more comfortable she felt being with him. He appeared attentive, patient, and respectful. He reminded her of some of her graduate students, particularly the ones that went on to become teachers themselves.

Al didn't answer. He needed time to reflect. Not necessarily to act, but to reflect on the psychology of treason and the reasoning behind it.

"After the Civil War, the Fourteenth Amendment to the Constitution asserted a doctrine of national sovereignty by defining citizenship as a national category," she continued in a soothing tone of voice. She was trying to make the history of secession sound as if it were a logical sequence of events which should inevitably culminate in the governors' demands. She knew that her presentation of the theoretical basis of secession sounded extremely compelling to him, just as it had sounded to the other governors what seemed like light-years ago.

"The recent arguments for secession are dependent on the earlier theories I just mentioned," she clarified, "as well as the fact that a large majority of the proponents of secession often regard the constitutional changes brought about by the Civil War as coerced and illegal."

"So many of these so-called 'patriot militias' and Posse Comitatus believe that the right to revolt against the federal government is implicit in our history and was certainly believed in by the founding fathers," Al summarized.

"That's exactly right," she confirmed. "Take a combination of alienated citizens, militia groups that believe in the right to bear arms, and patriots who feel that the Constitution was a reaffirmation of white Christians to remain the predominant power in this country and you have the basic ingredients for . . . treason, as you insist on calling it. The whole issue of police power is a good example of what you were just saying. The Posse Comitatus Act after the Civil War attempted to place some limits on the use of federal military power in the occupied South. And that act has been used as a justification for civilian law enforcement groups that call themselves the Posse Comitatus or 'county law,' when construed historically to be an alternative to federal law enforcement."

Al didn't say anything for quite a long while. He just let his horse meander side by side with hers. He was trying to collect his thoughts about the general dynamics of treason and defection, the two essential ingredients to this act of secession. He recalled the time when he had been part of a multi-disciplinary team of experts drawn from the CIA, DIA, NSA, and the State Department to study the increasing problem of defection and treason in the mid-1990s. He wasn't entirely certain that his medical expertise had been essential, but at least he had learned one important lesson. Defectors and traitors were *not* crazy. Such acts were not a function of someone's psychopathology but calculated and purposeful. Nobody ever defected because he was happy. Additionally, willingness to commit treason was usually an act of desperation, propelled by dissatisfaction, disillusionment, depression, and defeat. Defection and treason were responses to an overwhelming life crisis or to an accumulation of crises or disappointments. Contrary to what most people thought, ideology ranked very low on the list of motivations. Marital problems, mistress problems, sexual preference problems, drinking problems, money problems, and career problems were much more likely to influence behavior.

That's what made this situation different, Al thought. This secession—or defection—movement was happening because of ideological differences. But as in a divorce, were the differences so great that there was no possibility for reconciliation? What was beginning to concern him more than anything else was that defections and acts of treason usually accepted the potential risk to life and limb.

He wondered if he could create a situation that would make the governors' act of treason so self-destructive that they would have to stop. In other words, if their secession suddenly seemed injurious to their own cause. But that, of course, depended on whether as a group they were runners or fighters.

At one extreme, the runners were individuals whose motivations were shallow and were seeking an escape. Usually this type of individual had a history which contained a series of mini-defections. Whenever this individual saw a crisis approaching, he attempted to escape or flee. He always tried to avoid confrontations. Faced with a crisis, he runs.

In contrast, fighters were counterattackers. Early in the course of their lives when they saw a crisis coming they attacked. More often than not they were defeated but survived. So they modified their technique, first by sideswiping, letting the crisis seemingly roll by and, as it came abreast, swiping at it. By the time they modified their technique to backstabbing, they were ripe for defection. In fact, more often than not, fighters were not recruited by the intelligence community. They tended to volunteer. They usually sought out the principals to whom they would like to defect. They were always looking for opportunities to counterattack. They were individuals who were motivated by getting even, vengeance, and justification. For the most part, most defectors were in between both extremes.

As Al mused, Cheri prodded her horse once more and raced ahead of him. He took a deep breath and followed her lead. But this time, his lack of horsemanship caught up with him. He hit his head against a low-hanging branch and fell to the ground. The last thing he remembered was hearing a sharp crack and the sound of his horse galloping away.

33

GLEN CANYON DAM, LAKE POWELL, ARIZONA

Friday, July 4th, 6:15 P.M.

The men who built the Glen Canyon Dam knew that the natural sandstone walls of the Glen Canyon would one day contain a limited number of fissures that allowed the groundwater, or "leaks," from Lake Powell to leach through them. As a course of nature, these leaks would weaken the rocks that supported the dam and cause a certain amount of erosion of the sandstone. In order to counteract this natural weakening of the dam, long rock-bolts were inserted into the walls to create an artificial runoff through troughs placed at the base of the wall. This allowed the seepage to be routed directly into the river below.

Robby had understood this basic engineering approach as well as any engineer who had helped to construct the dam. But he also knew that the built-in tolerance for this type of runoff, which was considered more than adequate at the time the dam was built, was woefully lacking by current standards.

On this evening the water started to seep through the walls of the dam at a far greater rate and intensity than Robby or any of the treasonous governors could have imagined. For all their planning for a "controlled" flooding of the dam, the noise generated by the helicopter and rockets had loosened the rock-bolts that literally held the dam together. It was only a matter of time until man and nature formed an unwitting alliance to create chaos.

A fisherman sitting in his rowboat noticed that, unlike previous nights on Lake Powell, he was having a hard time keeping his fishing rod and boat steady. As was his custom, he would come out three evenings per week, just as the sun began to descend into the Western hemisphere, to fish for the cutthroat trout, named for the red marks on the lower jaws of its mouth. But the fisherman was having a hard time accomplishing the simple task of inserting the male ferrule into the female ferrule of the butt section of his expensive fly rod. God, he thought, if he couldn't insert one pole into the other, how was he going to adjust the leaders on his float or even consider using an artificial fly with its delicate antennae, topping, ribbing, and hackle as a lure for the trout? Or if he was really lucky, the Mountain Whitefish. There was no doubt in his mind that the increasingly turbulent waters would tear apart this delicate lure. Maybe, he thought, he should use the far simpler spinner, with its elliptical lead belly narrowing through the split link into a three-pronged, razor-sharp hook. But that was less sophisticated fly fishing and quite frankly less fun.

What bothered him the most was the fact that he couldn't understand what was happening. There was nothing unusual about the weather. The sky was a palette of dark red hues overlaid with a patina of orange, interspersed with a few clumps of white cotton balls of clouds scudding across it. This was not the type of celestial covering that would sanction a storm or forbode some imminent danger. The cool, pristine air maintained its customary formality of gently licking the sides of the fisherman's ruddy cheeks with a pleasant reminder of times past. Nothing was really all that different from the other nights he had gone fishing on this very same lake. And yet, despite all the familiar signs of a normal evening, the dark blue waters of Lake Powell appeared unbridled, incessantly agitated as if having been rudely awakened by some inexplicable force from its normally quiescent state. The boat was acting like a baby's cradle in water, rocking back and forth—but not by the gentle hands of a loving mother. Instead, he felt as if there were someone beneath the boat trying to tip it over.

For the first time in a very long time, he decided to put on his life vest. Could this be an earthquake? he wondered. Or was this part of the military exercise at the dam he was witnessing from the water below? He watched as scores of men in camouflaged trucks, tanks, humvees, and helicopters approached the dam area. He hoped that nothing they were doing would create permanent damage at the dam. Hell, he thought, if the dam ever broke and the water spilled into the river, it would destroy Lake Powell and the city of Page. That would affect about half a million inhabitants, not counting all the water and electric power that would be eliminated from people in seven different states. He shuddered at the thought.

Unfortunately, the fisherman was only partly correct in his suspicions. The plan concocted by the governors to scare the federal government into accepting their plans for secession had envisioned a highly controlled runoff of the dam's waters. Certainly, some towns would be flooded and some lives would be lost. That happened during the course of natural disasters like hurricanes and blizzards each year. But the feds would quickly realize that the fate of millions was in the hands of the state leaders who would use everything they could to make their point. A small price to pay for independence, the governors had decided. And the immediate legitimacy that would be given them by one major foreign country, and possibly more, would only enhance their cause.

How were the governors to know the advanced state of deterioration of the dam's sandstone walls? Certainly, some maintenance had been deferred over the last five years—every state had felt the pinch of cutbacks in federal funds. But the governors had all been given assurances that the amount of water released could be controlled. Enough water would be released to scare the feds into acquiescence, but not too much to do extraordinary harm. Although they did not yet know it, the water in Lake Powell was rising faster than anyone had anticipated. And their so-called controlled flood was going to be anything but controlled.

• • •

In fact, Page was soon to be submerged beneath the water from Lake Powell. Only the multi-varied rooftops of landmark residential and commercial buildings would serve as grotesque reminders that there once existed a vibrant life beneath the liquid pall. Who would have imagined that with so many different religious denominations and churches within the town that a biblical Armageddon would descend upon them so soon and so viciously? Even those atheists who professed an absence of spiritual belief would become righteously indignant at a Supreme Being in whom they had not really ever believed in the first place. The spunky editor of the *Page Gazette* was to write upon one of the rooftops the banner headline for the next edition of the newspaper: "God drowned in the Arizona desert." In contrast, the disc jockeys from the two local FM radio stations were to play music that they felt would embolden the citizens to their hardship, such as "We Shall Overcome," "God Bless America," "Yankee Doodle Dandy," and a medley of other lesser known songs from a variety of Broadway musicals. At one point, they would play the music from *Carousel,* especially the phrase "when you walk through a storm keep your head up high."

At the same time, the radio stations would act as a conduit of messages from one family member to another. Typical of the messages that were to come in was: "To Rene Sherman from Betty Adler—Please come and stay in our trailer five miles due west of town." That meant that between the two families there would be four adults and ten children ranging in age from five years old to eighteen years residing in quarters no bigger than a one-room studio apartment. But they would do it happily.

Ellen Butts, the svelte mayor of the town, would make a daily appearance on both of the FM radio stations and announce where food, shelter, and financial assistance could be obtained. She would reassure everyone that as soon as the water receded, everything would be back to normal. She estimated the loss of property at $2 billion. She didn't make that fact public for fear that it might depress everyone. Instead, she challenged the community to a race where the first family to completely rebuild their two-bedroom house would receive a ten-year state real estate tax abatement. But despite her brave facade, she couldn't help crying when she saw that the house that she had been born and raised in had been completely devoured by the flood. The toys and furniture with which she had grown up and eventually had become part of her psychological lattice floated by her with complete indifference to her beckoning sighs.

In contrast, Beverly Nadel, the owner of one of the radio stations, would wear a sweatshirt that said, "You ain't got nothin' left so you ain't got nothin' to worry about." Madeleine Fisher, the high school principal, would assure the high school senior class through the radio broadcasts that there would be a graduation ceremony despite the fact that the school in town was awash with the flotsam and jetsam of desks, chairs, lockers, textbooks, blackboards, and computers. The ceremony would be held two weeks late at their archrival's auditorium across the state lines in Utah. "And please," she added in her strident pedantic voice, "don't forget that Utah is one hour ahead of Arizona . . . with respect to time only."

As for the rest of the town, it would look as if it had been gutted by fire or explosives that left nothing but the facades of buildings gaping with see-through wounds of destruction that quietly implored complete demolition, followed by the inevitable reconstruction. Many of the G.I. veterans at VFW Chapter 473 thought that Page looked like the photographs they had taken of the wooden and cement remnants of the allies' firebombing of Dresden during World War II. Or more ominously, the gruesome aftermath of Hiroshima and Nagasaki, after the atomic bomb had been dropped. For almost all the citizens, Page would evolve into a wooden, steel, and concrete gargoyle of nature's response to man's arrogance.

At first, the fisherman held the gunnels of his rowboat tightly, watching the water eject from the base of the dam. It reminded him of an endless lineup of firehoses discharging the full blast of their respective water supplies with a vengeance. The water spurted from the hollow jet valves that were supposed to moderate the flow of the water, as if they were streams of fluids spewing forth from the mouth of the mythical water god Neptune. There was a viciousness in the way the water gushed, as if it were intentionally trying to destroy whoever and whatever was in its path. A child, a mother, a hundred-year-old oak tree, and a bulldozer all had equal moral value to the blind onslaught of this rushing water.

The fisherman started to yell up to the soldiers above in order to attract their attention. But he soon realized that the roar of the racing water was too loud for his voice to be heard. If he remained in the boat much longer, he would be in the direct path of a force intent on leveling everything in its way. Whatever advantages his mind and body might have had against the vicious torrents of mother nature were diminishing as the level and force of the water rose. He tried to rock the boat with the goal of being pushed by the flow of water to the other side of the lake where the water was still relatively calm. But the more he swayed the boat, the more at risk he felt, until he began to realize that no matter what he wanted to do, he was condemned to die.

The rowboat filled up quickly with water. Although the fisherman went through the motions of trying to bail out the boat, he knew that the effort was futile. In a matter of minutes, it would be all over. The water would tip over the boat and he would be thrown into the savage onslaught. He would die from exhaustion, although an autopsy would call it drowning. As a lifeguard he was taught that a person drowned out of fatigue. You became so exhausted in mind and body that you no longer could fight the elements. And you drowned.

As the water rose in the boat, the fisherman felt its coldness creep above his legs and thighs, onto his torso, and finally reach his neck. He looked up toward the blood-orange sky and was sorry that he would never again see the bright, shining stars.

34

GRAND TETONS, WYOMING

Friday, July 4th, 6:40 P.M.

"Are you all right?" Cheri asked, kneeling beside him.

"Who am I?" he asked jokingly. "What am I doing here? And who are you?"

"That bad, huh?" she asked. "Where does it hurt?"

Al tried to get up.

"Just lie there," she insisted, restraining him on the ground and liking it.

"Someone," he said, "either doesn't like me or my horse." He thought to himself that it sounded like a line from a country western song.

"That's a strange thing to say," she responded.

"I heard a crack before I fell. Like the sound of a gunshot. Then the horse tripped." He sang a line from the 1950s musical show *Call Me Madame.* "I hear music but there's no one there/I smell blossoms but the trees are bare . . ."

"So I've got a real musical star on my hands," she interrupted, ignoring what seemed to her like a paranoid concern about his life.

"How about this?" he asked as he spread out his arms, mimicking the posture of Pavarotti, the famous opera tenor, but singing a rock 'n roll song. "The Hunter Gets Captured by the Game. . . ."

"More than likely it was the sound of a dry branch breaking,'' she responded, looking for his horse. ''Your fall must have frightened your horse away.''

''Or maybe it was my singing,'' Al replied, deciding that the time was right to take full advantage of the situation. ''You don't have any chewing gum with you, do you?'' He added with mock seriousness, ''At times like this I have a dire need to masticate.''

''What do I have here?'' she chuckled, playing along with Al's ingratiating playfulness. ''Dick Clark's American Bandstand? Or maybe this regression to pubescence is some sign of serious neurological trauma secondary to your fall from the horse?''

''The Marvelettes, under the direct supervision of the incomparable Smokey Robinson, sang that song about the hunter,'' Al continued, relishing the absurdity of the moment. I'm lying on the ground, he thought, she's looking for a missing horse, someone may have tried to kill me, and I'm singing rock 'n roll in the woods while the country is falling apart. What else could he do to minimize the absurdity of the moment? Outbursts of rock 'n roll songs and trivia had always been his way of dealing with stress, anxiety, and uncertainty. As far as he was concerned, it was a lot cheaper than paying a shrink $175 per hour. Furthermore, his theory of neurophysiology had always held that if one is exposed to rock 'n roll at prepubescence, one becomes addicted to it until death. Of course, his neurology professors might not agree, but who really cared?

''Do you know what the Marvelettes' first major hit was?'' Al asked, sitting up. Someone who came on as strongly as she did had to, by definition, be a rock 'n roller. At least at heart. For Al, rock 'n roll wasn't simply a type of music, marked by heavy guitar, strong drum rhythms, simple melodies, and even simpler lyrics. It was a way of life, a zeitgeist, a way of thinking about life. It represented a very distinct American expression of defiance, independence, creativity, and playful insightfulness. And Cheri certainly was all of that, he thought. The heart of rock 'n roll represented the seamless infusion of African music, Gospel singing, country western twanging, folk music, Latin rhythms, unprecedented electronic advancements, and the plaintive cry of soulful alienation and personal pain mixed together with lyrics saturated with love, sex, and violence. Rock 'n roll was America, with all its discordance, cacophony, and mellifluous wishful thinking.

" 'Please Mr. Postman,' " Cheri responded, pushing him down, "recorded for Berry Gordy, Jr., in 1961 for his Tamla label after he had changed their name from The Casinyets." Pausing, she added eagerly, "Impressed?"

"Quite," he responded. She had a rock 'n roll soul after all.

"There wasn't much to do on a small ranch in Nowheresville, Texas," she interjected, "except listen to the radio and play 45 rpm records all day."

"Do you mind if I get up now?" he asked, starting to elevate himself.

"Yes," Cheri responded, enjoying the control she had over his prone body. "I do mind. What if you have a transection of the spinal cord, and you suddenly get up and become paralyzed? I could never have that on my conscience."

"What if I signed a liability waiver?" he asked. He relaxed long enough to start getting nervous again about being a target for someone with a gun. Or was the "shot" he thought he had heard only the snapping of the branch that knocked him off his horse?

"Do you know that you have very interesting lips," she said, just barely brushing over them with her finger. "Your lower lip is much thicker than your upper lip, which is thin and narrow." Pausing, she added, "Reading faces was a self-taught hobby I got into in high school when I ran out of listening to all the oldies but goodies. Believe me, in politics there is nothing more helpful than reading someone's facial expressions before they open up their mouth to ask you for something. Or they are about to screw you over with a smile."

"Should I surmise from your comments that you like my lips?" he asked, fascinated by this woman.

"The configuration of your lips tells me," she ignored his leading question, "that self-disclosure doesn't come easily to you. Whatever you think or say is very carefully thought out beforehand so that you will reveal only a certain amount and no more.''

''Anything else?'' he asked. ''Do you give séances also?''

''I'm serious,'' she said. ''The way you clench your jaw tightly,'' she continued, ''tells me that you have incredible tenacity, and that you don't give up no matter how hard the task might be.''

''What else?'' he asked, folding his arms beneath his head, enjoying the way she was focusing on him.

''In a crisis you become very aggressive,'' she continued, ''and strike out at your opponent's vulnerable points.''

''And what are your vulnerabilities?'' he asked, increasingly titillated by the touch of her hands and the sharpness of her mind.

''I'm certain,'' she said, ''that in due time you will find out.'' She ran her fingers over his thick, unruly, reddish-brown eyebrows. ''Let me finish. I don't often get a chance to analyze a doctor.'' Pausing, she added sarcastically, ''A healer of the mind and body.''

''I see,'' he said, beginning to wonder whether this horseback ride wasn't a setup. By Cheri? Or Josiah? Or Yvette? If he was co-opted, or out of the picture with a bullet in his brain, this whole secessionist problem could slide down the slippery slope toward civil war without any unnecessary negotiation.

''I don't think you can see anything,'' she said. ''Your eyebrows are so thick and low over your eyes.'' Her fingers attempted to smooth out the unruly brows.

''My God,'' he said, ''it sounds as if I have a terminal condition of the eyebrow, and who knows what else.''

''The thick eyebrows,'' she said, sounding as if she knew what she was talking about, ''also tell me that you are an extremely determined person.''

''Wait a minute,'' he blurted out, ''haven't we just established that fact with my tight-clenched jaw?''

''Perhaps,'' she said. ''But these wild eyebrows also show that you have wild, creative ideas.''

''You mean like thinking that I've been a target out here?'' he asked.

"Let's just say that you have a full appreciation for the spontaneous," she responded, suggestively. "You like to wheel and deal where anything and everything is possible."

"Governor Black," he asked disingenuously, "are you trying to seduce me?"

"You have a very high forehead," she continued, completely ignoring his question. "It's filled with intelligence. That's good. It also says that you are a man of ideas, a person to whom ideas are very real. As a matter of fact, ideas motivate you as much as power does. A deadly combination, Dr. Carter. For most people that makes you a very dangerous man."

"And for you?" he asked, reaching out to her highly arched eyebrows.

"It means that I have to be very careful," she said, drawing back slightly. "You tend to burn people out. You're Mr. High Intensity."

"I'm absolutely amazed that you can tell all this about me," he joked, "just from the lines and curves of my face."

"Well," she responded, "am I wrong about anything that I've told you?"

"Let me think . . ." He hesitated.

"Am I wrong?" she repeated, flicking his nose. "Don't be coy with me."

"What does it mean when you have high thin eyebrows over beautiful long eyelashes?" he asked, resisting the temptation to pull her down on top of him. Whatever else was happening around him was secondary to what he was feeling toward her.

"Do you really want to know?" she asked coyly, bending down toward him.

"Is it something that I shouldn't know?" he joked, playing along.

"Okay, you asked for it," she answered, bending even closer.

"You're not going to tell me," he said, "that you're a werewolf?"

"Arched eyebrows often mean a very deep capacity for very strong, intimate relationships."

"Often?" he asked.

"Often," she replied.

"And that cute little upturned nose?" he asked, inhaling the heat of her breath.

"An upturned nose," she uttered, her lips almost touching his, "designates an intense curiosity . . . usually about personal relationships."

"Usually?" he asked.

"Usually," she replied.

"And those heart-shaped lips?"

"That means"—she barely spoke the words as their lips touched—"that they want to tell you something."

"Talk to me," he responded, embracing her.

35

GRAND TETONS, WYOMING

Friday, July 4th, 8:00 P.M.

Cheri pulled away from Al, angered by her unexpected feelings for him. She hadn't made love in the woods since she was a teenager and she wasn't about to now. Her will softened as he drew her toward him again, caressing her neck and back, soothing anxieties and uncertainties. Why did she feel so drawn to this man? Particularly at a point in time when the country was about to blow apart. Didn't he see her as the enemy?

"Just let yourself relax," Al said, sensing her muscles tighten. "We don't have to do anything you're uncomfortable with. Let's just inhale the beauty of the moment. Here we are, two people, on opposite sides of a particularly sticky situation, attracted to each other. And in full view of the splendor of the Tetons."

"It's not the right time or place," she replied, pulling back again and straightening her clothes. "Even if it's something we both may want." She studied his disappointed face and realized just how much she was attracted to him. At some point during the afternoon meeting at the Lodge, she knew that she wanted his mind, his emotions, his wit, his talents. Now she realized that she wanted his body as well. But that was a complication she would not allow to influence the course of the next days' events.

Cheri smiled a mournful smile and tenderly touched his

furrowed brow with the tips of her fingers. "When this is all over, maybe we can talk about a rain check."

Al smiled in return, knowing that she was ambivalent but proud that she had made the only decision a true professional could make. He sat up and looked deep into her eyes. "I want you to help me."

Cheri flinched, visibly angry at Al now, rather than at herself. She had almost been manipulated by the oldest trick in the book. "So this is the great principle of crisis management?" she asked.

"There is a saying we have in crisis management," Al responded. "Shaft them before they shaft you. So to speak."

"I'm not amused," she said. "And don't change the subject."

"What are you talking about?" he said, trying to pull her toward him.

"Every time I ask you a serious question," she replied, having just experienced an epiphany, "you cleverly turn it away from wherever you don't want the conversation to go."

"I don't know what you're talking about."

"Oh, come on, Al," she added, "what difference does it make to you whether you and I become lovers? Another 'splendor of the Tetons,' so to speak," she said. "You couldn't care less. That's not your bag. You just want someone to take you on your own terms. And if they don't like it, as far as you're concerned, it's tough shit, pardon my French."

"You certainly have a way with words, Governor," Al responded, both amused and saddened. Perhaps when this whole episode was behind them he could show her that he was worthy of her trust.

"Listen, I didn't make it all the way up the greasy pole of politics because I bake great chocolate chip cookies," she responded.

"But I bet you can't do that as well as you can . . ." he said, reaching outstretched arms toward her in a purposefully dramatic gesture intended to lessen the tension that now existed between them.

"You are impossible," Cheri laughed, begrudgingly.

"What am I going to do with you?" She had been with countless men, all of whom she could categorize under one or another label and then expect them to act accordingly. But Al was different. So different that she couldn't find the appropriate tag. Determined? Yes. Calculating? Definitely. Manipulative? Without a doubt. Vulnerable? Seemingly, even though he tried to hide it. Controlling? More than most men or women in positions of power. Well, maybe they were both on par on that one.

"Since you enjoy playing games so much . . ." Al replied.

"No," she interrupted, hurt by his accusation. "I don't play games when I feel . . . this way. . . . But I'm afraid that you are."

"I'm what?" he asked, sensing that the conversation was turning serious before he had wanted it to.

"You heard what I said," she responded. "You remind me of an adolescent who wants to test his limits, just to throw his parents off balance."

"Thank you, Madame Freud. You happen to be right on the mark," he said, moving over and holding her tightly at arm's length. "I am a game player. But it happens that at this moment there is a fortunate or unfortunate confluence of feelings . . ."

"Christ," she interrupted brusquely. "Why do I think that I'm going to hear some bullshit? At least let go of my arms, because you are hurting them. And I'll be damned if I'm going to be subjected to two forms of torture at the same time."

"I'm sorry," he said, his voice unconvincing. "I have no intention of hurting you."

"Then why don't I believe you?" she asked, brushing herself off, yet savoring the thought of his body upon hers.

"Because sometimes I'm a sadistic son of a bitch," he replied, "and you sense it."

"Goddamnit!" she said, frustrated. "Why do you make it so hard for me to . . ."

"Governor Black," he said, trying not to sound insulting, "as a hardbitten politician, you should know better than anyone else that one swallow of passion does not a springtime of trust make.''

''Stop,'' she said, straightening her clothes needlessly, fearful about what might happen to her if she left him and even more frightened of what might happen to her if she didn't. The worst part of it all was that she couldn't help wanting him, even now.

''Cheri,'' he said, sensing her confusion and wanting to manipulate it, ''time is running out. I want to know whether you are with me.''

''So,'' she said sardonically, ''this really is the first principle of crisis management . . . try to fuck them and then enlist their support.''

His response was drowned out by the reverberating sounds of gunfire in the distance.

36

ROCKEFELLER LODGE, GRAND TETONS, WYOMING

Friday, July 4th, 8:45 P.M.

Pacing the conference room, Josiah felt restless. As an authoritarian governor he was not used to a process in which a decision was made and then not immediately implemented. At the close of the session the governors had given Alison Carter an ultimatum: get the Secretary of State to sign a paper which agreed with the right of the four states to secede. The power invested in Barbara's office, representing the President, would start the process. By the end of the holiday weekend, the President would be expected to issue an Executive Order to that effect. If he and the Vice President were still not back in the country, Barbara would be expected to sign it for him. The details of the actual secession would be worked out over a period of months by committees of lawyers and technical experts. If, however, no signatures were forthcoming, Phase II would be implemented.

It was clear to each of the governors that state referenda had not worked. While necessary votes for secession were certainly there, the U.S. Supreme Court had struck down the will of the people as unconstitutional. The highest court had asserted a doctrine of national sovereignty by defining citizenship as a national category, making the Executive branch of the federal government the sole guarantor of individual rights. By reversing this reasoning, it was argued by the states' rights lawyers that the President, or his duly constituted representative, had the legal authority, through the simple process of Executive Order, to grant the states their demands. Glaring at the governors seated at the conference table, Josiah was reminded that democracy was frequently a burden.

"Gentlemen," Josiah said, clearly agitated, "we have heard nothing from Dr. Alison Carter or from Governor Black. I think it is time to talk about carrying out Phase Two of our plan. Our next disaster, if you will. The Glen Canyon Dam has now been seized by our respective National Guardsmen and the flooding has begun. By now, Washington understands we are very serious. This will establish our credibility, once and for all. What we say and do is precisely what we mean."

"I wonder if we really needed to flood the dam before hearing from Reynolds," Andrew questioned, having told no one about the evacuation of Page he had witnessed. "When I think about the number of lives that will be lost . . ." he continued, disingenuously.

"I thought we settled this issue months ago," Josiah responded, trying to conceal his disdain for his colleague. Working with a wimp like Andrew, he thought, and not losing patience had been one of Josiah's major political accomplishments. "We're in a war, Andrew. A potential second American civil war. And there's an axiom of war that goes as follows: civilians die. We try to minimize it, but civilians die. In fact, they die for lesser causes than our own. In Bosnia. In Somalia. In Iraq. I don't mean to sound harsh, but didn't we all agree that despite casualties, we could make our supporters see that the cause of states' rights was worth it? And certainly, the end goal of secession. No more federal taxes. No more dictatorship from Washington . . ."

"I'm just talking about waiting," Andrew responded sheepishly.

"There will be no waiting!" Josiah stated. "We have waited long enough. We've talked this issue to death. We've agreed that we need to make our case—strongly."

"I agree with Josiah," Jim said. "Let's begin to focus on Phase Two."

"Perhaps," Andrew said slowly, "we should not be too hasty. No time clock is ticking other than the one that we impose upon ourselves."

"Andrew," Josiah said with disgust in his voice, "you are so typically bureaucratic—slow, ponderous, deliberate. What we need now is not some cautious state legislator imploring us to count nine times before making a stitch."

"Gentlemen," Yvette interjected cautiously, "I think that if we start fighting among each other . . ."

"My dear Yvette"—Jim burst out laughing—"would you please rest assured that the way your American colleagues relate to each other is nothing more than the manifestation of their affection for one another. And for democracy. Shouting back and forth, bargaining a little, taking a little bit here and giving a little bit there . . ."

"Yes," Josiah reiterated sarcastically, "real democracy in action. Just like World War One and World War Two, when France was bailed out both times by America."

"Faites attention!" Yvette said, waving her finger at him. "Be careful! You may have just stepped over the boundaries."

"On behalf of my colleague from Utah," Andrew said, "I want to apologize for him and certainly for our country . . ."

"Your country?" Yvette asked, laughing. "Perhaps you have forgotten why you are here."

"Well, it is still our country," Andrew responded defensively. "No matter what it's going to look like in a month from now. America is not just some sad collection of humans who are run by bureaucrats in Washington."

"You're starting to get maudlin," Jim said, slapping Andrew on the back. "I didn't know you had such . . . feelings. But you'd better get it straight. The U.S.A. as we know it will be *kaput,* finished, *fini.* It doesn't matter what you call it. It's all the same thing."

"I think it would be wise not to deceive yourself, Governor," Yvette said, concerned that Andrew's resolve was less than she had hoped for. "We are speaking here of forever altering the United States of America. Whether it's called the Confederation of States or the Union of Regional

States or nothing at all is not what is relevant. Just look at Canada. But for a few votes last year it would have been two separate entities—the country of Quebec and the country of Canada, minus one of its major provinces."

"Where, may I ask, is Governor Black?" Josiah asked, wishing to end all this waiting. "She left the meeting hours ago."

"I hope that nothing has happened to her," Andrew replied.

"You have an expression in English," Yvette said to no one in particular, "that she's a big girl and can take care of herself."

"And Al?" Josiah continued. "When will we hear from . . . ?"

Before he could finish, the Utah State Trooper with the prognathous jaw entered the room unannounced and walked directly to Josiah. As the guard whispered into his ear, Josiah nodded his head in agreement. From time to time, he shook his head in disapproval. "Are you certain?"

"Governor Brigham," Jim asked, "would you mind sharing what is transpiring?"

"Of course not, Governor McMinn," Josiah responded with a hint of apology in his voice. "The trooper has informed me that Dr. Carter was injured while horseback riding."

"I hope it isn't serious," Andrew responded, shocked.

"Apparently, Dr. Carter is not seriously hurt. He recovered quite quickly. Governor Black is tending to his wounds right now," Josiah responded, infuriated by the overly solicitous concerns from his supposed stalwart compatriots. If this was how they responded to one feeble accident, how would they respond if there were massive bloodshed? As usual, he would have to be the one who dealt with the problem. Andy was so typically Arizonian. Patronizing and self-assured, but squeamish. The state had been built upon mercantile interests hidden behind fancy politically correct theories. Arizona had spent centuries robbing and slaughtering the Navajo Indians, stealing their land and resources. And now they speak about preserving the integrity of their Native Americans. As for Wyoming, what could he say about a state of 400,000 people, less than 5 percent of the total Mormon population, who were willing to live in subfreezing, snow-filled days for ten months of the year? Not much. And as for that vain French peacock, Yvette de Perignod, Josiah wondered how much he could trust her, anyway. He didn't give a damn about what she said. It was true that in both world wars the United States had come to France's help and almost singlehandedly rebuilt the country with massive infusions of capital and manpower. But fifty years later, America was still having trouble wearing her title of superpower. With its financial, educational, and crime problems, America was, in fact, becoming a third-rate power. In all fairness to Yvette, France had come to the help of those young, brash, American revolutionaries during the War of Independence in 1776. And it was the mercenary German Hessian soldiers fighting on behalf of the British with whom the Americans were really engaged in combat on a day-to-day basis. How ironic, he thought, that France, informally representing Germany and England at this meeting, will turn history on its head.

"In fact," Josiah continued, with the gleeful grin of the cat who has finally cornered the canary, "our good doctor recovered so quickly that he and our beautiful Cheri were able to show the other animals in the woods how to copulate—and then some." He looked at the stunned faces in the room. Well, he thought, the "big lie" always worked in history. Why not the "little lie"?

37

DEPARTMENT OF STATE, WASHINGTON, D.C.

Friday, July 4th, 11:00 P.M.

Secretary of State Barbara Reynolds sat in her office watching the CNN broadcast of the floods. Unlike millions of other Americans, she was not shocked to see the ravaging waters from the Glen Canyon Dam rise high enough to look as if an entire town could disappear. Thank goodness she had been prepared for this. The citizens of Page, Arizona, and a score of small towns along the Colorado River had already been evacuated to safe, high grounds, several miles away from the flooded areas. Any damages that would be incurred throughout the crisis would be taken care of by federal aid to the disaster victims and towns. On the outside chance that the flood would get out of control and the damage be greater than expected, she could invoke an Executive Order requesting a State of Emergency. But for the moment, if all went according to plan, she didn't foresee that as a major problem. She still had bigger ones with which to contend. And having this endless pulsating headache didn't help.

The official story fed to the media was that a series of environmental needs of the area provided the perfect chance for the federal government to take the initiative and remedy potential structural problems of the dam as well. One expert witness after another was brought forth to testify that without government intervention, there was a disaster simply waiting to happen. The porous sandstone walls of Glen Canyon. The antiquated software in the main control room. The poorly designed steel vents. The tunnel holes that allow for air circulation. Each was viewed as a potential problem which the government had anticipated and solved.

Barbara's plan had worked. So far the problem was viewed as one of old engineering, not of secession. She knew from past experience in managing environmental disasters that the best way to handle them was to tell the story that created the least hysteria, and to project a sense of confidence that no matter how terrible things might appear, someone in government was in charge. She worked on the basic premise that images of disasters are eventually forgotten by the viewing public. While it was important to let the American people watch the disaster unfold, and empathize with the victims—in this case, people who had lost their homes to rampaging waters—they would eventually turn off the problem after hearing a surfeit of talking heads.

She had learned many of the principles of crisis management from Desaix Clark, an infamous senior State Department official and international crisis manager, who had been summarily retired to some local think tank, having been declared persona non grata out of China. The one lesson he had stressed over and over again was to restrict the media's access to the scene of a disaster so that the images that were transmitted were controlled as much as possible by the government. Barbara had seen, up close, the way the Bush administration had brilliantly executed a completely controlled media war against Iraq. For the most part, only a preselected pool of reporters was allowed anywhere near the site of combat. And the images that were allowed to be broadcast all over the world were ones that showed American rockets and planes taking off and hitting their respective targets in Baghdad. What was not shown were the hundreds of thousands of mutilated Iraqi military and civilian bodies, or wounded U.S. soldiers. From the media's point of view it had been an "asceptic" war. And that's what citizens saw on television.

That was what Barbara was counting on in the Glen Canyon Dam "accident." She had cordoned off the area, both on land and in the air, so that no reporters could come close to it.

Only a handful of key people—the President, the Vice President, the Secretary of Defense—knew about the conversation she had had earlier in the day with Utah Governor Josiah Brigham IV. What a lot of bullshit he handed me, she thought. At least an hour of socio-babble, trying to convince me that the Constitution framed in 1787 was not designed to solve the problems of the twentieth century. The very structure of the Constitution, according to Josiah, had resulted in legislation that does not serve the common good and a general lack of accountability on the part of those who legislate. Now she knew why she had always felt that state governors should stay out of national politics. They presumed that everything could run with the same small-mindedness as their smaller, less complicated political suzerainties. Brigham's diatribe had become a polemic on how the goals stated in the Preamble to the Constitution—establishing justice, promoting the general welfare, ensuring domestic tranquility—were being subverted. According to him and the other governors he claimed to represent, special interests reigned in Washington, D.C. No one took responsibility for anything. Delay, delay, and more delay seemed to be the credo of federal politicians, unlike in states, where officials are accountable for their actions. Nonsense, she thought. Government at the state level was no more accountable than the federal government. The only difference was the fact that if the states ran into financial or political problems they could always turn to the feds for help.

She had to admit that, until he reminded her, she hadn't given much thought to how an average bill becomes law. His explanation, however, was as torturous and tortuous as the real thing. First, a bill is introduced by either the House of Representatives or the Senate. Then it is referred to the appropriate Senate or House committee for hearings and recommendations. Then it is returned to the clerk of the House for debate. After that, it goes to the house in which it was not introduced, where it may be defeated, or passed with or without amendments. If passed, a joint congressional committee works out the differences between varying versions of the bill and arrives at a compromise. Finally, the bill goes to the President for his signature—or veto. Whew! It had reminded her why she preferred the political appointment route to power.

The long and short of their conversation was that the federal government had reneged on its obligations to the states in a big way, and was out of touch with the needs of the people. Too many hard-working people had no medical coverage. School children were not safe in school—or getting to school. No one was safe on the streets, especially after dark. A third of Americans were functionally illiterate, yet school budgets were being decreased. Every adult in every family worked—by necessity. Drugs were burning out the brains of fourteen-year-olds. And the federal government was seizing property, raising taxes, and bankrupting businesses of hardworking Americans. Brigham's list of federal abuses had been much longer, she thought, but it served to get down to his main demand—allow the states of Utah, Wyoming, Arizona, and Colorado to secede from the U.S.A. The legislatures of each state had already drafted and agreed upon articles of secession. Josiah was certain that a vote by the people in each of these states would support secession. The governors wanted no more delay tactics from Washington. The time was now. Certainly for secession by the states in exchange for no civil war—which might, he threatened, add more states to the secessionist movement.

There it was, as incredulous as it sounded, a secessionist statement by an extremely ambitious governor, speaking on behalf of equally ambitious governors. He had informed her that recognition treaties had already been worked out with representatives of several foreign governments. Reynolds now had only forty-eight hours to come up with a signed Executive Order. Or . . . There was no doubt in Barbara's mind that if the government's response to the governors wasn't all they hoped it would be, a second catastrophe would up the ante. But he had given her no clue about what disaster they would devise next.

Barbara had already informed the President, who had consented to an internal State of Emergency in which she was granted the authority to manage the crisis. The upper echelons of the federal bureaucracy had learned of this transfer of power through selected "No Dis/Eyes Only/Top Secret" memos and cables. No one could now question the authority or validity of her statements or orders. Both the President and the Vice President were still abroad and not returning calls on this subject. Not surprisingly, she smiled. She knew the President to be one of those politicians who, while they speak publicly about risks and consequences, was more than happy to lay both the responsibility and accountability onto others when times were tough. That's when she had called in Al Carter.

She was proud of her ability to manipulate people and systems without using the racial card. Unlike many women in positions of power, she was not afraid to recognize the importance of manipulation. Or to use people and situations as needed. In her own mind, she was elegant, a manipulator. Someone who exercised the craft with adroitness and finesse.

The flashing red light on her telephone took her mind off the images of the flood being projected by CNN.

"Yes," she said perfunctorily.

"I have Utah Governor Josiah Brigham IV on the telephone again," her secretary said. "What would you like me to do?"

"Patch him through," Barbara ordered, "but stay on the line and take handwritten notes of our conversation."

"But . . ." the secretary interrupted.

"No buts," Barbara reiterated. "I want the words verbatim. No memcoms."

"Can I use a tape recorder?" the secretary asked.

"No," Barbara responded. "That would be crossing a fine line." Since the Kissinger era, it was forbidden to have anyone record the conversations of the Sec State. Most Sec States had attempted to get around the restriction by ordering a memcom—a memorandum of conversation which ostensibly "summarized from memory" the salient points of the conversation. But it was understood that those memcoms were to be verbatim records of the ongoing conversation.

"All right. I'll patch him through," she responded.

"So, Josiah," Barbara said, dispensing with civilities,

"what's next? Let's get straight to the bottom line."

"My, my, Madame Secretary," Josiah responded, "there's no need to sound so brusque."

"We've already spoken. What else would you like to add that you haven't already said?" Barbara responded coldly. She knew that Josiah was laying odds that she would not send federal troops to the Lodge in Wyoming and possibly ignite an international incident. At least until she had more information. Who knows, thought Barbara, perhaps Josiah was going to disclose his plans to wreak an even greater catastrophe in the United States. At least this Glen Canyon Dam situation came equipped with the cover of plausible deniability, behind which many things could be hidden. Like an ersatz flood from an old dam.

"My colleagues and I want to be sure that you are entirely clear about our demands," Josiah continued, "now that you have seen our capabilities. We are not proud of what we had to do. And as a gesture of restraint, you must be aware that we could have turned off all of the electrical power going into seven states. But we didn't.

"Through an Executive Order"—Josiah spoke as blithely as if he were asking for bonbons—"we would like the President to affirm the right of states to secede. All that is required is a simple signature from the President or his duly appointed surrogate. Or"—he paused for emphasis—"we, I mean the states, will simply exercise what they consider to be their inherent right to secede and declare themselves independent from restrictive federal rules and regulations. The states will be very happy to rid ourselves of Washington's version of what our health care, our welfare laws, our environmental standards, and our transportation should look like. If we can't rid ourselves of your autocratic rule, our education and corrections systems will completely collapse. Federal pollution controls are bankrupting our businesses, closing our plants, causing an exodus of townsfolk, and shutting our schools. It has happened in much wealthier states like Ohio and Connecticut. What makes you think that it can't happen here? If we can't resolve our differences, needless death and destruction will follow."

"Governor Brigham," Barbara responded, already numb

to Brigham's repetitive litany of federal abuses, "do you really think that by the President's signing some little paper Congress will allow your states to accomplish something that we fought a war over some one hundred fifty years ago?"

There was no reply.

"And if not?" Barbara asked, knowing the answer.

"Then you and the country will witness another"—Josiah seemed to be searching for just the right term—"natural catastrophe. I guess you thought that you were very clever in evacuating the citizens of Page before we flooded Glen Canyon Dam. Please be certain that my colleagues and I will investigate how you found out about our little plan. But be equally assured that our next act of defiance will be bigger, and you will not have the luxury of time or knowledge to prepare a counterattack."

"I see," Barbara replied, sickened by his answer. "You wouldn't want to give me a hint of some kind, would you? Or are we going to play some cat-and-mouse game?"

"Madame Secretary," Josiah responded sternly, "there are three governors, and a slew of National Guards with me who are ready to enforce what we consider to be a major historical change in a nation and a government."

"Where's Alison Carter?" Barbara asked, becoming nervous at the thought of him among all these madmen. "May I speak to him?"

"I believe that Dr. Carter is in . . . conference with one of our governors."

Barbara keyed into the hint of frustration in Brigham's voice and realized that Al was beginning to implement their plan of divide and conquer. And what better way to start than with the most attractive governor . . .

"We have very little else to talk about at this point," Josiah responded. "You only have two days left to make your decision." He hung up the telephone.

There are always two sides to a knife, Barbara thought. And the strategy of how to retaliate had suddenly become clear to her. She pushed the button on her phone to her secretary's line. "Get me my special committee of operatives."

38

GRAND TETONS, WYOMING

Friday, July 4th, 9:45 P.M.

''Someone is trying to kill us,'' Al said, running for cover through the woods with Cheri trailing behind.

''Us?'' she repeated.

''Me. You. No difference at this point,'' Al responded. ''I'm afraid that our fates are now linked. And somehow my thoughts keep going back to Josiah.''

''If you're right,'' she asked, ''then why are we heading for the Lodge?''

''Because it's the only way out of here,'' he replied, weaving in and out of the trees. ''We need a car.''

''What makes you assume it was Josiah's doing?'' Cheri asked as they crouched in the underbrush.

''I'm not certain,'' Al responded, ''but I watched him throughout the meeting. My clinical senses told me that you are a direct threat to his leadership of the group. And, as for me, he would be happy to send a message back to Barbara that her messenger boy was worthless.'' They crept on their knees in the direction of the Lodge for what seemed to be hours. ''I have this strong feeling that once he thinks you are against him . . . He sensed that something was very wrong when we went out alone. There is a good chance that we were watched the entire time.'' Al had no need to explain any further what he meant. ''I wouldn't put it beyond him to try to eliminate . . . the competition, so to speak.''

"You deliberately brought me out here, didn't you?" she asked angrily. "You knew full well that if you kept me out here long enough you would compromise my participation in . . ."

"To be completely honest," Al responded, "you're very perceptive. But I also didn't hear any complaints on your part . . ."

"You bastard!" She stopped and smacked him across the face. "Who the hell do you think you are?"

"It's completely irrelevant who I think I am," he replied, "because if we don't get out of here soon we will just be a pair of rotten carcasses waiting to be devoured by whatever animals roam these woods."

"Boy," she said, "did I read you wrong. You really are . . ."

The sound of another gunshot rang out through the woods. This time Al pushed Cheri flat onto the ground.

"I don't think this is the time for recriminations," he said. "You'll have plenty of time for that when and if we leave here alive."

"Josiah isn't playing around, is he?" Cheri said rhetorically. "Is he?"

"The short answer is no," Al answered. "Even if he had only thought of getting rid of me," Al added, "he would still kill you. In his mind, you've been co-opted. So you have become dispensable."

"But he can't run this secession movement without me," Cheri said. "The governors won't accept it. Yvette is there only informally . . . for international legitimacy . . . and potential trade."

"If that's what you want to believe . . ." he said, stroking her hair, almost surprised that she didn't pull away.

"That's what I'm banking on," she said with conviction.

Al drew closer to her.

"I don't know if you're worth all this trouble. You sure as hell created more of a mess in my life than I had already," Cheri said.

"As the music says, 'Don't worry, be happy!' " he said.

"You stick with your music," she said, "but I'll hold you accountable for my safety. . . ."

"Done," he interrupted.

Through a break in the foliage, they could see the outlines of the Lodge. A large number of state troopers, body guards, and DSAs roamed the grounds. He was surprised to see the DSAs, who reported directly to the Undersecretary of State for Management Dick "the Moose" Brooks, a close acquaintance of Al's. He would have thought that all federal agents were persona non grata here. There was only one way out of this quagmire, Al decided. They needed a car to flee to the closest federal haven, which was a Ranger headquarters in Yellowstone National Park. There he could use a telephone to call Barbara. From there, he and Cheri could go by federal government helicopter to the Glen Canyon Dam, where, if he bet correctly, Cheri could assert her gubernatorial authority over her own National Guards. After this display by Josiah of raw power, he knew that Cheri realized she could no longer trust her co-conspirators. Josiah no longer needed her support. He was now running the show, and probably loving it.

From the prickly underbrush, Al recognized the face of a stocky DSA who had accompanied him on several overseas trips. As best as Al could remember, the man's last name sounded something like the famous German composer, Wagner. In sotto voce, Al started to hum "The Ride of the Valkerie."

"Excuse me, Pavarotti," Cheri said, placing her hand over his mouth, "but this is a strange time to decide that your true vocation is opera."

"You see that guy over there, the one with the flashlight in his hand?" Al pointed to the bushes nearby.

"Are you thinking of giving him a moonlight performance?" she asked. "Is this what you call strategy?"

"It's either my singing until I recall this guy's name," Al responded, "or it's Yvette and Josiah singing the 'Marseillaise' while dropping the guillotine on our lovely heads."

"So you want to know what rhymes with Wagner?" she asked, not sure whether to take him seriously.

The DSA walked over to them, waving the flashlight in the direction of the rustling noises coming from the bushes.

Al picked up a small stone, threw it toward the agent, and waited until he stooped down to pick it up before announcing himself.

"Dr. Carter! What are you doing in the bushes . . . with the governor? Remember me? I'm agent Roger Hagner. I accompanied you two years ago in Berlin and Budapest."

"Of course I remember. Pleased to see you again. The governor and I need to get out of here as quickly as possible . . . without anyone seeing us," Al responded.

"How may I help you?" Hagner asked. He was too well trained to ask anything more about the strange circumstances under which he was talking to a governor and a distinguished RMO. Whatever this was, it was none of his business.

"We need to get to one of those cars, undetected," Al responded, pointing in the direction of the limousines parked in front of the well-lit Lodge.

"Follow me," Hagner said with complete self-assurance.

"What does he think he is doing?" Cheri whispered to Al as Hagner motioned them to walk behind him along the forested areas at the edge of a dirt path. "How do you know he won't betray us?"

"We have to trust someone," Al responded, holding her hand tightly as they came closer to the perimeter of the Lodge. "Anyway, I told you his name sounded like Wagner."

"So what does that have to do with anything?" she asked incredulously. It would be like Al to give her a discussion on DSA loyalty at a moment when their lives were in danger.

"Nothing. But I also like opera," he answered. "Unless you can tell me that you trust one of your own state troopers, we have no other choice but to go with Hagner."

"What if he takes us back to Josiah?" she asked.

"We'll have to cross that bridge when we get there," he responded.

"Or *if* we get there," she added ominously.

As they were about to veer away from a group of troopers lounging in front of the Lodge, Hagner turned around, pulled his gun out of his holster, and announced in a loud voice: "You're under arrest."

39

GRAND TETONS, WYOMING

Saturday, July 5th, 12:05 A.M.

''Please follow me,'' Hagner ordered. With his gun pointed at their backs, he steered both Al and Cheri toward the Lodge. The governors and Yvette were standing on the porch as if they were on a receiving line at a diplomatic reception.

''Welcome,'' Josiah said, greeting them. ''It's so good of you both to return. We were so concerned about you. I was tempted to send out a search party.''

''You mean a hunting party,'' Al retorted. ''Fortunately for us, your hunters weren't very good shots.'' The state trooper with the prognathous jaw stood beside Josiah. The trooper's glare told Al all he had to know.

''Oh, come on,'' Jim said. ''You can't be serious.''

''Yes, Governor McMinn.'' Al looked contemptuously at him. ''I have no doubt there's a great deal about this affair that you may not know.''

As he and Cheri stood on the grass in front of the steps to the Lodge, Al looked around to assess their options.

Cheri looked at the governors and realized that in her absence she had relinquished control to Josiah. But the strange smile on Yvette's face bothered her. France's economy was in shambles. A prohibitively expensive social welfare system, which entitled every French worker to six weeks of vacation, six months of maternity benefits, free education, free medical care, and sizable retirement benefits, had for all practical purposes bankrupted the country. While Cheri knew the extent of France's problems, the country had refused to admit to the world that it was nearing financial default throughout the 1990s. Instead it had created all types of disguises to cover it up. Rather than declare a particular enterprise bankrupt, for example, the government would shift the workers from that business to another location, where the government would rebuild the very same bankrupt factory with tax money. This way the government saved face in unemployment statistics and transformed what was a true economic disaster into an apparent success. Cheri began to wonder just how much, and in what ways, the French were counting on regaining a foothold in the secessionist states.

She looked at her co-conspirators with a feeling of sadness. Certainly, what had brought these governors together was the realization that the President was really irrelevant to the everyday workings of the ordinary citizen. And her feelings about this would never change. Two decades of American Presidents had been weak and ineffective, be they Republican or Democrat. It was always the same pattern. Heavy spending on a Presidential campaign for an individual who could and would promise anything and everything to everyone in order to get himself elected. Once elected, the President would manage to break every promise he had made to be voted into office. For a long time now, people had stopped caring what the President said or did. In fact, the position of President was becoming obsolete. The shift of power to the states, away from the federal bureaucracy, had begun almost a decade before when the governor of Michigan defied orders from the Justice Department to provide more jails, at a time when the state could barely afford to meet state payroll. So he challenged the U.S. Attorney General to come to his state and try to implement the federal edicts that the governor felt were both unconstitutional and prohibitively expensive. It was really the governors who were essential to the economy of the state and the maintenance of their constituents' well-being. But I've certainly misjudged my colleagues, she realized. With absolute power, they might be more despotic than Washington.

"Clearly, you have doubts," Josiah said in his distinctively patronizing fashion, "but that's no reason to discard your"—he paused to search for the right word—" 'proper' intellectual home."

"You had no need to be concerned," Cheri responded, distancing herself from Al. "If you feel that I wandered too far afield with Dr. Carter for a very brief moment, I can assure you that it will not happen again."

"I'm so glad to hear that," Josiah said. "We're glad to have you back, aren't we, gentlemen?"

Cheri looked around at the nodding heads and all she could think of was a toy she had when she was a child, in which a plastic bird perched on the rim of a glass all day, nodding its head back and forth as if it were drinking water from the glass.

"C'est très bien, ma chérie, de t'avoir encore," Yvette said, embracing Cheri and whispering in her ear. "It's so good, my dear, to have you back again."

"We do have some decisions to make right now that we hadn't planned on," Cheri said, trying to sound authoritative and in control.

She stared at Al as she spoke. "I'm convinced that Dr. Carter is not authorized to speak for anyone in the federal government, despite what he has told us. He is simply here to stall for time while Washington regroups, configures its strategy, and organizes its forces. He revealed to me that the federal government never had any intention of negotiating with us. The President, Vice President, and Speaker of the House are all away for the July Fourth weekend."

"Well, you certainly have developed an acute attack of verbal diarrhea," Al responded, wondering what Cheri had in mind since he hadn't told her anything of the sort.

"Fresh!" Cheri slapped him across the face and walked over to Yvette.

However with one quick move, Cheri grabbed Yvette from behind and held her throat in a hammerlock position. There was no way that the governors would ever trust her again, she thought. Being a target for a gun-happy trooper was not the path to states' rights. And there was no longer any doubt in her mind that the little romantic episode in the woods with Al had planted seeds of co-option that would never give her an equal voice again. Al had been right about her changing sides, but for the wrong reasons.

The Utah State Trooper with the prognathous jaw responded by unholstering his gun and aiming it straight at Al's head. Hagner acted intuitively and pointed his gun at Yvette. It was what the cowboys in this region had once called a Mexican stand-off.

Al smiled inwardly, pleased that his instincts were still accurate. He had made the right calculation that Hagner could be trusted.

Governor McMinn was obviously agitated. He was beginning to have doubts about the entire venture. It had all seemed so abstract and legalistic before. For the first time he realized what it meant for Americans to kill fellow Americans, and the sight before him was nauseating. It was one thing to go to war on behalf of your country and kill some demonized enemy. But it was a completely different matter to kill your friends and neighbors in the name of the Constitution.

In an unexpected move, Hagner swung his gun from Yvette to the Utah State Trooper and shot him in the shoulder of the hand holding the gun. He fell to the ground, writhing in pain.

"Take it easy, guys," Hagner said, his gun circling the crowd. No one seemed willing to take him on. "The three of us are going to borrow one of Uncle Sam's Torinos and try to prevent an unnecessary bloodbath." He waved Al and Cheri toward the driveway in which several cars were parked.

As the three backed toward the cars, one of the other troopers in the crowd raised his gun and opened fire. Hagner fell to the ground, clutching his chest and firing back wildly. Yvette fell to the ground and lay in a pool of blood.

Al and Cheri ran into the first car that had keys in its ignition and headed toward Yellowstone National Park.

40

YELLOWSTONE NATIONAL PARK, WYOMING

Saturday, July 5th, 1:15 A.M.

Cheri braced her hands against the dashboard as the speedometer registered 90 mph. If an onlooker didn't know any better, this string of cars, with their headlights blazing, might have been a high-speed funeral procession in a grade B movie.

The greatest problem, however, was that Al wasn't sure where he was headed. The two-lane highway they were on wove its way around mountains, rivers, and hillocks as if it were a snake slithering toward its final attack. At best, when it was daylight and he was acting like a normal tourist, he would frequently lose his way. But now, in the midst of a pitch-black night, he felt as if he were driving like the toad in *The Wind in the Willows.* And it didn't feel good. Every time a patch of fog set in it forced Al to slow his speed. Whenever he thought he was lost, the bright headlights in his rearview mirror reminded him that there were those who knew exactly where they were going.

"I feel like Bonnie and Clyde," Cheri said, sensing that Al must be extremely tired from both the physical and mental stress of the situation. Neither had spoken for the twenty minutes they had been in the car.

"That's a hell of an analogy," he responded, veering abruptly to the right to miss a large branch lying in the center of the road.

His eyes were beginning to burn from the strain of their concentration. He swerved the car again, this time avoiding the mutilated carcass of a dead animal.

"Listen, Sterling Moss," she continued. "If you insist on driving any farther to the right, we'll be swimming in the Snake River."

"That's not a bad idea," he responded.

"What's not a bad idea?" she asked.

"Maybe we should leave the car here," Al said, rubbing his eyes, "and paddle down the river."

"To where?" she asked, realizing that she should have kept her mouth shut. "Not that we have a paddle . . ."

"We swim down the Snake River," he replied in seriousness, "to Lewis Lake where there is a Forest Ranger Station and call for help. From the feds. Forest rangers. Park police. Federal troops. Somebody!"

"First of all, Superman," she said, "trying to swim in the Snake River at this time of the night is like voluntarily submerging yourself in a deep freezer."

"And . . . ?" he asked.

"Second, by the time you muster the cavalry," she continued, "it might be too late."

"Too late for what?" he asked.

"Too late for the dénouement of Josiah's great plan," she said, turning around to see how close the pursuing cars were getting to them. "And although you and I will never agree on the issue of states' rights," she said emphatically, "I have a feeling that while our movement sounds good on paper it will suck on implementation. Or be perverted in some way by my former colleagues. Especially that sanctimonious Mormon." She smiled at Al.

"Don't tell me that this civil war is some type of Mormon revenge for the way the Mormons were treated some one hundred years ago," Al asked.

"Not at all," she responded, shaking her head. "Between you and me, I'm beginning to doubt that Josiah's even related to the founders of his church. It's not anyone's conspiracy. Just a movement whose time has come. Anyone who has read the newspapers over the last ten years could have predicted it. After the federal courts proved unsympathetic to our states' concerns, the real problem for us governors was how to get the President's attention. The Glen Canyon flood was only the first part of the threat. I have to tell you that there is more to come.'' She looked at Al's face, waiting for his reaction.

''What's next?'' he demanded, astounded at the thought that the Glen Canyon Dam incident would merely be a prelude to others.

All of a sudden the car started to careen from one end of the road to another. ''Oh shit,'' Al shouted. ''A tire must have blown. We'd better get out of here before we end up as a tree ornament.''

The lights from the pursuing cars evolved into beacons, flooding the area with visibility.

''Put both feet up against the dashboard, unbuckle your seatbelt, and brace yourself,'' he said.

Al swung the steering wheel all the way to the right, smashing through tree limbs and bushes, and crashing against rocks and boulders like a bumper car in a carnival. They jumped out of the car when he reached the count of ''three'' and lay on the moist ground watching the car roll down the hill like an overworked Tonka toy headed for certain destruction.

Cheri checked herself for injuries. ''Let's get down to the river.''

''One minute,'' Al replied hesitantly. His examination revealed a left ankle that was beginning to swell. Probably tendons twisted as he jumped out of the car. ''Uggghh,'' he groaned, trying to put weight on the foot.

''Christ,'' Cheri uttered, ''you're injured!'' She lifted his right arm and draped it over her shoulders. As they tried to move down the hillside, she realized that she was going to have a lot of trouble getting Al all the way to the river.

''Listen,'' he said, pushing her away, ''this isn't going to work. The hunters are coming over the crest of the hill. You've got to get to the Forest Ranger post downriver. I'm just slowing you down.''

''I think you've watched one too many war flicks,'' she answered, balancing him by tightening her grip around his waist. She tried to be a convincing liar and minimize the gravity of the situation, but the reality was far more frightening than she could reveal to Al. The men who were chasing them were Josiah's personal bodyguards, all members of the Utah State Police. But each man, prior to his entrance into the police force, had been attached to an elite U.S. military unit like the Special Forces, SEALS, and the DIA. Their common bond was that they were trained killers, each one specifically selected by Josiah for his ability to maim, neutralize, or destroy a target. And as far as Cheri knew from the captain of her own Colorado State Troopers, each one of their hunters had sworn an oath of personal allegiance to Josiah. They were, in short, his personal hit team. Whenever there was an impending problem that could potentially embarrass him, the hit team took care of it. Their mandate was to neutralize a problem before it became public, even if it involved violating the law. No questions were asked. No excuses were provided. Cheri knew that the men who were chasing them had no qualms about taking out both her and Al.

She recalled an episode several years before when Josiah's personal financial manager had absconded with some funds. A few days later he was found dead in Moab, Utah, the apparent victim of a horrible motorcycle accident. The mandatory autopsy revealed absolutely nothing, except for those contusions, fractures, and mutilations one might expect from such an accident. The only strange part of the entire episode was the persistent rumor that Josiah's financial manager had never ridden a motorcycle in his whole life. Needless to say, the fearsome reputation of Josiah's hit team was further enhanced. The investigating officer, and current leader of the hunters behind her and Al, was none other than the man with the prognathous jaw. Only God knew what other extraordinary atrocities this man and his buddies were capable of, thought Cheri as she maneuvered Al to the bank of the river.

"Sorry to become an inconvenient cripple," he apologized as he hobbled through the foliage.

They both stiffened at the sound of a gunshot.

"Goddamn it!" he uttered, accelerating his pace.

"Gunfire is an underestimated motivator," she said, unable to avoid the graveyard humor.

"It's either the firing squad or hypothermia and drowning," Al said, referring to the Snake River below.

"I think we've finally come to a moment of existential choice," Cheri said. "Either a quick death or a slow, painful one. Sartre would be very proud of us."

"Well, I'm certainly happy to know that a dead French philosopher would take great pleasure in my present situation." Al spied their car at the base of the hill. It was completely destroyed. Tires, glass, and metal were strewn all over the ground and bushes.

"Great thinkers often frame difficult life problems in simple, comprehensible terms," Cheri countered.

More shots were fired in their direction. While they missed their targets, both Al and Cheri knew that the next ones might be more accurate. The existential choice would be completely eliminated by the forceful persuasion of a bullet.

Al picked up a semi-inflated spare tire that had been in the back of the car. "How about a midnight swim?"

"Now how could I refuse such a lovely invitation?" she responded. "Only a gentleman of the finest breeding and unspeakable desperation could come up with such an obviously ludicrous suggestion."

"Well?" Al asked, looking up the hill toward the clearly delineated outline of men descending.

"On the other hand," she said, grabbing one end of the rubber tube, "it's time for us to enjoy the full spectrum of nature's wonders."

"Madame," Al shouted as they both held onto the rubber tube and jumped into the river, "I admire both your courage and your unique way with words."

"Oh, my God," Cheri shouted as she hit the water. "Don't forget to meet me at the nearest Forest Ranger Station. I'll wait for you or you wait for me. Promise?" Her words were dissolved by the ravage sounds of the Snake River.

They were quickly swept into the rapid flow of the freezing river. The water raged around them like a restless lion intent on devouring its prey. It was impossible to think of anything except the infernal noise of imminent destruction.

Cheri, who had taken many rafting trips down the Colorado River, motioned to Al to copy her, and lie prone with his feet pointed downstream. If they were to hit any rocks, his outstretched feet would absorb the initial shock of the crash.

Al, who was at best a mediocre swimmer, followed Cheri's example and extended his feet out ahead of him. To his pleasant surprise, the ice cold water had numbed his left ankle so that he couldn't feel any pain. He was almost content to be bobbing up and down, thrown from rock to rock, like a ball in a pinball machine, rather than feeling the pain of his twisted tendons. "Let the good times roll," he repeated to himself as he swallowed his first mouthful of water. He was tempted to sing a few verses of Tina Turner's famous lyrics, "Rollin' . . . rollin' . . . rollin' down the river . . ." to control his fear, but the shock of the water eliminated any lyrical notions.

Suddenly, he was caught in a small whirlpool, spinning around and around as if in a washing machine, together with the debris left by tourists grinding away at him, scratching, tearing, cutting his skin. Blackness overwhelmed his coldness. He felt like a human corpse caught in a moment of nature's revenge. No longer able to hold his breath, he passed out.

Cheri was having a hard time keeping her head above water, despite her rafting experience. She saw Al in the distance, assaulted by turbulent currents of water, but there was very little that she could do to help him. In fact, there was very little she could do to help herself as she was pulled down the river at six miles an hour, choking on the water she swallowed. Her faith in their ability to survive the freezing cold and jutting rocks was waning.

Odd, she thought, what seemed important to her when her life was in danger. As a doctoral student of philosophy, she had focused on the concept of "faith," the one element in her life that had allowed her to proceed from brash graduate student to governor of a powerful state. Faith in God. Faith in herself through a failed marriage. And faith in an improbable political career. And at one time, faith in her country. But the latter had begun to shatter years before, like a sealed window glass under the relentless heat of a desert sun.

Her dissertation, in retrospect, had been entirely too academic in nature. The word "faith" was derived from the Latin *fidere* (to trust), a belief that transcends objective reality. She divided faith into two categories: those beliefs relating to religion and those that were inherently nonreligious, unexpected from a woman who had been strictly reared in the Catholic Church. *"Credo quia absurdum est,"* she thought to herself as she coughed up water, "I believe because it is absurd." Certainly, that characterized her present situation. Here she was, fleeing for her life, from the very people who only hours before were her staunch allies. And to preserve an idea in which she was no longer sure she had faith.

She was drifting downstream toward life or death in defiance of those Greek philosophers for whom reason was the determinant of what was to be believed.

Credo ut intelligam. I believe in order to understand, she thought. St. Augustine's thesis that faith had the determinative role, in contrast to reason, was far more appropriate to the situation. She smiled to herself for the first time since the shots had shattered the peace in the woods. Her life as a doctoral student had been magical. How much she had learned. How smart she had felt. St. Thomas Aquinas, in his more esoteric writings, had said that reason could carry some people further than others, but there were always articles of faith beyond the reach of the reason of any man. Bonaventure believed that faith helped those ones to pose the right questions and to avoid false assumptions. Herbert de Cherbury argued that one should begin with reason, proceeding afterward with faith. Pascal, the mathematician/philosopher, believed that faith related more to an *esprit de finesse,* to intuition, rather than a geometry of logic.

The philosophers and their ideas came rushing into her head, mirroring the increased speed with which she was traversing the river. John Toland believed that faith requires the confirmation of reason. Ritschl proposed that faith and reason were autonomous, each being preeminent in their respective spheres of influence. Troeltsch, to whom Cheri was especially attached because of his strong Catholic convictions, believed that Christian faith emerged from a dialectic between historical studies and the religious life. But this proposition had been contradicted by the famous Spanish philosopher Unamuno, who thought that the conflict of faith and reason led to the "tragic sense of life."

But it was the "I-thou" relationship of the Hebraic philosophers, particularly Martin Buber, for which Cheri was really reaching. That special relationship between man and God. That personal covenant individual man had made with God. It was within the folds of Hebraic thinking that she wanted to scream out, "Please God, don't let me die this way. It's unbecoming. It's absurd."

She was about to promise all types of compensation to God in return for salvation, until she hit a rock with such force that her legs crumbled in front of her. Her right shoulder bashed against something ragged, and she saw a small stream of her own blood trailing her in the water. As she pushed away from the rocks, she thought of the twentieth-century philosopher Santayana, who believed that "animal faith" was the primary drive that took man out of his moment of absurdity. It was her last thought as she spilled over a twenty-foot drop.

41

YELLOWSTONE NATIONAL PARK, WYOMING

Saturday, July 5th, 3:00 A.M.

Al regained consciousness to the insistent sound of Hagner's voice asking, "Can you hear me? Can you hear me?" and realized that for some reason that could only be explained by the miracle of human endurance, he, Al, was still alive. At least his heart was beating and his brain was transmitting neurological signals to the rest of his body. Perhaps it was the extreme coldness of the water that had acted like a natural deep-freeze mechanism, slowing his metabolism down so that he had needed only a fraction of the oxygen, nutrients, and metabolites normally required to stay alive in his frozen condition.

The complicated medical phenomenon of hypothermia had changed the physiology of his body, Al concluded. His body temperature had probably fallen below 35 degrees Centigrade. A man with his physique should have lost consciousness in ten minutes in the water and should have died thirty minutes later. Most of the medical studies done on hypothermia had come from patients who had been induced into that state as a prelude to cardiovascular surgery and neurosurgery. As the body approached 30 degrees Centigrade, there was a diminution in all physiological functions. Pulse rate, blood pressure, and metabolic rate fell drastically. Although shivering, hallucinations, and narcosis sometimes occurred, this was also the zone of maximal benefit to the surgical patient since the body's oxygen requirement was reduced 40 percent, allowing safer occlusion of the circulation.

His aching body convinced him that after being caught in the eddy he had bounced from rock to rock in a semiconscious state. He had no idea how long he had been lying on the banks of the river.

Hagner leaned over Al and shook him again. "Can you hear me?"

Al struggled to nod his head in assent.

"Great!" Hagner responded, turning toward a scholarly looking man standing next to him. "Al, meet Tommy, our friendly forest ranger."

Al nodded his head and managed a "hi."

"You're near Grant Village, a camping village with a country store and a group of tents," Tommy said. "Hagner and I will take you to my cabin and fix you up."

"Where's Cheri?" Al asked before he lapsed into a period of semiconsciousness. He was barely aware of the two sets of hands which carried him to a warmer place among the bushes, undressed him, wiped his body down with warm towels, dressed him in dry clothing, and wrapped him in blankets.

As Cheri fell over the twenty-foot waterfall she couldn't resist looking down. It was almost as if the laws of nature were running in reverse. Instead of gravity pulling her down, the swirling waters and jagged rocks were being pushed up. It was less a matter of Newtonian physics than some Darwinian imperative of nature's revenge. Cheri tried not to panic. If she became agitated in any way, what little oxygen she had retained in her lungs would be needlessly consumed. She would fall prey to the natural dynamic of exhaustion and drowning.

She shot through the cold water feet first, legs straight together, using them as natural shock absorbers. As soon as she hit the rocky bottom of the river, she shot back up again. With the force of the water tugging at her from all directions she started to swim toward the bank. She knew that drowning in water like this was not simply a matter of exhaustion but just a momentary lapse in her desire to remain afloat, because of all the effort it took. But the more she swam, the farther away the shore seemed. When she realized that she was still making no headway, she knew that she had to reevaluate her strategy. If she continued to swim in the same direction, she would simply exhaust herself to death. If she tried to swim across the river, she would never reach the other side. If she allowed herself to float downstream, she would be at the mercy of the jutting rocks and the next set of falls. And next time she might not navigate them so successfully.

The only reasonable approach left was to collect all her thoughts and energy and focus on some point across the river. Using the Australian crawl, her most powerful stroke, and with the determination that can only arise from desperation, she placed one fatigued arm out in front of the other, followed by the next. Right. Left. Right. Left. Her shoulders ached. Her hands were beyond the point of feeling. She wasn't sure that her legs were actually responding to her desire to kick. Her neck was a continuous punching bag for the unrestrained fury of the river. The pain all over her body was so intense that she had to consciously force herself from retching. The only thing she kept focused on was a space on the shore between a rock and a twisted tree. She didn't even care whether the rock or the tree were real or simply hallucinations. All she knew was that she had a goal, a purpose, a destination. And if she didn't keep her focus, she would be finished.

It took Cheri what seemed to be an eternity to enter calmer waters and swim to shore. She lay on a small strip of pebbles, cold and wet, trying to figure out where she was. And if Al was alive.

She had crawled out of her watery grave convinced that she and Al must stop the insanity the governors had started. She felt remorse for the citizens of Page who would soon lose their property and their lives by the act of terror committed against the federal government. Casualties of war. The innocent victims of a major power play that she had finally decided was unnecessary.

She sat up, pleased that all of her limbs were intact. Now

if she could just find her way to Grant Village and the Forest Ranger Station. From there, she could . . . She wasn't sure what she would do. Try to find Al? Find her own security agents? Alert Washington? But of what?

She had walked no farther than fifty yards down the beach when she came upon three familiar men huddled together. "If I didn't know any better, I would wonder who had brought the burgers and buns," Cheri announced as she picked up a dry towel. Her wet clothing wrapped around her like a mummy. Her skin was wrinkled and had been completely bleached of all vitality by the water.

"Cheri!" Al stood up and with Hagner's help they both rushed over to her. Each one was more solicitous than the other. Their overlapping dialogue and concerns forced her to plead with them to stop so that she could be heard.

"Guys, I appreciate your attention. My needs are quite simple—dry clothes, a hot shower, a large steak with a baked potato, followed by strongly brewed coffee. And then about three days of sleep under fourteen layers of blankets."

"I think we can accommodate you on almost all your requests," Al said, "except for the fourteen layers of blankets. I believe we have only thirteen left." He took her in his arms and gave her a big hug. "You should never go swimming without your buddy. Didn't you learn that in swim class one-oh-one?"

"I'm really glad to see you, too," she said, shivering from the cold. "But let go, or you'll be sopping wet."

"That's all right," he replied, holding her face in his hands. "Next time don't forget to wear your life vest."

"Call me Tommy, your friendly forest ranger," Tommy said, shaking Cheri's wet hand. "I think that I can certainly provide the dry clothes, if you all follow me to my cabin."

They walked as quickly as one limping man and one shivering woman could to a small log cabin only a quarter of a mile away. The wood-burning stove, four unmade bunk beds, four semibroken chairs, and one combination table/desk looked better to them than any page from *GH* magazine. The yellow-tainted poster of Smokey the Bear on one wall, warning about the dangers of forest fires, completed the picture of a no-nonsense ranger station.

Tommy quickly wrapped Al's ankle in an Ace bandage and poured two cups of tea into two metal cups for Al and Cheri. "We've got to get you out of those wet clothes before you get pneumonia." He pulled a green duffel bag out from under one of the beds and took out a pile of dry clothing. "I think you'll find something in here to change into," he said, giving them to Cheri.

Cheri separated the items in the pile. "Let me see what the latest fashions are in this part of the country. Well, we have one pair of oversized denim pants, a man's plaid flannel shirt, mismatched socks, rust-stained underpants, and a thick woolen sweater peppered with moth holes."

"Will that be cash or credit?" Al asked, unable to hide the sheer joy he felt in seeing her again. For a moment, while he was recovering on the beach, he thought that his life would be dreadfully empty if Cheri didn't show up again. And now she was here. All spit and fire.

"I'm sorry, sir," Cheri responded playfully, dragging the clothes to the corner of the cabin, where she changed behind a towel. "But I'm afraid I've lost my credit cards."

"A likely story," Al responded. "Hagner, arrest her and book her on charges of attempted fraud."

"Yes, sir." Hagner laughed. He, too, was pleased to see both Al and Cheri safe and together again. God forbid anything should have happened to them. How would he explain to the Sec State that he had lost not only Barbara's favorite doctor but the governor of Colorado?

"Tommy, do you happen to have something useful around here like makeup?" Cheri asked jokingly.

"As a matter of fact . . ." Tommy rummaged through a shoe box marked Lost and Found and pulled out a cracked compact containing face powder, a red-orange lipstick, and a bottle marked Eau de Toilette. He enjoyed the look of surprise on Cheri's face.

She took the items and attempted to transform herself into her image of a governor.

Although watching her primp was enjoyable, Al was acutely aware that time was moving on.

"By the way, Hagner, that was some quick thinking on

your part,'' Cheri said, wondering what Al might have found out from Hagner.

''Thank you,'' Hagner said. ''Sorry about my having to pull out my gun and place you both under arrest. . . .''

''That's okay,'' Cheri interrupted brusquely. ''You had to do whatever was necessary to get us out of that impossible situation. We were surrounded by nothing but the governors' henchmen.''

''By placing you both under arrest,'' Hagner continued, ''I was able to throw Josiah's men off balance. It allowed them to continue to think that I was still with them. At least it bought me enough time for both of you to get away.''

''But the last time I saw you,'' Al said, sipping his third cup of tea, ''you were sprawled out on the ground, wounded by a bullet.''

''It's amazing how effective these bullet-proof vests are,'' Hagner replied, tapping his chest. ''It's composed of Twaron 2000, microfilament fibers. I'm sure you're interested to learn that my life was saved by a combination of 60 percent polyester and 40 percent cotton.''

''But how did you get away?'' Al asked.

''The same way you did,'' he answered. ''I managed to 'borrow' a car, too. I figured that you'd head toward the only Forest Ranger outpost within one hundred miles,'' Hagner continued, ''which means that your final destination had to be this luxurious cabin.''

''Considering that I felt totally lost myself, you did a great job of tracking us,'' Al said, wondering whether there was something important that Hagner was not revealing. There were a lot of missing pieces to the puzzle which still had to be filled in.

''It really didn't take all that much. I saw the car go off the road,'' Hagner replied, ''knew the direction and speed of the currents, and made some quick calculations about how fast and far you could go. . . .''

''Assuming we would still be alive,'' Al interrupted.

''You sound as if you are interrogating the poor man,'' Cheri said, ''instead of being grateful for his having saved your life.''

''Our lives,'' Al added.

"That's right, Al," she corrected herself. "Our lives."

"I stopped along the road from time to time," Hagner answered. "With the large searchlight that was in the car I would run to the shoulder of the road and watch you both floating downstream past me."

"On behalf of the both of us," Cheri said in a conciliatory voice, "I want to thank you for having watched out for us and made certain that we would come out of this melodrama alive."

"No thanks are needed, Governor," Hagner responded, blushing. "I was simply doing my duty." He paused and added, "By the way, Tommy, where's your telephone?"

"Sorry," Tommy replied. "The power lines have been down for a couple of days and there are no portables. Budget limitations have ruled out my having a fax, or a cellular. The nearest phone is ten miles from here."

"Well, ladies and gentlemen," Hagner announced calmly, "that's not good news. By my calculation, Josiah's boys are only a few minutes away from finding this cabin. If I found you both . . ."

Al turned toward Tommy. "Is there any way that you could put me into direct contact with someone from the local Indian tribe?" Al asked. "Or to a Washington representative of the Bureau of Indian Affairs?"

"As I told you before, not without a telephone," Tommy responded.

"Do I sense a strategy forming?" Cheri asked, naively.

"Strategy number two, to be exact," Al responded.

"There are over three dozen tribes between here, the Rocky Mountains, and the Mississippi River. The Arapaho, the Arikara, the Blackfoot, the Cheyenne, the Crow, the Hidatsa, the Iowa, the Mandan, the Osage, the Pawnee, the Sioux, the Wichita, the Kiowa-Apache, the Plains Cree, and Sarci. To name a few. Which one are you interested in?" Cheri asked.

"You'll know soon," Al responded cryptically, making it very clear that he still had his doubts about her. "But it would help me out to know what the governors are planning next."

"I don't know," she responded apologetically. "If Josiah

has plans, he hadn't shared them with any of the governors, including me.''

''And you really don't know what the next disaster will be?'' Al asked again.

''No. Each governor was responsible for working out the details of his own part in the secessionist plan. It was an extremely compartmentalized operation. We were going to be sharing plans during our meetings at the Lodge. I had planned the flood. Josiah was to develop plans for Phase Two, but he had been very closemouthed about the details. Whenever I asked him about the several scenarios the governors had previously discussed, he'd brush me off saying, 'Let's hope we don't need to get to Phase Two.' I'm afraid that our momentous horseback ride came before we governors could share our plans with each other.''

''You've gotten to know Josiah pretty well by now,'' Al said, sensing that she hadn't revealed everything she knew. ''If you were he, what would you do next?''

Before Cheri could answer, Hagner put his index finger up to his lips in a gesture of silence. He walked to the window and pressed his face against a pane of glass, peering out into the darkness. ''There are half-a-dozen flashlights, two hundred yards away. And I don't think they are interested in hot tea.''

''Let's get the hell out of here,'' Al said.

''I can't go,'' Tommy stated flatly. ''Someone from the Forest Rangers has to be here, by law. Sorry, guys, I've got a job to do.''

Tommy shut the lights in the cabin, shook hands with each of them silently, and gestured toward the window at the back of the cabin.

''What about the next disaster?'' Al asked Cheri again as they climbed through the window that faced the woods in the back of the cabin.

''Hoover Dam, I think,'' she muttered, with a sense of panic in her voice. ''Five times the magnitude of Glen Canyon in its flooding and power capacity. This time it will be very clear to the country—and the world. . . . And the federal government will be forced to capitulate . . . or go to war.''

"I appreciate that bit of information," Al said, trying to sound conciliatory.

"By the way," Cheri said as she walked quickly in the dark. "Don't be surprised if we meet a very handsome Indian along the way."

"And who might that be?" Al asked, puzzled by her statement.

"Just the elected leader of the tribes I mentioned a few minutes ago," Cheri replied. "He lives close by here. And I think he's just the man you want to see in order to implement your Phase Two."

"How do you know about him?" Al asked.

"Let's just say that a woman of discretion and fashion," she responded coquettishly, "still has to retain some secrets in her personal life. Otherwise the man she loves might not find her all that alluring." She proceeded to run ahead to catch up to Hagner, leaving a slightly limping Al behind.

"Would you mind repeating that again?" Al called out, stunned. Had he heard correctly? At this moment of extreme danger to both of them, had she just professed her love to him?

"Which part?" Cheri shouted back.

"The one about . . ."

Al's words were interrupted by the sound of a gunshot reverberating through the night.

42

PARIS, FRANCE

Saturday, July 5th, 11:45 A.M.

Lighting up a Gauloise cigarette, the diminutive man with the carefully coiffed mustache fastened the metal handcuff to his right wrist, put the key in his pocket, and placed the worn, deep brown leather courier pouch on the front seat of his green 1980 Volvo. He turned the ignition key on and pressed a radio station that played French oldies but goodies. The man sang along with the words of a song by Johnny Holliday, one of the 1960s teen idols, as he pulled out of the American Embassy. The African-American Marine guard at the gate waved him forward. As the antiterrorism metal barrier lowered into the ground, the man behind the steering wheel laughed to himself. If a terrorist wanted to either enter or leave the American Embassy, that barrier was the most worthless deterrent in the world, especially with formidable new variations of the C4 plastique explosive. But Americans will always be Americans, he thought, and smiled again. They only learn from major catastrophes. But in all honesty, so did his own countrymen, the French, or more precisely those inhabitants from around Toulouse-Albi-Carcassone, the Languedoc region. A region as different from Paris in culture and manner as New York City was to Mobile, Alabama.

He drove carefully into the chaotic traffic circle known as the Place de la Concorde, glancing at his leather briefcase to make certain that it would not be unnecessarily jarred from the frequent stops. While the radio blared his favorite song, "Un Million de Chinois et Moi," he put his foot on the accelerator and maneuvered his way into the center of traffic. This was a prescient song that twenty-five years ago had depicted the tragic state of overpopulation in China. But the overpopulation had not changed. Except that now the problem was all over the world. Even the Americans had a problem of illegal immigrants. Somehow they had learned how to incorporate these people into their society. One way or another, these illegal immigrants became productive members of the United States. In France, things didn't work out as well. The politicians allowed unlimited access to the North African countries, from which immigrants displaced workers all over the country. Especially in his city, Toulouse, the center of Aerospatiale, a French-British-German consortium that produced the Airbus 330 and the Concorde. Instead of creating new jobs for the African immigrants, the French government, using governmental subsidies, displaced French nationalists with illegals. No wonder he had become a member of the Toulousean Secessionist Movement, a quasi-political/terrorist organization that had been in existence for over five years. He truly believed that Toulouse and other regional hubs would at some point in the foreseeable future secede from France and set up a separate confederation. Much like in Belgium, where the country was partitioned into several segments in 1993, with a newly written constitution which empowered all of the minority parties. Because there had been no fighting or violence, no one in the world took any notice of it. Certainly not CNN or the American public. But soon they would take notice of the Toulousean Separationist Movement. "Un million de Chinois et moi . . ."

He carefully maneuvered his way around the stone obelisk that Napoleon had stolen from Egypt, across the way from the Rodin Museum on Rue de Varenne.

He drove over the Pont de la Concorde. Just his luck, today was one of the hottest days of the year and his goddamn air conditioner didn't work. He turned the little knob that controlled the flow of cool air, but nothing came out.

How he wished that he had one of those big beautiful Cadillacs with all the comforts and pleasures that only a full-sized American car could provide. He made a right-hand turn onto Pont de l'Alma toward the Quai d'Orsay, the French Foreign Ministry.

As he drove along the Seine, glancing at the artists with their easels, the booksellers, and souvenir peddlers, he knew that he would miss it all. Despite his antipathy to the overly centralized French government, he still was a French patriot whose father had fought in the World War II French Resistance, Le Maquis, and whose mother was a third generation "pied noir." Very early on in life his mother would nurse him on the importance of self-sufficiency and autonomy. In part, he had gotten his rebellious streak from his mother who, if truth be known, was part Corsican and part Italian. So when she talked about Toulousean independence to him, he couldn't help but think that she was really referring to the independence of Corsica, the island where Napoleon Bonaparte had been born.

As he turned into the guarded Quai d'Orsay, a French policeman asked him for identification and, once reviewed, nodded his head to indicate that he was pleased with what he saw. He motioned the car forward.

The man parked in the space marked Courier. At the front desk, he introduced himself to the seated policeman and informed him that he was the official courier for the American Embassy. The policeman wanted to know why the American courier was French and not American, but when the man threw down a slew of identification cards and papers in righteous indignation, which was the only attitude to assume with obdurate bureaucrats, the policeman was satisfied. He had concluded that the Americans were still subcontracting all of their support services to French companies. The second thing that the policeman wanted to know was what was in the briefcase. Playing coy, the man said that it was nothing of importance to the policeman but belonged upstairs in the Department of Couriers where all sensitive information was stored. If the policeman wanted to inspect the contents of the briefcase, he contended, he would have to give him a receipt that showed that the package had been delivered to the Quai d'Orsay. Seeing no harm in this simple bureaucratic demand, the policeman signed the paper and bade the courier good-bye, if not good riddance.

The courier walked quickly to his car and started the ignition. Even the guard at the gate was surprised at how hastily this diminutive man left the Foreign Ministry.

This time the driver drove down the Avenue de la Tour Maubourg, parallel to the Boulevard des Invalides. As he parked the car in a run-down garage, he heard the explosion. He quickly melded into the crowd at the subway entrance and boarded a train for Orly Airport where he would take a direct, nonstop Air-Inter half-hour flight to Toulouse.

Mon dieu, he thought, *comme ces Américans sont malins.* My God, he thought, these Americans are so mischievous.

43

YELLOWSTONE NATIONAL PARK, WYOMING

Saturday, July 5th, 6:10 A.M.

Daylight brought with it the clarity of danger that surrounded Al, Cheri, and Hagner. Even the sign a few hundred yards from the cabin they had just left was a warning written in large, bold-faced type: DANGEROUS THERMAL AREAS: BOILING WATER; THIN CRUSTS; ALWAYS STAY ON CONSTRUCTED WALKWAYS.

Al looked at both Cheri and Hagner, who in turn were looking at him for leadership.

"*Quo vadis, Domine?* Wherefore goest thou, Lord?" Cheri asked, parodying the question that Peter had allegedly asked Christ.

Al took what seemed to be an interminably long five seconds to assess the landscape. In front of them stretched what looked like miles of walkways constructed of wooden planks, branching out in several directions. The walkways sat about one foot above an area called Fountain Paint Pot, a geological variation of a witch's cauldron. Everywhere he looked, Al saw geysers, bubbling mud pots, hissing steam vents, or boiling springs. Here and there were patches of algae, small shrubs, and vegetation, which Al could only identify by its rainbow colors. What little botany he recalled from his college days reminded him that the different colors on the surface of a liquid were formed from bacteria and algae that could live in very hot water. In fact, the green, yellow, and orange mats of color that surrounded him served as temperature indicators. Not all bacteria died in hot water. There were certain types of hot-springs bacteria, called cyanobacteria, which lived in water 167 degrees Fahrenheit. At this temperature the bacteria appeared as yellow organisms but became progressively darker as the water became cooler. At temperatures significantly less than 167 degrees, the bacteria turned a rust or brown color, enhanced by deposits of sulfur, iron oxides, and arsenic sulfide. This meant that some areas in front of them were cool enough to walk through.

From where he stood, the sounds of men searching the cabin were audible to Al. Within minutes, their pursuers would figure out that they had left and would be on the trail behind them. And from the flat, dull sameness of the terrain, he, Cheri, and Hagner would be perfect targets.

As they stood there, deciding which way to go, the sound of a bullet whizzed by. Al started running as fast as he could on the wooden boards and Cheri and Hagner kept pace. But Al knew that as long as they stayed on the walkway it would be like shooting sitting ducks.

"On the count of three," Al yelled to Cheri and Hagner, "I want you to jump over the railing and start running through this muddy basin. If we just aim for the dark patches, we'll be okay. If any one of us gets into trouble, the others must continue to dry land. This muck must end somewhere!"

"Wait a minute," Cheri said with astonishment. "That's scalding water. Either we'll burn to death or we'll sink and die."

"You'll just have to trust me," Al yelled back. "Three, two"—Al started to climb over the railing as another bullet screamed by—"one," and he jumped onto the rust-colored hydrothermal turf.

"I'm not going down there," Cheri proclaimed, watching Al sink about three feet into the mud.

"Over you go," Hagner said, pushing Cheri over the side. He knew that Al was correct. If they stayed on the walkway it was only a matter of time before a bullet hit one of them.

Then Hagner climbed the railing, hoisted himself over,

and landed on a patch of what looked like rust-colored moss. Once his legs hit bottom, he felt as if he were standing on an air mattress with no firm backing. When he picked up one leg to walk, the other leg would sink farther down. But he realized that he was in no danger of actually drowning.

"Are you guys all right?" Al asked as he slugged through the mixture of mud, moss, and hot water. It was hot, as he had guessed correctly, but not scalding.

Cheri started to laugh. They were all covered in a layer of brown slime. So much for her newly applied makeup.

Hagner's grimace made it quite clear that he was not enjoying the experience.

"I've often wondered whether a mudbath really enhances beauty." Cheri laughed, rubbing some on her face. "I guess I'm going to find out."

"Now you're getting the hang of it," Al said, realizing that Cheri was creating a very effective camouflage. He started to rub the mud all over his face and body. Hagner followed suit.

From the assassins' perspective, Al, Cheri, and Hagner were becoming indistinguishable from their environment. Except for the variety of sounds coming from the thermal area, all objects on the horizon were now some shade of brown. It was getting increasingly more difficult to fix the runners in their gun sights. Hell, thought the Utah State Trooper with the prognathous jaw, hunting humans was a hell of a lot more challenging than hunting animals.

Al moved as quickly as he could through the hot, muddy, bubbling springs. A row of trees seemed to be in the near distance at the edge of the basin. He needed to get to them . . . fast. And from there, a road and a telephone. Barbara Reynolds needed to know about Hoover Dam.

Al decided that their pursuers were probably more concerned with killing Cheri than either he or Hagner. She was now not only a traitor to the secessionist cause, but Josiah knew she had information that could possibly prevent the second catastrophe. And with the rest of her knowledge, she alone could destroy the movement.

"We've got to get out of here before we become archaeological specimens to be dug up in a thousand years," Cheri said, stepping from one muddy brown patch of algae to another, thankfully missing the small geysers of hot water which shot straight up into the air at random intervals.

"This stuff is like glue," Al said. He grabbed Cheri's hand and, in the process of trying to help her, tripped and brought them both facedown in the proverbial mudhole. "So much for the helping hand," Al said, exploding into laughter.

Within another five minutes of struggling through the mud, a shoreline clearly emerged. Al, Cheri, and Hagner headed toward it with the speed and deliberation of thirsty men in the desert heading for an oasis. Al was the first one to drag his body from the mud to the rocks. The others were right behind him.

"Welcome," a tall man with a ponytail greeted them. "You had better hurry up." He extended his arm to each, helping them climb onto higher ground. He was surrounded by ten men, each carrying a rifle or semiautomatic weapon.

"Daniel!" Cheri blurted out as she stood up. "I can't tell you how happy I am to see you." She looked at her mud-soaked clothes. "Ordinarily, I'd give you a big hug . . ."

"Mud or no mud, I'm not going to miss a hug from my favorite governor," Daniel Bloodhawk said, pulling her toward him.

"All right, you're on," Cheri said, running into his arms. "When are you going to stop being so goddamn attractive?"

Cheri adored Chief Daniel Bloodhawk, part Apache, part Navajo, presently elected leader of the Western Council of Native-Born Americans. Not only was he extremely good-looking, he was also politically shrewd and totally dedicated to the cause of Native American rights. And she enjoyed his ability to laugh at himself and his cause. It made him real.

"Chief Bloodhawk," she said, "I want you to meet my two companions. You know DSA Hagner . . ."

"Good to see you again," Bloodhawk said, extending his hand in greeting. "I'm glad to see that you're still taking good care of the governor."

Al looked at Hagner, finding Bloodhawk's comment strange—DSAs were, by law, assigned to foreign officials.

And, as far as Al knew, Colorado was not yet a foreign country.

"It's always a pleasure to work with you," Hagner responded.

"And this is my new traveling companion, Dr. Alison Carter," Cheri added, pulling Al over to her and personally planting him in front of Daniel. "He represents Secretary of State Barbara Reynolds."

"Ah, a good person, your boss," Bloodhawk responded. "An honor to meet you, Dr. Carter."

"Good to meet you, chief," Al said, shaking Bloodhawk's hand. "In fact, I've come with a message from the Secretary . . ."

"I'm sorry to interrupt you," Bloodhawk said, "but my first task is to keep you all safe." He nodded his head in the direction of the muddy springs and his men provided covering firepower while Al, Cheri, and Hagner followed him into the woods. Within two minutes of rushing through trees and underbrush they arrived at a dirt road with several waiting cars.

"I need to discuss an important matter with you," Al said to Bloodhawk as their jeep sped down the road.

"Let me guess," Bloodhawk said, pushing his foot down on the accelerator. "You want to ask me if I, as the chief representative of the Western Council of Native-Born Americans, can support Washington, D.C., in its endeavor to maintain the integrity of the United States."

Al didn't say a word. He looked at him with a host of questions that he, Al, couldn't answer. How had Bloodhawk known what he had come for? In fact, how had Bloodhawk known that they were coming? Clearly, Bloodhawk had worked with Cheri before. But why did he know Hagner?

"I'd say that that was an awfully good guess," Al responded. "How did you know?"

"Let's just say I was informed," Bloodhawk answered cryptically, not thinking it necessary to make his source known. After all, he, Bloodhawk, was the chief.

44

GLEN CANYON DAM, PAGE, ARIZONA

Saturday, July 5th, 8:30 A.M.

From Brigadier General Jason Montague's perspective the assault on the Glen Canyon Dam was a soldier's nightmare.

Over the past few hours, working from the National Military Command and Control Center in Washington, D.C., Jason had to hastily assemble a group of soldiers. He knew what type of troops he needed, but he wouldn't have the time to integrate them into one cohesive fighting force.

Jason's assault unit was composed of the 4th Cavalry Division, five Special Forces units from Fort Bragg, components of the Air Force, Navy SEALs, and, most important, the newly created unit of cyberstrategists located at the Army Intelligence and Security Command at Fort Belvoir, Virginia. He had put them all together into a fighting unit nicknamed "Jason's Raiders" for want of a better designation. The mission was coded "Operation Dambuster." And the glue that held the entity together was Jason's personal relationship with the commanders of the different components. He had been given carte blanche from the Sec Def and priority clearance to secund anyone he wanted in "quick time." But he knew from previous experiences in the world's hot spots—the Persian Gulf, Somalia, Bosnia, Liberia—that there was no more effective organizational glue than that of professional respect, personal comradery, and shared battlefield experience.

If most generals had to worry about the cloud of war during a battle, the uncertainty and confusion that normally arises during an ongoing firefight engagement, Jason had to worry about the cloud of war before the firefight even began. Because of the speed with which the groups had been secunded, there were no clean lines of command and control. Weapon deployment was scattered, battle-unit configuration was confusing, and there was no tactical clarity of operation. To Jason's disappointment, there just wasn't enough time to prepare this motley group of volunteer soldiers, all of whom were willing to risk their own lives to preserve the integrity of the Union. But each man knew that if he failed in securing the dam, there would be no second chance.

Jason rode in the forward UH-60L Blackhawk along with eight Special Forces soldiers dressed in their "chocolate chip" (Battle Dress Uniforms), a tan-based fabric with various shades of brown and gray to help personnel "disappear" against the desertlike topography of the terrain.

Jason had done what countless numbers of his predecessors had done in similar crises around the world. He had combined, on an ad hoc basis, several Army, Navy, Air Force, winged and armored cav units into one hopefully seamless fighting unit that had a clear mission statement. In this case, the objective was to secure the Glen Canyon Dam as swiftly as possible with the least amount of casualties on both sides. Limiting casualties, he thought, was definitely going to be a problem. The fact that his troops were attacking in daylight was certainly detrimental to the element of surprise which most field commanders relied on for a strategic advantage over their adversary. He was also denied the advantage of tactical flexibility because of the limited space within which he could operate. There were only so many maneuvers that he could engage in at the dam. But the fact that he had the best fighting troops anywhere in the world, bar none, gave him an immense amount of consolation. The closest thing to the perfect soldier, he smiled, was once defined by a Marine Commandant as "one without a mother."

Looking out of the helicopter door, he realized that they were over the Colorado River, approaching Lake Powell. In less than two minutes they would be over the dam. Only one thing really bothered him. This would be the first time in more than one hundred years that American soldiers were about to engage other Americans on American soil. Not since the Civil War had American fought American. It took World War I to heal the wounds of the Civil War by allowing Northerners and Southerners to fight together once again against a common enemy, the Germans. Perhaps it would take another war against a foreign enemy, maybe against China, he speculated, to heal the divisive wounds within his country. But he couldn't worry about that problem right now.

He raised his left hand and tapped his index finger against his watchface to indicate that in one minute they would be over the dam.

According to Operation Dambuster, the following things should have happened before Brigadier General Jason Montague landed at the dam, all orchestrated by Colonel Nicholas Holland, commander of the Army Intelligence and Security Command. In the first part of the operation, a Delta Force commando unit should have detonated a nonnuclear electromagnetic-pulse device the size of a suitcase. The EMP bomb, which was to be placed near the Information Center at the dam, should have fried the opponents' command, control, and communications capability, making it impossible for any one part of the National Guard Forces to communicate with any other part. According to SIGINT and ELINT that Jason had just received, no electronic transmission of any sort had been picked up by the NSA. That type of intelligence meant to Jason that the soldiers on the ground were either in complete radio silence or their computer and electronic capability had been knocked out as planned.

The second part of the "info-attack," as Jason liked to call it, had been tasking the CIA to insert computer viruses into the switching networks of all the National Guard headquarters. This should have been easy to accomplish, since in order to continue the degradation of the different state communication systems, the CIA specifically bred electronics-eating microbes.

The third part of the strategic plan of this "cyberwar" included using Commando Solo, a slow, chunky, propeller-driven aircraft, to jam the communications on the dam and substitute its own messages on any frequency. Jason had pulled this workhorse from the 193rd Special Operations Group, a Pennsylvania Air National Guard Unit. He recalled how successful the 193rd had been during the Persian Gulf War when the crew broadcasted radio reports to Iraqi soldiers eager to hear uncensored news of the war. As a result of broadcasts of the next areas to be targeted by U.S. bombers, many Iraqi soldiers deserted those positions. Commando Solo had also been effective in preparing Haiti for the U.S. intervention when it beamed into the island radio and TV messages from deposed President Jean-Bertrand Aristide. As Jason prepared to lead, specialists from the Army's 4th Psychological Operations Group were already preparing the tapes for Commando Solo which used morphed images of all four governors to convince the soldiers on the dam to give up because the secessionist movement had been defeated.

Fourth, the strategy included using logic bombs, carried by flying mechanical drones, to shut down computers that ran the railroad, trucking, and support systems and to redirect the supplies to another site that would normally have gone to the rebel soldiers on the dam.

Jason stood over the open hatch of the Blackhawk, holding on to one of the three rappel ropes that hung on each side of the helicopter as it hovered over the rim of the dam. At this point, the helicopter and the men inside were extremely vulnerable to groundfire or Stinger missiles.

He motioned to his colleagues to start descent. At precisely 830 hours Operation Dambuster commenced. The future of the United States of America was about to be determined.

General Montague and six of his Special Forces rappelled down the ropes onto a dam walkway in precisely six seconds. Although commanding generals were forbidden from leading an assault, Jason had made it a condition of his employment to be able to lead the battle if he was to plan the strategy. Barbara and Phil knew better than to argue with Jason.

As the crackle of gunfire surrounded them, Jason cradled

his 5.56mm M16A2 Armalite assault rifle in his arms. He directed his men to secure the dam's crest quietly and quickly and was pleasantly surprised to find that the crest of the dam was guarded with far fewer rebel forces than he had been told. In contrast to the one hundred or so men that were supposed to be on guard at the top of the dam, there were, at most, two dozen rebels. Not very impressive, he thought.

As he looked up into the skies, Jason was emboldened by the sight of countless Special Forces soldiers rappelling from numerous helicopters hovering in the air. To the civilian hostages, he thought, it must look like an invasion of giant black locusts beating their wings in a cacophony of whirring engines and straining metal. It was one of the most beautiful sights he had ever seen. Just for sheer numbers and coordination of attack, he knew that he had chosen the right unit. The 4th Air Cavalry Squadron hovering above him was as special as the reputation which preceded it. In all, the sky was blanketed with seventy-four helicopters—twenty-six attack, twenty-seven scout, eighteen transport, and three electronic warfare. And from each of the helicopters, men, equipment, or supplies were being lowered onto the dam and over the Information Center.

Rebel forces with their arms raised high up in the air were being disgorged from the bowels of the dam. They, in turn, were followed by civilians who had been held hostage, who were hugging and kissing the soldiers who had come to liberate them.

"General, behind you!" a Special Forces Staff Sergeant shouted with anxiety in his voice.

Jason swung around and without a moment's hesitation opened fire, letting loose 30 rounds of 5.56mm ammunition at a 950 rpm cycle.

A man in his early sixties dropped face forward onto the ground. His body was splattered with blood. As far as anyone knew, Robert Benson, the town eccentric, had become the first and only casualty of the assault on the dam. An innocent bystander, in the wrong place, at the wrong time.

45

CAMBRIDGE, ENGLAND

Saturday, July 5th, 11:45 A.M.

The attractive woman in her early thirties wore the prerequisite attire of the Cambridge University graduate student, who reluctantly apes those "untutored Americans": blue jeans, a loose transparent blouse, sandals, and a huge backpack containing books by the pound. In this case, Birdie, a code name used for this assignment, carried contents far more dangerous than the accumulated knowledge she was presumed to have gathered from her philosophy books. She walked along the banks of the Cam River unimpressed by the buildings comprising one of the oldest institutions of learning in Great Britain.

Her advanced degree in political science was, possibly, less important to her than her skills in the martial arts, explosives, and covert actions. At the "farm," the CIA's training grounds in Virginia, she had been considered one of the best and brightest in her class. While in training, she had spent many weekends at Williamsburg, a reconstructed eighteenth-century village depicting the living conditions of the American colonialists during the Revolutionary War period. How ironic, she thought, as she crossed the Silver Street Bridge into Queens College, that two hundred years after the American Revolution she was now part of another revolution, and once again directed against England. The real irony this time was that England was America's closest ally and what she was about to do could tear that alliance apart. But she had no choice. Based on this morning's briefing, as part of a team of American counterinsurgents sent all over England from London, to Cambridge, to Oxford, and to the munitions factories in the city of Manchester, their objective was clear: inflict enough damage so that Prime Minister Sir Reginald Lowell would think twice about his continued participation in a secessionist movement against the federal government of the United States.

As she passed a group of madrigal balladeers singing Elizabethan songs, she wondered if the Prime Minister would realize that the violent actions to be taken against England within the next twenty-four hours would be executed by American agents and not some terrorist group like the Irish Republican Army. One of her compatriots was already organizing a massive demonstration to be held in Trafalgar Square, denouncing the Prime Minister's ineffectiveness and inattentiveness to domestic problems, some of which she was helping to create. The rest of the plan was unknown to her. There was just no need for her to know. The one principle determining access to knowledge that had been ingrained in her throughout her training, and which she respected as necessary, was the "need to know." Soon, the British Prime Minister would know that these simultaneous acts of terrorism were directed against his country by the United States, when Barbara Reynolds would tell him, in no uncertain terms, that his support for the secessionist movement had to end. Of course, Reynolds would publicly condemn the "sudden rash of irresponsible violence" in an ally country.

Birdie had argued that on a tactical level the Americans had to choose their targets very carefully. Too much damage inflicted at the heart of England might definitely backfire against the United States. The targets had to be more symbolic than actual in importance. And most important, the Americans had to make certain that the targets they chose would not incur British retaliation. Birdie knew that British intelligence and counterintelligence were impressive. The Zimmerman Telegram was just one example of their brilliance. By intercepting a German message to the Mexican

Government, which encouraged a Mexican invasion of the United States, the British were able to counter American isolationist sentiments and force the President of the United States to enter World War I on the side of the British. Britain's MI-5 and MI-6 helped the United States to develop its own intelligence service, beginning with "Wild Bill" Donovan's OSS and ending with the creation of the CIA. To be sure, almost every major British official involved in helping the U.S. to develop its own intelligence service, including Kim Philby and Sir Anthony Blount, was primarily an NKVD or GRU Soviet intelligence operative, but that wasn't found out until fifty years later. So it was no accident that the Russians knew about the development of the atomic bomb from the very beginning.

So in some vague sense Birdie felt very little guilt about what she was about to do. In her judgment, the British had always been, at best, an untrustworthy ally. In fact, without stretching the point too far, she could rationalize that despite a shared common language and heritage, the British were the ultimate exploiter, manipulator, and traitor to U.S. interests at home and abroad. And their assistance to an American secessionist movement was the final straw that broke the camel's back.

Birdie's immediate objective was simple: leave the backpack in one of the small bookstores at Cambridge University which specialized in books on the American Revolutionary War period. The target was symbolic, highly irreverent, if not sacrilegious, but no one would get hurt. And senior British officials would understand that this small unfortunate incident was simply a warning to them to stay out of U.S internal affairs. In one way, she was merely reenacting the part her ancestors had played in Waltham, Massachusetts, when they drove the British out of the colonies. But this time, because of the low-intensity level of the operation, the chance of British retaliation against America was minimal.

As she entered the courtyard of Queens College, founded by the wife of Henry VI and the wife of Edward IV, she watched a group of students play high-speed Frisbee. It was hard for her to believe that the very steps she was walking on were the same ones that Newton, Darwin, and Cromwell had walked several hundred years before.

The university ambience reminded her of her undergraduate days in California at Stanford University. After a grueling four semesters she was finally able to relax with a Frisbee and her friends in front of Hoover Tower. But she wondered what it would have been like if some innocent-looking co-ed, like herself, had simply walked into the Stanford bookstore when it was closing and then set off a bomb. She consoled herself with the fact that she was not destroying either valuable manuscripts or human lives.

Tiger lilies swaying in the breeze, bicyclists racing across campus, missing each other by a hair's breadth, buildings which had focused a country's meaning for centuries were all irrelevant, and possibly emotionally cumbersome, if one dwelled upon them too long. The Gothic towers and stained-glass windows of the buildings made Birdie feel as if she were entering some variation of Disneyland. It helped her, in some small measure, to minimize the human aspect of the "minor accident" for which she would be responsible.

It was two minutes before closing time and most students were exiting as she walked through the arched entrance of the small campus bookstore into a musty dark room totally filled with books relating to the American Revolutionary War. She laid her backpack down on the table farthest from the door and set the timer on the C4 plastique. Everyone had already left, including the one lackadaisical salesperson, who appeared completely indifferent to her appearance at the end of the day.

"Excuse me, miss," said an old gentleman sitting in a chair near the door. "The store is closing in one minute. You really must be leaving. As you can see, you and I are the only ones here."

"Oh," Birdie responded as courteously as she could. "I'm so sorry. I didn't realize the time."

"You're from the States," the security guard asked, "aren't you?"

"I'm from San Francisco," she responded, checking her watch. She had only forty-five seconds to depart. This kindly man wanted to befriend her at the wrong time.

''How do you like it here?'' he asked, standing up and almost blocking her way out. ''I've been working at this store for five decades and I've seen a lot of Americans come and go. As a matter of fact, one of your presidents came to Cambridge.''

''I didn't realize how late it is. I really must be going,'' Birdie responded, trying to walk around him. She had wanted to correct him, tell him that former President Bill Clinton had gone to Oxford and not Cambridge, as if that had any significance. But she really needed to extricate herself from this dangerous situation. She checked her watch again and saw that she had only fifteen seconds to clear the area. Without another word, she sprinted out the door and into the street.

''How rude those Yankees are,'' the old man began to say out loud.

Before he had finished his sentence, the small bookstore at Queens College was a heap of rubble. The explosion had gone off on time. As planned, the rest of Queens College remained completely intact, especially its famous library of antique books.

Birdie raced through the streets, clearly attracting attention. But she couldn't worry about that right now. The old man was right, she thought, we Americans are rude . . . when provoked.

46

WESTERN COUNCIL OF NATIVE-BORN AMERICANS, WYOMING

Saturday, July 5th, 8:45 A.M.

It was not an accident of fate that at the relatively early age of forty-five, Daniel Bloodhawk was the effective leader of all the major Indian tribes west of the Mississippi. Through a combination of skillful maneuvering, selective patronage, and respect for the multitude of differences among the tribes, he had also cultivated the proper bureaucratic connections at the Bureau of Indian Affairs and at the Bureau of Land Management.

In the hour it took Bloodhawk and his guests to arrive at his reservation, west of the Fountain Paint Pot, he had already made certain that lodging, food, dry clothing, and showers had been prepared for them.

The reservation, housing two thousand Indians, resembled a typical recreational park, filled with aging trailers, an assortment of log cabins, a common bathroom facility, and a local grocery store. The fifty-acre compound was dominated by a large red brick building in which Bloodhawk and his fellow chiefs from all over the western United States convened twice a year. It was in the auditorium of this building that he, Al, and Cheri chose to discuss strategies to counter the secessionist movement. Representatives from various tribes followed them in and took seats along the back wall, a respectful distance from the discussion.

"Let me repeat your request so that I'm sure I understand

it,'' Bloodhawk said, staring at his two clean, tired, and thankful guests who, despite their obvious fatigue, were trying nobly to stay awake. ''You want me, and the other leaders of the major Indian tribes of Arizona, Colorado, Wyoming, and Utah''—he gestured to the tribal reps—''to formally request from the governors of those states that the Indian tribes be allowed to secede from their respective states. Quite novel,'' he said, walking to a large map of the United States which hung in the front of the room. ''What do you intend to accomplish by our action, if we should agree to it?''

Al thought for a moment, taken with the irony of the situation. As an RMO, he was always interacting and negotiating with the host-country physicians and diplomats. Here he was, negotiating with citizens of his own country, about whom he knew very little. While he had lectured to the Foreign Service officers about negotiating styles of nations around the world, this was a first for him. He could tell when the Chinese would invoke the concept of *quanxi,* a ''friend of China,'' in order to impose pressure on their counterpart. Similarly, he could tell how an Alawite Syrian, less than 5 percent of Syria's indigenous population, might lie out of force of habit so that every yes meant no. But he knew nothing about the negotiating style of the Native American. Because he knew little of their customs, he had to resort to the assumption that Bloodhawk would negotiate in the same manner that he would—that Bloodhawk would accept his strategic assumptions, that they would reach an understanding quickly, and that Bloodhawk was capable of implementing their final agreement. Unlike the Russians, American negotiations were typically result-oriented, put less emphasis on process, tended to develop superficial bonds of friendship, and made heavy use of time pressure and media manipulation.

''Secretary of State Barbara Reynolds wants to talk to you,'' Bloodhawk said, handing Al a cellular phone.

''Thanks,'' Al said, taking the phone and going off to an empty corner of the room. He wondered who had gotten in touch with Barbara to tell her where to reach him.

''Al, how are you?'' Barbara asked in her most maternal

voice. "Are you okay? Cheri okay? Hagner?"

"I'm fine, Barbara," he responded, curious whether Cheri, Hagner, or Bloodhawk had contacted her earlier. "Everyone is doing well, a bit tired and worn, but that's to be expected." Either he was becoming paranoid or someone had easier access to Barbara than he had. "More important, what's been happening there in the past twenty-four hours?"

"Al, we're on an open commercial line. So whatever I'm going to tell you will be short and sweet," Barbara replied, with obvious relief in her voice.

" 'Hey, Mr. Postman, deliver da letter da sooner da better,' " Al replied in a mocking singsong pattern of famous rock 'n roll singers. "Just give me a brief sit rep." The Sit Rep, or situation report, was a standard short bullet-form in which a policy official was kept abreast of ongoing events. It was the written version of a CNN ten-second spot.

"General Jason Montague has been successful in retaking the Glen Canyon Dam," Barbara began. "I see you're going to get a chance to implement part two of the strategy we discussed in Washington. My initial probe indicates that Bloodhawk is amenable to working with us. But you've got to button down the deal."

"I hear you loud and clear," Al responded, his voice somewhat interrupted by static on the line. Al couldn't help wondering whether anyone was trying to intercept this telephone conversation.

"You've got to reach a settlement with the governors soon," Barbara continued with an unexpected threatening tone of voice. "Al, we only have until Sunday, at midnight, before the governors release their second major disaster upon this country."

"From what I understand," Al added, "the Hoover Dam will be the next target."

"Where did you get that information from?" Barbara asked, sounding extremely skeptical.

"Barbara, we're on an open commercial line," Al responded. "Let's just say, from a reliable source."

"Just be careful," Barbara reiterated. "And don't forget that Governor Black was a founding leader of the secessionist movement. Weigh everything you hear from her. Do you understand me?''

''Roger,'' Al responded, straining to hear her last words as their conversation was prematurely cut off. He walked back to Bloodhawk and returned the cellular phone.

''So what did the Sec State have to say?'' Cheri asked.

''Nothing much,'' Al responded. ''She just wished us good luck and wanted to make sure that we weren't in any further danger.''

''And what did you tell her?'' Cheri asked, annoyed by the way he was brushing her off.

''That we're okay,'' Al responded. ''Should I have told her something else?''

''You really didn't answer my question,'' Cheri repeated in a stern voice.

''You and your honorable colleagues,'' Al said, ignoring Cheri's demanding tone and returning his attention to Bloodhawk, ''are the leaders of approximately 14.5 million Native Americans, including the Sioux, Navajo, Apache, Dakotas, Pueblos, and many other distinguished tribes. When I look at the map of the United States, I am amazed at how much land you and your colleagues control.

''If I'm not mistaken,'' Al continued, pointing to the map, ''the tribes control approximately three hundred reservations and a total of close to 100 million acres of land in the states we have been talking about. Is that correct?''

''Give or take a few million acres,'' Bloodhawk laughed. ''But for the most part, that is correct.''

''If you were to officially withdraw the areas you control from those states,'' Al continued, his strategy now crystal clear to him, ''what would happen?'' It was at times like this that he enjoyed the rush of excitement of his own creativity and cleverness. But he knew he had to be careful not to appear too excited, or he might find himself at a serious disadvantage in any negotiation with Bloodhawk.

''In less than twenty-four hours,'' Bloodhawk responded, anticipating where Al was headed, ''we could literally cripple every state west of the Mississippi. We'd stop its flow of water, shut down its hydroelectrical powergrids, and reduce much of its air, land, and water traffic. In short, we would be able to deny resources, food, transportation, and water to a particular state because of the land, air, and water rights we technically own. Through existing treaties we have bequeathed rights—for due consideration—to each state. But we can always rescind the agreements and take back physical possession of those rights."

"In short," Al continued, "you could totally destroy a state's ability to function as a service entity. Is that right?"

"To put it bluntly, yes," Bloodhawk answered. "We could do to the states what they have tried to do to us for centuries." He looked up at some of his colleagues who were sitting in the back of the room. "Am I right?" Four chiefs of major tribes and a small retinue of aides nodded their heads in agreement.

"Is it true that you are under federal and not state jurisdiction?" Al asked the question rhetorically, knowing the answer full well. Barbara had briefed him well beforehand. Apparently, Al thought, she had also briefed Bloodhawk. Al still thought it odd that Bloodhawk had been waiting for him in Yellowstone. Somebody had been able to track his movements at a time when Al, himself, wasn't sure he'd make it through this mission alive. Things were happening fast and there were too many unanswered questions. But for the moment he had no choice but to go with the flow of events, making certain that above all else he was not being set up. By anyone. A crisis, by its very nature, was governed by all kinds of variables, dynamics, and individuals which could not be controlled or even understood. Living with uncertainty was the price he had to pay to be part of the game. But way down, he was hoping that someone on his side had some control over the situation.

"It's a little more complicated than that," Bloodhawk responded. "Imagine the Indian tribes as small sovereign nations living within a larger sovereign nation called a state, which in turn exists within an even larger sovereign entity called a country. While we are largely responsible for our own existence, we do receive federal assistance in the form of grants and loans to encourage our people to work their farms or set up businesses." Bloodhawk decided not to go into the extensive legal description of an American Indian tribe and what prerogatives they did and did not have. But from early on in his political career, he had lived and breathed the precise definition, criteria, and legal precedence that gave the Indians their sovereignty. To him, it was his citizenship papers in America.

Bloodhawk knew that the American Indian tribes had been legally defined by the Supreme Court in 1831 in *Cherokee Nation* v. *Georgia.* In this famous case, the Supreme Court defined the Indian tribe as "domestic dependent nations." Federal recognition of a tribe meant that the U.S. government acknowledged that the tribal nation exists as a unique political entity with a government-to-government relationship to the United States. As far as the federal government was concerned, recognition entailed certain rights reserved for, or granted to, Indian nations by treaties, Executive Orders, special acts of Congress, or rights determined by the courts to be available to the tribe and its members. In *Worcester* v. *Georgia* (1832), the court handed down decisions in which tribes were viewed as autonomous governments retaining inherent power not expressly ceded away by the tribes or extinguished by Congress and essentially independent of state control. In *Williams* v. *Lee* (1959), the court recognized Indian tribes as permanent governments within the federal constitutional system. The Supreme Court had said in a series of judicial rules that treaties, agreements, and statutes be construed as the Indians would have understood them, that ambiguities be read in their favor, and that Indian laws be read liberally in favor of the Indians. In effect, the Supreme Court reaffirmed the doctrine that Indian tribes possess all the powers of any sovereign state.

"What would make you take a step to reaffirm your sovereignty in a meaningful way?" Al asked diplomatically, anticipating what he thought would be the answer.

"Many things," Bloodhawk responded. "But the most important would be a direct insult to our integrity or a desecration of our ancestral burial grounds."

"What else?" Al pressed forward.

"Dr. Carter," Cheri interrupted him. "Bloodhawk just told you."

"Perhaps you can help me to understand what you are

getting at, Al, since you are the skilled representative of this wonderful country,'' Bloodhawk said with just a bit of sarcasm, and not quite certain where Al's thoughts were going.

''One of the first things the federal government grants a sovereign nation which has complied with our wishes,'' Al explained, ''is immediate foreign aid in the form of direct loans, credits, and grants. In the case of the Indian tribes, I would say something close to what we would spend in the Middle East to maintain our strategic advantage . . .'' He halted, looking straight into Bloodhawk's narrowing eyes. ''Should we say $10 billion per year for the next five years?''

''Perhaps something along the lines of twice that amount,'' Bloodhawk retorted, knowing that Al was in no position to argue. He had neither the time nor the energy left. Bloodhawk was relying on Barbara Reynolds's word that Al was authorized to pledge those amounts of money without a written order from both the legislative and executive branches of the government. According to Barbara, the country was in an official State of Emergency.

''Let's split the difference,'' Al said. ''Fifteen billion dollars for you to demand formal secession from Arizona, Utah, Colorado, and Wyoming. That means in the next twenty-four hours, you and your people will threaten to shut down those states. You will block the highways that go through your lands from all incoming and outgoing traffic, including shipments of food. You will picket the state capitols so that the governors are forced to return to their respective states in order to deal with the problems that you have created. At the same time, you will prevent the movement of any National Guard troops. Period.''

Bloodhawk looked once again to the other tribal chiefs and their counselors. All nodded their heads in agreement.

''Agreed.'' Bloodhawk reached out and shook Al's hand. ''But there are two problems I see immediately. One, who will protect us if we get into direct confrontation with the states' National Guard? And how do we know that you will be good for that amount of money?''

''The first problem will be solved by my getting on the phone with the Secretary of Defense,'' Al responded, ''who will directly order federal troops to proceed to your reservations and lands. These troops will be there to protect your citizens.''

''And the second issue?'' Bloodhawk asked, impressed by Al's self-assurance.

''That will be guaranteed by Secretary of State Barbara Reynolds who, for the next forty-eight hours, represents the full faith and credit of this government.''

''You have a deal, Al,'' Bloodhawk said, clasping Al's shoulders as a sign of a task already accomplished. ''But if for any reason your promises fail to materialize, and we have put ourselves on the line needlessly, then all those wonderful things that you said that we Indians can do against the state governments will be directed against Washington, D.C. Is that clear?''

''Perfectly,'' Al responded. ''Only one more thing. Could you encourage your Indian colleagues in French Quebec and British Vancouver to rattle their sabers a little? At least that would help us to divert French, and possibly British, attention away from America.''

''Anything else, Al?'' Bloodhawk laughed, knowing that he had already been asked to accomplish the near impossible.

''I think we've done enough for one day,'' Al said, relieved for the first time in twenty-four hours. Al glanced at Cheri, whose cryptic smile made him decide that it was too soon to relax.

47

FRANKFURT, GERMANY

Saturday, July 5th, 12:04 P.M.

The drive between Wiesbaden and the city of Frankfurt is extremely pleasant if one has both the time and inclination to enjoy a countryside filled with vineyards. The region around Wiesbaden is primarily known for its sweet, fruity-tasting Zinfandel wines. The other unique feature of the region is its location as a mecca for the tired, the weary, and for those in need of extreme self-indulgence. For the spas of Wiesbaden were some of the most popular ones in the world. Whether it was the mud or the sulfur waters which accounted for the cures, the Wiesbaden spas were well-immersed in the alchemy of sand, water, and soothing hands which massaged away whatever real or imagined pains one might have.

But the man who was driving the Porsche 928S, the only one of its class manufactured with an automatic transmission, making it an incredibly unreliable car, was concerned less about the wine and the cures than that he was running ten minutes behind schedule. Traveling at close to 140 kilometers per hour on the Autobahn Route 41 from Wiesbaden to Frankfurt, he prayed silently that he would make it in time to place the package sitting on the seat next to him on Lufthansa Flight 135 bound for Denver, Colorado. Unlike most flights that left Frankfurt, one of the central hubs of passenger travel all over Western Europe, this was a freight airplane that carried heavy machinery parts to states in the Midwest. The man who drove the Porsche knew all too well that Flight 135 was, in fact, carrying a sundry assortment of military equipment, ammunition, field guides, medical supplies, heavy artillery, and battle vehicles. But even as Patrick, his code name from the DDO who had once been his boyfriend, raced down the autobahn, he wasn't sure that he had enough time to arrive in Frankfurt, find the airport (which he knew from previous experience was buried in a labyrinth of concrete highways), and then locate the freight delivery entrance for Lufthansa. He wasn't a novice at executing last-minute off-line orders, but neither could he achieve the impossible. He had been told only two hours ago that the flight would be departing on time and that he had to ''build'' a package which could safely pass through German Customs.

The needle on the speedometer was all the way up to 160 kilometers per hour when he entered the principal thoroughfare surrounding the downtown financial center of Frankfurt. Just as he recalled from earlier trips to Germany, there were signs in both English and German, as well as signs with the silhouette of an airplane.

Patrick, who had once taken a job right out of college as a New York City taxi driver, had never forgotten his aggressive driving skills. He wove in and out of traffic until he reached the main terminal of the Frankfurt airport. Because his reading German was less proficient than his spoken German, he slowed down to pay attention to directions.

''Papers, please,'' the security guard at the entrance of the freight delivery area asked in German.

''I have some here,'' Patrick responded, handing him a group of disheveled papers. ''These are the invoices for the package and those are my identification papers.'' As many times as he had gone through Customs in Germany, he never stopped imagining himself to be in one of those World War II films where the Nazi soldier asks the innocent bystander for his identification papers in order to have the necessary pretext to arrest him. In this particular case, Patrick knew all too well that he was neither innocent nor a civilian and that the papers he had just given the guard were forged, done

one hour after he received his instructions from his Station Chief. When he had asked whether there was a "finding" and whether what he was about to do was legal, he was told in no uncertain terms that he had no choice but to execute the assignment—or leave the service. Since the CIA was an "excepted service," he served at the pleasure of the DCI, the Director of the Central Agency. He could be fired at will. Of course, there was no congressional finding for this extremely sensitive operation. But he was told that the Sec State would bear the burden of any legal transgressions because there was a real State of Emergency back home. All he had to do was to keep his wits about him and act professional. In short, Patrick had no choice.

"May I see the package, please," the guard asked.

"I would love to show you the beautiful glass blown in Wiesbaden, but my flight is leaving in ten minutes. If I don't get it on the flight I will lose an absolute fortune in sales and be fired."

"Please, get out of the car," the guard ordered, "and bring the package with you."

Patrick decided he could do only one of two things. Either he could comply with the guard and lose the possibility the package would make the plane. Or he could ram through the gate with his Porsche and incur the possibility that both he and his package would be destroyed before he ever got it on the plane.

"What are you looking for?" Patrick asked him. "Maybe we can strike a compromise so that I can make the plane on time."

"Please, get out of the car!" the guard repeated. This time he pointed a 9mm Beretta at Patrick.

"All right," Patrick responded, opening the door of his Porsche slowly. "By the way, which gate leads to Flight 135?"

The guard pointed toward a 747 airplane straight ahead, only about three hundred yards away. The cargo door was being closed. There was very little time to discuss the matter further. Patrick decided to take the second option. Without warning, he slammed his door shut, stepped on the accelerator, and knocked the guard over as he went through the gate.

The airplane had started to pull back from its docking area. In a few minutes it would be airborne. In his rearview mirror, he saw four guards with semiautomatic weapons racing toward his car.

He was calculating that within a minute he could reach the airplane as a bullet hit his right shoulder. He pressed his foot down on the accelerator and held the leather-wrapped steering wheel tightly with both hands. He ignored the blood that was starting to pour out of his shoulder. When the car started to swerve, he realized that a bullet had punctured his left rear tire. Holding the steering wheel steadily, he pushed down the button near the transmission marked Electric Power, the turbo-charger for the car. He felt the car jolt forward as he accelerated straight toward the moving 747.

He aimed the car at the right wing of the plane, the wing that he knew would be filled with forty thousand gallons of highly flammable jet fuel. He pulled a .38 Smith & Wesson gun from its holster and shot three bullets into the package next to him.

The red 928S Porsche and Flight 135 exploded into a phosphorescent flame of death.

48

NYE COUNTY, NEVADA

Saturday, July 5th, 11:40 A.M.

''Secure the courthouse area as quickly as possible,'' FBI Special Agent Angela Rodriguez ordered, ''but no shooting unless you have to.'' She watched from the ground as three dozen FBI agents armed with semiautomatic weapons were methodically extruded from the bellies of Apache and Blackhawk helicopters hovering above. Looking at her watch, she realized that many of her most trusted subordinates were engaged in similar jumps in Wyoming, Utah, Colorado, and Arizona. Hopefully, these assaults would serve as a warning to the other groups throughout the States.

''Make certain there are no media personnel within a mile of this area,'' she continued, confident in the abilities of her agents. If only the American viewing public could witness the assault, she thought, they would be very impressed. It was going to look like a typical hostage rescue scenario, the type that the public had become inured to through their constant exposure to television news and second-rate TV movies. Frequently, the central drama of the situation was lost because the eventual outcome had been played out so many times. The audience had learned to expect either an ecstatic or depressing denouement. But for Angela the scenario was a real zero-sum equation. Either she won by having a hostage released without harm or she lost when the hostage was killed. Eventually her agents had to engage in a massive firefight, if only to extract vengeance. That's not exactly what she had been taught, but it came pretty close to it. Without saying a word, Barbara had made it quite clear to Angela that she was to make an example of this incident, as well as the massive undertaking to neutralize all of the False Patriots groups that had been identified in the four states.

Angela knew from HUMINT and ELINT that Sandy Evers, an ATF agent, was being held captive in the red brick courthouse by Darrell Hayeck, the unofficial ''judge'' of the citizens' court, County Commissioner Larry Teague, and Nevada State Police Captain Robert McElroy. Intelligence estimated that two dozen citizen soldiers were also in the building and that everyone was armed with semiautomatic weapons. There was no doubt in Angela's mind that if she didn't play this correctly any fiasco at Nye County would make Ruby Ridge a footnote in the textbook of FBI mishaps.

Looking toward the horizon, she was surprised to see how lush the vegetation was in this part of the country. Born of Puerto Rican parents and raised on 135th Street and Columbus Avenue in Manhattan, her landscape was the defaced empty brick buildings indigenous to the five boroughs of New York City. After receiving her B.S. in Criminology at Northeastern University, she went on to the FBI Academy and found that she had special talents for management, organization, and leadership. As one of the few Hispanic women in the Academy, she was quickly spotted and put on the fast track for promotion. As far as her superiors were concerned, they felt no sense of defensiveness about what they were doing with Angela. She was talented, and it was made very clear that the Bureau placed expectations upon her. That meant for the last fifteen years she had performed, as she would say, on ''maximum octane.'' Since she didn't have her own family and was not burdened by the concerns of marriage, or child-rearing, or any nagging thoughts about self-direction, if she played her cards correctly she could be a Deputy Director of the Bureau within ten years. Not bad for a thirty-eight-year-old Puerto Rican woman whose parents didn't speak any English.

God bless America, she thought. Where else could the

daughter of non-English-speaking immigrants become important? In Puerto Rico, where her family had been considered respectable and middle-class, the most that she could have hoped for would have been to be a real estate agent or a reservations manager for an American franchise hotel. In America, she had learned to want more from life. And though she would never become rich, public service fulfilled any dreams she might have entertained as a child. Her two younger sisters had respectable jobs in local banks and were very happy with their lives. As might be expected from a tightly knit family, her parents were extremely proud of her achievements in their adopted country. But those accomplishments could suddenly evaporate if she didn't manage to neutralize these rebel groups without attracting any media attention.

"This is FBI Special Agent Angela Rodriguez," she shouted through a bullhorn once her agents were in position. "I would like to talk to whoever is in charge. I'm here to discuss the release of ATF Agent Sandy Evers."

"I'm Darrell Hayeck," a voice responded from a bullhorn in the building. "I'm the person you have to deal with."

"Judge Hayeck," Angela continued, "what exactly will it take to resolve this situation peacefully?" She knew that Darrell was no more a judge than she was the Director of the FBI. But she decided to exploit a first principle of hostage negotiations: demonstrate respect toward your adversary.

"We want two things," Darrell replied, now standing in front of the open door of the courthouse. "One, we want all of our lands which are presently controlled by the federal government to be returned to state and local authority. Two, in response to the will of the citizens, we want to continue to prosecute our own criminals, including Sandy Evers, two forest rangers, one BLM official, and several IRS officials."

"Anything else?" she asked rhetorically. Even though his requests were totally out of the question, she knew that she needed to allow him the opportunity to express them—a second principle of hostage negotiations. This way everyone could say that this group had been given a chance to make their demands known.

''Yes,'' Darrell added in a foreboding tone. ''If you don't comply with all of our demands, I can assure you that Sandy Evers will receive more than a superficial wound the next time. We are prepared to retaliate against the feds through any means possible including explosives, guns, and shutting down federal operations.''

''You mean Project Worst Nightmare?'' she asked, determined not to provoke him but at the same time wanting to make certain that he would not get away with any disrespect toward her. Project Worst Nightmare was a plan circulating throughout all of the militia groups which eventually wound up in regional FBI offices around the U.S.A. The plan outlined the steps that the secessionist militia groups would follow to shut down government operations if the feds used force on any of them.

''Agent Rodriguez,'' he responded, ''I'm impressed that you do your homework.''

''Thank you,'' she replied, pleased that she could follow another important principle of hostage negotiation—setting limits on his need to debase her.

''Before we make any concessions,'' she said, ''I want to make certain that Sandy Evers is in good health.'' She wondered if Darrell knew that she was following the time-tested script for hostage negotiations. If he didn't comply, there would be very few options from which to work.

''That's the least I can do,'' Darrell responded in a courtly fashion. He brought out a blindfolded Sandy Evers, flanked by two men carrying semiautomatic weapons.

Angela recognized one of the men holding Evers from HUMINT photos as Larry Teague. She recognized the other man from his FBI file as Robert McElroy. From his militaristic appearance, she concluded that he had transformed himself into a staunch supporter of the secessionist movement from the cautious, law-abiding police officer he had been earlier in his career. He had gone from someone upholding the Constitution to one insistent on defying it. She directed her sharpshooters to fix their sights on Sandy Evers.

''Now that you've seen him,'' Darrell said, ''what do we get in return?''

Darrell clearly understood the game, Angela thought.

Every favor granted had to be matched on equal basis by the other side. Nothing was for free. Not even human life. Someone had to extract a price for survival. And someone had to concede to that price whether they liked it or not. In the world of practical exchange, human beings were transformed into commodities, measured only by their ability to extract concessions. The rest was irrelevant, no matter how much each side professed the importance of human life or the sanctity of federal government policy. The only thing that would not be forgiven was if a major slaughter of American citizens by the FBI was witnessed by the media and put before the public. That was why Angela had made certain that spokesmen for the media were kept completely away from the confrontation sites thoughout the country. So no matter what happened, it would be simply her word versus the adversary's.

"Please understand," Larry said, "we are not looking for an armed confrontation with the federal government. All we want is to resolve any differences that we have with the federal government in a peaceful manner. We are simply engaged in a long democratic tradition of civil disobedience."

"I understand you perfectly well, Commissioner Teague," she responded, "and I'm certainly not looking for a confrontation. But I am concerned about the weapons you and your friends are holding."

"Agent Rodriguez," Larry said with a voice cracking with anxiety and fear, "we don't want anyone to act precipitously."

"On that point," she replied, "we are in full agreement." She whispered into the ear of her principal sharpshooter who was lying in the grass next to her.

He fired a shot and Sandy Evers collapsed onto the ground as if his legs had buckled under him. The sharpshooter aimed again carefully. This time, County Commissioner Larry Teague fell to the ground, his forehead splattered by blood. He was the second victim of the nonexistent civil war.

49

NYE COUNTY, NEVADA

Saturday, July 5th, 12:10 P.M.

''Shoot a couple of canisters of tear gas into the building.'' Angela motioned her men to move forward carefully. ''We'll need a medivac for Sandy Evers. And remember to have someone notify the next of kin that Commissioner Larry Teague was killed resisting federal officers.'' The sight of blood running down from Sandy's right thigh made her uncomfortable. She had been in several shootouts around the barrio in New York City and never really flinched when she saw someone was injured. But over the years whatever psychological defense mechanisms had been built up to protect her against feeling the full force of her emotions were beginning to wane.

''Hey, boss,'' Seth Merril, a former DIA operative, said, moving alongside of her to offer her firepower cover with his specially outfitted M-16. ''Please be careful. We can't afford to lose you at this point in the operation.''

''You mean,'' she responded, ''at the end of this assault it's okay?''

''Yeah,'' he replied, ''just not on my watch.''

''Thanks a lot,'' Angela said, drawing her 9mm Beretta as they approached the house, now seething with tear gas. She took a handkerchief out of her pocket and covered her mouth. Seth put on his gas mask and offered her the one he carried for her.

"Take it, boss," he said. "Once we go through that door, all hell is going to break loose."

"Seth," she asked, smiling, "what exactly have we been in so far?" She motioned the other agents to close in on the building. Evers and Teague had been left outside where they fell. Teague's body was carried away by the first agent to reach the building and Evers was placed on a stretcher. Hayeck and McElroy had disappeared inside the building. Angela motioned three of her colleagues, each dressed in standard blue fatigue suits and wearing bulletproof vests, to bring the wooden battering ram forward. They rushed the front door with the ram and smashed it open. Angela and Seth rushed into the gas-filled room, accompanied by backup FBI agents.

"Where the hell did everyone go?" Angela asked, looking around an empty room. She ordered her men to break open the windows so that the gas could be cleared out. Except for a few pieces of old, run-down furniture, there was nothing in the room that could help her. She had expected to find maps, papers, documents of one type or another, communication equipment, and an assortment of firearms. But there was nothing here that might criminally incriminate anyone.

"Ladies and gentlemen," Angela announced, coughing slightly from the remnants of the tear gas, "let's look for an escape route. . . ."

"It's right here!" Seth shouted, lifting up the metal handle that was concealed within the floorboards under a wooden chest. "There is a wooden ladder leading about five feet down into a pretty large tunnel."

"Welcome back, Vietnam!" Derek Butts shouted. He was a handsome ex-Vietnam veteran in his mid-fifties whose specialty had been counterinsurgency and counterterrorism. His job in Vietnam had been to figure out how his opponent thought and what type of unorthodox action he might take. "Cover me, Angela," he said as he descended the ladder, "and I want some heavy semiautomatic weapons behind me. I don't want a bunch of you women bottling up my escape route. What I could use is a flamethrower to prophylactically clean out my way as I go through the tunnel.''

''Hey, you better watch your foul tongue in the presence of a lady,'' Seth said, looking at Derek, who laughed and understood his word-game. ''We don't talk about prophylaxis and sex. Not here and certainly . . .''

''Okay, guys,'' Angela interrupted, ''thanks for the commercial break, but it's time to tune into the main show.'' She looked around to check the status of her men and was satisfied. ''Before some of us go down this rat hole, I want the rest of you to cover the perimeter and try to uncover the exit route for the tunnel. If we're lucky, which I don't suspect we'll be, you can arrest anyone who comes out. Except Derek, of course. I shouldn't have to mention it, but I would prefer that we take everyone alive—you heard it, all of you hotshots. Alive.'' She felt she had to emphasize it, since it was always a hunter's basic nature when he found his prey to try to kill it rather than contain it. ''All right, let's start going down, but be careful. These zealots are motivated by blind hatred. So don't take anything for granted. Let's just check on each other from time to time to see how we are doing.''

''Here goes nothing,'' Derek said, descending into what he knew in the back of his mind could be a one-way ticket to hell. Seth was behind him carrying his automatic. Angela and a half-dozen men brought up the rear in single file.

''Keep against the wall,'' Derek ordered, darting from one alcove to another. All tunnels look alike, he thought, whether they're in Vietnam or the United States. It's as if there was one designer of tunnels from time immemorial who went from country to country, plying his trade. All narrow, cold, and damp. From what he saw around him, he was now exploring a class-A tunnel.

''How far do you think the tunnel goes?'' Angela whispered.

''There's no way to know,'' he replied, ''but the longer they wait to attack us—if they're still down here—the more sophisticated I know they are. It just means they are waiting to set us up until they can extract maximum damage.''

"In short," Angela added, following closely behind him, "we might be sitting ducks."

"Not quite," Derek replied, "but I would say that we were a close second cousin." He raised his nose in the air. "I smell cordite and diesel. We're getting pretty close to a mother lode of firearms. Be prepared to open fire with everything you've got."

Angela passed the message on to the rest of the team.

Shots whizzed through the tunnel. Then silence.

"Take cover," Derek shouted, recalling his days as an all-American quarterback on the Columbia College football team. Although he couldn't see anyone, he knew from his days in Quan Tri, ferreting out "gooks," that there was always a moment of silence before the enemy opened fire. He felt that his moment was about to come. And he wasn't wrong.

A second hail of bullets ripped through the tunnel.

Derek began to rush through a long passage in the tunnel when an eerie whooshing sound hit his ears. The noise was accompanied by a bright yellow-blue flame. "Flamethrower!" Derek shouted, waving the FBI back.

Suddenly, the distance between Derek and the False Patriots was filled with the smell of cordite, benzene, and burning flesh.

"Aaaaagh!" Derek screamed and lurched forward, blasting his weapon at anyone who might be in front of him. If he had only a few seconds to live, he'd be damned if he wouldn't take a bunch of those sons of bitches with him.

When the flames subsided, Angela and her team ran toward Derek, unloading their weapons with the full fury of those who can smell the sweet scent of revenge. By the time the fight was over, twenty-four False Patriots were dead. FBI agent Derek Butts had been burned alive. Darrell Hayeck and Robert McElroy lay facedown on the ground, their bodies riddled with bullets.

Angela and her agents continued to search the area. The tunnel opened up into a room that looked like an underground warehouse, about two hundred feet long by seventy-five feet wide. In it were boxes marked "Ammunition," and unmarked boxes of communication equipment, propaganda material, and blueprints. All of the boxes had been shipped from an organization called A.P.R.L., located in Salt Lake City, Utah. The room itself housed an elaborate communication center filled with computers, television cameras, and radio equipment. Wooden crates stenciled with large red letters spelling "Fragile," filled with hate leaflets and floppy discs, were in the process of being sent to France, England, Germany, and Corsica, a French colony.

A map of the United States was tacked across several crates with the names of militia groups written on a legend at the right lower corner that corresponded to colored push-pins on the map. An additional chart described each group's modus operandi, its strength, and listed its address.

"Take down that map," Angela ordered Seth, "and relay the information to the Director of the FBI, Secretary Reynolds, and to our other field units. New Hampshire, Michigan, Indiana, Montana, Idaho, Arizona, Colorado. You know the routine. Instruct all of our units to start preparing strategies against these extremists. ASAP. Make certain that you tell them to be prepared for confronting big-time weapons—flamethrowers, amfo, napalm."

"Yes, ma'am," Seth replied, feeling depressed but knowing that this was no time to let his emotions cloud his ability to act. He looked again at the charred and blood-splattered bodies. What a desecration of the American dream, he thought, to be killed on American soil, by a fellow American, for a supposedly American cause. This was not supposed to happen here. This was supposed to happen in far-off places fighting people who were different from us.

With tears streaking down his face, Seth came to the only conclusion he could come to: God had a real funny sense of humor. But no one in the room seemed to be laughing.

50

BASTIA, CORSICA

Saturday, July 5th, 1:10 P.M.

The Mediterranean island of Corsica, considered one of the world's most beautiful resort areas, is located 120 miles southeast of Nice, France. Although considered part of France, the island has always been plagued by violent demonstrations for independence. Despite the fact that one of France's greatest leaders, Napoleon Bonaparte, was born here, the people of the island have had, at best, an ambivalent relationship with France. Considered one of the poorest regions of France, it has been subsidized by billions of dollars in aid which, like most aid delivered around the world to the needy, had probably lined the pockets of the very wealthy. In short, corruption, violence, and a strong nationalist movement have festered on the island for centuries. More than one Prime Minister of France, including Yvette, concluded in private that "Corsica isn't worth the trouble it's causing." But the truth of the matter was that most Corsicans, in a total population of one quarter of a million people, no longer wanted independence. Those who had sympathized with the Corsican Independence Movement realized that the recent spate of violence on the island had an extremely debilitating effect on the island's important industry.

The French National Assembly in Paris had recently proclaimed that "no one has a miracle recipe for returning the island to absolute calm.'' They were at that point in their frustration where one more major act of violence might tip that scale and force the French government to grant one of its historical acquisitions complete independence. The government's fear, however, was in starting a trend where France would divest itself of La Reunion (in the Indian Ocean), the islands of Martinique and Guadeloupe (in the Caribbean), and several islands in the Pacific Ocean, not to mention those parts of its own country that wanted to become independent: Toulouse, Brittany, and Alsace-Lorraine.

Etienne Verde, a pseudonym for an American operative who had been sent over to Corsica to foment the ''mother of all insurrections,'' had been given one specific order by his handler in the U.S. Embassy: ''Make certain that France has no doubt about pulling out of the Midwest.''

Etienne Verde drove a medium-sized Peugeot to navigate the narrow roads of the rocky mountainside. The goddamn island was nothing more than one rock chipped away by the elements, he thought. Corsica had all of the characteristic features that would place it in travel books as one of those ''interesting tourist hideaways.''

As he drove carefully around the hairpin turns, he thought that it would have been a lot wiser for France not to have acquired Corsica from the Republic of Genoa in 1768. It really wasn't worth the trouble for the French to maintain even the basic infrastructure of the island. It was too expensive and too extensive. On the other hand, Etienne Verde knew that it wasn't a one-sided relationship. For hundreds of years, disenchanted Corsicans looking for upward mobility had left their undeveloped island for the mainland, where they served in such noble professions as policemen, administrators, Foreign Legion troops, and the infamous gangsters often seen along the Côte d'Azur.

No one was as tough as the Corsicans when it came to the underworld of crime. It was rumored that half the fashionable French Riviera was owned or controlled by Corsican gangs, including racetracks, restaurants, nightclubs, prostitution, extortion, and gambling. And that was probably just the surface of their involvement in the fiber of French corruption. It was said that they, the Corsicans, had no equals.

Not the Italian Mafia nor the French "macro."

Over the years, the Corsican nationalist thugs had split the island into two counties, obtained Corsica's first directly elected territorial assembly, established a university, and extracted funding from the central French government. They had also decided to extort monies from their suffering compatriots by imposing a "revolutionary tax," which added to the cost of doing business and sparked major turf wars among competing Corsican gangs. Their ideological fervor was modeled upon revolutionary groups around the world. Over a five-year period, total nationalist thugs accounted for more than four thousand incidents involving explosives, murder, destruction of property, and over six thousand cadavers.

After a two-hour ride on a primarily dust-covered road, Etienne Verde stopped at a winery named after the town in which it was located, Aleria. The plan was quite simple. He was to create a natural disaster. The French would assume the perpetrator of the crime was a Corsican Nationalist because the Aleria winery had been a political hot potato for several years. The winery was owned by a "Pied Noir" (Black Foot), a French immigrant from Algeria who received low-interest loans from the French Central Bank, a privilege that most Corsicans were deprived of because of their high-credit risk. The Corsican Nationalists had previously tried to destroy this winery as an example to the central government in Paris of what would happen if Corsica continued to be treated as a third-world country. So Aleria was a target of opportunity. And Etienne's assignment was to make it a cause célèbre that would push the French into granting Corsican independence.

Etienne got out of the dust-covered Peugeot at the side of an enclosed vineyard. He opened the trunk and took out a red can marked "Flammable." The black woolen hood he pulled over his head was typical costume for the Corsican Nationalists. He pulled wireclippers from his fatigue pants, cut the sharp wire at the property line, and crawled along the ground. The vineyard was twenty miles long and several miles wide. He could see about a dozen workers in the fields. He always marveled at how such a luscious fruit could be born from so arid a land. He laughed to himself. He was a farmer, of sorts, spreading the seeds of destruction wherever he went. He let the contents of the can spill out slowly as if he were pouring maple syrup on a stack of pancakes. In fact, the contents of his can were not too different in viscosity from maple syrup. Napalm was a sticky liquid that would allow a fire to keep burning despite all attempts to put it out. He had to be very careful that once he ignited the napalm he would not become entrapped in his own inferno.

It took about twenty minutes to empty the contents of the can along several rows of vines. Then Etienne took out his Bic lighter and set each row of napalm on fire. He purposefully dropped the lighter with its insignia of the Corsican Liberation Party on the ground. If it didn't melt entirely, it might be useful as incriminating evidence.

But Etienne Verde didn't kid himself. He wasn't supposed to. The French government would know that this was an act perpetrated by an American operative. It was coming within twenty-four hours of the explosion at the Quai d'Orsay. Etienne Verde reentered his Peugeot and drove away, undetected. He knew that this was part of the charade called covert operations. As he drove back over those same dusty roads, he watched, with some remorse, as four French helicopters appeared on the horizon dropping chemicals to retard the lashing flames of Aleria.

51

ROCKEFELLER LODGE, WYOMING

Saturday, July 5th, 4:05 P.M.

Every war develops its own myths and icons. Who could forget the F-4 Phantom jets streaking over a village somewhere in Vietnam, dropping napalm and then swooping upward as the flames licked the bottom of their sleek carriages, racing skyward? In the Gulf War, the icon became the myth, or vice versa. Since no one, by definition, could see the F-117A Stealth fighters, the noncombatants—most of whom through the process of wishful thinking weave the fabric of bits of information into fanciful stories—spread the tale of an invisible plane which wreaked havoc by dropping smart bombs onto strategic locations. Much like the haunted-house paradigm that most philosophers like to play with, it was impossible to prove or disprove an ethereal presence such as a ghost.

And so it was for this secessionist non-war that a new icon arose—military maneuvers that never existed, to practice for a civil disturbance that never happened, to squelch an ideology belonging to some fringe groups who, as a result of these operations, no longer existed. If asked years later whether there had ever been recorded evidence of a conflict between federal and state troops, the answer by force of necessity had to be—no. There was no second American civil war. And more important, it could never happen.

For Brigadier General Jason Montague, the shibboleth of this non–civil war was the 4th Air Cavalry Squadron which had been effectively used to take back the Glen Canyon Dam. He was also employing the 3rd Armored Cavalry

Squadron to suppress the insurrection. One group of the 3rd Cavalry had just been sent to the Lodge to apprehend the leaders of the movement. He had deployed the second group to Lake Mead in order to protect the Hoover Dam. SIGINT, HUMINT, and ELINT indicated that there was an inordinate amount of National Guard activity around that dam. While a report from Special Agent Angela Rodriguez speculated that the next major catastrophe could be the dam's destruction, she still needed confirmation from a second source.

Jason wasn't about to chase a decoy. There were so many other attractive targets around the country which secessionists could threaten. Primary electrical power grids. Large nuclear reactors. Major hub cities where air, land, and sea transportation intersected, like San Diego, Seattle, Miami, and New York. His major concern right now was with executing a surgical strike on the Rockefeller Lodge with the least amount of collateral damage . . . and hoping it was the best target he could aim at without wasting his resources and manpower.

From his position in the passenger's seat on the AH-64 Apache helicopter, Jason could see the configuration of his ground forces surrounding the Lodge. Forty MIA2 tanks, six mortar carriers, forty M3A2 tanks, scores of UH-60L and OH-58D helicopters, and about one hundred humvees mounted with anti-tank guns, machine guns, and recoilless rifles were already in their places. From his vantage point some five hundred feet above the ground, he was confident that there was very little that his men would have to do to secure the Lodge and arrest the governors. According to intel, there was very little protection in the woods around the Lodge itself. The governors had probably assumed that the focal point of federal activity would be in the Glen Canyon Dam area. Furthermore, intel thought that American state troopers would not really be prepared to kill their federal equivalents if a decision had to be made.

Both of these assumptions would have proven correct if Jason had not encountered the barrage of fire he did as he landed.

"Bring me down far enough so that I can jump," Jason said, turning toward the helicopter pilot.

"Sir," the pilot responded, "it's a red zone. We will be sitting ducks if I come down too close or if you rappel down the rope."

"Take me down. That's an order," Jason shouted above the roar of the rotary blades. "Just choose the type of Duck Sauce you want—in the air or on the ground."

"Yes, sir," the pilot responded. "But let me call in some backup firepower."

"We've already got some Blackhawk helos behind us," Jason responded.

Suddenly his helo started to shake. A stinger missile had hit its underbelly. The glass-bubble cockpit burst into flames.

"Sir, we may have to make a crash landing. The helo's on fire. It's been seriously damaged."

"Just bring her down," Jason said.

"Yes, sir," the pilot replied.

Within seconds the helo landed and Jason jumped out. The pilot was not as lucky. The helicopter exploded into a fiery ball as he was unfastening his shoulder straps.

Mortar rounds chased Jason as he ran toward a clump of trees and jumped on top of the turret of a camouflaged M1A2 Abrams tank.

"What the hell happened?" Jason asked Second Lieutenant Murray Brown, a bald-headed, red-faced soldier just out of West Point.

"Sir," Brown responded with a prominent lisp, "I don't know. This area was supposed to be completely clean."

"Clean?" Jason repeated the word. "This is a goddamn hornet's nest. And as far as I know, they're firing at us from every direction."

"I don't know, sir," Brown responded, with his pronounced sibilant *s*. "Would you like me to make a coordinated attack on the Lodge?"

"You're in charge," Jason said. "Do what you are supposed to do."

"Yes, sir," Brown responded, ordering his tank crew to fire while he moved his own tank forward.

The combined noise of a 7.62mm Coaxial Machine Gun and an M256 120mm Main gun forced Jason to cover both of his ears with his hands. He had to admit to himself that the M1A2 Abrams tank was a formidable fighting machine. During the Gulf War one of his men, with one M1A2, took out six Russian-made T-72 tanks in eleven seconds. From that day on, Jason never looked at the Abrams without respect. And now he had three of them at his immediate disposal, all coordinated to attack one simple target—an immobile wooden and stone building.

But something was very wrong, he concluded. As the tank he rode in advanced, a barrage of gunfire came at it from his rear. He realized that he had been fooled by what appeared to be his own strategic advantage. He should have been suspicious of the fact that he was unable to detect any counterforce. Where the hell were the shots coming from? he wondered. An enemy didn't suddenly appear out of nowhere. Yet this enemy seemed to be everywhere. The more his tank advanced, the greater the barrage of fire he encountered. Every time he marked a position of incoming fire, it would invariably be one of his own tanks. But that wasn't possible, he thought.

Jason recalled the famous line from Pogo, a comic book character: "I have seen the enemy and the enemy is us." How stupid, he thought. The 3rd Army Cavalry Regiment was composed of National Guard units from Utah, Arizona, and Colorado.

"You're under arrest," Lieutenant Brown said, turning toward Jason and pointing his 9mm Beretta at his commander. "Please put down your sidearms, General Montague."

52

GRAND TETONS, WYOMING

Sunday, July 6th, 10:05 A.M.

The roadblocks set up by Chief Bloodhawk, his fellow Native American chieftains, and their thousands of followers from tribes all over the region created an effective logjam of civilian and military traffic all the way from Yellowstone National Park to Jackson Hole, a distance of almost thirty-five miles.

"What the hell is going on here?" a colonel riding a humvee asked Bloodhawk as he stood in front of a human barricade.

"We are protesting the presence of foreigners on our sacred native soil," Bloodhawk replied.

Al, Cheri, and Hagner stood alongside Bloodhawk as witnesses to the civil disobedience, a tactic that had proved successful throughout the civil rights movement of the '60s and the Vietnam War protests of the '70s.

"What the hell are you talking about?" Colonel Andrew Cole asked indignantly, scanning the convoy of supply trucks that were reinforcements for the secessionist units surrounding the Rockefeller Lodge. "And who the hell are you?"

"I am Chief Daniel Bloodhawk," he replied. "And this is Governor Cheri Black of Colorado and Dr. Alison Carter. Governor Black represents the western state governors and

Dr. Carter represents the Secretary of State in Washington, D.C.''

''Stand down, Colonel,'' Cheri ordered. ''Chief Bloodhawk is a head of state now. He is asking you and your men to get off his . . . country's . . . property.''

''As far as the federal government is concerned,'' Al confirmed, ''Chief Bloodhawk has the full power and authority of a sovereign leader to order you off his land.'' He added, gilding the lily somewhat, ''Both the governor and I are here to negotiate a treaty with Chief Bloodhawk in order to clarify the relationship between our two nations.''

''Is this some kind of a joke?'' Colonel Cole asked, waving his men forward, all of whom carried M-16s. ''This is the same goddamn road my men and I take every other day on our military maneuvers. Now you are telling me that because this guy, who calls himself a chief, has decided that this is Indian property . . .''

''Native American property,'' Bloodhawk interrupted. ''I'm certain, being African-American, that you appreciate our political sensitivity.''

''Right,'' Cole responded, frustrated. ''Native American property. That means we no longer can traverse this terrain because it's on what you call 'foreign soil.' ''

''That's a pretty good summary of the situation, Colonel,'' Al reaffirmed.

''I've got a convoy of thirty-three supply trucks, fifteen M1A1 Abrams tanks, twelve 155mm Howitzers, and countless other equipment,'' Cole repeated, ''and you guys are telling me that I basically can't do jackshit with them.''

''Not only that,'' Cheri added, enjoying their ability to manipulate the situation with nothing more than their wits and bluff, ''but you will be in serious violation of state, federal, and international law if you insist on passing through.''

''How do I know that what you're telling me is true,'' Colonel Cole asked, ''and how do I know you have the ability to enforce it?''

''Good questions, Colonel,'' Al responded. Anticipating that his authority would be questioned somewhere down the line, Cheri had called Sec Def Grahn and Sec State Reynolds for a briefing on the situation. "We have your commanding officer on the phone," Al added, handing the colonel the portable phone. Even though the National Guard was in open revolt against the federal government, Al had a feeling that the colonel would buckle in as soon as he heard the voice of the Sec Def. Al had learned a long time ago from his experiences as a roving RMO that it was much easier to acquiesce to the direct orders of an authoritative figure than to defy something for an abstract principle.

"This is Colonel Andrew Cole, commanding officer of the Wyoming National Guard, on detail from the Third Armored Cavalry Regiment." Cole spoke briskly into the phone. "Whom may I ask am I speaking with?"

"Colonel Cole," Phil responded, "you are speaking to the Secretary of Defense of the United States, Phillip Grahn."

"Yes, sir." Cole snapped to attention as if he were in the actual presence of the Sec Def, responding just as Al had suspected he might.

"Just in case you have any doubts as to who I might be," Grahn continued, "let me read out key code words under which you are presently instructed to operate: Opus. Withdrawal. Secession One. Secession Two. Do you need any more evidence?"

"No, sir!" Cole snapped to attention again. "How would you have me and my men proceed?"

His almost instantaneous transformation from defiance to obedience, thought Al, was directly due to the socialization of the professional military officer who, through time immemorial, was taught that he was always responsible to the highest civilian authority above him. That was why most Sec Defs were usually civilians and not military officers. The President, a civilian, was the ultimate Commander-in-Chief.

"You are to follow the command and authority of Dr. Carter," Phil continued, "who represents the direct authority of the Sec State. Above all, please remember to respect the territorial integrity of the sovereign status of Chief Daniel Bloodhawk. We are in delicate negotiations with him and other tribal chiefs at this time."

Phil waited but did not receive any further questions . . . or protestations. "Is that clear, Colonel?"

"Yes, sir," Cole responded.

"Do you understand that if you pledge your loyalties to parties other than the U.S. government," Phil added, "it will place you in direct line for a court-martial? We are all aware that some elements of the Third Armored Cavalry Regiment, possibly National Guard units like your own, have pledged their loyalty to a secessionist cause."

The colonel did not respond for fear of incriminating himself.

"Could this be the case?" Phil asked.

"It could very well be, sir." Cole responded despondently, already imagining an immediate court-martial and subsequent execution.

"Well, Colonel Cole," Phil responded, "somehow I feel that you could make a difference for those few men who have had their heads turned in the wrong direction. How would you like to make that difference?"

"I would appreciate that opportunity, sir." Cole responded with the alacrity of a child who had just been offered the choice between going to bed without his dinner or gorging himself before the television set.

"Then, in front of Dr. Carter, Governor Black, and Chief Bloodhawk, you must swear your allegiance, and that of your men, to uphold the Constitution of the United States," Phil continued. "Please don't take this as a threat, but if you fail to do so immediately, you will be taken into custody and tried for treason."

Although no one asked him to, Cole raised his right hand while holding the telephone to his ear with his left hand. "I swear, on behalf of myself and my men, to uphold the Constitution of the United States. And if I fail to do so, I will give myself up to be tried for treason and dealt with in an appropriate manner."

"Please pass me on to Dr. Carter," Phil ordered.

"Yes, sir," Cole replied. He handed the phone to Al, who put his head together with Cheri to listen to Phil. Bloodhawk listened in on the conversation on his own telephone.

"I think we've made a good start, Al," Phil said. "I've

got Barbara on the line so we can all go over our next steps.''

''As you may already know,'' Bloodhawk interjected, ''Major Jason Montague was taken prisoner by elements of the Third Armored Cavalry and is being held at the Rockefeller Lodge. That's why we set up our roadblock in front of the road that leads to the Lodge. There can be no reinforcements or retreats.''

''Smart move,'' Phil responded. ''If you're not careful, we may make you a three-star general.''

''Going from a head of my own state,'' Bloodhawk retorted, ''to a three-star general in your Army is quite a letdown.''

Everyone laughed for the first time that day.

''I understand,'' Barbara said, ''that you have deployed your fellow chieftains to Utah, Arizona, and Colorado to apply pressure on both the National Guard headquarters and state legislatures.''

''That's right, Secretary Reynolds,'' Bloodhawk responded.

''Barbara,'' she corrected him, ''if you don't mind.''

''Then Barbara it is,'' Bloodhawk repeated. ''As far as I know, we have been quite effective in all of the states you just mentioned. The legislators in those states are requesting that their governors return from 'vacation' to deal with the problem.''

''Good,'' Barbara said. ''But now I have both bad and good news to tell you all.''

''Is that a prelude to a joke?'' Al asked.

''Unfortunately not,'' Barbara replied. ''The good news is that Operation Trident is ahead of schedule. International pressure is working on foreign governments to change course and pull out of this madness.''

''How so?'' Cheri asked.

''The offices of the Foreign Ministers of England and Germany, and the President of France have all lodged major complaints against the United States for a variety of reasons,'' Barbara continued. ''I've read more diplomatic demarches in the past twelve hours from these countries than I've had in the past six years.''

''So they've finally felt the effect of the United States' reaching into their respective homelands?'' Al asked. It always helped to have a covert arm of the government to persuade other world leaders of the consequences of their past, or in this case, intended behavior.

''General Patton wasn't wrong when he said that the best military or diplomatic strategy was to hold your adversary by the nose and kick him in the ass,'' Barbara said.

They all laughed again. Al was only sorry that he couldn't have been part of the planning and execution of Barbara's retaliation. If nothing else, it would have been a creative session.

''Yvette has been medevacked to France,'' Barbara continued, ''and she has persuaded the Foreign Ministers from Germany and England that it would not be a good idea to even contemplate aiding the secessionist movement. Our covert messages to them—highly incendiary, so to speak—were quite effective in persuading our allies to back off from supporting any movement that might divide the United States.''

''That sounds good to me,'' Cheri replied. ''What's the bad news?''

''We didn't have enough time to vet all of the members of the Third Armored Cavalry to determine who were loyal to the states and who were loyal to us,'' Phil replied. ''Jason was taken prisoner and our contact swears that if an agreement for secession doesn't come soon, Jason will be killed and a second catastrophe unleashed that will make the mess in the Glen Canyon Dam seem like child's play. We have until midnight tonight to comply.''

''Not much time,'' Al responded, thinking that they still had twenty-four hours left. He wondered what could be accomplished in such a short period of time. Not very much, he concluded.

''We've lost twelve agents already, Al,'' Barbara replied. ''And we've sent Special Agent Angela Rodriguez and an FBI team to the Hoover Dam, where we suspect that our 'patriots' may have planted enough dynamite to destroy the dam several times over.''

"Christ," Cheri declared, "you're talking about unleashing the forces of Lake Mead . . ."

"That's right," Barbara interrupted.

". . . so that means bye-bye Hoover Dam, Davis Dam, Parker Dam, and Imperial Dam, all of which are located along the Colorado River. And good-bye Nevada, California, Arizona, and Mexico," Cheri continued.

"Keep going," Barbara said. "What else does that mean?"

"Millions of lives," Phil added, "billions of dollars in property damage, and the entire southwest section of the United States becomes an economic, political, and psychological wasteland."

"Do we know for a fact that Hoover Dam is the next target?" Al asked.

"No, Al," Barbara replied. "But we've picked up a lot of intelligence during Agent Rodriguez's raid to suggest that it very well may be the next target."

"In all fairness," Cheri added, "that was part of the governors' original plan. But no one suspected—especially me—that we would ever get to this stage or that it was even a feasible operation."

"Al, that's why I want you to get inside the Lodge," Barbara continued, "and start a face-to-face negotiation with Governor Brigham, whom we suspect is the present leader of the secessionist governors. Does that sound reasonable, Cheri?"

"Yes," Cheri answered. "We won't know where the next target is unless we get inside the Lodge."

"We have until midnight tonight, right? About fourteen hours left?" Al asked Barbara, checking his watch.

"Not exactly," Barbara said. "You have precisely eleven hours left."

"How do you figure that?" Al asked.

"Fourteen hours was based on eastern standard time," Barbara replied, "and we are three hours ahead of you. You have until 9:00 P.M. tonight."

53

GRAND TETONS, WYOMING

Sunday, July 6th, 11:45 A.M.

"Governor Brigham." Cheri spoke into the portable telephone with a definite tone of authority. "You've got what we used to call a Texas stand-off."

"Charming and manipulative as ever, Cheri," Josiah responded with the supercilious tone of voice of someone who knows quite well that he is in control.

"Stop acting like a horse's ass," Cheri responded, making certain that Al, Bloodhawk, Cole, and Hagner could hear her end of the conversation. "It was a good try but we lost. At least let's end this thing without any more loss of lives. Your troops are surrounded by those elements of the Third Armored Cavalry Regiment that are loyal to the Union."

"Nonsense," Josiah said, calling Cheri's bluff. "You were always a good poker player. But not that good." He added, "As you probably know by now, we have as our guest General Jason Montague, one of Secretary of State Reynolds's personal representatives. So that you might be properly informed, he is well and at my side, as are my other colleagues who are listening into this conversation through a speaker phone."

Cheri handed the telephone to Colonel Cole. "Please inform the governor from Utah of the military elements he is surrounded by at this very moment."

"Sir," Cole spoke into the telephone as if he were addressing the Chairman of the Joint Chiefs of Staff, "I am Colonel Andrew Cole, Commander of the Wyoming National Guard, the main force of the Third Armored Cavalry Regiment. At my disposal, I presently have surrounding your own rebel troops the following capability: thirty-three supply trucks; fifteen M1A1 Abrams tanks; twelve 155mm Howitzers, each with twelve rocket tubes; fourteen M2 Bradley infantry fighting vehicles; five OH-58 Kiowa Warrior scout/attack helicopters; five AH-64 helicopters; and fifteen M270 Multiple Launch Rocket Systems. If you have any questions about the veracity of my inventory, I urge you to ask your guest, General Montague, whether I am exaggerating my forward force deployment. The general can also inform you that whatever I may be lacking at the present time can be corrected within minutes. Over and out."

"Nice work, Colonel," Cheri said, taking the telephone back. "Well, Josiah, are you now convinced that if this is not a Texas stand-off it is certainly going to become a Mexican stand-off? One side is going to bite the dust. And it ain't going to be pretty."

"Hold your horses, Cheri," Josiah said. "You know that I don't like to be pressed."

"What are you waiting for, Josiah, an epiphany?" Cheri was purposefully provocative. "Don't tell me that you want to go down in the annals of Mormon history as the first Utah governor to have ordered his constituents into an illegal action and, as a result, had them massacred. All because the great governor of Utah wanted to become a martyr for a secessionist movement—that ultimately failed. Not to mention the fact that your entire behavior has been condemned by the senior deacons of your church. As a matter of fact, I understand that they are seriously contemplating throwing you out of the church for abusing your position and illegally using the church's properties for personal gain."

"I don't know if you're bluffing, but I'm touched by the fact that you are so concerned about my religious future," Josiah interjected.

Al was certainly impressed by Cheri, even if Josiah wasn't. Where was this woman when I needed her all around the world? he thought. Pressuring Josiah to make a quick decision and attacking his narcissism might just get Al into the Lodge to negotiate directly with him. Which was what both he and Cheri wanted.

Josiah responded as expected, clearly irritated by Cheri's insistence and insult. "I'm ordering my troops to stand down while you approach the Lodge. Who do you plan to bring with you?"

"I'm bringing Dr. Alison Carter," she responded, "whom you know represents the Secretary of State. Also Colonel Andrew Cole, Chief Daniel Bloodhawk of the Shoshone nation, and my personal bodyguard Robert Hagner will be coming in. I don't expect any problems getting into or out of the Lodge. Is that understood? I would hate it if Colonel Cole's orders to his deputy commanders to assault and destroy would have to be implemented."

"Please, Cheri," Josiah replied. "I'm a little too old and experienced to be threatened. Remember, my dear, the Glen Canyon Dam was only our first . . . project. I'm sure you wouldn't want anything to happen to me, either."

"As I said," Cheri replied, "this is truly a Mexican standoff."

"Two mutually assured disasters," Al whispered to the group, "are what are maintaining the stability of the crisis right now. Seems to me like a new variation of the old Cold War. Then we had the mutually assured destruction of two countries and their cities held hostage to the threat of atomic devastation. Nothing seems to change."

"You're the expert on human nature," Bloodhawk interjected. "You tell me why."

"Man needs war to give meaning to his existence," Al replied, wondering whether Bloodhawk considered him an expert on human nature because of his medical background. "He only stops fighting when he is physically and emotionally exhausted. The rest is nothing but the futility of the world to rationalize its own cowardice and compensate for its inherent inadequacies by developing lofty principles. Meanwhile, people around the globe are routinely slaughtered en masse. Witness Cambodia, where Pol Pot effectively massacred from one to two million of his own people yet rested comfortably for years in Battambang province protected by the Thai military. Or Burundi and Rwanda, where over two hundred thousand people were massacred in less than two weeks. And one week later, several thousand so-called relief organizations suddenly appeared like vultures on carrion to collect their financial tribute for posturing as a collective entity of concerned world citizens. I don't know which is the greater travesty, the massacre of innocent people or the financial rewards given to those who feed on their bodies. The rest is simply rationalization."

"Thank you," Cheri said. "Now you're Seneca, the father of the school of Cynicism and Stoicism." She had to admit to herself that she admired Al's knowledge and opinions. It brought her back to her wonderful years as a Ph.D. candidate.

"I take that as a backhanded compliment," Al retorted with the intellectual vigor of a graduate student. "Actually, Seneca was the founder of neither the School of Stoicism nor Cynicism. He was a tutor to the Roman emperor Nero but espoused stoic values that later entered into Christianity: follow virtue, distrust emotions, and overcome evil with good."

"I certainly stand corrected," Cheri responded in a nondefensive manner. "I just think that beneath that innocent exterior and convoluted verbiage, you are really a romantic."

"Cheri," Al added, "with you around it would be hard for me to practice Seneca's belief in asceticism."

"I wouldn't want you to . . ." Cheri responded, touching his cheek.

"I hate to interrupt," Bloodhawk interjected, "but I have a call for Al."

"Who is it?" Al asked, taking the telephone receiver.

"Angela Rodriguez," Bloodhawk replied. "That FBI agent the Secretary of State . . . I mean Barbara . . . mentioned."

"Hello," Al said. "This is Dr. Alison Carter."

"Sir," Angela replied in a hurried manner, "I'm Special Agent Angela Rodriguez, assigned by . . ."

"Your name and your task have been mentioned to me," Al responded. "How can I help you?"

''Right now,'' Angela said, ''I have over one hundred FBI and other federal officials carefully examining Hoover Dam for any explosives or possible situations that might lead to another . . .''

''And . . . ?''

''And''—she still wasn't sure how to say what she had to—''after three hours we have found nothing to indicate that this dam could be the next target.''

''What?'' Al asked, incredulous. ''Both Governor Black and the Secretary of State indicated to me otherwise.''

''I know, sir,'' she reponded hesitantly.

''Then what is the problem?'' Al asked, a clear tone of confusion in his voice.

''Well, sir,'' Angela continued, ''a few hours ago we raided one of the main headquarters of the False Patriots in Nye County, Nevada, only a few miles away from the Hoover Dam . . .''

''Yes,'' Al asked, impatiently.

''. . . and there were maps of the Hoover Dam,'' she continued, ''as well as maps of the Davis Dam, the Parker Dam, and the Imperial Dam.''

''Are you saying that one of those other dams may be the next target?'' Al asked.

''We have agents combing every inch of those dams as well,'' Angela replied, ''and we still have found nothing.''

''Special Agent Rodriguez''—Al sounded brusque—''I have a feeling that you are trying to tell me something, but you are very reluctant to say it. What is it?''

''When we raided the Nye County Headquarters''—Angela tried to choose her words carefully—''we picked up several taped telephone conversations between Governor Black and . . .''

Cheri motioned for Al to hurry up. ''Josiah expects to see us ASAP.''

''I'll be there,'' Al responded to Cheri, walking with the telephone. ''Please continue, Ms. Rodriguez.''

''The telephone conversations were between Governor Black and . . .''

Suddenly the line went dead.

54

ROCKEFELLER LODGE, GRAND TETONS, WYOMING

Sunday, July 6th, 1:05 P.M.

Alison Carter walked through the front doors of the Lodge for the second time in two days. This time, however, he was not alone. Accompanying him were a former leader of the secessionist movement, Governor Cheri Black; the head of the Western Council of Native-Born Americans, Daniel Bloodhawk; DSA Robert Hagner; and Colonel Andrew Cole of the United States Army. But Special Agent Rodriguez's conversation had been very disconcerting. Was he really walking in with allies? He knew he would soon find out.

Al knew also that this would be the last face-to-face meeting at which he would be able resolve the crisis without incurring more bloodshed. Or precipitating a civil war. At this point, the military situation was at a stalemate, but the political situation was completely in flux. Without Yvette, who had been medevacked back to France, or Cheri, the secessionists were being led by the governor of Utah, Josiah Smith Brigham IV. Or were they? It was for Al to determine to what degree Brigham controlled his colleagues.

Looking around, Al realized that over the last two days the secessionists had created a formidable command and control center out of the Lodge. The entry area alone was filled with weapons, personnel, and computers. He estimated that it would take at least five hundred troops to overtake this makeshift fortress.

"Greetings," Josiah said, reaching out his hand in a sign of friendship. He was almost surprised when Al shook it. "I'm glad to see you're looking fine, Cheri. You too, Al, considering all the personal hardships you've encountered."

"I'd like you to meet Chief Daniel Bloodhawk," Al said, ignoring Josiah's facetious tone of voice.

"I've heard quite a lot about you . . . and your people, of course," Josiah responded, gritting his teeth. He knew that Bloodhawk and his tribe were responsible for creating the stalemate he found himself in now.

"I also want you to meet Colonel Andrew Cole," Al continued, "and DSA Robert Hagner."

Josiah acknowledged them by nodding his head. "Now let's meet the rest of my group." He led everyone up the Lodge's opulent staircase into the room in which they had held their previous meeting. And then he stopped and stared past Al as if he were fixed on an object at the other end of the room.

Al observed the silence and stare closely and realized that Josiah's immobility had all the markings of a minor epileptic seizure. If Al was correct, consciousness and mental and physical activity would return as abruptly as they left. Although he hadn't treated many cases of epilepsy, he knew that treatment often involved only a mild sedative like phenobarbital or an amphetamine like Benzedrine. The cases he had seen were precipitated by unusual stimuli or stress. Flashing lights. A sudden change in weather. An emotional shock. That explained why Al hadn't noticed any seizure activity before. While Josiah felt in control of the situation, he was fine. But now the strain of the crisis was mounting incrementally and he was beginning to somatize the stress.

As suddenly as his attention had drifted, Josiah refocused on the group and continued walking them into the room.

"Well, well," Wyoming Governor James McMinn said, greeting the group. "I always look forward to cheerful reunions. Al, you've certainly managed to gather a motley band of followers. And this must be the Robin Hood of the Grand Tetons." He walked over to Bloodhawk and held out his hand. "You've definitely caused me an immense headache. My constituents are screaming about the traffic tie-ups and demonstrations all over the state. I hear your people are telling the citizens of Wyoming that they are no longer legitimately there. Instead, they are being asked to observe your Indian laws and requirements for citizenship? Otherwise your people will expel my people from the state?'' He added, nervously, ''Very clever strategy. Very clever.''

''Good to see you again, Cheri,'' Arizona Governor Andrew Paul said, walking over and shaking her hand. ''I'm sorry that we've had to go through all this nonsense. I'm not certain that we've accomplished anything other than to destroy a dam and demolish a town. Maybe you can help us figure it out.''

''Andrew,'' Josiah interjected, ''you'll have plenty of time for self-flagellation later. Now is not the time.''

''Easy talk for you, Josiah,'' Andrew said indignantly, ''but I didn't notice any towns in Utah disappearing.''

''Enough!'' Josiah commanded. But it was clear to everyone in the room that he didn't have as much control as he would have liked. If Yvette were still here, Josiah thought, it would have been very different. Instead, he had to manage a bunch of disgruntled whiners who squealed like pigs every time pressure was applied to them. He wondered how long he could hold this loose coalition of malcontents together. How ironic, he thought, that he felt like a dam holding back an oncoming flood.

''How is Yvette?'' Al asked. He motioned to his team to sit down at the rectangular table opposite their presumed counterparts.

''If I didn't know who was asking me that question,'' Andrew responded, clearly despondent, ''I would have laughed in his face. I think you know the answer. My God, have you no civility? Of all places—Cambridge University. Isn't anything sacrosanct?''

''Hold it, Andrew,'' James interrupted indignantly. ''I was an Oxford scholar as well as a Harvard undergraduate. There's no comparison. Cambridge in Massachusetts is far more impressive than Cambridge in England.''

''All right, guys,'' Josiah interjected. ''We're not here to fight among ourselves.''

''Well, I see that I can't leave you boys alone. Certainly

not for more than a few hours,'' Cheri said with a broad smile, ''otherwise you will destroy yourselves.''

''But isn't that what you want?'' James asked in his usual understated sarcastic tone of voice.

''Jimmy,'' Cheri replied, in her softest, most reassuring voice, ''all I want is what you should have wanted for you and your constituents all along. Peace. Prosperity.''

''Oh, Christ!'' James uttered. ''Now she is Mother Teresa, giving me a fuckin' lecture on the moral politician. Did you forget, Governor Black, that it was you and Josiah here who encouraged us to break away from the federal government? You seem to have forgotten all that palaver about states' rights, the Tenth Amendment, that which was not granted specifically to the federal government remains within the states' rights.'' He paused, his face flushed with a combination of anger and excitement. ''You're a real piece of work. On that ride in Breckenridge you made it clear that the time, the place, the plans, which by the way were yours, were all in place. And if we didn't do what you suggested—take over the Colorado River starting with the Glen Canyon Dam—we would be losing a historical—or was it hysterical?—moment in history. You challenged us to become 'real politicians.' You even mocked our dear colleague Andrew here with, if I may quote from your own words, 'How do you expect to control your own state if you can't control your own horse?' Do you remember that, Cheri? It was only three days ago. That's not a very long time in the history of politics.''

''All right, Jimmy,'' Josiah interrupted. ''We're not here to attack one another on an ex cathedra basis.''

''Ex cathedra?'' James repeated, mocking Josiah's high-pitched tone of voice. ''What the hell does that mean?'' Looking at Al and knowing his role fully well, he spat out, ''Is ex cathedra like in ex cathedra Cambridge University?''

''You son of a bitch!'' Josiah screamed, standing up ready to strike James. But he didn't. He simply stood staring at him for three seconds. When he refocused, he sat down again.

''If I didn't know any better, boys,'' Cheri said, ''I would say that you're very definitely falling apart.''

"Very astute observation, Governor Black," Andrew said with a sigh of resignation. He, too, had come to the same conclusion. The tide had obviously turned, and he was too savvy a politician not to know when to come back to shore. His most important concern was to return to his state capital as quickly as possible. With the destruction of the Glen Canyon Dam, the presence of federal and National Guard troops, and a new surge of Indian disturbances on the reservations, his obligation as governor of Arizona was his primary one. His involvement in a civil war now seemed ludicrous. But maybe it always was. Whether you were a county executive in Texas or the President of the United States, the principle of accommodating your local constituents was the universal truth of all politics. As far as he was concerned, the quicker they could resolve this prickly issue, about which he now had second thoughts, the quicker he could leave this Lodge.

"I think we should begin to seriously discuss the final resolution of our situation," James interjected, clearly annoyed by the unruly manner in which they were all behaving. "One way or another we must, I repeat, we must settle it, here and now." His outburst was accompanied by applause from several members of both sides of the table.

Al sat silently watching the dynamics of the group evolve. Only two days ago, the secessionist movement had been led by a highly disciplined group of domestic leaders with the direct support of a foreign country. But without Cheri, and to a lesser degree Yvette, the unity had dissolved into a cauldron of disorder and discontent. Collective political ideals were subsumed by personal expediency. A common ideological purpose which could have changed the course of history had been buried in competition and backbiting.

Al checked his watch. He had less than eight hours to stop this lunacy . . . at least according to Barbara. Or did he? Angela Rodriguez's incomplete sentence still rang in his ears, "Governor Black and . . ." Who had really been planning the secessionist movement? he wondered.

55

ROCKEFELLER LODGE, GRAND TETONS, WYOMING

Sunday, July 6th, 1:20 P.M.

''Gentlemen, can we try to focus on the heart of the matter?'' Al asked. ''It's time to discuss the basis for an . . . agreement.''

''Whoa,'' James said. ''Hold your horses, partner. I don't think we're anywhere near the point of talking about one yet.''

''Does anyone else in this room agree with Governor McMinn's evaluation?'' Al looked around the table, examining each of his adversaries' faces very carefully. More than anything else, he sensed that they were tired, if not exhausted. The past seventy-two hours has been far more traumatic than they had initially envisioned. So why were they still stalling?

''I can't believe that after all that has transpired you want to repeat the Glen Canyon episode!'' Cheri asked. ''Don't you have any feelings for the citizens of Page and what has happened to their lives? We all know that unless we come to terms here and now, innocent citizens of your states are going to suffer. And lose their lives. And their property. And then there will be no turning back.''

''Are you trying to threaten us?'' Josiah asked in a defiant tone of voice. ''I don't think that you are in any position to dictate any terms.'' He paused and added, ''*Any* terms!''

''I would hope that neither you,'' Al said firmly, staring

straight at James's face, "nor any of your colleagues would construe what we are about to do as dictating terms, certainly not before we know precisely where each side stands."

"I agree with Al," Andrew interjected, obviously anxious to leave. "We have to start somewhere."

"All right," Josiah responded, realizing that unity among the governors was in danger. "Since you seem confident about where you stand, Dr. Carter, why don't you summarize the situation as you see it."

"Gentlemen," Al responded, looking from governor to governor, "each of you is now confronted with a simple risk-reward ratio."

Cheri smiled to herself. She enjoyed listening to Al. He seemed to have a way with words that made anything he said seem credible without sounding slick.

"What do you mean 'risk-reward ratio'?" James asked. "It sounds like a banking term."

"Governor McMinn." Al spoke slowly, certain that if he could split the governors of Arizona and Wyoming away from Josiah, he could convince them that it was in their respective interests to acquiesce to the demands he would eventually lay out. "Your state's interests, despite your earlier beliefs, are not in having America divided."

"And what should our interests be?" Andrew asked in a mock sarcasm so that it wouldn't look as if he were the first one to throw in the towel.

Al responded as if he had been practicing law for the last twenty years, rather than medicine. "Your interests, as well as those of your European allies, lie in preserving the physical integrity of your states and the viability of your respective state governments. All, of course, within the context of a federal constitution. Let us speak frankly."

"That's certainly refreshing," James responded.

"I understand from conversations with Washington"—Al ignored James's provocative comment—"that there has been an unfortunate accident in the French Ministry on the Quai d'Orsay. Several French diplomats and senior civil servants died in an act of terrorism." Al looked around the table. It was clear that everyone there understood precisely what he was talking about. He didn't have to spell out the federal government's abilities when threatened. And he wanted the governors to be able to save face.

"How are you so certain?" Josiah asked.

"Will you try and listen a little," Andrew interjected. "It would save us all time, energy, and money . . . and maybe our jobs."

"I suggest you let Dr. Carter finish," Bloodhawk said, "so that we can finalize a . . . peace treaty, for lack of a better word." He smiled inwardly at the irony of the situation. How many worthless peace treaties had his ancestors signed? At least now, he was on the side of those dictating the terms.

"How do you like that?" James shouted. "We're already being told that we have an agreement-in-progress. And the only thing left to do is to implement it." James stood up as if he were ready to leave the table.

"Sir," Colonel Cole said, "I think it would be a good idea for you to remain seated until we've finished."

"Thank you, Colonel," James responded. "That really makes it complete. I've just been threatened by a medical doctor, an Indian chief, and an Army colonel."

"Sit down," Cheri said, "and shut up. Stop making an ass of yourself."

"I have also been informed by the Secretary of State," Al continued in a calm tone, as if no altercation had taken place, "of an unfortunate accident at the Frankfurt airport, where a 747 Lufthansa carrying unspecified cargo to the United States was set afire by an unknown arsonist. That was most unfortunate." Turning toward Colonel Cole, Al asked, "Approximately how much does it cost to replace one of those jumbo 747s?"

"About fifty million dollars per plane," Cole replied.

"That's a lot of money," Bloodhawk added. "Imagine if an airport suffered damage by having a fleet of planes blow up . . . by accident. That could put a real dent in a state's budget, its tourist economy, its business travelers. . . . Each of you governors operate your own airports, isn't that so?"

"Thank you, Chief Bloodhawk," Al said. "You took the

words out of my mouth.'' He got a secret pleasure out of the ashen color on Andrew's face.

''Are we now going to hear,'' Josiah interrupted Al, ''that your Secretary of State was most regretful upon hearing about the terrible accident at Cambridge University?''

''As a matter of fact . . .'' Al responded.

''Please save us from your Secretary's personal condolences,'' Josiah continued. ''Whomever set fire to a bookstore, no matter how small, at Queens College committed a heinous deed. It was a barbaric act unworthy of a superpower, let alone one founded upon the First Amendment.'' In point of fact, Josiah couldn't care less about England's loss. But he was extremely concerned that the same thing could happen to the records stored by the Mormon's Genealogical Society and now wondered how much the federal government might know about them.

''I certainly can empathize with your sentiments,'' Al added. ''Most tragic. When I heard about it, I immediately thought of all of those libraries and warehouses around our country, and in your states, gentlemen, that house books and records.''

''Let's cut the crap,'' Josiah responded. ''Am I to presume that these accidents will continue until Utah . . . we . . . decide to withdraw our support . . .''

''. . . and subsidy,'' Al added.

''. . . from these secessionists?'' Josiah concluded.

''That is correct,'' Al replied, uncomfortable with the threatening posture he was taking. Diplomacy, to him, should be reasonable men reaching reasonable compromises because it was the only reasonable thing to do. ''Therefore, as your states' duly elected governors,'' Al said, looking straight at Josiah, ''I'm certain that there are many more important things for you to do than to stir up trouble for the federal government and involve your states in a no-win situation. I find it hard to believe that there aren't enough internal state and local issues to deal with without trying to take on the country and the Constitution.''

''As a matter of fact, James,'' Cheri interjected, eager to put salt on the wound, ''your state already has problems with Chief Bloodhawk and his nation. As I understand it, it's an issue of having usurped the rights and privileges of another nation state. Is that correct, Chief Bloodhawk?"

"To put it bluntly, so that no one in this room can misinterpret what I am saying," Bloodhawk replied in a clear voice of authority, "the Native Americans of Wyoming, Colorado, Arizona, and Utah have decided to secede from the states in which we are located. Our rights as sovereign nations have been violated by the insensitive, crass, and heavyhanded ways that state officials have dealt with my colleagues and their constituents. So we are demanding that you return the lands that we lease to you. If you persist in this secessionist movement against the federal government we Native Americans, all the way from Mississippi to California, will have no alternative but to secede from your states, take back our land, and requisition all those appurtenances located upon the lands—hydroelectric plants, power lines, railroad tracks, airports, highways, waterways . . ."

A National Guardsman walked into the room and quietly handed Colonel Cole a note. The colonel broke into a broad smile.

"We get the idea, Bloodhawk," Josiah interrupted. "And you, Colonel? What threats do you have for us?"

"None at all," Cole responded. "I have just been informed by one of my field commanders that the troops surrounding the Lodge have surrendered without firing a shot. No one was hurt and certainly no one was killed. So, gentlemen, you . . . we . . . are now completely surrounded by loyal federal troops."

"For all practical purposes . . ." Al said.

". . . we are defeated." Andrew finished Al's sentence for him.

"In effect," Cheri responded, "yes."

"No thanks," Josiah added, "to traitors to the cause."

Al looked at Cheri's radiant face and couldn't help wondering which traitors the governor from Utah had in mind.

56

ROCKEFELLER LODGE, GRAND TETONS, WYOMING

July 6th, 1:45 P.M.

"Gentlemen," Al said, "it's time to reach some understanding about how we will proceed from this point on. Our primary objective," he continued, taking several folded papers out of his jacket, "is to sign a formal document that will conclude the hostilities." He passed the papers from governor to governor for their review. After minutes had passed, and the papers had been returned to him, he continued, "Are we in agreement?

"Are you on board?" Al looked at Andrew, purposefully picking on the weakest governor. With Cheri's defection and this governor's signature, the secessionist movement was seriously fractured.

Andrew looked at Josiah and Jim before he responded. He clearly needed some support or reassurance that what he was about to do was acceptable to them. But neither gave him any encouragement.

"As the governor of Colorado," Cheri said, picking up a pen, "and one of your former leaders, I am going to be the first governor to sign this document which, for want of a better working title, is called 'Settlement of Differences.' "

"Very clever, Al," Josiah interjected, irritated by the outflanking maneuver.

"Well, will the Arizona governor," Cheri asked facetiously, "tell us what future generations will think of the fact that you were willing to sacrifice the safety and well-being of the citizens in your home state?''

''Don't let them intimidate you into agreeing with something that you don't feel comfortable with,'' Josiah said forcefully.

''May I take a few minutes to think about it?'' Andrew asked, pushing his chair back from the table.

''Take as much time as you want,'' Al responded, ''as long as we leave this room with a written document which delineates the points needed for a full and complete agreement between Washington and your states.''

''What's the alternative?'' James asked, in a less than conciliatory tone of voice. ''Suppose we don't sign the agreement?''

''Then you have the serious problem of dealing with my people,'' Chief Bloodhawk responded. ''I think I've given you a very clear picture of what would happen if my people decide to secede from your states.'' It seemed to Bloodhawk that James was stalling for time. But why? The longer he waited to sign, the more he could hurt his position.

''In other words,'' James responded, ''we don't really have much of a choice.''

''On the contrary,'' Al responded, ''you can play out the scenario as it exists now and see what happens. But how many innocent lives and how much property will have to be destroyed before we arrive at this very same point? Or you can capitulate now, save lives, save face, and avoid going to prison for seditious or treasonous acts against the federal government.'' Pausing, he added, ''I definitely think you have a choice. In all fairness, you have more of a choice than you all were offering to the feds . . . or me.''

''If you could only understand the situation from our perspective,'' James retorted, realizing that the game had been lost, and wondering just how much personal and professional respect he could salvage at the eleventh hour.

Al directed his response toward Josiah. ''You literally attacked the United States of America. You were prepared to declare war against your own country. You forged alliances with international conspirators. Those acts in and of themselves constitute treason and a violation of the law of sedition. Well, it didn't work, thanks to many factors,'' Al said, turning to Cheri to pay tribute. ''It would be fair, yet blunt, to state the obvious. You have lost. The secessionist movement has been thwarted all the way from its grass roots to, hopefully, the very top of its highest branches.''

As if she had waited for her cue, Cheri signed the settlement and passed the document and pen to Andrew. After a few moments of silent deliberation, he nodded his head in agreement. ''Count the governor of Arizona as one of the governors who is reaffirming his commitment to the Union.''

''Andrew,'' James said, ''all they are asking for is a yes or no. They don't need a speech.''

''When it's your turn to decide,'' Andrew answered, ''then do whatever it is you want to. But don't tell me what to do.''

''You'll get your chance,'' Cheri said to James. ''And then you're next, Josiah.''

''Not quite,'' Josiah shouted. ''Not quite!''

Al wondered if he had finally accomplished what he had wanted—to provoke Josiah into blowing up and revealing those pieces that were still missing from Al's complete picture of the movement. Why had Cheri turned away from the movement so readily? What had been the next target for destruction? Who, besides the governors in this room, was involved in this secessionist movement? As Josiah shouted out only a half hour before, Cheri wasn't the only traitor. But did the other one, if there was another one, reside in Washington, D.C.? Barbara Reynolds's name kept haunting him. But why would she have helped precipitate a secessionist movement?

''I'm not going to be the fall guy,'' Josiah shouted. Reaching into his cowboy boot, he pulled out a small Derringer pistol and fired it twice.

57

ROCKEFELLER LODGE, GRAND TETONS, WYOMING

Sunday, July 6th, 2:05 P.M.

Colonel Cole pulled out his 9mm Beretta and took aim, but there were too many state troopers surrounding Josiah to have a clear shot at him.

"Colonel," Josiah screamed, "don't do anything foolish. A lot of people will die and nothing will have been accomplished."

"Sir," Cole responded with more bravado than reason, "please give yourself up and prevent any further bloodshed. The secessionist movement is over. You have nothing to gain from this."

"Don't come any closer!" Josiah ordered, backing away from the group with his entourage.

"Again, Governor, I ask you to surrender," Cole shouted back. "Please don't force me to fire on you and your men."

"Colonel," Josiah responded defiantly, "my men and I are leaving here, either on foot or in body bags. But we will not surrender. If you kill me, you will make me a martyr to the cause. I would certainly prefer that type of exit from this world than that of a coward who was trapped like some common criminal."

"On the count of three," Cole interjected, "I will fire at will."

"Stop!" Al shouted. "Governor Brigham is right. Put down your gun. The last thing we want is to create one more martyr. If we kill the governor in cold blood, the press will make the ATF mishap in Waco, Texas, look as if it was a precision military exercise. A killing wouldn't serve anybody's purpose."

"But Dr. Carter . . ." Cole implored.

"He's got us by the short hairs, Colonel," Al responded.

"Dr. Carter is right," Cheri added. "If we shoot him, we will be playing right into his hands. For the moment, there is nothing to do but to release him and his men."

"But, ma'am . . ." Cole responded.

"No ifs, ands, or buts," Al reiterated. "You heard the governor of Colorado. Let them all go." Al had concluded that nothing would be gained by Brigham's death. If anything, he would lose the opportunity to find out the answers to his questions about the secessionists and to ferret out Brigham's co-conspirators.

"Is that an official order, sir?" Cole asked Al, as the ranking member of the federal government at that very moment.

"Yes, it is," Al responded brusquely. "An official order as conveyed from me to you, reinforced by the backup authority of the Secretary of State and, in turn, the Commander-in-Chief of the United States Armed Forces." That should assuage Cole's concerns, Al thought.

"May I have that in writing, sir?" Cole asked, acting like the good federal bureaucrat that he was.

"Of course," Al replied. "Now put down your gun and send the governor and his men on their way. And tell your men outside the Lodge to let them through unharmed. Is that understood?"

"Yes, sir!" Cole responded, snapping to attention.

"Thank you, Colonel," Josiah said. "I knew you were a smart man, Dr. Carter. Otherwise our wily Secretary of State wouldn't have chosen you to come here. And Cheri wouldn't have worked with you to defeat our cause. My compliments to all of you."

After Josiah left, Al focused on the thin trail of blood that trickled down his cheek. The bullet meant for him had merely grazed his forehead and the superficial wound above his right eye needed only washing with soap and water and a simple Band-Aid placed over it to heal perfectly. He was far more concerned about the wound in Cheri's right shoulder, although she didn't seem as if she were in any pain.

Al wiped the blood away from his forehead, and he heard the governor and his troopers drive away. Then he heard Cole's men stomping up the stairs of the Lodge.

Cheri was still slightly dazed from the shock of the whole episode and collapsed to the floor. A red bloodstain on her blouse was clearly visible and enlarging. Without waiting for permission, Al lowered the top of her blouse and examined the wound. It was deeper than he would have liked it to be. Although the bullet had passed through her shoulder cleanly, and lodged somewhere in the wall of the conference room, she would need to have the wound sutured within the next twenty-four hours or it would become infected.

"Hagner," Al said, "you're going to have to send Cheri to the nearest ER while I track down Josiah. I'm certain that we haven't heard the last of him. Colonel Cole, send information on Josiah to all FBI offices and appropriate federal agencies. Instruct them to inform you when he is spotted. Do not have anyone attempt to capture or shoot him, unless he shoots first." Al then placed two Band-Aids that Hagner handed him over his forehead and right eyebrow in order to stop the slight oozing of blood.

"Yes, sir!" Cole responded, ordering his men to disperse and proceed accordingly.

"You're not going anywhere without me," Cheri said feebly. "This isn't the first time I've been shot at or had a minor scratch." She looked at Al with the intensity of someone who would stop at nothing to accomplish her aims. "If you leave me here, you know you'll just worry about this little flea bite in my shoulder. If I'm with you, I'll make sure you don't."

"Cheri, that's a pretty bad wound Josiah inflicted on you," Al lied. While she certainly needed medical attention, he also wanted her to get some badly needed rest. Furthermore, he still wasn't certain what role she had really played in this crisis. By removing her from the scene, at least he had one less problem to deal with.

But he just couldn't help himself and planted a kiss on

Cheri's forehead. She looked like a pouting ten-year-old who would do anything to get what she wanted, even if it meant exacerbating her wound. Suddenly, Al was angry at himself for having allowed her to manipulate him. This Texas transplant with her mouth, moxie, and occasional truck-driver demeanor had a compelling quality about her. She was coy without being cloying. She was attractive without being self-conscious. She was smart without being a smartass. She was exceedingly feminine without having to show herself off. And she was not afraid of power, either, in someone else or in herself.

"Aren't you a medical doctor?" she asked.

"Yes," he replied.

"Then, you sew it up for me," Cheri responded emphatically.

"I don't have any surgical equipment," he said, looking for any way out of the situation. As much as he might want to help Cheri, he would be wasting valuable time. Or would he? She definitely knew more than she was still willing to tell him. But she was right. For the moment, he had no other choice. He wasn't going anywhere without her.

"Gentlemen," Cheri announced as if she were about to make an ecclesiastical pronouncement, "please find Dr. Carter a bottle of vodka or gin, a needle, and some thread. ASAP. I'm certain that if you ask the people at the front desk, they will tell you where to find everything." Watching Hagner and Cole leave the room to do her bidding, Cheri looked at Al like a schoolteacher showing a student who is boss. "In the meantime, you are going to prepare me for surgery."

"And how do you recommend I do that?" Al asked, realizing that they were now alone in the conference room. Cradling her chin tenderly in his hands, he brought his lips to hers. They inhaled each other's passions. Gently, he stroked her face, neck, and the outlines of her small breasts. He could feel her nipples harden beneath his touch.

"Leave your hand there," she said, resting her hand upon his. "You see, Doctor, what a wonderful healing skill you have?"

''I'm not sure you call that part of the healing arts,'' Al whispered as he nibbled at her ears.

''I can't tell you how wonderful it feels,'' she continued, kissing his stubbled face. ''I don't think I even need the operation now.''

''Love heals all?'' he responded.

''That's what they say,'' she said, ''and I wager you to prove me differently.''

''Excuse me,'' Hagner said, clearing his throat as he walked into the room. ''I've brought all the necessary items for surgery. Absolut vodka. One needle. Black thread.''

''Hagner,'' Cheri said, disappointed, ''didn't you ever hear of timing?''

''Yes, ma'am,'' he responded, his face flushed, ''but I was led to believe that it was imperative that we gather all the necessary equipment ASAP.''

''Do you always follow orders?'' she asked.

''Yes, ma'am,'' he responded, placing the items on the conference table. ''Especially when it involves your well-being.''

''Oh, you're such a gentleman,'' she replied mockingly. ''Now I have two men to worry about me. That's not bad for a Texas girl.''

Cole and Bloodhawk walked back into the room carrying a bottle of antiseptic, a pillow, and a blanket.

''I think that you will need something to rest on,'' Bloodhawk said, trying to make her feel more comfortable on a chair.

''I'm going to need you both to hold her against the back of the chair,'' Al said to Bloodhawk and Cole.

Al threaded the needle and soaked it in the bottle of vodka in order to sterilize it. ''Hagner, you will have to crouch down and hold her legs together so that she doesn't kick me while I'm sewing.''

''How much of this stuff am I supposed to drink?'' she asked between swigs of vodka.

''At the rate you're pouring on the anesthetic,'' Al responded, ''I don't think you will have to worry about anything. Now, guys, hold her tightly.''

Al cleaned the wound on her shoulder with iodine, swabbing it back and forth until her entire shoulder was brown. He poured alcohol over both of his hands and then took the needle and placed it close to the uppermost parts of the lip of the skin. "Hold on, baby!" he said as he passed the needle through the folds of her shoulder.

"Aaaggghhh!" she screamed. "Oh Christ, I never thought sewing was such a painful pastime." Everyone smiled, grateful that she could keep her sense of humor.

"Good girl," Al said. "Ready for another stitch?" He passed the needle and thread through her skin with the skill of a seamstress who sews for her livelihood.

"Oh, Mother Teresa!" Cheri shouted in a loud voice as the three men held her tightly against the chair. She was trying to be as strong as possible because Al would finish the suturing no matter how she felt. That was the nature of being a professional. The task had to be accomplished at all costs. And that was why, she realized at that very moment, Al would stop at nothing to get to the bottom of their current problem with Josiah. No matter who might be injured in the process. A settlement with some of the governors may have been signed, but she knew that Al's mission was not yet over.

"Aagggghh!" Cheri screamed before she blacked out.

58

SALT LAKE CITY, UTAH

Sunday, July 6th, 5:35 P.M.

"Tell me again why we've come here?" Cheri asked Al as they rode in the military convoy led by Colonel Cole.

It was an eight-car procession of motorcycles, MP vehicles with flashing red lights, and truckloads of fully armed federal soldiers. During the two-hour plane trip from Jackson Hole to Salt Lake City International Airport there had been no bleeding or inordinate pain for either of them. Fortunately, the military paramedics on board the C-131 cargo transport were able to provide Cheri with liberal doses of local anesthetic. She had slept for most of the trip.

Al checked her right shoulder to evaluate the progress of his post-operative surgery. All that work in his understaffed clinic had paid off. At least for performing minor operations under less than optimal conditions. He had the medics give her a tetanus booster shot and an antibiotic in order to prevent any tetanus or post-operative infections.

She responded by placing her head on his shoulder. The half bottle of vodka she had drunk during the operation had made her groggy. But she was clearheaded enough to know that how she felt about Al was not the product of inebriation.

Al liked the feel of Cheri so close to him. But his thoughts had to be elsewhere—wherever Governor Josiah Brigham was! Nothing prevented Josiah from precipitating the second catastrophe that both he and Barbara had alluded to. And

Al was certain that at that very moment Josiah was attempting to put some act into motion that required precision timing.

Al withdrew two rumpled, faded pieces of paper from his pants pocket. They were hate flyers that Jaime had given him at the clinic only days before—and now seemed like ancient history. FBI Agent Gonzalez had reaffirmed to him during their brief telephone conversation that all of the hate mail, armaments, and militia instructions were coming through Salt Lake City, and possibly from within the Mormon complex. The information provided to the FBI by its informers convinced Al that Josiah was now a loose cannon. A renegade. Any Mormons who were working for Josiah must be disaffected members of the church, Al thought, or extremist sympathizers who could be found in any religious group. Unfortunately, charismatic leaders were always very attractive to those poor souls who were thirsting for meaning and direction in their lives. All that Al had to go on right now to track Josiah down were these two pieces of paper and his own clinical instincts.

"It's been quite a while since I let a man take care of me," Cheri murmured.

"Don't start handing out kudos until we've completed our mission," Al answered, brought back to the moment by the warm, physical presence leaning against him.

"You sound anxious," she said, gently touching the Band-Aids on his face and feeling helpless. There was nothing that she could do for him now. He would have to play out the final scenes of a scenario that she had helped set in motion.

"That's probably because I am," Al answered. "And to answer your first question, we're here because I think this is where Josiah fled to. Cole checked air controllers in Wyoming and confirmed that Josiah was on his way to Salt Lake City. The real question we should be asking is, 'why?' "

"That's a very good question," she said, bringing his face down to her lips. "But did I ever properly thank you for having been so good to me?" When Al did not respond, she decided to stop playing her game and play his. Al was obviously completely engrossed in his pursuit of Josiah and nothing was going to sidetrack him.

"But why are we racing to the Temple?" Cheri asked. "Why not to the governor's mansion or to the capitol?"

"Here's my assessment," Al said with conviction. "Your governors' plan didn't work. Thanks to the military expertise in retaking the dam, FEMA's evacuating Page, our coopting of the media, and Defense's maintaining order among the National Guard, we were able to contain the crisis very quickly. In fact, unbelievably well."

"You're still not telling me why we are here," she reiterated.

"I'm trying to explain to you the reasoning process I went through," Al responded. "The immediate support structure for the secession was destroyed with the collapse of the governors' solidarity. The financial interest in your states by our so-called allies will now be more closely monitored by the federal government. Of course, Bloodhawk and his colleagues played no small role in the collapse of the secessionists movement." As he abbreviated all that had taken place over the last three days, he realized that a lot had been accomplished in a short time. "Here, take a look at these two pieces of hate mail that came from here. If you need any further convincing about why we are here, just look at the area code at the bottom and the contents of those leaflets."

The caravan stopped in front of the Mormon complex at 50 North Temple Street.

"So that's why we're here," Al concluded his discourse. "We've stalemated Josiah at every turn. But what is the only card left that he can play? The one that can rip this country apart."

59

SALT LAKE CITY, UTAH

Sunday, July 6th, 5:55 P.M.

''Separation of Church and State?'' Cheri reiterated his conclusion, walking quickly to keep up with Al.

''You got it,'' Al responded, realizing that according to Josiah's timetable there were only forty-five minutes left to prevent a second act of destruction. And there was no doubt in Al's mind that Josiah would be true to his word. If Josiah wanted to be remembered for anything, it would be for the fact that he was a credible leader who had created a real movement of secession and, having failed, destroyed his adversaries in the process.

Fortunately, the grounds of the Temple complex were relatively empty of tourists. Only the occasional stroller looked with quiet astonishment at the soldiers rushing through the paths and stationing themselves at the entrances and exits of each of the buildings.

''Josiah has to be in one of these buildings,'' Al stated, looking around. ''He may be heavily armed and he may have a contingent of state troopers with him.''

''What are the Rules of Engagement for what we're doing?'' Cole asked, unsure whether he and his men had military or civilian authorization. Given the situation, he preferred a CYA by making the Sec State's personal representative responsible for anything that happened.

''It's simple,'' Al replied. ''If the governor gives up, take him in with the least amount of harm. If he doesn't give up, protect and defend your men at all costs. But shoot only if you have to. I'd like to avoid having to explain to the media why the federal government killed a state governor."

"Yes, sir." Cole saluted.

Al looked at the spires of the Temple at the other end of the grounds. He had visited here about twenty years ago, after he had graduated from college. He had always been impressed by a spiritual movement that grew from one man with a vision to a worldwide religion with eight million members, most of whom happily paid a tithe of 10 percent of their income each year to support the infrastructure of the church. What he had always liked about Mormonism was its heavy reliance on family values and the two-year missionary work performed by its young adult members as mandatory service to the church. So he was not surprised to find well-dressed young employees scattered around the Temple grounds, with name tags announcing both their name and state of origin. Several of the guides were from different countries. All were beatific. Smiles never left their collective faces. For Al, Mormonism was synonymous with professionalism, efficiency, loyalty, and dedication to family, church, and country. The only problem was that Governor Josiah Brigham IV was a uniquely dangerous aberration.

Al stopped several guides along the path and asked whether they had seen anyone who fit Josiah's description. Everyone smiled and asked Al where he was visiting from, but no one proved helpful.

With Cheri at his side, they entered the Tabernacle. At the far end was a large wooden stage holding rows of wooden benches which faced the benches in the audience. The Tabernacle, where the famous Mormon Tabernacle Choir sang each week, was less impressive than he had remembered. He and Cheri walked in and out of most of the rows until Al was convinced Josiah was not there.

When they left the Tabernacle, they walked toward the Temple. The side door was locked and the sign on the front of the door read: "Open 9 A.M. to 5 P.M. to Preapproved Members of the Mormon Church."

Al was about to motion to the soldiers stationed at the doors to break them down when Cheri waved them away. She took Al by the hand and walked him around the corner of the building, out of earshot. "I know you're frustrated. And anxious. But remember the reason you came here!" She paused for grudging acknowledgment. "Separation of Church and State. A basic principle of the American Constitution."

"I know," he replied nervously, "I know. What are you trying to tell me?"

"You came here for a reason," Cheri said firmly. "What was that reason?"

"I suspect"—Al sounded impatient even to himself—"that as a governor of a Mormon state and as a deacon in the Mormon Church, Josiah could abuse his powers and really try to screw the country. Like confusing the boundaries between politics and religion. As it is, religious fanatics are already filtering into political life through school boards, grass-roots political organizations, stealth candidates . . ."

" 'Stealth candidates'?" Cheri asked. "What do they do, drop out of stealth bombers?"

"Don't play the naive politico with me, Governor Black. You know exactly what I mean. Stealth candidates are offered on the ballot by a particular group. But once they get elected, they switch their political alliances. Like someone who gets elected to the school board and then turns around and attacks the very people who helped him get elected. Proponents of book censorship have been doing this for years. They seem conservative, but reasonable. But once elected they try to ban every book that has ever offended them, and their real radical backers creep out of the woodwork. Many stealth candidates are controlled by religious extremists and their power base can be in another country or state."

"Are you saying that Josiah could be a stealth governor?" Cheri asked.

"Exactly," Al replied.

"Then neither the Tabernacle nor the Temple itself," Cheri suggested, "will provide us with much useful information. They are merely specific locations where religious rituals are practiced. How can those rituals undermine the American way of life?"

"I can't tell you for sure," Al responded. "I'm not clear about it myself. I just felt that Josiah would come here." Al was aware of the irony in what he was saying, even as he spoke. How could peaceful, beautiful surroundings such as this complex be related to something that could undermine the very foundation of the Constitution? And eventually break up the United States through violence, hatred . . . and eventual secession? Maybe religion wasn't the major issue. He looked at the pieces of hate mail again. They had to have been distributed from somewhere close by.

"I've only got a half hour," Al said, looking at his wristwatch. "I know that what I'm looking for is staring me right in my face, but I can't see it."

"Maybe you have to be a Mormon to appreciate what you are not able to see," Cheri said.

"That's it!" Al shouted. "You beautiful, brilliant genius. When in Rome . . ." He took Cheri's hand and approached a young brown-haired girl with a guide's tag that read "Henrietta, Mormon Guide, Holland."

"Excuse me, Henrietta," he said, "but could you tell me where I could find out who is or is not a Mormon?"

"Of course, sir," Henrietta replied in a welcoming tone. "You want to go across the street to the Family History Library. You can trace your heritage . . . your ancestors. All the way back to"—she paused to think—"to the sixteenth century, I believe."

"And what else can you learn there?" Al asked as Cole and several of his troops approached.

"We have records on everyone who has ever lived or died in the United States," she replied, careful of her choice of words. "All the way back to the times before the Pilgrims' arrival. Their original religion, birth dates, parents, grandparents, great-grandparents, racial group . . ."

"But the Mormons have only been around for about one hundred years, give or take a decade," Cheri interrupted.

"Yes," Henrietta responded, realizing that she was speaking with non-Mormons, "but we Mormons believe that everyone who converts to become a Mormon can bring along thirty-five generations of their ancestors in one baptism.''

''So if I were to become a Mormon,'' Al clarified, ''you would have to know my former religion, and lots of other information about me and my family members for as far back as there was a written record.''

''Yes,'' Henrietta replied, ''and it really doesn't matter what religion you are. You can be Catholic, Baptist, Jewish, Moslem, Hindu, Shinto . . .''

''And you have all that information in the library across the street?'' Al asked.

''Yes,'' she replied. ''It doesn't matter what color you are—black, white, yellow—or what your religion is, we will have it in our records.''

''Thank you, Henrietta,'' Al responded.

Al and Cheri, with Cole and his men trailing them, ran across the street before Henrietta could tell them that the building was closed.

60

SALT LAKE CITY, UTAH

Sunday, July 6th, 6:20 P.M.

''The building is locked,'' Al said frustrated, pulling on the front doors of the Family History Library. He peered through the glass but couldn't see anything. It was pitch black inside.

''There's no one in there,'' Cheri said. ''Perhaps we should look elsewhere.''

''Al,'' Cole added, ''Cheri might be right.''

''He's got to be in here!'' Al snapped. ''I'm telling you that he's in here, using the names of my ancestors and your ancestors for the wrong purposes, without the Mormon Church knowing anything about it. Otherwise they would have had him thrown out of the church a long time ago.''

''What do you mean?'' Cheri asked, suddenly realizing that Al might be on to something much bigger than salvaging his own reputation for being right. The fate of the nation just might lie in his hands.

''He has access to all those names,'' Al said. ''Imagine what he could do with a computer and a data base that contained your race, religion, sex, and family history.''

''You could target specific groups,'' Cheri added, ''to solicit contributions . . .''

''. . . to create hate mail,'' Al interrupted. ''You see why I'm certain he's in there? Target a Catholic group from the data base, for example, and make them the object of hate mail by, let's say, a Baptist sect somewhere in the deep South, also using data taken from the data base. You could cause a lot of damage between these two religious groups. Or it could be between two racial groups.'' He waved the hate mail he had been carrying all the way from Dupont Circle. ''One of my patients in Washington was almost killed because of these flyers.''

''It's PSYOPS!'' Cole reflected.

''Yes, the ultimate Psychological Operation,'' Al affirmed, motioning to Cole to have his men break down the door. ''Divide and conquer. Imagine the combinations of religious and ethnic groups you could set against one another—Catholic against Baptist, Episcopalian against Jew, Hindu against Moslem. Imagine Josiah with a list of the names of Moslems living in Maryland and a list of Baptists living nearby. And he starts to create literature, pamphlets, commercials, computer messages, all fostering hate between these two groups. And then add the false imprimatur of the federal government through a 'study' showing how much more successful newly arrived Moslem immigrants are in Maryland than their Baptist neighbors. All the while he's disseminating his hate propaganda. Then, through press releases and intensive media exposure, he shows how ineffective the federal government is at stopping outbreaks of ethnic and racial violence. Remember how ineffective the federal government appeared to the public when it was unable to stop the spate of African-American church burnings in the 1990s?''

''I certainly remember the studies funded by the federal government,'' Cheri added, following Al's train of thought, ''showing how recently arrived immigrants from Asia were smarter and more successful than African-Americans or poor Appalachian whites. Anyone who wanted to stir up trouble could have insinuated that the Asians were sneakier and more devious and didn't live by the rules of fair play.''

''And you've created another Yugoslavia,'' Cole added, realizing the incredibly destructive force of misinformation. ''Formulate a policy called ethnic cleansing and then pit Serbs against Croats, Croats against Muslims, and Serbs against Muslims. With all the diversity that exists side by side in America, someone could create quite a Balkanization of the United States."

"And what do you get? America at war with itself. Killings. The migration of populations. Possible foreign intervention. In short, the destruction of a country united by the Constitution, and which above all else stands for tolerance of differences in race, religion, sex, and income levels. Wipe away that tolerance of diversity by eliminating the cohesive glue of this country—the Constitution and the federal government itself—through a code term like states' rights or by a group called the True Patriots and you've created a second civil war. But it would be more like the massive slaughters in the Balkans than the neat ideological divisions of the first Civil War. No North versus South. Or Gray versus Blue. All this purposefully manufactured hatred would become Red Blood versus Red Blood, in the false name of patriotism."

Al paused to see whether his little speech had fallen on deaf ears. It had not. It was now clear to all that whatever Josiah was planning to accomplish with the help of the governors, he had also had his own agenda, which he was now going to try without their help. In short, the governors had been played for fools.

"Somehow, with the information in this building," Al continued, "and the use of modern communication technology . . ."

"It's frightening," Cheri said, clasping her hands over her ears as one of Cole's men shattered the glass panels of the front doors with a burst of machine gun fire. "Is it really possible to do all that damage in the next half hour?"

"You should see how easy it is to win an entire war using sophisticated computers, satellite links, and electronic jamming devices," Cole responded. "Twenty years ago, when I was stationed in Iran as a young lieutenant, the Ayatollah Khomeini brought down the Shah and his entire country by simply using taped cassettes of his speeches and transmitting them over public commercial telephone lines from France throughout the bazaars of Tehran, instructing his followers how to overthrow the Shah. And there was nothing we Americans could do to stop it, short of cutting off the country's entire power source.'' He stopped for a moment, conscious of the old anger rising up in him. ''Ten years later the demonstration in Tiananmen Square in Beijing was exacerbated by CNN television coverage and the use of fax machines from Hong Kong. We didn't quite succeed in bringing down the corrupt Chinese Politburo, but we came pretty close,'' Cole added.

''Now just imagine the weapons and ammunition that Governor Brigham may have amassed and distributed to his 'constituents' all over this country along with his hate mail,'' Al added. ''I believe this man will stop at nothing to destroy our country, as we know it, and bring in some bastardized form of his religion. Only without its values.''

''So you really don't know what Josiah's next move will be?'' Al turned toward Cheri.

''No,'' she responded, hurt that Al hadn't believed her in the first place. ''I told you that the governors had originally planned to destroy the Hoover Dam as a backup strategy. Not that I'm proud of that particular idea. The picture you're painting would be completely Josiah's idea. None of us knew about it. Believe me.''

''I think I do,'' Al said.

''Come on!'' Cole shouted, waving his flashlight around the lobby of the library. ''We've got to find the SOB.'' Cole led Al, Cheri, and his troops through the doorway and down the darkened hallways.

In every room they entered they found the same thing. Shredded microfiche. Torn library stack cards. Ripped books. Torched genealogical charts. It looked as if a tornado had struck. Or someone had made certain that no one could use the information again. Presumably after the person who did this had digested the information he wanted.

61

SALT LAKE CITY, UTAH

Sunday, July 6th, 6:45 P.M.

Looking at the aftermath of what had been a destructive rampage, Al had no doubts that Josiah had gone to a lot of trouble to be thorough. But if he had wanted to destroy the contents of the building, then why hadn't he simply burned the building down? Al concluded that the answer was obvious. Because the destruction wasn't about the information at all. It was about power. About Josiah's wanting Al to see what he had done. Josiah was throwing it up in Al's face. Yes, Al thought, this was open defiance. Part of whatever game Josiah was playing.

Al looked at his watch, almost feeling the second hand beating away. The game was progressing and Al still wasn't certain what it was about.

"I know he's here, somewhere," Al proclaimed, more to convince himself than to convince anyone around him.

"If it's true that he copied the files and then destroyed these," Cheri said, "then it would also follow that he would want to protect whatever other information is left."

"What do you mean?" Al asked, sensing that Cheri was getting at something important, but still not able to put his finger on it.

"In most libraries where you have precious documents or fragile papers, like the ones that I used for my doctoral research," Cheri replied, "there is usually a backup copy stored in some other building for safekeeping."

Al looked at Cheri as if she had delivered the Gettysburg Address backward.

"I adore you," he said, hugging her and planting a kiss on her cheek.

"Hey," she screamed, "don't forget the shoulder, doc. It is still tender."

"You're right," Al responded, all smiles. He turned toward Cole. "What type of location would you pick if you had to store sensitive backup material?"

"Well," Cole responded, looking around, "I would want something that was not apparent as a storage building from the outside and was not easily accessible to the general public. Someplace that wasn't too far away from here . . ."

"He's right," Cheri said, spreading out a tourist map of Mormon places of interest she had picked up as they walked through Temple Square. The legend at the side of the map listed the important buildings and places to visit. Right under "Family History Library," the building they were in at the edge of Temple Square, was a listing for "Family History Library-Archives," which was located a short distance beyond the limits of Salt Lake City.

According to the description of each place of interest, the library was "Open to the Public," while the Archives was "By Advance Reservation Only."

"There!" Cole yelled out, as if he had found gold. He pointed through the broken window to the hills beyond the city. "See those two hillocks? They look innocent, inaccessible, and provide a natural safety environment for sensitive data in whatever format it's being stored. And that's just where the Archives should be according to the map."

"You're right," Al agreed, his mood clearly boosted by the discovery. "But how can we be certain . . ."

"Help!" a faint voice shouted from beyond a locked door.

"Who is it?" Cole demanded, pointing his M-16 rifle at the door.

"I'm Herbert Oaks," the voice responded. "Please help me . . . ," and his voice trailed off.

"Stay away from the door," Al ordered. "We're coming

in.'' He nodded to Cole, who proceeded to shoot off the doorknob. When the door was finally opened it revealed a heavy-set man with blood pouring from his chest, sitting on the floor, leaning against several bullet-ridden bodies stacked one upon the other. From the stiffness of the rigor mortis and the stench of decay, Al estimated that they had been dead for about two hours. Only Oaks was barely alive.

''Call for medical assistance,'' Cole shouted to one of his men.

Al thrust his fist into Oaks's sternum in order to stop the bleeding. ''Who shot you?''

''The . . . go . . . ver . . . nor.'' Oaks pronounced the word distinctly, as if he knew it might be the last one he might ever utter. ''We tried to stop him . . .''

''Don't talk,'' Al said, replacing his fist with the sleeve of a soldier's jacket. ''You'll be fine. We will be moving you to a hospital. Where is the governor?'' As he asked the question, Al could hear the whirring sounds of helicopters landing in Temple Square. Ambulance sirens were not far behind.

''The . . .'' Oaks paused, his chest heaving up and down like an air pump trying to suction in as much oxygen as possible. ''The . . .'' He repeated the word again as he saw the penumbra of the impending darkness descend. ''Vault . . . mountain . . . twenty miles.''

''Don't talk anymore,'' Al said. Turning toward Cole, he added, ''Find a mountain or locale designated 'The Vault,' twenty miles outside the city.''

''Sir,'' Cole responded, looking at Cheri's map, ''I believe that the 'Vault' and the Archives are one and the same. It's just difficult to pinpoint where it is from this map.''

''Wait a minute!'' Cheri interjected. ''Move your finger over toward this mountain range, about one mile from the mouth of the Little Cottonwood Canyon. What do you see?''

''Ma'am,'' Cole replied, ''you have better eyes than I do. I'm afraid I don't see anything other than some mountains with some letters on them.''

''Colonel,'' Cheri asked, ''can you read those letters?''

''Well, let me see,'' he responded, squinting closely at all kinds of religious icons and symbols. "I think I see the letter *C*."

"And what else?" she asked, trying to confirm what she already suspected.

"I think there is a letter *T*," Cole responded, "and . . ."

"And what?" she prodded him, urging him to make the final pronouncement.

"*P*," Cole replied.

"Are you certain?" she asked. "Look again!"

"Listen, guys," Al said, walking over to them. "We're not playing Treasure Island here." Oaks had died, but he didn't want to say a word to anyone. That was the code he lived by. Death carried its own silence. But somehow, in a strange, almost bizarre way, he felt responsible. Maybe if he hadn't pressed Josiah so hard, or made him feel so desperate, he wouldn't have killed all of these people. But even Al realized he was simply rationalizing Oaks's death. He died the way he probably lived, at the will and whim of Governor Josiah Brigham IV.

"Is that a *P*?" Cheri asked Carter.

"What difference would one goddamn letter make?" Al asked.

"Please look," Cheri insisted. "Is that a *P* or an *R*?"

"It looks like an *R* to me."

"Then that's the place you'll find Josiah," Cheri blurted out. "That's the Vault. I'm certain of it." Cheri grabbed the map and ran down the stairs with Al and Cole trailing behind. They climbed on board a waiting Apache helicopter and Cole showed the pilot the coordinates on the map. He was told that they would be there in less than five minutes.

"What the hell is this all about?" Al asked Cheri, knowing that there was no time for error. "And why does the letter *R* make the difference?"

"That mountain area," Cheri responded, her cheeks flushed red, "twenty-one miles southeast of Salt Lake City and one mile from the Cottonwood Canyon was the only one marked specifically as a Mormon site."

"With the initials CTR?" Al asked, his voice barely audible above the whirring sounds of the rotary blades.

"The initials CTR," Cheri responded, "mean Choose

The Right. Every Mormon child and adult has worn that monogram on a ring, or a license plate, or a pin, or a T-shirt. It's precisely the location where Oaks designated the Vault would be found."

62

LITTLE COTTONWOOD CANYON, UTAH

Sunday, July 6th, 8:25 P.M.

As the two Apache helicopters landed uneventfully in an open meadow, Cheri, Carter, Cole, and a dozen Special Forces soldiers fully equipped with explosives jogged toward the mountain excavation known as the Vault.

Attached to the large, burnished steel doors were several bold red signs: NO TRESPASSING. PRIVATE PROPERTY. HAZARD. HIGH VOLTAGE.

''Now that's pretty unfriendly for a religious organization,'' Al blurted out, breathing heavily from the short run. ''Cole, bring your explosive experts forward. We're going to need a lot of C4 plastique to open these doors.''

''What happens if there is no one inside?'' Cole asked, his bureaucratic side coming to the forefront again. If Josiah wasn't there, Cole wanted to be able to inform whomever might ask him questions in the future that he was simply following orders from a superior.

''Cole, for God's sake!'' Al shouted. ''Time is running out, and you're pulling a CYA on me.''

''Okay,'' Cole responded with alacrity, shouting orders to his men. ''Bring the Bomb and Explosives boys forward. Let's get rid of these metal mousetraps ASAP! You two guys go around and cut any wires or cables that appear to be coming in or out of the Vault. If you're not certain what it is, cut it anyway!''

"Yes, sir!" a soldier and his partner shouted back.

Sergeant Highfill quickly unpacked his plastique and with the help of his colleagues wrapped the colorless clay around the perimeter of the steel door. After he placed a tiny detonator in the clay, he pointed to an embankment and told everyone to clear the area.

"On the count of three, we'll detonate. But what if there are civilians in there?" Highfill asked Al, mindful that the lowest man on the totem pole would be the first one to be indicted for crimes committed against civilians.

"In war," Al responded emphatically, "there is an inevitability that civilians will die. And we are at war." Al wasn't sure he was right about being at war, but they had to get into the Vault one way or the other.

"Three . . . two . . . one . . ." Highfill shouted right before the door blew open.

Sergeant Highfill and his colleagues ran into the fog of war, their M-16s at the ready. Al looked at his watch. According to his calculation he had twenty minutes to prevent a national calamity of major proportions.

"Oh Christ!" Al shouted. "We've got another set of steel doors!"

"Don't worry," Cole responded. "These are only nine-ton doors. The other ones were fourteen-ton doors. Sergeant Highfill, let's get rid of these impediments. This time with feeling."

"All right, sir," Sergeant Highfill responded, ordering his men to place the C-4 around the doors, "but all of you have to get out of here—back to the embankment. Otherwise, the flying debris will end up decimating our group before we can even get inside."

"Okay," Cole ordered, "everyone out, except the B & E boys."

Just as everyone was about to return to the embankment the small steel doors opened. The soldiers stood at their ready, rifles pointed.

"Lady and gentlemen," Josiah said in a very calm, self-assured, inviting tone of voice, "there is no need for such unnecessary noise and destruction of state property."

"Hold your fire," both Al and Cole yelled out simultaneously. Al needed the governor alive in order to find out what plans he had put in motion.

"Thank you, Dr. Carter," Josiah said in response to Al's action. "I must commend you for your decision. Killing me before the magical hour would have been extremely counterproductive."

"We've seen some of your 'productive work,' " Al responded, "at the Family History Library building. Your slaughter back there was both barbaric and unnecessary. So, I think you can understand why we are a little nervous."

"You are quite right, Dr. Carter," Josiah responded, congratulating himself inwardly for his own restraint. There was no need to be a bully or take advantage of the present situation. Irrespective of the amount of firepower available to Al and his men, nothing would change the course of history as he was going to play it out in the next few minutes. As a matter of fact, who better than Al and Cheri could appreciate the devastation he would wreak without the use of any armaments? He was so proud of his achievements that he wanted them all to appreciate his ultimate weapons—PSYOPS and High Technology. No bullets could stop him now. His creation was far beyond the scope of conventional thinking. And like all great creators of new inventions, he needed witnesses to his genius.

"Forgive my manners," Josiah said, pointing quite specifically to Al, Cheri, and Cole. "Please come in!"

"Thank you," Al responded. "The three of us will be pleased to follow you."

"Unarmed, of course," Josiah ordered.

"Of course," Al responded.

Both Cheri and Cole looked to Al, who had already started walking toward Josiah.

"What the hell are you doing?" Cheri whispered to Al.

"Trying to find out," Al responded, "what he's up to." He added, "You know, you can remain outside with the soldiers. I'm certain, as Josiah is, that troop reinforcements will arrive quickly."

"I don't understand why you're doing this," Cheri said, "but I'm coming with you."

''So am I, Dr. Carter,'' Cole added, putting down his weapon.

Al whispered in Cole's ear, who in turn instructed Sergeant Highfill to redeploy his men to the embankment, but to assault the Vault with full force if none of them returned within thirty minutes.

''I must say, Dr. Carter''—Josiah spoke with a broad Cheshire smile—''you certainly have a knack for sticking with the game!''

''Let's just say that your invitation is quite compelling,'' Al replied, ''so I have very little choice but to accept your terms.''

''Thank you,'' Josiah said, leading them into a poorly lit tunnel. ''Please attempt to follow me. I assure you that you have nothing to worry about. Your well-being is completely in my hands.''

63

LITTLE COTTONWOOD CANYON, UTAH

Sunday, July 6th, 8:30 P.M.

"Stay as close to the wall as you can, please," Josiah whispered as they pressed along the semilit hallway in silence. "I don't want any live human targets, just in case one of my soldiers mistakes you for enemy intruders."

"What in God's name is all this?" Cheri whispered to Al, looking at twenty-five-foot-high tunnel walls lined from floor to ceiling with spools of tape, books, maps, metal casings, and storage boxes.

"Those are all the backups," Al replied, "to everything you saw in the Family History Library. And I'll bet you any amount of money that they've already been programmed to create a massive amount of chaos in this country."

"You're quite right, Dr. Carter," Josiah interjected, signaling to his state troopers that everything was fine.

The tunnel opened up into a room filled with all types of electronic equipment, fluorescent computer screens, and printers spitting out material which fell in rolls onto the floor. The area was nothing less than a high-speed command, control, and communication center which, when activated, was capable of reaching any part of the United States, or for that matter any part of the world, in nanoseconds. It was the media control room of the future. A twenty-first-century electronic mortuary.

On a desk set in a large alcove sat all the accoutrements

of a professional workspace—scattered papers and pens, a telephone, framed photographs, manuals, and a pitcher of water. In the alcove stood a console that, Al guessed, controlled all or some of the nonauxiliary electronic equipment in the room. Next to the console were tanks marked "Hazardous Gases." Two metal boxes with external pull-down handles were attached to one wall. To Al, the small area in which Josiah stood reminded him of a modified Operations Center at the State Department.

"In ten minutes all the information you saw destroyed in the Family History Library will be automatically disseminated by a series of high-powered Cray Computers through all the media: telephone, fax, radio, television, cable, satellite, worldwide Internet . . ."

"We get the idea," Al interrupted, noting the emergency backup lights ringing the perimeter of the ceiling of the main Vault.

"So the ultimate destruction of the United States is psychological warfare. A disinformation campaign that will rip at the core of different groups around the United States. What is it, some made-up incident of police brutality that will result in another riot in Watts? Some hate-mongering preacher spewing forth intolerance in the guise of justice? Or some poor white trash taking out their feelings of inadequacy by burning schools and churches of minorities who are trying to make a decent life here? You don't even need the incident, now do you? Just program garbage and lies throughout the telecommunications industry, and presto! It's as good as if it happened. Everyone reacts. No real rape of the white lady by the black man, but it causes a riot anyway. No real burning of the Mt. Zion Baptist Church, but it calls forth retaliation. What we have here is a virtual incident and a truly bloody outcome!"

"Well, well, I'm very impressed that you figured out my plans. I hope you appreciate my creativity," Josiah responded. "But please don't forget that we do actually ship real weapons, ammunition, transportation vehicles, communications and intelligence equipment all over the country. Well, perhaps I certainly show a little favoritism to the militia and paramilitary groups in Wyoming, Utah, Arizona, and Colorado. But just to make you feel that I am an equal-opportunity leader, I think you should know that we supply both sides of a racial or ethnic conflict with the supplies necessary to kill each other."

"That's quite considerate and politically correct of you," Cheri responded, facetiously.

"So which will it be, Josiah? A race riot? A new religious inquisition?" Al continued. "A massive cleansing of our society of all those people infected with AIDS? The withholding of drugs to the aged and infirm? Tell us what wonders you've created, as you say, to tear apart the country. An ethnic cleansing of Hispanics, African-Americans, Asians, Jews, Catholics, Moslems? I guess your little romp with the other governors to divide four states from the federal government was only the beginning of your plans."

Josiah looked at Al with the crazed expression of a man who is inebriated with some mythical notion of absolute power and the self-delusion of absolute control over a greater Mormon America.

"You realize you are completely surrounded," Josiah said, reaching for one of his state troopers' M-16s and pointing it at Al. He motioned to his troopers to check Al, Cheri, and Cole for weapons, but they found none.

"I appreciate your concern for our safety," Al laughed, "but I assure you that I'm perfectly harmless, as are my companions. And unlike you, we represent absolutely no physical threat to anyone here. You invited us in as your guests, assuring us complete safety. Now, Governor Brigham," Al added sarcastically, "it certainly wouldn't look good to your men or our people if you went back on your gentleman's assurance."

"That gun is certainly very reassuring," Cheri said sarcastically. "I really feel a lot safer with you pointing that M-16 at us, Josiah."

"Josiah," Al said, "might I suggest that you and your men put your weapons down. I would hate to have someone get hurt accidentally."

"Namely you?" Josiah asked, checking his watch. With exactly seven minutes left to begin Operation Chaos, he put down his rifle and ordered his men to do likewise. It was unnecessary for him to use or even demonstrate the use of force. He was completely in control of the situation.

Al checked his watch as well.

''Ah, I see,'' Josiah said, ''that, as usual, you have some practical concerns, like the fact that time is running out. Let me save you the mental gymnastics of figuring out what will happen next.''

''In other words,'' Al said, ''you are going to tell us what you are going to do and why we can't stop you from doing it.''

''As usual, Al,'' Josiah responded, ''you're right on target.'' He poured a large glass of water for himself, knowing that the time lost in any extraneous acts or dialogue exasperated Al.

''If you don't find me too presumptuous,'' Al goaded him, ''would you mind sharing with us what our strategy should be and what our options are?''

''Not at all, Al,'' Josiah responded, looking around a room filled with obedient state troopers. Everyone was at his mercy, and that's how he liked it. That old axiom that the pen was mightier than the sword was true, Josiah thought, but with a modern twist: modern communications were far more powerful than a crate of M-16s. The military had a fancy new term for what he was doing: Strategic Information Warfare. Using electrons converted into information ''bullets'' passed through computers, telephone wires, cable lines, optic fibers, and satellite transmission into a complex telecommunication-based society like America with the goal of disseminating false information in order to destroy the social, economic, and political foundations.

Al checked his watch again. Ten minutes left. Why shouldn't he just jump Josiah and try to destroy the equipment? The answer was as simple as the question. Only Josiah knew precisely what he had set into motion and what would counteract it.

''The computers,'' Josiah began, sipping slowly from his glass of water just to be sadistic, ''have been automatically set to disseminate information on virtual incidents that will be picked up immediately by the *New York Times*, the *Washington Post*, the *Los Angeles Times*, as well as countless other newspapers around the country. I am confident that the virtual graphics will create a race riot in at least four cities in the Southwest, among both legal and illegal immigrants, and the destruction of property by gang members who have recently established roots in several rural towns. Maybe it's just as well that our little escapade at the Glen Canyon Dam didn't work out exactly as we had planned. Maybe regional differences aren't strong enough to divide the country. So as a backup I set up conditions for Americans to fight each other along the more . . . classical . . . lines of hatred. It's only a short step until Big Brother steps in, pardon the pun, and the groups vent their hostility toward the federal government. For the groups' collective ineffectiveness. For the official audacity of the feds. It really doesn't matter why. Whether we win or lose this round, the seeds of chaos are there. If we lose, we start up the militia groups again. Representatives from certain foreign governments return to assist selected areas of the country. Secessionist movements arise again. And next time we western governors succeed where we had failed. However, if we win, the entire secession process is speeded up with many more states joining in. The Constitution, as we know it today, is completely rewritten. The federal government is abolished or terminally weakened. All power devolves to the state and local level."

"Don't tell me that this whole diabolical plan was devised just so that the citizens in four western states don't have to give up their guns to the feds. Or open their public schools to all citizens," Al continued. "Your vision of a new and better Constitution. One written closer to home."

"What do you think?" Josiah responded. "You're not that naive. Government is about power. Power to rule its citizens. Power of the state to reclaim lands that were given to the Indians or were unilaterally taken by the federal government, crippling Utah's ability to develop as a major economic force. Power to decree Mormonism as a state religion. Our secessionist movement is about bringing values back to the people. A Utah that ruled itself would be a model for every other state.

"We Mormons are prosperous without federal subsidies,'' he continued. ''We own property in Wyoming, Colorado, Utah, and Arizona, as well as in other states and foreign countries. Our cities are clean. You can walk down the main street of our largest cities without fear of being mugged, robbed, or murdered. Our schools, hospitals, nursing homes, and social services are rated among the top in the nation. We are, you might say, the Singapore of the United States.

''But in order to run such a clean, efficient, prosperous, and safe state, we need a strong, authoritarian regime . . .'' Josiah paused, and then asked, ''Is it clear to you now why I had to do what I did?''

''It's clear, all right,'' Cheri muttered to herself, reaffirming to herself how important it was to stop this madman.

''You can kill me right now,'' Josiah said, ''and nothing will change.'' He ran his fingers around the rim of his glass of water. ''The computers are already preset to start my own brand of virtual reality.'' He added, ''Please don't even think about your forces on the outside. All of my programs have been cross-referenced, cross-indexed, duplicated . . .''

''I think you've made yourself clear,'' Al said, looking around the room one last time. He had precisely seven minutes left. And he was scared. There had to be a way of stopping Josiah's brand of psychological warfare. Because it could work. It could tear the country apart.

Cole was doing everything he could to hold himself back from personally attacking Josiah. But what good would it do anyway, stopping this one man? There were thousands like him all over the country who had to be stopped.

''Cheri,'' Josiah said, ''had you not turned your back on our movement, we might not be facing each other the way we are today.''

''Right!'' Cheri responded, noticing that Al was transfixed by the metal box marked ''Emergency Lights.''

''By the way, I should inform you that any amount of undue noise—translated into your men's unwise attempt to storm the Vault—will actually trigger Operation Chaos ahead of schedule. Call it one of those particular electronic quirks.''

''Josiah, what if you give me one more chance to relay

your demands to Secretary of State Reynolds?'' Al asked.

''Oh come on, Dr. Carter.'' Josiah laughed. ''Prolonging negotiations is such an old, outmoded technique. There is nothing she can agree to now that she didn't before.''

''That's not true, Governor Brigham,'' Al answered. He had just discovered a hole in Josiah's reasoning and he had nothing to lose by exploiting it.

''What do you mean?'' Josiah asked.

''Barbara has no idea of either the nature or extent of the damage you intend to create,'' Al replied. ''I think it's only fair that you give her a chance to respond to your demands of secession, explaining to her precisely what you just told us.''

''You're a clever man, Dr. Carter,'' Josiah said, completely mistrustful of his intentions but realizing that Al might be correct. He, Josiah, had never conveyed his current plans to the Sec State or what the consequences would be. With the flooding of the Glen Canyon Dam, he certainly had demonstrated the potential of his threats. But, as Al said, Barbara was completely unaware of the severe consequences of his next actions. What did he have to lose by talking to her? Everything was in place. If she called in a military assault, it would be too late. And what if Al was right? What if just by postponing his deadline and talking to her for a few minutes he could gain acceptance of secession? He would be known as a hero. The man who averted a great natural tragedy. Perhaps a leader of the confederation of individual states. ''Get her on the phone, Dr. Carter. But don't be too clever. It may cost you and your companions their lives a lot sooner than necessary.''

''Governor, you give me more credit than I deserve,'' Al responded, picking up the phone and dialing the Sec State's direct number. ''I graduated at the bottom of my medical school class. And that was not easy to do with only fifty students.''

''I think we can dispense with the unnecessary commentaries,'' Josiah said in an irritated tone of voice. There was something too flippant about Al, considering the situation he was in. Josiah hoped that Al was not trying to exploit some loophole that he, Josiah, might have overlooked.

"Watch what you say to her. No names, no places."

"Barbara," Al said, talking on the speaker phone, "this is Dr. Al Carter . . ."

"Is that really you, Al?" Barbara asked, pressing the button on her console that would activate her tape recorder. Al put his hand over the mouthpiece of the receiver and turned toward Josiah. "I'm afraid she won't believe it's me unless I give her our code."

"Do what you have to in order to convince her," Josiah said.

"I'll say it this way," Al said into the receiver. "It's your Little Richard, high up here in the mountain of love where the Osmond twins still live one mile from Palisades Park."

Barbara knew that Al was trying to convey some information using rock 'n roll metaphors, but she was never as good or as quick at this game as he was. On a legal pad she wrote:

mountains—where?
Utah—the Osmonds were Mormons
Palisades Park—an extinct amusement park in New Jersey
Who sang and wrote it?
Freddie Cannon.Cannon = guns?

But why would Al inform her of what she already knew? There were guns in the Utah Mountains. It had to be something else, she thought. Could Cannon = Canyon? Canyon—one mile from where?

"How are you, Al? I've been very worried. Where are you?" Barbara responded.

"We're all fine, stayin' alive as the guest of Governor Josiah Brigham IV, who wants to speak with you. Our spirits having flown, because love is a battlefield," Al replied.

Josiah shook his head, warning Al not to say anything about their location.

Barbara added to her list:

We're all fine—Al, Cheri, anyone else?
Josiah—Salt Lake City?

Stayin' Alive—The Bee Gees
B.G.—Battleground.
Our Spirits having flown—also Bee Gees
Flown? Battleground in the sky? Is Cole there also and the 442nd Airborne Division?
Love is a Battlefield—song by Pat Benatar.
Meaning—To commence air/ground battle using the 442nd Airborne Division?
Love—This is the end?

She looked at the sheet of paper, frustrated. Tears started to well up in her eyes. If she was reading his message correctly, Al wanted her to start military action immediately against Josiah. But it might cost Al and the others their lives. Or maybe she wasn't deciphering the message correctly at all. She put the pencil down. Her head was throbbing. It was 11:55 P.M. She reached in her desk drawer for her pills.

"But the truth is that I miss you terribly, especially our rides through the tunnel of love," Al continued.

That helped, Barbara thought. He's in a tunnel, in a mountain, one mile from the mountains surrounding Salt Lake City? She knew the area well. Little Cottonwood Canyon. Tunnel of love = a tunnel in the mountain? All of a sudden it all made sense. The backup records to the Family History Library that had been pillaged were outside of Salt Lake City. So that was Josiah's center of operations. But how could she do what had to be done without sacrificing her friends?

"What the hell is going on here?" Josiah asked, grabbing the phone from Al. "I warned you not to be too clever. That rock 'n roll code isn't going to help you. I wasn't born yesterday."

"You have it wrong, Josiah," Al replied. "That's the way Barbara knows it's really me. Anyone could fake my voice. But not our special way of communicating. It's just a way of making sure that she is who she says she is and I am who I say I am."

"Madame Secretary," Josiah shouted into the telephone, "this is Governor Josiah Brigham IV speaking."

"Yes, Josiah," Barbara said, "speaking louder doesn't

make you sound any more coherent.'' She was waiting to hear his demands but damned if she would extend the courtesy of calling this madman governor.

As Josiah became engrossed in his conversation with Barbara, Al realized that he had to act. Even if the proverbial cavalry was on its way, it would be too late. Josiah's dynamics were all there for anyone to see. Just as he had to ruin the Family History Library to show what he could do, he'd never agree to scrap his elaborate plans to bring the country to the point of civil war. He couldn't give up all that power.

Al scanned the alcove again. If his initial assumption was correct, the unmarked gray metal box on the wall next to the one marked ''Emergency Lights'' was a power transformer that controlled the computers in the Vault. The electrical mother of all mothers. Destroy the transformer and the entire system becomes irrelevant. But how?

''I may be able to extend the deadline for . . . two minutes?'' Josiah laughed into the telephone, sipping from his glass of water.

Al took a chance on his clinical sense. He sprang forward, pushing the governor aside, and pulled down the levers on both metal boxes on the wall. As the room darkened, the backup lights on the ceiling started to flicker on and off as Josiah's reserve generators kicked in. The syncopated beats of light disoriented everyone in the room. Josiah stood transfixed, completely paralyzed, undergoing a petit mal seizure, brought on by the strobe effect of the flashing bulbs.

Al lunged forward, ramming the half-filled glass of water into Josiah's face, and jamming it upward into the cribriform plate of his frontal lobe. Blood spurted from Josiah's eye socket as the glass crushed his nose. His head smashed backward. The desk was splattered with water, blood, shards of glass, and small remnants of flesh, brain tissue, and spinal fluid. The transformer on the wall erupted into a giant sparkler of electricity, fire, and smoke as gunfire from the state troopers ricocheted all over the room. A massive fire erupted from a stray bullet which had pierced the wrong cable.

Al grabbed Cheri's hand and they both started to run back through the tunnel. Cole was right behind. They had to get out before the flames engulfed them from behind or before they would be caught in the crossfire between the Utah State Troopers and Cole's 442nd Airborne Division breaking through the steel doors upon orders from Barbara.

64

DEPARTMENT OF STATE, WASHINGTON, D.C.

Monday, July 7th, 9:00 A.M.

"The three days that saved the country," Cheri said to Al as they stood in the waiting area of the Secretary of State's office.

"It was very close," Al answered. "But thanks to Cole, Hagner, Bloodhawk, and . . ."

"And . . ." she repeated, looking him straight in the eyes.

"And you," Al continued. "Without you . . ." She looked so beautiful, he thought, dressed in a very lawyerlike blue suit. Only the sling over her right arm, which wouldn't come off for another week, marred a perfect appearance.

She ran her fingers through his hair and smiled knowingly at the tiny red scars left over his eyebrow. He looked so handsome, she thought, in his pin-striped, double-breasted suit. With his drawn, tired face, and slight limp, he looked like an ambassador returning on TDY from a war-ravaged country.

"May I remind you," Al responded, tracing his fingers over her angular face, "that you're being very closely watched." He pointed to the oil portraits of past Secretaries of State that adorned the walls.

"Do you think Henry Kissinger or Cyrus Vance"—she continued running her fingers down his back—"ever got turned on standing here in front of their predecessors?" Maybe it was the residual emotional effects of having been so close to death that made her feel so alive now and excited by Al's presence. Recalling Josiah's gruesome death in the electrical fire in the Vault had certainly reinforced her desire for life. She, Al, and Cole had escaped death by literally seconds. All of the Utah State Troopers had died in the fire. Several of Cole's men had been injured. And as far as they could discern, none of Josiah's files or equipment remained intact. But the most important thing was that a second civil war had been averted. Those who had participated in its preparation were being arrested as she and Al spoke. For the moment, the United States of America remained intact.

"I didn't think that being in charge of foreign affairs," Barbara said, greeting them both, "meant that I was responsible for creating domestic affairs."

"Barbara." Cheri pulled away from Al's arms and flew into Barbara's. "I'm so glad to see you."

Al was surprised. He had suspected that they were friends but never suspected that they were as intimate as they seemed to be.

"For a moment there," Barbara responded, "I wasn't certain that I was ever going to see either one of you again. Maybe I'll start calling you 'the Big Bopper,' Al. It might suit you better than 'Little Richard.' " She motioned to them to follow her into her office.

"So, Al," Barbara said when they stepped inside, "aren't you going to greet me properly?" She reached out her arms and tried to hug him. "Come on, baby, let the good times roll," she laughed, paraphrasing a 1950s rock 'n roll classic.

But Al wasn't responsive. His mood had changed completely after seeing Barbara hug Cheri. He was seething with anger and suddenly realized why.

"It's good to see you again, Madame Secretary," Al responded as he took a seat on the couch next to Cheri.

Barbara sat down opposite them in the wing back chair.

"Why so formal?" Barbara asked, anticipating what was about to happen.

"You're my boss," Al replied, "and that's the appropriate address for my superior."

"Congratulations on a job extremely well done. When the

President returns from his trip, I would like to commend you for a special award."

"What kind of award do you have in mind?" Al asked with a clear edge to his voice.

"Something reflecting your courage and intelligence," Barbara responded, realizing a confrontation was imminent, "in having saved the country from ideological fanatics."

"That's wonderful," Cheri burst out. "More than any other person, Al deserves that recognition." She tried to hug Al, but he pulled back from her, too.

"What type of medal would you give to Governor Black?" Al asked sarcastically. He stood up and paced the room slowly.

"From what I gathered from our Situation Reports," Barbara responded, "she will receive recognition for assisting in containing the secessionist movement and for providing you with invaluable assistance."

"Isn't that nice, Governor Black?" Al asked facetiously. "You and I are going to receive special recognition for our outstanding services to this country."

"What's wrong, Al?" Cheri asked, hesitant to hear the answer. "Why are you so angry?" She saw that he could no longer contain himself. It was only a question of time when his emotional valves would blow.

"My God!" he shouted. "Did you both think that I wouldn't figure it out?" He rushed over to Barbara's chair and stuck his face right up to hers. "Did I really seem that much of a shmuck to you?" He paused, looking at both of them. "Isn't there some kind of medal for being a stooge, a patsy . . ."

"Enough!" Barbara stood up and removed herself from his arm's reach. "So you don't want a friggin' medal. That's fine by me. But remember, Dr. Alison Carter, Regional Medical Officer for the United States State Department, you are still addressing your boss, the Secretary of State. If something is bothering you, stop that sniveling. I'm a big girl, I can take it—despite my malignant hypertension." The added guilt, she hoped, might dampen his blast a little. He deserved to be upset. And quite frankly, if she were in his position, she probably would be doing the same thing.

"Please, Al," Cheri pleaded. "Leave well enough alone."

"What about all's well that ends well," he replied. "That's also a good one."

He took a deep breath and continued. Even if he had been deceived, Barbara was his boss. But more important, she was also his patient. And the reminder of her malignant hypertension was a reality that he had to contend with as a physician. If he did not control his outburst, he could cause her to have a stroke. And then what would he have accomplished?

"How long have we known each other, Barbara?" he asked in his most professional voice.

"A long time," she responded, equally self-controlled. But she could not resist swallowing an anti-hypertensive pill while he was talking, just as an extra measure of protection.

"Then why didn't you tell me?" he asked. For the first time his voice had the true timbre of pain resonating within it.

"There was nothing to tell you," Barbara replied, walking toward her desk.

"How can you say that?" He followed her, leaning over her desk with both hands planted firmly on its top.

"Did you ever hear of a 'need to know'?"

"Of course," he replied. "If I request any sensitive information, I must first demonstrate a need to know."

"Very good," Barbara responded. "So let us be clear about whatever thoughts and speculations you might have about me or anyone else. Keep them to yourself. You didn't—and don't—have a need to know."

"Are you telling me that I didn't have a need to know when my own life, which . . ."

"That's enough!" Barbara interrupted. "You've done a great job. No, a formidable job, given the constraints. I thank you. I'm certain the President will thank you upon his return. And I'm certain that the country thanks you. That's it, Dr. Carter! There is nothing more. Not now. Not then. The episode is completely over. Who did what to whom and why it was done are no longer relevant. Forget whatever thoughts you might have had about them. Today is another day. It's as simple as that. The crisis is over and the case is closed."

"Why can't we talk about it?" Al asked. "The possible dissolution of a country isn't just an idle 'episode' that's over in a few days. It's not just another hostage crisis. This could have been the final chapter in our history. And you're treating it as another routine assignment that was successfully completed. Even when there are important pieces still missing in the puzzle."

"Dr. Carter," Barbara responded coldly, "the world doesn't seem to respect your hurt pride. We've got other problems to worry about now. Is that clear?" She handed him a file marked "Top Secret." "Do I still have my personal physician, acting as my special emissary, working strictly on behalf of the Secretary of State?"

He grabbed a piece of blank paper from her desk and scribbled down a few words.

"Here's my response, Madame Secretary," Al replied, handing the paper to her and storming out of the room.

" 'I regret to inform you that as of today I can no longer serve as a Regional Medical Officer or Special Emissary for the Department of State,' " Barbara read aloud. " 'Alison Carter, M.D.' "

65

VIETNAM VETERANS MEMORIAL, WASHINGTON, D.C.

Monday, July 7th, 10:30 A.M.

''Wait for me!'' Cheri yelled, catching up to Al as he walked through the C Street exit of the State Department.

''How long have you known about it?'' Al asked, trying to control his temper.

''Probably from the very beginning.''

''Why didn't you tell me?'' he asked.

''I didn't want to compromise the entire operation,'' she said.

''Horseshit!'' he replied, continuing to walk at a rapid pace down Constitution Avenue until he reached the Vietnam Veterans Memorial. ''Compromise the whole operation! That's a joke.'' He stopped and looked at her, anguished. ''This entire operation was compromised from the very beginning.'' He bit his lower lip. ''The entire secessionist movement was instigated, created, and fomented by none other . . .''

''Please.'' Cheri placed her fingers on his lips. ''It's over. Don't look backward.''

''Why is it so hard for you to hear what I'm about to say?'' Al continued.

''I'm afraid,'' Cheri replied.

''Afraid,'' he repeated, ''of what? After all we've been through, you're still afraid? Of what could you, the tough, gunslinging governor of Colorado, and former leader of the

Western Governors' Council, be so afraid that you were willing to risk my life, your life, and this nation's destiny?''

''I was afraid of you,'' she responded.

''Of me?'' he repeated the question, incredulously. ''I think it would be more appropriate to say that I should be afraid of you and Barbara.''

''I was afraid of losing you,'' Cheri said, surprised that the words would ever come out of her mouth.

''You were afraid of losing me,'' Al said, ''so you decided to keep me in the dark even though you knew that I had to suspect something all along.''

''Then why didn't you confront me before?'' she asked.

''I asked you repeatedly,'' Al replied, ''but you simply deflected the questions, stonewalled me, or played with me. You were so persuasive about seeming concerned about me that you warned me in the most elliptical manner to 'get out' of the crisis while I could. At least I knew where Josiah was coming from—hell and destruction. Yvette even tried to warn me early on, but I was so imbued with doing my duty for God and Country that I wouldn't listen to her. She specifically warned me about Barbara and her Machiavellian ways. But I was too loyal, too obedient, too professional. One rarely questions authority or one's superior, especially when it involves matters of national security. But today my suspicions about you, Barbara, and the entire contrived crisis finally proved correct. When I saw you and Barbara, so buddy-buddy, it all clicked. I realized what a real jerk I must have appeared to you and her.''

''I can understand that your pride is hurt,'' she said. ''But that will pass, if you give it a chance.''

''I tried to give it a chance,'' Al continued, ''but you saw it yourself. Barbara didn't want to admit to anything. She didn't want to admit that it was she who created this whole strategy of a secessionist movement, using you as her shill. And she used me as her patsy to give the whole crisis an air of legitimacy, because as her personal emissary, everyone, except you, of course, assumed that I was really sent to negotiate a real deal and avoid a crisis. Instead, I was sent to divert everyone's attention from the real underlying issue, which was that the entire secessionist crisis was created by and for Secretary of State Barbara Reynolds with the quiet compliance of the conveniently absent President, Vice President, and key members of government. Sure, it may have happened on its own in time. But it certainly was no accident that this crisis was precipitated on July Fourth. Everyone knows that no senior government official is in town then. Only tourists. And the rest of the country is too busy celebrating Independence Day to be concerned about real news. So you, Governor Cheri Black, expressly created the Western Governors' Association for the sole purpose of creating a secessionist movement within it, directed behind the scenes by none other than your comrade-in-arms, Barbara Reynolds."

"Don't make it sound so evil," Cheri said, holding onto his arm. "Listen to me, Al. Then form your own judgment as to whether your friend . . ."

"My friend," Al smirked. "Ha!"

"Yes," Cheri continued, "Barbara Reynolds was and still is your friend. So she hurt your pride. So what? Don't you think my self-esteem took a beating when she first asked me to create an organization at the governors' level that would have enough credibility to promote and provide cover for a secessionist movement? It's true. She was the originator. She was the organizer. She was the brains behind the whole operation. But the movement had to be created to smoke out those people all across the country who would have pushed us into a civil war anyway . . . but on their terms. All Barbara did was to co-opt an already existing movement and organization and speed up the process. Leading to its demise. She did it with the President's permission on the condition that it could be implemented and concluded while he was away and Congress was in recess."

"So she also planned the destruction of the Glen Canyon Dam?" he asked, incredulous. "And the death of innocent citizens of Page?"

"In fact, the flood at Glen Canyon Dam resulted in only one or two civilian deaths. The flood itself was completely managed by the federal government," Cheri replied somberly, staring at the Memorial. "The Glen Canyon Dam was set up as a primary target because we knew that the real troublemakers were looking toward the Hoover Dam, where countless more lives might have been lost. At least we could control the Glen Canyon situation.''

''A few civilian deaths in Page was acceptable to both of you?'' Al asked.

''Of course not,'' Cheri replied, trying to control her emotions. She knew that there was no good way to defend death. Especially to a doctor. He would leave her no matter what she told him. ''We debated that point again and again. But we knew that to stop a much greater potential of death and destruction we had to incur some casualties. That is inevitable whenever you deploy military forces. And believe me, we took every precaution humanly possible to minimize the collateral damage. But we were at war. Except this was a war to prevent a second civil war.''

''Fifty thousand American boys died for a goddamn lie in Southeast Asia,'' Al responded, pointing to the names on the black granite. ''First, it was President John Kennedy who lied to convince them to give their lives in a godforsaken place no one ever really gave a damn about—until the first American casualty occurred. Then it was President Lyndon Johnson who swore we were fighting this war to save the world from communism. Then his cowardly, depressed Secretary of Defense, Robert MacNamara, reassured the American people that we had to lose these lives because the war was a benchmark in American foreign policy. Then came Nixon and his intellectual minions . . .''

''Including your previous boss,'' Cheri interrupted, ''Henry Kissinger . . .''

''. . . who assured our country that victory was in sight and all we had to do was to fight a little while longer,'' Al continued, his jaws clenched in anger. ''But they forgot to tell us that the entire purpose of waiting was to make certain that we could withdraw with dignity after the reelection of President Nixon. Then, to make their necessary deaths a real mockery, that coward, former Secretary of Defense Robert MacNamara, writes a memoir asking the American public to forgive him because he basically felt the war was a sham, and realized that he had to lie in order to maintain that big lie. What hypocrisy!''

"Al," Cheri retorted, "I can't change history. And I can't justify the deaths of those people in Page. I'm not even going to try. In war, the killing of innocents is inevitable. We had no other choice. In this case, we sent a few civilians to their deaths to preserve something more important—the Union."

"But it was Barbara's war," Al said. "Just like it was Kennedy's War, or Johnson's War, or Nixon's War. She started it, not knowing how many countless civilians might die. And I was one of those potential civilian losses. From the moment Barbara sent me to New York . . ." He stopped and realized what he was about to say. "I was expendable. She had no intention of having me successfully negotiate a peace agreement. All she really wanted to do was smoke out militia groups at the grass-roots levels, soldiers who were sympathetic to the secessionist cause, Foreign Ministers who had an interest in the dissolution of this country . . ."

"That's right, Al," Cheri agreed. "Think of Barbara as someone who simply sped up the clock. Just the way that President Franklin Roosevelt sped up the clock by creating different programs to support our allies fighting the Nazis, like the Lend Lease ships we sent to England. That was really done so that we wouldn't have to enter World War Two until we were militarily prepared. In the same way, Barbara knew that this anti-federalist movement had been festering for years, if not decades. She had made a convincing argument to the President to co-opt the process, using me as the focal point. She and I have been friends since college. She knew that I could be trusted. And she suspected that, if given the opportunity, Josiah would be the one to try to bring down the entire country."

"Why didn't the FBI do something? Or the President?" Al asked, knowing the answer.

"Come on, Al," Cheri responded with a smile. "That one is too easy a softball to swing at."

"Okay. So he is too political and too weak," Al said. "But he didn't mind if she did his work because that way he could take credit if the plan succeeded or fire her if it failed."

"That's it, slugger," Cheri said. "The same thing with the Vice President. And certainly key members of Congress. They were all too thrilled to be out of town for the July Fourth weekend."

"They were all on one of their typical overseas junkets," Al added. "Very clever. That explains the news blackout. A dam breaks. Innocent people caught in a tragedy of nature. Even the troop movements were perceived as military exercises. A civil war would seem both preposterous and highly improbable. Especially if one were standing around a barbecue pit, ritually preoccupied by whether the hot dogs or the chicken were grilled enough."

"That was the overall idea," Cheri said. "That's why you were so important to the plan being credible."

"I was the glue that held this entire strategy together," Al said. For a brief moment, he realized that he might have served a noble purpose but at the cost of his life. He thought of the "honey trap," a technique used in the spy trade to entrap a victim. In the jargon of the spy trade, he was acting as the "sparrow," the trained courtesan who entraps the victim in a recorded illicit interlude in order to compromise him or her.

"You weren't the only one who was hurt," Cheri said. "You owe that grande dame on the seventh floor of State an apology. She put more trust in you than maybe you deserve. She believed in your loyalty enough to accept that whatever you uncovered, you would understand had to be that way. She couldn't compromise herself by giving you a blow-by-blow explanation. Nor did she want to compromise me. Or you. She is concerned that some day this might come back to haunt you. She told you no more than you needed to know." She looked at him with sadness, wishing she could kiss away the pain she saw written all over his face.

"This is the beginning of a long war," Cheri continued. "We've just won the first battle. There will always be another person or group around to fill the vacuum. All that we really accomplished was to buy some very precious time. You saw what Josiah was prepared for. Today it was using the Mormon Church for nefarious purposes, against its own knowledge and will. Tomorrow it will be something else.

It's only beginning, Al. Just think about what good you just did."

"Hagner, Bloodhawk, Cole . . ." Al added. "They were all part of Barbara's inside group?"

"Hagner was sent to protect me and keep an eye on things in case they got out of hand," Cheri responded. "Bloodhawk had worked with Barbara before and had tried to pull that secessionist ploy on her under different circumstances. That's when she got the idea of co-opting the whole damn business. Colonel Cole was luckily co-opted by us."

"And my attempts to divide and conquer the governors?" Al asked.

"What about them?" she asked, stroking his brow over the little red scar.

"Were they contrived?" Al asked. "Or were they real?"

"You tell me," Cheri replied, thrusting her arms around his neck and kissing him.

"Josiah," Al asked, holding her at arm's length. "He was the wild card?"

"We had some information on him," Cheri replied, "but not enough to know what he would do and when. So, in that sense, he was very much a wild card."

"I have one more question. Do you like rock 'n' roll?"

"Yes," Cheri lied. As far as she was concerned, there was only one kind of music—country western.

"Good," Al responded, "I'm taking you . . ."

"Before we go anywhere else," she interrupted, "I think we should first go back to see Barbara. And apologize to her. And take back that foolish note."

"On one condition," he responded.

"What's that?" she asked.

"Don't ever lie to me again, please," he said. "If you don't like rock 'n' roll, tell me. My feelings won't be hurt."

"No more lies," she said, holding his hand. "I hate rock 'n' roll and all that loud electronic drum-beating music."

"What about some country western two-step?" Al asked.

"Now you're talking," she replied.

They crossed the street and headed back toward the State Department.

As he entered the building, Al glanced back in the direction of the Vietnam Veterans Memorial and wondered whether it would ever be possible to protect national security without having to hide behind a lie.

THE #1 *NEW YORK TIMES* BESTSELLER!

A startling glimpse into what makes our government tick...
...and what makes it explode.

Tom Clancy's Op-Center

Created by Tom Clancy and Steve Pieczenik

__TOM CLANCY'S OP-CENTER 0-425-14736-3/$7.99
__TOM CLANCY'S OP-CENTER: MIRROR IMAGE 0-425-15014-3/$6.99
__TOM CLANCY'S OP-CENTER: GAMES OF STATE 0-425-15187-5/$7.99
__TOM CLANCY'S OP-CENTER: ACTS OF WAR 0-425-15601-X/$7.50
__TOM CLANCY'S OP-CENTER: BALANCE OF POWER 0-425-16556-6/$7.50

ces slightly higher in Canada

yable in U.S. funds only. No cash/COD accepted. Postage & handling: U.S./CAN. $2.75 for one k, $1.00 for each additional, not to exceed $6.75; Int'l $5.00 for one book, $1.00 each additional. accept Visa, Amex, MC ($10.00 min.), checks ($15.00 fee for returned checks) and money ers. Call 800-788-6262 or 201-933-9292, fax 201-896-8569; refer to ad # 559

nguin Putnam Inc.
). Box 12289, Dept. B
wark, NJ 07101-5289
ase allow 4-6 weeks for delivery.
ign and Canadian delivery 6-8 weeks.

Bill my: ☐Visa ☐MasterCard ☐Amex_______(expires)
Card#_______________
Signature_______________

ll to:

me_______________
dress_______________ City_______________
te/ZIP_______________
ytime Phone #_______________

ip to:

me_______________ Book Total $_______
dress_______________ Applicable Sales Tax $_______
_______________ Postage & Handling $_______
te/ZIP_______________ Total Amount Due $_______

This offer subject to change without notice.

#1 *NEW YORK TIMES* BESTSELLING AUTHOR

Tom Clancy

__**EXECUTIVE ORDERS** 0-425-15863-2/$7.99

"A colossal read."—*Los Angeles Times*

__**DEBT OF HONOR** 0-425-14758-4/$7.99

"Spectacular...Clancy's passion is overwhelming. His sense of cliffhanging is state of the art."–*Los Angeles Times*

__**WITHOUT REMORSE** 0-425-14332-5/$7.99

"A confident stride through corridors of power, an honest-to-God global war game...a pyrotechnic finish."–*The Washington Post*

__**THE SUM OF ALL FEARS** 0-425-13354-0/$7.99

"Vivid...engrossing...a whiz-bang page-turner!"
–*The New York Times Book Review*

__**CLEAR AND PRESENT DANGER** 0-425-12212-3/$7.99

"The reader can't turn the pages fast enough to keep up with the action."–*Publishers Weekly*

__**PATRIOT GAMES** 0-425-10972-0/$7.99

__**THE HUNT FOR RED OCTOBER** 0-425-13351-6/$7.99

"Flawless...frighteningly genuine."–*The Wall Street Journal*

__**THE CARDINAL OF THE KREMLIN** 0-425-11684-0/$7.99

__**RED STORM RISING** 0-425-10107-X/$7.99

Prices slightly higher in Canada

Payable in U.S. funds only. No cash/COD accepted. Postage & handling: U.S./CAN. $2.75 for o book, $1.00 for each additional, not to exceed $6.75; Int'l $5.00 for one book, $1.00 each addition We accept Visa, Amex, MC ($10.00 min.), checks ($15.00 fee for returned checks) and mon orders. Call 800-788-6262 or 201-933-9292, fax 201-896-8569; refer to ad # 190

Penguin Putnam Inc.
P.O. Box 12289, Dept. B
Newark, NJ 07101-5289
Please allow 4-6 weeks for delivery.
Foreign and Canadian delivery 6-8 weeks.

Bill my: ☐ Visa ☐ MasterCard ☐ Amex ________(expires)
Card#________________________
Signature________________________

Bill to:
Name________________________
Address________________________ City________________
State/ZIP________________________
Daytime Phone #________________________

Ship to:
Name________________________ Book Total $__________
Address________________________ Applicable Sales Tax $__________
City________________________ Postage & Handling $__________
State/ZIP________________________ Total Amount Due $__________

This offer subject to change without notice.

Tom Clancy's Power Plays

POLITIKA

A new Soviet Union. A new political arena. A new adventure in military strategy that only Tom Clancy could have conceived...

_0-425-16278-8/$7.50

TOM CLANCY'S POWER PLAYS: ruthless.com

Created by Tom Clancy and Martin Greenberg

_0-425-16570-1/$7.99

'rices slightly higher in Canada

ayable in U.S. funds only. No cash/COD accepted. Postage & handling: U.S./CAN. $2.75 for one ook, $1.00 for each additional, not to exceed $6.75; Int'l $5.00 for one book, $1.00 each additional. Ve accept Visa, Amex, MC ($10.00 min.), checks ($15.00 fee for returned checks) and money rders. Call 800-788-6262 or 201-933-9292, fax 201-896-8569; refer to ad # 765

enguin Putnam Inc.
.O. Box 12289, Dept. B
'ewark, NJ 07101-5289
ease allow 4-6 weeks for delivery.
oreign and Canadian delivery 6-8 weeks.

Bill my: ☐Visa ☐MasterCard ☐Amex_______(expires)
Card#________________
Signature________________

ill to:

ame________________
ddress________________ City________________
tate/ZIP________________
aytime Phone#________________

hip to:

ame________________ Book Total $________
ddress________________ Applicable Sales Tax $________
ity________________ Postage & Handling $________
tate/ZIP________________ Total Amount Due $________

This offer subject to change without notice.

Praise for Steve Pieczenik and Pax Pacifica

"Insightful . . . A page-turner with plot twists. Pieczenik provides a keen insight into the world of international diplomacy."
—*Denver Post*

"Another absorbing glimpse from a professional of what goes on inside the corridors of power."
—Frederick Forsythe, author of *Deceiver*

"An astounding story . . . Pieczenik reigns supreme as America's leading geo-psychological novelist."
—James Grady, author of *Six Days of the Condor*

"Few authors have dramatized the protracted struggle between East and West as well as Pieczenik . . . He draws on his experience as an important actor in the struggle, and then creates a complex plot of high intrigue, deception, shifting loyalties, and war and peace in Asia."
—James R. Liley, former CIA chief in Beijing, former U.S. ambassador to South Korea and current director of Asian Studies at the American Enterprise Institute in *The Washington Post Book World*

"A wealth of fascinating detail . . . Pieczenik's ability to excavate ever deeper layers of character motivations is on full display."
—*Publishers Weekly*

"A masterpiece of storytelling. An endlessly innovative, exciting, and extremely prescient psycho-political thriller about the Far East, written by a master craftsman and brilliant international strategist."
—Dr. Richard H. Solomon, President, United States Institute of Peace, and former Assistant Secretary of State for East Asian and Pacific Affairs, U.S. Department of State

"Pieczenik combines the sophisticated savvy of the Washington bureaucratic scene with the insights of a psychiatrist [and] the extraordinary talents of a storymaker."
—Ambassador Morton Abramowitz, former Assistant Secretary of State for Intelligence and Research, U.S. Department of State

"Stunningly realistic, richly detailed . . . a riveting narrative."
—Ronald Kessler, author of *The FBI*

Also by Steve Pieczenik

THE MIND PALACE
BLOOD HEAT
MAXIMUM VIGILANCE
PAX PACIFICA

Created by Tom Clancy and Steve Pieczenik

TOM CLANCY'S OP-CENTER
TOM CLANCY'S OP-CENTER: MIRROR IMAGE
TOM CLANCY'S OP-CENTER: GAMES OF STATE
TOM CLANCY'S OP-CENTER: ACTS OF WAR
TOM CLANCY'S OP-CENTER: BALANCE OF POWER